A Family Surprise for the VILLAGE NURSE

BOOKS BY TILLY TENNANT

THE VILLAGE NURSE SERIES
A Helping Hand for the Village Nurse
New Dreams for the Village Nurse

THE LIFEBOAT SISTERS SERIES
The Lifeboat Sisters
Second Chances for the Lifeboat Sisters
A Secret for the Lifeboat Sisters

AN UNFORGETTABLE CHRISTMAS SERIES
A Very Vintage Christmas
A Cosy Candlelit Christmas

FROM ITALY WITH LOVE SERIES
Rome is Where the Heart is
A Wedding in Italy

HONEYBOURNE SERIES
The Little Village Bakery
Christmas at the Little Village Bakery

The Little Island Flower Stall
Eden's Comfort Kitchen
Christmas in Paris
A Home at Cornflower Cottage
The Cafe at Marigold Marina

My Best Friend's Wedding
The Hotel at Honeymoon Station
The Little Orchard on the Lane
The Time of My Life
The Spring of Second Chances
Once Upon a Winter
Cathy's Christmas Kitchen
Worth Waiting For
The Waffle House on the Pier
The Break Up
The Garden on Sparrow Street
Hattie's Home for Broken Hearts
The Mill on Magnolia Lane
The Christmas Wish
The Summer Getaway
The Summer of Secrets

TILLY TENNANT

A
Family Surprise
for the
VILLAGE
NURSE

bookouture

Published by Bookouture in 2025

An imprint of Storyfire Ltd.
Carmelite House
50 Victoria Embankment
London EC4Y 0DZ

www.bookouture.com

The authorised representative in the EEA is Hachette Ireland
8 Castlecourt Centre
Dublin 15 D15 XTP3
Ireland
(email: info@hbgi.ie)

Copyright © Tilly Tennant, 2025

Tilly Tennant has asserted her right to be identified as the author of this work.

All rights reserved. No part of this publication may be reproduced, stored in any retrieval system, or transmitted, in any form or by any means, electronic, mechanical, photocopying, recording or otherwise, without the prior written permission of the publishers.

ISBN: 978-1-83618-383-9
eBook ISBN: 978-1-83618-382-2

This book is a work of fiction. Names, characters, businesses, organizations, places and events other than those clearly in the public domain, are either the product of the author's imagination or are used fictitiously. Any resemblance to actual persons, living or dead, events or locales is entirely coincidental.

For my wordy girls – thanks for the tea, booze, endless encouragement and freezing dips in the sea!

CHAPTER ONE

As Ottilie drove past the hill that marked the border of her home village of Thimblebury, the sun caught the diamond on her new engagement ring, and a broad smile lit her face. She smiled a lot lately, but it was hard not to when there were such exciting prospects in her future. She hadn't expected Heath's proposal, but she'd accepted it without hesitation.

She'd realised he was up to something when he'd suggested they drive out to picnic by the shores of Lake Windermere and had packed the sort of luxury food they'd never usually take on a picnic. It wasn't exactly the weather for al fresco eating either. While it was a clear spring day, they'd had to wrap up in jackets and boots, and sitting in the shadows by the lake as the sun had dipped below the hills had been chilly. Ottilie had wanted to suggest they leave and head to a warm pub somewhere, but she hadn't. Deep down, she'd sensed something was different. He'd been far more jittery than normal, and she could tell he had something to say, something that meant she shouldn't tell him she was cold until he'd said it. And then he'd got down on one knee and opened a small box to reveal a beautiful diamond ring.

'Yes!' she'd cried as she'd flung her arms around him – so loudly that it had echoed across the water. 'Yes I will!'

Whatever they'd gone through in their time as a couple, they'd survived it, and her love for him was stronger than ever. She couldn't wait to be his wife, for a second chance at happiness.

'Do you mind if we have a party?' she asked Heath, who was in the passenger seat now.

He turned to her, his face lit by a low sun which wove bronzed highlights into his hair. 'For the engagement?'

She nodded. 'Unless you think it's too much fuss?'

'God, no!' He smiled with such affection she didn't think her heart could take it. 'You can have anything you want.'

'You don't mind?'

'Why would I mind? It's a brilliant idea. When were you thinking?'

'I suppose it depends how big we want it to be,' Ottilie said, admiring her beautiful ring.

'How big do *you* want it to be?'

Ottilie was pensive for a moment, her eyes fixed on the road. 'I want it to be as big as we can do by next week. I want to keep our engagement a secret until then, but I can't wait much longer! The party should be the announcement.'

'Don't you think people will want to know what they're going to a party for?'

'I suppose so, but that's part of the fun. We can tell them we're not going to tell them until the day... if you see what I mean.'

'Hmm...' He smiled. 'Am I allowed to say that's not like you?'

'It isn't, is it? It must be the new improved me that you've helped me to find. For once, I want to make a fuss. I want a big fanfare. I think something this good deserves it.'

A Family Surprise for the Village Nurse

'Me too,' he said, reaching to squeeze her thigh. 'I can't wait to tell everyone.'

'At the risk of sucking the romance right out of this conversation,' Ottilie added as the outskirts of Thimblebury came into view, 'I need to call at the shop for some milk before we go home.'

'That's certainly a segue,' Heath said with a low chuckle. 'But if you need to get milk, then we'd better get milk.'

A couple of minutes later, Ottilie pulled up outside the post office and shop run by Magnus and Geoff.

'You might as well wait in the car – I won't be long,' she said as she unclipped her seat belt.

'You say that, but don't forget who works in that place,' Heath replied. 'If there's any gossip, I'll see you sometime next week.'

Ottilie grinned and opened the door, but Heath called her back. 'And if you want to keep this engagement secret until the party, you ought to leave your ring with me while you go in because there is no way Magnus or Geoff will miss that.'

'Good point.' Ottilie pulled it off and handed it to Heath with a look of regret. 'I already hate not wearing it, though.'

'It was your idea to keep it a secret. Wear it for me – I want to shout it from the rooftops.'

'It'll be worth it.' Ottilie leaned in to kiss him. 'Keep it safe for me.'

Heath put it back into the presentation box while Ottilie dashed into the shop.

Magnus was stacking boxes of teabags onto a shelf. He turned with a bright smile as Ottilie pushed open the door, setting the little bell above it tinkling. 'Hello! We were just talking about you!'

'I thought my ears were burning,' Ottilie glanced to the counter to see Geoff leaning on it, a bookmarked novel at his elbow. 'What have I done wrong?'

'You're as angelic as always,' Geoff said. 'We were just saying we were going to message you about the next film-club pick.'

'Oh, it's mine, isn't it?' Ottilie went to the fridge and collected a bottle of milk. She took it to the counter and got out her purse. 'Sorry, clean forgot. How long do I have to let you know?'

'As soon as you can, just in case it's something difficult to get hold of.'

'How about I choose something that's not difficult to get hold of?'

'You could,' Magnus said, 'but where's the fun in that?'

'Speak for yourself,' Geoff said, putting Ottilie's milk through the till. 'Anything else, my love?' he asked her.

'No, just that.' She gave him the correct change, and he nodded his thanks.

'How's Heath?' Magnus called over.

'He's...' Ottilie broke into a broad smile as she thought about him waiting for her in the car, with that beautiful ring and a promise in his pocket. '*Amazing.*'

'Wow.' Geoff shared a grin with Magnus. 'Someone looks like the cat who got the cream.'

'Someone feels like that too,' Ottilie said. She chewed on her lip, her news threatening to burst from her, despite what she'd told Heath about keeping it to announce at their party.

'You feel like sharing it?' Geoff asked.

'I will.' Ottilie picked up the bottle and headed for the door. 'By the way, I might be having a party in the next week or two. Is there a date that you can't do?'

'A party?' Magnus asked. 'Oh, you know us – we're always available for a good party. What's it in aid of?'

'You'll find out at the party,' she said in a tone that sounded every bit as mischievous as she felt. 'But in the meantime I'm going to keep you guessing.'

'You can try,' Magnus said as she opened the door to leave. 'But we'll get it out of you.'

'Good luck with that!' Ottilie laughed as she left them and went back to the car.

'That was quicker than I expected,' Heath said as she got in.

'Yes, but they've already worked out something is going on,' Ottilie started the engine. 'I'm never going to keep this secret until our party.'

'I'm not expecting you to,' Heath replied. 'And if you don't, I won't mind one bit. I love you, and I want everyone to know how much.'

Ottilie paused, hands on the steering wheel as the engine ticked over, a sudden frown on her face. 'Do you think Flo will be upset we didn't tell her straight away?'

'It had crossed my mind, to be honest. You can never tell with her which way it's going to go. She'd keep it to herself if you wanted to tell her sooner rather than later.'

Ottilie nodded. 'Yes, you're right. She can be discreet when she needs to be. Let's go over later and tell her.'

'Later is good because there's a bottle of champagne in your fridge and I want to open it. We've got more celebrating to do before anything else.'

'Don't be getting me drunk!' Ottilie said. 'I've got work tomorrow.'

'And you haven't had a bit to drink this afternoon because you've driven, so you have to have at least enough to make you hiccup before we go over to Gran's. In fact, I'd say you need a stiff drink just to go over there at all.'

'She's not that bad!' Ottilie said with a laugh. 'Don't be so mean – that's your gran you're talking about! Don't forget we wouldn't be together at all if it weren't for her.'

'True, but even then she was an absolute menace,' he said, making Ottilie laugh again.

'That's one word for it. Considering how happy we are now, we'll let her off just this once, eh?'

Heath popped the cork from the bottle, and Ottilie gasped as it pinged across the room to ricochet from the wall.

Heath laughed. 'The champagne's more excited than we are!'

Ottilie wore a grin as she went to find it.

'Looks like it.' She held it up to him. 'We should keep it. A souvenir.'

'You're a sentimental one, aren't you?' he said, pouring two glasses.

'I just know that when I'm having a bad day, sometime in the next few years, I'll be able to dig it out and look at it and feel happy again.'

'I'm going to do my best to make sure you don't have bad days.'

'Even you can't keep them all away.'

'Watch me,' he said, pulling her close. 'You're going to have the life you deserve from now on.'

'Why does that seem slightly threatening?' she said, laughing as he leaned in to kiss her.

'I'm going to look after you, Ottilie. I'm going to make you as happy as it's in my power to make you. Whatever you need, I want to be there to help you get it. I've been an idiot in the past, and I want—'

She pressed a finger to his lips to silence him. 'We were both idiots. It's in the past, and that's where I want to keep it.'

'You're right,' he said. 'I only... I didn't know what I had until I nearly lost you, and that was all my doing. I want you to know, that's all, just how much you mean to me and how conscious I am of how I almost ruined it. I count myself a lucky man – you'd have been in your rights not to forgive—'

'Really,' she cut in, not wanting to dredge up memories so sharp they would pop the balloon of her happiness in an instant. The betrayal she'd felt after discovering that Heath had kept his connection to her husband Josh's killer a secret had been a hard thing to get past, but they had. She didn't want to keep going back to it to feel those emotions all over again. She wanted only the happiness that their future now held, a future with all that mess behind them. 'Heath, stop. I don't want to think about all that. This, here and now, will be a good memory. Don't spoil it by bringing up things that don't matter any longer.' She reached for the glasses and handed one to him before holding hers up for a toast. 'To *good* memories.'

'Good memories,' he echoed with a smile.

There was a knock at the front door, and then a voice carried down the hallway through the letterbox.

'Ottilie... Heath? Are you in?'

Heath grinned at Ottilie as she put her glass down. 'Doesn't miss a trick, that one. She was probably watching for the car.'

Ottilie laughed lightly as she opened up to find Heath's grandmother, Flo, on the doorstep. 'I thought I saw you come back,' she said, stepping inside.

'Come in,' Ottilie said wryly as the old lady tottered down the hallway to the kitchen, any invitation a formality she'd already assumed.

'Did you enjoy your picnic?' she asked Heath. And then her gaze fell on the champagne and her eyes narrowed. 'Someone's got more money than they know what to do with.'

'Would you like some?' Ottilie asked.

'No...' Flo folded her arms. 'Not interested in that muck.'

'Take a seat then,' Ottilie said, going to the kettle. 'I'll make you a tea.'

'It's a shame you don't want any, Gran,' Heath continued in the impish tone he'd had moments earlier for Ottilie. 'Because I'm sure you'd hate to miss out on our celebration.' He glanced at Ottilie, and she nodded her agreement. 'I've just proposed to Ottilie. And she said yes.'

Flo stared at them both. 'You're getting married?'

Heath grinned. 'Looks like it.'

'Oh!' Flo rushed to hug him and Ottilie in turn. 'That's wonderful! Have you set a date? Will it be summer? I'll have to go shopping... Can you take me to that dress shop in—'

'Steady on!' Heath laughed. 'We don't have a date yet, so there's plenty of time for shopping.'

'But you won't leave it too long? Because I'm not getting any younger,' Flo sniffed. 'It'd be just my luck to die before the big day.'

'Next year, maybe?' Ottilie said, glancing at Heath for approval.

He nodded. 'I'd say next year too.'

'You'll have a proper one, won't you?' Flo asked. 'None of this silliness in football grounds or whatever.'

'You mean a church?' Ottilie filled the kettle and switched it on. 'We haven't even thought about that yet.'

'We haven't had time to think about any of it yet,' Heath said. 'Two hours ago, I didn't even know I'd be having this conversation with you.'

'Of course Ottilie was going to say yes!' Flo gave her hand a vague waft, as if she'd never heard anything so mad in her life as Ottilie daring to refuse Heath's proposal.

'Still, I wasn't going to assume anything.'

'But she's right,' Ottilie smiled. 'I was always going to say yes.'

'That's what I said!' Flo folded her arms with a look of triumph. 'What did your parents say?'

'We haven't told them yet,' Heath said. 'You're the first person we've told.'

'Me?' Flo's look of pride was enough to make Ottilie glad she was the first to know, even if they were only telling her now because she'd barged in on them.

'We were planning to come over to you later,' Ottilie said. 'But you saved us the trouble.' She put Flo's cup of tea onto the table and was about to take a seat across from her when the sound of her phone ringing came from the handbag she'd left on the counter. 'Hang on,' she said, looking at the caller ID. 'This is Stacey – I'll take it in the other room so you two can talk.'

'You're back!' Stacey sounded breathless as Ottilie went into the sitting room and answered. 'I saw the car go past.'

'Yes. Why are you so knackered?'

'Oh, aerobics. YouTube, you know.'

Ottilie grinned. Her best friend was in the middle of a reluctant health kick. 'And you couldn't wait until you'd got your breath back to call me?'

'No because you were having some fancy picnic with Heath and I want to know what happened.'

'Nothing happened.'

'So he just decided to buy three of the shop's most expensive bottles of fizz for no reason?'

'Who told you...?' Ottilie's grin spread. 'Geoff. It was a bit daft of Heath to buy it from the shop here, wasn't it? Your brother didn't say a word when I just went in for milk.'

'And you told him you were planning a party.'

'He didn't waste any time getting on the phone to tell you, did he?'

'I'm his sister and your best friend – of course he was going to tell me. What I want to know is why *you* didn't tell me.'

Ottilie laughed. 'I've only just found out I'm having a party myself! I would have told you once I had a minute. I take it Chloe's out with Mackenzie and you're bored?'

'Yeah, gone over to Oliver's house. He's a sweetie, you know. I'm so glad she's found a nice lad. He treats Mackenzie like he's his own kid. Do you fancy coming over for an hour? Simon's got things to do and he can't make it for ages yet.'

'I'm sorry, I'd love to, but I can't. Heath's still here, and Flo's just turned up. You can come here if you like.'

'Flo's there? No thanks – I'd rather do more aerobics.'

Ottilie laughed. 'Right then. In that case, I'd better go. I'll catch you tomorrow.'

'You'd better. I want to know what this party's for, you know.'

'It's a secret until the party. Then you'll know.'

'With everyone else – that's no good!'

'Sorry, but—'

'I'll get it out of you.'

'That's what Geoff and Magnus said. Good luck then.'

Ottilie was still laughing as she ended the call and went back to join Heath and his gran.

'What's so funny?' Heath asked.

'Stacey. She wants to know why we're having a party. Geoff's been on the phone to her – I think they're working together to get it out of me.'

'You can tell them if you want to,' Heath said.

'I could, but at this rate it'll be a surprise announcement to absolutely nobody. We've already told Flo. And I ought to phone my mum really – it's only fair if Flo knows. And you will want to tell your parents…'

'They'll keep it to themselves,' Heath said.

'Your scatty mother won't remember you told her in the morning,' Flo cut in.

'Seems a bit harsh,' Ottilie said mildly, looking at Heath, who hadn't taken offence at the comment either. Flo made no secret of her feelings for her daughter-in-law, and Heath had grown used it over the years.

'I'll call my mum later,' Ottilie said, 'after we've had our drinks.' She turned to Flo. 'Are you sure we can't tempt you with a glass of fizz?' She glanced at Heath with a wry smile. 'Stacey tells me you bought three bottles from Geoff's shop.'

'You can't do anything around here without it getting noticed, can you?'

'Serves you right for being lazy and not driving out to the supermarket.' Ottilie picked up her glass and took a sip. 'I'll let you off, though. There's one thing about Magnus and Geoff's shop – it might be small and local, but they know how to choose the best things to stock – this is lovely!'

Once they'd had a few drinks and an excited discussion of initial wedding ideas, Ottilie and Heath had seen Flo back to her house. They'd bid her goodnight, reminded her that their engagement was a secret for the time being, and now walked the lanes of Thimblebury, hand in hand. Ottilie was pensive as they passed from pool to pool of warm lamplight coming from the streetlights overhead.

'You're OK?' Heath asked. 'You've gone quiet. Not having second thoughts, are you?'

'God, no! I'm so happy. I don't know why I'm quiet. A bit exhausted with all the excitement I expect.'

'You're thinking about Josh too,' he said shrewdly. 'It's all right – it's only natural a day like this would bring back memories.'

'A bit,' she admitted. 'I didn't want to say so – thought it might take the shine off our day.'

'It doesn't. I don't want to erase the life you had before me; I only want to share it from now on.'

'I'll cheer up as soon as we're in.'

He pulled her close. 'You don't need to do anything of the sort. Do you want to visit his grave soon?'

Ottilie nodded, a smile that was all at once melancholy and yet full of love. 'I think so, yes. Thank you.'

'For what?'

'For understanding.'

They arrived at the darkened gate of Wordsworth Cottage and pushed it open. Ottilie rummaged in her pocket for her keys while Heath whistled faintly, staring into a cloudless sky strewn with early stars. 'Shall I light a fire?' he asked.

'It's a bit chilly, but will we be downstairs long enough to make use of it?'

'In that case, sod the fire.'

Ottilie laughed. 'I didn't mean it that way. I only meant it's getting late and we both have work tomorrow. You' – she prodded him playfully in the chest as she pushed open the front door – 'also have a long drive back to Manchester before you start your day.'

'It's not that long,' he said, catching her by the waist. 'And hopefully not for much longer.'

'But you still have to get up early. You light the fire. You're right – it's a bit chilly. I need to talk to Mum anyway, and then we'll decide whether we feel tired or not.'

With the sounds of Heath bustling at the hearth, Ottilie went into the kitchen. Sitting at the table in her coat, she got out her phone, noticing her mum had already sent a text a few minutes earlier. Instead of replying to that, she dialled the number.

'Hello, Mum. How are you?'

'Oh, hi, love. I just sent you a text message.'

'I know – I saw it. I thought I'd call instead.'

'What have you been up to? We've had lovely weather here – almost nice enough to sit out.'

'I have been sitting out. Heath took me for a picnic at Windermere.'

'That's nice. Lucky you. I cleaned out the compost bin.'

Ottilie laughed. 'I bet that was exciting for you.'

'You went to Windermere? Just a picnic or did you do some walking? The boat trips are nice there – are they running yet, or is it too early in the year?'

'I'm not sure; we didn't see any. No, no walking. Just eating. Actually... I've got something to tell you. Heath asked me to marry him, and I said yes.'

'Ottilie, that's wonderful news! Was that today? At the lake?'

'Yes. He had it all planned out. Do you know what, I felt like he was up to something, and then he did it. Down on one knee and everything.'

'You must be so happy.'

'I am, Mum. I can't tell you.'

'And after all you've been through... This one's in a safe job too.'

Ottilie tried not to frown. It was a throwaway comment, and her mum wouldn't have meant it to be as tactless as it sounded. But the fact was Josh, the husband she'd lost before she'd come to live in Thimblebury, had been a policeman, killed in the line of duty, and it was something that still haunted her. Even though Heath had a safe job, as her mum called it, Ottilie still had nightmares where she'd get a phone call to say some disaster had befallen him as he'd driven to work, or from work, or at work. When she couldn't see his safety for herself, it was always there in the back of her mind.

'I'm sorry.' Ottilie's mum seemed to realise her mistake. 'I didn't mean...'

'It's all right; don't worry, Mum. I know what you meant.'

'Forgive me. I say the stupidest things sometimes.'

'You don't. Listen, I'll come over at the weekend,' she said. 'We'll go shopping, get some ideas for the wedding. I'd love your input. If you're not busy, that is.'

'That would be lovely. I'm not busy.'

'I'm sorry if I've been neglecting you.'

'Don't worry, Ottilie. I'm sure your job keeps you occupied. I don't expect you to be here all the time, especially when it's such a drive.'

'I know, but that's no excuse. Sometimes it's easy to overlook family, isn't it? When things get hectic, I mean.'

'Will you bring Heath over?'

'No,' Ottilie said. 'I think it should be just us.'

'You can bring him if you like – it'd be lovely to see him.'

'He needs to go and see his mum and dad, and I wanted to go to the grave too – if you didn't mind coming there with me.'

'Of course. I took some flowers last week, you know.'

Ottilie nodded. It was a great source of guilt that she didn't take flowers to Josh's grave as often as she'd like, but she was over an hour away and life was often hectic, even in a tiny village like Thimblebury. 'Thank you,' she said.

'Well, I thought you might not be able to get there. But if you're coming next week, we'll get some more – I expect mine will be wilted anyway.'

'That sounds good,' Ottilie said.

'He'd be happy for you.'

Ottilie nodded. She was sure her mum was right. Josh would have wanted her to be happy, and she was, but that didn't mean she thought life was always fair. It certainly hadn't been to Josh.

CHAPTER TWO

It was usually Ottilie's colleague, Lavender, the receptionist at the surgery who went out to get coffee and tea for the surgery. But today she'd been snowed under at work and a couple of no-shows had left a gap in Ottilie's clinic schedule, so she'd offered to nip out to get their supplies.

The day was as bright as the one before, the air like cut crystal as the spring sun bounced from the rooftops of the village. After two years living here, Ottilie took the clean air and green hillsides for granted too often, as she did the twisting roads and lanes that had no idea what a traffic jam was. Today was no different, though she took a moment to admire a row of cherry trees where the first pimples of blossoms were bursting from the branches. A trio of women from the mother and baby group passed by with their prams and pushchairs and said hello. Ottilie presumed they were taking advantage of the good weather to let their little ones loose on the playground outside the community centre where they normally held the group.

At the shop, Magnus was cleaning some low shelves. He was grumbling, dipping his hand into a bucket of water that probably needed changing, but at the sight of Ottilie he brightened.

'Hello, Nurse!'

'Morning.' Ottilie made a beeline for her supplies.

'Did you enjoy your evening?'

Ottilie grinned as she turned to see him look up at her from his spot on the floor, trying, but failing, to look as if his question was innocent. 'Very much, thank you.'

Geoff came in from the back room and went to the counter. 'Hello. I thought I heard your voice. Is he grilling you for information already? He's obsessed with getting this secret out of you.'

'I only told you about the party yesterday afternoon.'

'I know – that's how quickly he's become obsessed. He hasn't stopped talking about it.'

'That's not true,' Magnus huffed. 'You make me sound like crazy town.'

'You are crazy town,' Geoff told him.

'What about your party?' Magnus got up from the floor, drying his hands on an apron as he walked over to join them at the till. 'Where are you going to have it?'

'I don't know. I suppose we might hire somewhere, not sure where. There aren't that many places locally. I'll have to see what ideas Heath has. We haven't got that far yet.'

'We thought,' Geoff said, 'you might like to have it at our place.'

'Oh,' Ottilie began, 'it's kind of you, but '

'You already know it's plenty big enough because we have film club there,' Geoff interrupted. 'Everyone knows where it is and can easily get there. It makes sense. Otherwise it's the grotty community centre, or somewhere out of the village that will cost your guests a fortune in taxis.'

'I wondered whether we could do it at my place,' Ottilie said.

'Are you only inviting yourselves and a couple of fleas?' Magnus asked.

Ottilie laughed. 'I suppose Wordsworth Cottage is a bit on the small side. If we had the weather, we could—'

Geoff held out the card reader for Ottilie to pay. 'Why are you putting up a fight? It's the perfect solution, and we'd love to have you.'

'We would,' Magnus agreed. 'It will be a good excuse to catch up with Heath. He doesn't come to film club often.'

'He's busy, you know,' Ottilie said, 'at work. He doesn't get as much time to come as he'd like.'

The real reason Heath didn't go to film club was that he thought it was silly and they didn't show the films he wanted to see. It had been a point of contention between them from time to time. Perhaps, once he moved to Thimblebury and felt more a proper part of the community instead of a part-timer, he might be better disposed to the club and its members. Ottilie didn't always want to see the films that were chosen, but she'd treated it as a place to keep up with friends and neighbours, and she looked forward to their monthly meet-ups.

'Magnus only wants him to come so he can drool over him,' Geoff said.

Magnus prodded him with a chuckle. 'I do not drool. I only said once he looks like a very handsome boy I went to school with. My first crush, in fact.'

'*Heath* does?' Ottilie asked. 'How did I not know this? God,' she added with a smile, 'I hope it's not him. That would be awkward.'

'You know,' Magnus said, 'I think he does look a little Icelandic.'

'Does he?'

'I think it's the teeth.'

Ottilie burst out laughing. 'The teeth? He'll love that when I tell him! So you might be long-lost cousins?'

'You never know,' Magnus said, tapping the side of his nose. 'And then you'd be my cousin too.'

'How do you work that out?'

'When you marry him.'

'Who said I was going to marry him?' Ottilie's tone was coquettish. She was in the mood to put questions into their heads and then not give them the answers.

'Pft!' Geoff waved his hands. 'Of course you will! And don't listen to Magnus – he thinks everyone looks a bit Icelandic.'

'We probably all are,' Ottilie said. 'Way back. I expect if you go far enough back, we're all a little bit of everything.'

'Vikings,' Magnus said sagely, making Ottilie laugh again.

'I don't think there's much Viking in me. They'd have kicked me out for being soft.' She scooped up her coffee and sugar. 'I'd better get back, or I'll be kicked out of my job by Fliss. See you later.'

'Don't forget what we said,' Geoff reminded her as she made for the door. 'Ask Heath, but you're welcome to have the party at our place.'

'I will.' Ottilie stepped outside. She didn't want to put Magnus and Geoff out, but she couldn't deny that it did seem like a very good idea.

Some things never changed at Thimblebury surgery. Though Fliss, the chief partner and GP, had cut her hours to spend more time with her husband Charles after his heart attack, and Simon had become their regular full-time GP, they'd agreed to keep their daily work routine largely as it had been for all the years Fliss and Lavender had worked together. Which meant closing up at lunchtime – barring emergencies – and downing tools to share a meal together. Fliss had always seen it as time to bond them as colleagues and friends, and while it was unconventional in Ottilie's experience – there had hardly been time for a sip of water on shift when she'd worked as a ward nurse at a Manchester hospital – she'd grown to love these moments. During their lunch breaks together, she'd learned more about her co-workers and their lives than she'd ever known about anyone she'd been on shift with at the hospital, and the surgery team was as close as any she'd worked with as a result.

'No Mrs Icke this morning,' Lavender said as she filled the kettle. 'I bet you're relieved about that.'

'Yes,' Ottilie said, pulling some plastic tubs from the fridge. 'That's one way of putting it. I might just have to check the calendar to see if it's my birthday and I forgot.'

'Don't push your luck – she'll probably turn up this afternoon to demand an audience. Doesn't know what an appointment is.' Lavender looked up at the clock. 'If those two don't get down here soon, there'll be no point in them starting lunch at all.'

'It seems like it's been one of those days when the schedule goes out of the window. I've had my share of overruns today.'

As if in response, Fliss barrelled into the kitchen. 'Honestly! Five minutes means five minutes, doesn't it? It certainly does to me, so why do so many of my patients think it's all right to take twenty explaining the lump on their toe that's hardly there at all and then remind me of every other illness they've ever had?'

'Because you let them,' Lavender said. 'You need to be more assertive.'

'Any more assertive I'd be throwing them through an open window,' Fliss grumbled. 'I always thought the words: *our time is up; I have more patients to see* meant just that. Unless I've been speaking Greek this whole time and nobody told me.'

'Well, you're not alone by the looks of it,' Ottilie said. 'Simon isn't done with his last patient either. I think it's been one of those sorts of mornings.'

'Let's hope it doesn't continue into the afternoon. Thank God for our lunch breaks – if not for them, I'd lose my sanity.'

Fliss washed her hands and then took a seat at the table, Lavender immediately putting a plate of salad in front of her.

'I plated it up a few minutes ago.' she said in reply to Fliss's look of faint surprise. 'I thought you'd probably be along shortly.'

'Where would I ever find a receptionist as good as you?' Fliss picked up her fork and began to eat.

Lavender raised an eyebrow as she spooned some coleslaw onto her plate. 'Considering that everyone in Thimblebury knows you, it won't be from round here.'

'Oh, Lavender!' Fliss put a hand to her chest and pretended to be wounded. 'Straight through the heart! How could you?'

Ottilie reached for the coleslaw tub, laughing softly. She loved the gentle, teasing banter that Fliss and Lavender shared. They'd worked closely together for many years, and it showed. Fliss trusted Lavender to run the administration side of her surgery like nobody else, and she loved her like a family member too. When Ottilie had first arrived, she'd wondered if she'd ever be a part of the surgery in the same way. She'd been happy to find that it hadn't taken long for her to feel if not quite as indispensable as Lavender, liked and valued almost as much.

'What's with the posh coffee in the cupboard?' Fliss added.

'Blame Ottilie – she went to the shop today.'

Ottilie poured some water into a glass. 'They didn't have the usual stuff, and I thought I'd be fired if I came back with the value brand.'

'Wise choice,' Fliss said. 'And how were the dynamic duo today?'

'The usual. Magnus was doing his best to wind Geoff up, as he does.'

'They're a funny pair, aren't they?' Fliss said, and Ottilie reflected on the irony of that statement. If anyone asked most residents of Thimblebury who the funny pair was, they'd point the finger at Fliss and her husband, Charles before they zeroed in on Magnus and Geoff.

'Magnus is a terrible flirt,' Lavender said. 'Remember when Simon first came to work here. Poor Geoff.'

'Yes, but everyone knows he adores Geoff,' Ottilie said. 'It's just his way; he can't help it. He was even telling me today how he thinks Heath is a bit of all right' – Ottilie sipped at her water – 'to use a phrase my mum would be proud of.'

Lavender got up and searched the cupboard, coming back a moment later with a salt cellar. 'No filter, that's Magnus.'

'Yep, whatever he's thinking is coming straight out,' Ottilie agreed. 'He said he thought Heath might be Icelandic. He said he looks a bit like it.'

'He thinks everyone might be Icelandic,' Fliss said.

'Said it was the teeth.'

Fliss let out a roaring laugh. 'Now I've heard everything! Perhaps you ought to get his teeth tested, just to be certain.'

'Imagine! I might find he's related to Magnus. How funny would that be?'

'You might get a discount at the shop. Worth a DNA test just for that, the prices they charge.'

Lavender and Ottilie exchanged a grin.

'I was thinking of getting one of those done, actually,' Lavender said. 'My friend did it – found all these relatives in America. She's going there next month to stay with some of them in Oregon. Lucky, eh? Free holiday. Knowing my luck, though, all my long-lost relatives would be in Hull.'

'At least you wouldn't have to go far to see them,' Ottilie said.

'True. But would I want to?'

'I've done one,' Fliss said. 'After Charles's heart scare, we both did one to see if there were any more genetic surprises lurking in our futures.'

Lavender gave a melodramatic shiver. 'I'd rather not know if anything is coming for me.'

'I'd say it's wise to know.'

Lavender rolled her eyes. 'You would.'

'I was telling Simon about it only the other day. For the cost,' Fliss continued, 'I think it's a good investment. I found mine fascinating in lots of other ways too.'

Ottilie ripped open a bread roll and started to butter it. 'Did you? Like what?'

'You'd be amazed at what they can tell from your DNA these days,' Fliss said. 'Finding your ancestors is only the tip of the iceberg. They can tell from your DNA what your hair colour ought to be, your eye colour... without even having seen you! You have to admit that's clever. There's even a section about sporting prowess. Apparently, genetically I'm a good long-distance runner.'

Lavender burst out laughing. 'You've never run as far as the length of this kitchen!'

'That might be true' – Fliss wagged her fork at Lavender, not a bit offended – 'but I could if I wanted to – my genes say so.'

'I think you'd have to train first,' Lavender replied.

'And that's the bit I have the problem with,' Fliss shot back, causing Lavender to laugh again.

The door opened and Simon came in.

'Trouble?' Fliss asked.

'Mrs Salt,' he said. 'I've sent her for a nasendoscopy – don't like the look of a blockage in her throat.'

'I'll keep a look out for the results and get them to you as soon as they're back,' Lavender said.

Simon shot her a grateful, if weary, smile.

'This looks nice,' he said, turning his attention to the plate of salad Lavender pushed towards him.

'It could do with some chips,' Fliss said.

'You've got bread,' Lavender replied serenely. 'That's the only carb option I can do – sorry.'

'Thank you, Lavender.' Simon picked up his fork. But even as he tried to look cheerful, Ottilie could tell that he was not. She could guess at the reason. Simon worried too much about his patients. It was a quality that was both admirable and a problem for someone tasked with the care of a community, someone like Simon who took every failure personally, who looked after every patient as if they were a relative. Despite trying to put it away until the test results were available, he was worrying about Mrs Salt.

'I'll keep an eye on her,' Ottilie said.

Simon looked up from his lunch.

'Mrs Salt,' Ottilie continued. 'I'll call in over the next few days and make sure she's bearing up OK. She's on my way home anyway. As for the rest...' She shrugged.

'I know,' Simon said. 'It's in the lap of the gods. I get more frustrated than I ought to about things I can't control. Hopefully she'll get her procedure done quickly and it will be good news. She's such a sweet old thing.'

'Better behaved than some,' Lavender agreed. She glanced at Ottilie. 'Like Flo, for instance.'

'Flo's a kitten when you know what makes her tick,' Ottilie said.

'Rather you than me having to do that,' Lavender replied.

The thought of Heath's cantankerous grandmother reminded Ottilie that, in an in-law way, she would soon become *her* cantankerous grandmother too. All thoughts of troublesome patients and hidden family diseases were momentarily forgotten, replaced with excitement. She and Heath had agreed to keep their engagement a secret until the party they were planning to throw to announce it, but Ottilie was finding it hard to keep such good news to herself, particularly at moments like this, where she sensed the table could do with something positive to talk about. It wasn't like they'd kept it entirely to themselves – Flo knew, though Ottilie and Heath had asked her to keep it to herself for the time being. They'd agreed they could be confident that she would, but then again, she'd been as excited as they were. There was a chance, given the right circumstances and the right gossip partner, that she'd let the secret out before they did. Their parents knew too. Would it matter if Ottilie told her colleagues – who could be trusted to keep it out of the village grapevine far more than Flo could? Besides, she'd been the one wanting to keep it a secret; Heath had been happy to shout it from the rooftops.

Before she'd had time to consider the matter further, impulsivity had taken hold and the words were out.

'Heath and I are having a party.'

'What for?' Fliss asked.

Ottilie's smile was so bright it seemed to light the room. 'We got engaged.'

'He proposed?' Lavender leaped up and pulled Ottilie into a hug. 'That's amazing! Congratulations!'

'About time,' Fliss said.

Simon nodded. 'Congratulations, Ottilie.'

His mood seemed immediately lighter, and Ottilie was glad to have shared her news, if only to see it. Simon had been a good friend to her and the village since his arrival, and he'd had his share of tragedy before then. More than anything, she'd wanted to see him find happiness here, as she'd done. He had, in the form of Stacey, her best friend, but for them love was still new in comparison to her and Heath.

'When was this?' he asked.

'A few days ago,' Ottilie said. 'We wanted to announce it at the party and, to be honest, we were intending the party to be a lot sooner than it probably will be. As usual, things seem to be getting in the way. We've got a venue now, though, if we want one, so that's one job off the list.'

'Where are you having it?' Simon asked.

'Magnus and Geoff's place.'

Lavender and Fliss both grinned.

'Of course,' Fliss said, going back to her meal. 'If there's attention to be had...'

'I don't think it's quite like that,' Ottilie replied. 'They made a good point, that apart from the community centre, their place is about the only one big enough to hold more than a dozen people. And I think we'll invite more people than that.'

'I can't believe you managed to keep it to yourself all this time.' Lavender grabbed Ottilie's hand and frowned at it. 'Where's the ring?'

'She couldn't very well wear it if she was going to keep the engagement a secret, could she?' Fliss cut in. 'I think one of us might have asked if we'd noticed an iceberg on her finger.' She shot a sideways glance at Ottilie. 'I trust he *has* bought you a diamond the size of the iceberg that did for the *Titanic*?'

Ottilie smiled. 'Not quite. I'll bring it to show you tomorrow, but I won't be wearing it just yet, not until it's official. Please keep it to yourselves for now. I probably shouldn't have said anything, but I couldn't help it.'

'We will,' Fliss said, giving Lavender a pointed look.

Simon reached for the salt. 'Heath won't mind that we know?'

'Of course not...' Ottilie speared a tomato with her fork. 'It was my idea to save the announcement. It turns out I'm not very good at saving announcements after all.'

'You're happy,' Fliss said. 'It's only natural you want to share it. Nobody will hear it from my lips until your party. So when are you thinking about having it?'

'I'm happy to do it sooner rather than later. I'll talk to Heath later, see how he feels about Magnus and Geoff's offer, and once I know, I'll let everyone have invites.'

'I take it he'll be moving to Thimblebury then?' Fliss asked, and in her tone now Ottilie detected some anxiety. It was hardly surprising. The last time Ottilie had mooted the idea of leaving the village and her job at the surgery, Fliss had taken it badly. They'd formed a close working relationship and friendship too, and Ottilie hadn't realised just how much that meant to Fliss until it had been threatened with her leaving.

'We haven't got that far in our plans yet, but I think so. There's been some discussion with his boss about remote working, and he had his place in Manchester valued just in case, so...'

'Good,' Fliss said. 'It'll be nice to see him around more often.'

'Nice for me too,' Ottilie said. 'Long-distance is all very well, but it takes its toll on you after a while.'

'I couldn't be having all that toing and froing,' Lavender said.

'Quite,' Fliss agreed. 'Not that Charles would ever have been worth the effort.'

Ottilie shared a grin with Lavender and Simon. Fliss said things like that about her husband, but she didn't feel them. They had what some in Thimblebury viewed as a strange marriage, but nobody could argue that they weren't devoted to one another. He'd suffered a heart attack the previous year and her reaction to it had cemented the fact for anyone who'd doubted it.

'Does Florence know about your engagement?' Fliss asked.

Ottilie nodded. 'She was the first person we told.'

Lavender reached for a roll and bit off the corner. 'Can you imagine if she hadn't been?'

'She might have had something to say,' Ottilie agreed.

'Something to say?' Lavender put her knife down. 'We'd never have heard the end of it!'

'I think it's the most wonderful news,' Fliss said. 'It's nice to have something cheerful to talk about at the table – too often it's this person's biopsy or that person's post-nasal drip.'

'Ugh,' Lavender said primly. 'Post-nasal drip – not at the dinner table, please.'

'Would you rather have stool samples?' Fliss asked impishly.

Simon and Ottilie both laughed while Lavender grimaced at Fliss. 'Tomorrow, you can plate up your own salad!'

CHAPTER THREE

Ottilie had just showered and changed when Heath arrived at Wordsworth Cottage. After a quick kiss and enquiries about their working days, he opened a tote bag onto the kitchen table, a pile of shiny magazines sliding out.

Ottilie picked up the top one and burst out laughing. '*Dream Weddings*? Someone's keen!'

Heath's grin was sheepish and he shrugged. 'One of the girls in the office has just got married. She had these on her desk for the recycling, and I asked if I could have them.'

'So you can pick out your dress?'

He laughed. 'Yes. That's exactly it. But I thought it might give us some ideas.'

Ottilie flicked idly through the magazine. Every page contained dreamy bouquet ideas, evocative photos of magical venues and impossibly romantic dresses. 'Since when did you care about this kind of thing?'

'Since I cared that you might care.'

'Thank you,' she said, putting the magazine down and tidying the pile. 'We'll look at them after we've eaten.'

From another bag, he took out a bottle of milk. 'I called at the shop, just in case you were short. We'll always use it.'

'We will when you're around,' Ottilie said. 'I think in a secret life you were an extra in *Bugsy Malone*.'

Heath laughed lightly. 'I like milk, what can I say? Geoff told me what he'd said to you about using their place. I told him if you were happy with it, then so was I. He tried to pretend you'd told him what the party was for so I'd slip up, but don't worry, I was smarter than that.'

Ottilie grinned. 'Little bugger.'

'So I think that's the venue settled?'

'Then we can talk to him about what date suits them and we can send our invites! I'm properly excited now! It's lucky they both love you so much.'

Heath put the milk in the fridge. 'I think it's you they love. I'm just the carry-on baggage.'

'No.' Ottilie prodded him playfully in the chest. 'Magnus has convinced himself you're Icelandic. Wishful thinking, I think they call it.'

Heath laughed. 'Me? I'm sure I'm about as Icelandic as a pineapple!'

'He said it was the teeth.'

Heath shook his head. 'In fairness, for all I know I might be, but I doubt it. I've never really thought about it before.'

'About being Icelandic? I don't suppose that's everyone's waking thought.'

'I've never even thought about ancestry. Everyone's doing those tests in our office. I wasn't bothered – I'm fairly certain I won't find anything interesting.'

'Me neither, apart from some Irish on my dad's side.'

Heath rolled up his sleeves. 'Irish? You never said.'

'We never talked about it before. So you're quite sure you're not a bit Icelandic?'

'You'd have to ask my parents. Ask my gran and she'd tell you I'm half Martian on my mother's side.'

Ottilie let out a giggle. 'Your poor mum – Flo really has it in for her.'

'Gran would have me taking a DNA test just to be sure I'm not.'

'Fliss said she did one and it was really fascinating – guessed her hair colour and everything. And Lavender was saying her friend found loads of relatives in America and she's going to visit them. It's crazy, isn't it? Imagine saying all this to someone when we were kids – they'd have thought you were mad.'

'Relatives in America, you say?' he asked, rubbing his chin and pretending to ponder. 'Perhaps we ought to do one. That'd be the honeymoon sorted.'

Ottilie turned on the tap to wash her hands. 'Knowing our luck, we'd have long-lost relatives in some place that was at war. Though I must admit, I'm a bit curious.'

'I suppose it would be interesting. We've got enough on our plates right now, though.'

'Not really. Now we've got Magnus and Geoff on the case, we'll hardly have to worry about anything as far as the party is concerned. You know what they're like – they'll want to get involved in everything. Might as well just hand it all over to them.'

'As long as they're not planning to get involved in the wedding, I'm fine with that.'

'I bet they'd arrange a lovely wedding. They do great parties, after all. You'd have to ask Magnus to be your best man – seeing as you're almost certainly Icelandic and probably his long-lost cousin.'

Heath grinned. 'If that's the case, it might be better if none of us know. Shall I make a start on dinner? What do you fancy?'

'I'm not massively hungry. Pasta and tomatoes would do me, if you're happy for something light.'

'That's fine with me too. We could go out for a walk later if you like.'

Ottilie nodded and went back to the pile of wedding magazines. She opened one up. The page showed the banquet room of a Highland castle, decked out in lights and white linens.

'You know...' Heath's voice caused her to look up. 'You can have anything you want.'

'I don't want a lot,' Ottilie said. 'These magazines are all very well, but they're dreams, aren't they? That's why they're in magazines – they're aspirational; they're not meant for ordinary people.'

'What I mean to say is, whatever you want, I'll try to give it to you.'

'Thank you. I expect we'll be talking about it a lot over the next few months.' She was silent for a moment, head turned back to the page. And then she looked up at Heath, who was chopping onions. 'The only thing I really wish, the thing I can't have, is my dad, walking me down the aisle. It makes me sad you and him never got to meet.'

'Yeah. I'm sure I would have liked him.'

'He'd have loved you.'

'You think so?'

She nodded.

Heath was silent again, only the sounds of his knife against the chopping board filling the kitchen. Ottilie went back to her magazines.

'Did he get on well with Josh?' he asked after a time.

'They had their moments. He had a lot of respect for Josh; I know that much.'

'I suppose he would – Josh was a policeman after all.'

'That wasn't it,' Ottilie said. 'Josh went out of his way to be there whenever anyone needed him, and my dad had a lot of time for someone who did that. It's why I know he would have liked you because you do that as well.'

'Not always,' Heath said. 'But I'm trying to be better.' He smiled up at her. 'You make me want to be better. I suppose all this family stuff has made you think about that?'

'Yes.' Ottilie closed the magazine. 'I think about my dad all the time, obviously, the same way I make certain to keep Josh in my thoughts, but it's strange – as the years go by, I can't help but feel I'm losing the memories of him. I have that sense of what sort of a man he was, the way he'd look at a certain point, stories of growing up with him, but...'

'I get it,' Heath said. 'How long has he been gone now?'

'Ten years... or thereabouts. That's another thing – you lose track. It makes me feel like a bad daughter, but I can't help it. Life just gets in the way, doesn't it? Drags you along with it.'

Heath smiled. 'Again, I get it. God, sometimes I lose track of what day it is, let alone how many years have passed since a thing happened. And each year just goes by that much quicker...'

'We sound old, don't we?'

Heath chuckled. 'Ancient. I think we'd better go and listen to some rave music or something, just to remind ourselves we're not quite one foot in the grave yet.'

'I never listened to rave music when I was young,' Ottilie said. 'If the truth be told, I've always been boring.'

'Not boring,' Heath said. 'Just quiet. Sensitive...'

'Dull,' Ottilie cut in. 'You can say it; I know what I am.'

'Whatever you think you are, I like it.'

'Only like it?'

'I love it. I love you, and I want to spend the rest of my life with you.'

She went to stand behind him and circled an arm around his waist. 'Me too.' Ottilie kissed his neck lightly, and then let go and went to the kitchen doorway.

Heath turned to look. 'Where are you off to now?'

'To get my notebook. So we can make some plans.'

'You have notebooks?'

'You never noticed my notebook obsession?'

He laughed. 'No. Clearly I haven't spent enough time here.'

'Don't worry,' she said, blowing him a saucy kiss from the door that made him chuckle, 'we'll be putting that right soon enough.'

During a brief lull between patients, Fliss put her head round Ottilie's office door. 'I've forwarded an email to you,' she said briskly.

'Oh, right... anything I need to action urgently?'

'Nothing work-related – don't worry. I only thought I'd mention it in case you thought it was spam. It's a half-price offer from those ancestry people I used. You seemed interested the other day, so I thought you might want to see it. Don't worry if you're not bothered – just delete it; I won't be offended.'

Without waiting for a reply, Fliss disappeared again. Ottilie opened her inbox to see the forwarded email at the top. She opened it up.

She'd never been one of those people obsessed by where they'd come from or who their ancestors might be, but the more she'd discussed it over the past few days, the more curious she was. Perhaps her age had something to do with it too. As she grew older, she thought about her family more and more – people she'd lost, people she'd known only briefly in childhood.

She wondered whether Heath might find it interesting. He'd joked about it being boring, but wouldn't it be funny if he did find he was a bit Icelandic? With a smile at the thought, Ottilie clicked through to the company's website and ordered two. They'd do them together. She was looking forward to comparing them, even daring to imagine what it might mean for their children – if it wasn't too late to think about having them.

No sooner had she submitted her order than there was a knock at the office door.

Lavender put her head round it and grimaced. 'Sorry... your favourite patient is in and wants to know if you can bump her up the list.'

'My favourite patient?'

'Mrs Icke.'

Ottilie pulled a face as she checked her online diary. 'She's not due until this afternoon.'

'You know what she's like – swears blind you told her this morning.'

'Her selective deafness strikes again, eh?'

'You mean her non-existent deafness?'

Ottilie glanced down her list and then nodded. 'I shouldn't keep doing this for her, but I suppose I could fit her in quickly if I skip my cuppa.'

'I'll make you a cuppa. I'll make you ten if you get her miserable face out of my reception.'

Ottilie gave a weary smile as Lavender went to get the old lady. On the bright side, at least that was one less patient to see later.

CHAPTER FOUR

Two weeks passed, filled with party planning and wedding discussions. Ottilie and Heath had agreed on an autumn date, but that was about all. Heath gave the impression of wanting to go along with Ottilie's choices, but she could tell he was holding his own opinions back. When she'd said she wanted small and intimate, he'd agreed, but he'd seemed disappointed.

It would sound odd and unreasonable to Heath, no matter what he said, and so she didn't say so, but part of her didn't want a big fuss. She didn't want to feel like she was upstaging the first one with Josh, that this marriage was more important to her, more worthy of her time and effort. It was a battle she'd have to work out for herself, one that Heath couldn't hope to understand because even she would struggle to explain it. They'd started to draw up a guest list so they could have numbers for prospective venues, but even that had been more difficult than either of them could imagine.

'Where do you draw the line?' Heath had asked as they sat together at the kitchen table of Wordsworth Cottage, staring at a page full of names.

Ottilie had twiddled the pen in her fingers and sighed. 'I

know. If I invite those cousins' – she tapped the page – 'I have to invite all the other ones. And to be perfectly honest, I don't really like the others.'

'Same with friends. I've known Guy since college, and we were best mates with David. I haven't seen David for years and he was always a bit of an idiot, to be quite honest, but if I don't invite him, Guy will want to know why because they're still good friends, and I can hardly say I didn't ask him because I think he's a dickhead who never grew up, can I?'

'It's not supposed to be stressful, is it?'

'If it is, nobody told me.' He sighed. 'How many people does that venue in Buttermere hold? You know, the one with the jetty by the lake? I can't quite remember.'

'They had two rooms for hire. One held about a hundred and fifty and the other…' Ottilie scrunched up her nose. 'Hang on – I emailed them; I'll check their reply.' Ottilie scrolled down the list but then stopped at something that wasn't from a potential venue. 'That was quick.'

'What?'

'The DNA test. The results are back.' She looked up at Heath. 'That's exciting, isn't it? I might find I'm related to royalty.'

'I don't think it tells you stuff like that.'

'Well, I might have more exotic heritage than I thought. Ireland and Manchester – not the most exciting combo, is it?'

'I don't think I even have anything other than British ancestry, so…' Heath shrugged.

'I'll open it later,' Ottilie decided.

'Open it now. I can tell you want to.'

'But we're busy with this.'

'It'll take two seconds to look it over. Open it. Hang on…' Heath took out his phone and scrolled through his own inbox. 'Mine are in too. Shall we open them together?'

Ottilie smiled as she clicked the link. 'See – you play it cool, but you want to know as much as I do.'

'Well, if we do have long-lost relatives somewhere exotic, that's the honeymoon sorted, isn't it?'

Ottilie prodded him with a laugh. 'Honestly, I can't tell whether you mean that or not.'

'Oh, I do, trust me.'

'You first,' Ottilie said, her tummy bubbling with anticipation. She hadn't cared up until this point – not really. Once they'd sent their samples, she'd barely given it a second thought. But now there were all sorts of possibilities, new things to discover about one another.

'Huh…' Heath read in silence.

'What?'

'Well…' He looked up. 'I'm sorry to say, but I'm not Icelandic. English and Welsh – that's it.'

'Welsh? Did you know?'

'No, but it's only twelve per cent. How about you? Any exciting honeymoon destinations in yours?'

Ottilie scanned the information. 'Strange,' she said after a few minutes to process it. 'And a bit disappointing. Totally English.'

'Why's it strange?'

'Because I know my dad's family are from Ireland. Some of them still live there. But there's nothing about Ireland here at all – not even a tiny percentage.'

'Let me see…' Heath leaned in to look. 'You're right. What's that there? Norway, three per cent.'

'I don't know. I suppose if we're British, we've all got a bit of Viking in us, right?'

'I suppose so. So they can trace pretty far back?'

'Generations. I read the info pack when I sent my sample and I think it's a couple of hundred years.'

'Weird. Could it be his family were Irish but they'd gone there from Britain and so their DNA is showing as British?'

Ottilie paused. 'As far as I know there's at least three generations in Cork, but I don't exactly know how this works. I suppose that could be it. Well...' She locked her phone. 'That's that. Honeymoon in Manchester it is!'

Up in the hills, it was colder than it had been when Ottilie and Stacey had left the village. Even though it was bright and dry, the air sweet and clear, Ottilie was glad of the fleece she'd picked up last minute. She was, however, regretting her choice of shorts, wishing she'd put long trousers on too. Stacey didn't seem to be struggling quite as much with the temperature. In fact, there was a sheen of sweat on her brow as they trudged up their planned route.

'Whose idea was it to start hiking?' Stacey paused on the track, holding her side as she caught her breath.

'I believe it was yours,' Ottilie said, taking a sip from her water bottle. 'You said you wanted to get into shape, you didn't want to drive for hours to a gym where you'd hate everyone there, and that we had a natural gym right on our doorsteps that we never use.'

'Did I really say all that?'

'I'm paraphrasing, but that's about it.'

'Next time I say something that stupid, remind me of today.' Stacey wiped a sleeve across her forehead and squinted up at the hillside. 'How much further is it?'

'I have no idea. You've got the map.'

'About that...' Stacey looked sheepish as she turned her phone screen to Ottilie. 'I lost signal about a mile back. I thought we might get it back further up, but...'

Ottilie threw a look of concern at the screen. 'Will we be able to find our way down?'

'We haven't found our way there yet.'

'I vote we turn around, get in the car, find that little bakery we passed on the way here and stuff our faces.'

'I'd say that's the best idea I've heard today. We can start our hiking routine again next week, right?'

Ottilie raised her eyebrows. 'Whatever you say.'

'We will!' Stacey insisted as they scrambled down the hill, rocks and scree coming away beneath their feet. 'That's if we don't die getting down here.'

'We'll be fine. Just talk less and look more at what you're doing.'

'Easy for you to say. I'm pathologically incapable of shutting up – everyone knows that.'

'Have you ever been tested for ADHD?'

'Don't you start – Chloe's always going on about that. I think I only have a lot to say because people keep asking me things.'

Ottilie grinned up at her. 'Want me to stop?'

'I didn't say that... whoops!'

Ottilie had to laugh as Stacey slid on a patch of wet grass and onto her bottom. 'I take it back – it's not ADHD; you're just scatty.' She went back and offered a hand to help her up, Stacey grinning sheepishly as she took it.

'If we do come hiking again, maybe we'll pick somewhere on the flat?'

'Thimblebury high street?'

'Sounds good to me. Can we just have a minute? I'm sweating buckets here.'

Ottilie nodded, and they picked their way over to a tussock where they could take a seat and look out from the hillside.

'It's been worth the effort for that view, hasn't it?' she said.

'I suppose so. This was what I meant. We've said it before, but we live in this amazing place and we don't see nearly enough of it. Sometimes I feel guilty. I bet some people would kill to live here; I don't even think about how lucky I am half the time.'

'You're busy. There's a difference between living in a place and holidaying there – everyone knows that. You can go on holiday and dream of moving there, but the reality for most would be they'd still have to work and cook and clean and whatever else. And don't forget you've got Chloe and Mackenzie to think about, not just yourself.'

'True. And Ollie now – he stays over every weekend. I keep asking when they're going to get their own place.'

'Can they afford to?'

'I don't suppose they can, but it makes more work for me when he's there. Simon's great, of course – he helps out when he can, but he's got a big workload at the surgery, so...'

Ottilie took a packet from her backpack and offered it to Stacey. 'Diet biscuits,' she said with a grin.

'I sound like I'm complaining about nothing, don't I?' Stacey said, munching on a biscuit, her gaze on a vista where sunlight and shadow chased one another across distant hillsides. 'I've got nothing to moan about really.'

'It does us good to get things off our chest. Doesn't matter whether they're big or small.'

'How's the party planning?'

'Good. You know Geoff and Magnus – I'm hardly lifting a finger. They've got the food covered, buying from their wholesale suppliers and insisting they do a lot of the cooking – because we know they love cooking – and they've got that amazing sound system at the house so no need for me to worry about music... all I've got to do is invite people. I almost want to ask them to step back and leave me something to do because it doesn't feel like our party at all at the moment.'

'It's a tricky one.' Stacey crammed the rest of the biscuit into her mouth and reached for another one. 'But I know my brother and that sounds about right. Take advantage of it. You get an easy ride, and him and Magnus get to indulge their inner party animals.'

'Hmm...' Ottilie bit into a biscuit. 'I suppose you're right. People pay good money for this sort of service.'

'Exactly. What's Heath said about it?'

'He's happy enough.'

'There you go then.' Stacey got up and brushed a hand over her shorts. 'I think those biscuits have made me hungrier than I was before. Shall we go and find that bakery?'

CHAPTER FIVE

For most, it was easy enough to send invites to Ottilie and Heath's party via social media, but for the odd exception, it was necessary to write one out and deliver it the old-fashioned way.

Just after work, Ottilie was climbing the hill to Daffodil Farm to see Corrine and Victor with their invite. She was hoping to see their alpaca herd too. Victor often took her over to the field to feed and fuss them, and Ottilie looked forward to those visits, especially when she got to see their newest addition, which they'd named Ottilie in her honour.

She was looking forward to seeing the herd but even more so to a slice of Corrine's fruit cake. Victor's wife never stopped baking, but there were plenty of takers, so it never went to waste. Ottilie was always treated to a slab and a cup of tea on arrival at Daffodil Farm, and then sent away with extra for her and Heath when she left. It had come to the point that if she didn't manage to visit the farm for a couple of weeks, Heath would be so disappointed not to have cake that she'd have to arrange to go up there just for him.

When she was in a rush and the path would allow it, Ottilie drove up there. Today, even though the sun was low in the sky and would likely set before she made it back down, she still left her car at the bottom and walked. Already, the clear spring sky was changing, tinged with pink and peach and indigo, and the hollows were shadowed, and the air was so clean she couldn't get enough of it after being in a stuffy treatment room all day. If it was dark when her visit was over, she was sure Victor would run her back down in his faithful Old Banger – the ancient Land Rover that seemed to defy all laws of physics simply by still being in one piece.

At the farmhouse, Corrine opened the door before Ottilie had even knocked. How lovely to see you! You should have said you were coming… Victor's over at the field, but I'm sure he won't be long.'

Corrine wiped her hands on her apron as she ushered her in. As usual, Ottilie could smell cinnamon and sugar on the air of the warm kitchen. If she hadn't spent a few weeks staying with Corrine and Victor when her own cottage had been flooded shortly after she'd arrived in Thimblebury, she'd be of the firm belief that Corrine didn't bake anything other than her signature cake. However, on good authority Ottilie could say that Corrine did, in fact, cook many other dishes and they were all as good as her fruit cake.

'I'm sorry I didn't warn you, but I had a spare half hour after work and I wanted to come up to give you this…' Ottilie took an envelope from her jacket pocket and handed it to Corrine, who took it with a questioning look. 'It's an invite,' Ottilie explained as Corrine opened it and read the page within. 'We're having a party – Heath and me. We'd love you to come. All of you – Penny and Melanie and their other halves too, if they can make it.'

'I'm sure they'd love to. Victor and I will definitely be there. Is it for a special occasion?'

'It might be,' Ottilie said, tapping the side of her nose.

'What sort of occasion?'

'I can't say now, but all will become clear.'

'Oh... well, do we need to bring anything?'

'Yourselves – that's all we need.'

'But if you're celebrating something we can't turn up empty-handed!'

'Of course you can!' Ottilie said. 'And besides, I must have cost you a small fortune in flour, eggs and sugar since I arrived in Thimblebury – you've spent more than enough on me without buying me gifts.'

Corrine put the invite on the kitchen table and went to boil the kettle while Ottilie took her usual seat and gazed out of the window. 'It's a lovely sunset from up here,' she said.

'It'll be a frosty night, though,' Corrine said. 'A bit late in the year too – always a problem for the garden.'

There was a beat of silence as Ottilie's gaze went back to the square of peach-and-gold horizon she could see through the window. When she looked back, Corrine was staring into space. Not admiring the sunset, as she was, but fixed on a spot on the wall as if deep in thought.

'Penny for them,' Ottilie said.

Corrine shook herself and smiled vaguely. 'Sorry.'

'Don't be. Is everything all right? You seem...'

Ottilie couldn't put her finger on it. Corrine had been her usual welcoming self, but now that she paid more attention, Ottilie could see that something wasn't right. She wasn't quite her usual self, even though she'd done a good job of pretending.

'You're not ill, are you?' Ottilie asked, her mind immediately going to Corrine's recent recovery from skin cancer. 'It's not... there's nothing troubling you? No more moles or—'

'Oh, no, nothing like that,' Corrine said. 'I'm fine – no relapses, nothing to worry about.'

Ottilie was about to ask more but then the back door was flung open by Victor. A complaint about something or other hung from his lips, but he stopped as he saw Ottilie and broke into a smile.

'Hello, stranger! What brings you to our corner? Or have you come to see my girls?'

'I'm never going to turn down a chance to feed the alpacas,' Ottilie said. 'If it's not too late in the day.'

'I'd just fastened them in for the night, but I expect I can undo the shed again this once, seeing as it's you.'

'Have a cup of tea first,' Corrine said.

'There's a spare in the pot for me, is there?' Victor kicked off his boots and sat them on a coconut mat at the back door.

'Isn't there always?' Corrine replied.

'What brings you up here then?' Victor asked Ottilie as he joined her at the table.

'We have an invite,' Corrine cut in, putting the envelope in front of him. 'To a party. We don't get so many of these nowadays, do we?'

'Not so many parties I can be bothered with nowadays.' Victor took up the envelope and pulled out the page.

'Will you come?' Ottilie asked. 'We'd love to see you there, but if you don't—'

'We'll come, lass,' Victor said, folding the page again. 'Only because it's you, mind. Is this open to us all? Penny and Melanie too?'

'Of course,' Ottilie said. 'You and your daughters and their husbands, and even the alpaca if you want to bring them!'

Ordinarily, he would have laughed at her joke – at the very least had a quip of his own – but Victor shot a strange and doubtful look at Corrine, and this time Ottilie knew something wasn't right.

'We'll tell them,' he said, turning back to Ottilie. 'I can't say whether they'll be coming or not, but I expect they'll let you know themselves.'

'We'll have enough food either way, so we'll leave it up to

them,' Ottilie replied. She gave Corrine a grateful smile for the cup she'd just put down in front of her. She then went to give one to Victor.

'No cake?' he asked, looking up at her.

'Give me a minute!' Corrine said impatiently as she went to the pantry. 'Honestly! I don't know how you aren't rolling down those hills with the amount you eat!'

'I work it off, don't I? Not like some, sat in this kitchen all day.' He winked at Ottilie, who returned it with a grin, even though she probably oughtn't to have done.

'Cheeky bugger!' Corrine snapped as she put a chunk of fruit cake in front of him. Her tone was gentler for Ottilie. 'You're having a slice?'

Ottilie smiled. 'As if I'd say no!'

'And you'll take one for your Heath,' Corrine added, a statement rather than a question, confirmed by the fact that she didn't wait for Ottilie's reply, instead pulling a roll of parchment paper from a drawer and wrapping a slice before putting a second one on a plate and giving them both to Ottilie.

'That'll make his day,' Ottilie said. 'He'd never say it to Flo, but I think yours is his favourite cake in the world.'

Corrine flushed and bustled at the sink. She didn't acknowledge the compliment, but Ottilie knew she was secretly pleased and proud to hear it.

The following morning, Ottilie made her usual call at Hilltop Farm before work. Ann and her son, Darryl, who lived at the farm, were Victor and Corrine's nearest neighbours – though there was a fair distance between their lands. But while Victor and Corrine's farm was a thriving business, Ann's was dilapidated and constantly close to bankruptcy. Somehow, she managed to keep things going, despite the challenges of Darryl's learning difficulties and her husband's untimely death. Ottilie worried more about her than Darryl, though she always made her daily visits about him so that she wouldn't make Ann feel guilty for taking the time from her day.

As always, she knocked lightly to announce her arrival and then let herself in through the unlocked back door. She stepped into the kitchen to find Ann at the stove – as always – and Darryl in his usual spot at the kitchen table with his favourite two books about trains open in front of him.

Ann turned from where she was frying bacon. 'Good morning!'

'Morning.' Ottilie smiled at her and then turned to her son. 'Darryl...'

He looked up at the sound of his name, gave the vaguest of nods and then returned to his books. It didn't worry Ottilie – she was used to this sort of response from him. If anything, it was reassuring. It meant he felt comfortable in her presence, that he trusted her. If there were any other reaction, if he was actually taking note of her and what she was doing, she'd be far more concerned.

'We're having a good one this morning,' Ann said. 'He's being very cooperative.'

'He's had his insulin?'

'Yes, no problem. I'm just doing his breakfast now. There's spare if you have time to stay.'

'I'm sorry. I'd love to, but I called to check on Darryl, of course, and also to give you this...'

Ottilie took an envelope from her bag and held it out.

Ann wiped her hands on her apron and took it from her. 'What's this?'

'An invite to a party we're having – me and Heath. I'd love you to come, but I completely understand if you can't make it for any reason...' she added, glancing at Darryl, who was still poring over his books.

'We'll do our best,' Ann said. 'What's the occasion?'

'A surprise,' Ottilie said.

'For Heath? Is it his birthday?'

'I mean a surprise for everyone else. We're celebrating a thing which we'll tell you about on the night.'

'Ah...' Ann smiled. 'Am I allowed to guess what it might be?'

'No,' Ottilie said, grinning back at her.

'Then I shall only wish you a huge congratulations and keep my guesses to myself,' Ann replied, her own smile growing. 'It's wonderful news. I hope you'll be very happy. Are you inviting everyone?'

'All the film club, some of my patients, everyone at the surgery, of course. I think Corrine and Victor will be there, so that will be someone for you to chat to if you do come.'

'That's good. Have you seen them recently then?'

'Yesterday.'

'Ah...'

Ottilie tried not to frown at the leading nature of Ann's short comment. 'Is there something I should know about?'

'Of course not.'

'Did you...' Ottilie paused. 'Do you know if all is well with them?'

'I think they have a lot of worries at the moment,' Ann said. 'I've seen Corrine a couple of times this week and she wasn't herself. I asked if she was all right and she said it wasn't her – something to do with one of her daughters. I don't know what exactly, but it sounds like marriage trouble to me.'

'Corrine said that?'

'Not as such, but, you know, reading between the lines...'

'I suppose that must be a worry,' Ottilie agreed. She fastened up her bag. 'I'm glad she's got you to talk to about it.'

'You won't tell her I said anything, will you? I'd hate her to think I was gossiping.'

'My lips are sealed. I'm glad to know I wasn't imagining it yesterday. I hope it works out for them, that's all. They're such lovely people they don't deserve all the troubles they seem to have. Anyway...' Ottilie readjusted her bag. 'I'd better get on my way if everything is nice and calm here.'

'Are you sure you won't take a sandwich?' Ann asked, nodding at the pan of bacon.

'Delicious as that smells, I don't have much time to wait for it to be cooked, I'm afraid. But thanks for the offer.'

With a last goodbye to Darryl, which he barely noticed, Ottilie took the road down the hill, the sun cresting a row of distant peaks to bathe the land in gold. She would never get bored of this view, not for as long as she lived. It was strange to imagine there was a time in her life when she'd never seen it. Soon, the happiness she'd found in Thimblebury would be complete. Heath would be living there with her, and everything would be just about perfect.

CHAPTER SIX

Magnus was wearing an apron depicting a muscled torso over his Hawaiian-style shirt and, despite its primary function being to keep his clothes clean, he wiped it down the moment a tiny speck of food splattered onto it. Geoff was more relaxed, chopping salad in a corner while he belted out a Frank Sinatra song.

Ottilie had been grateful for the offer of the large space of their home for her party, but taking up the favour had inevitably meant they were going to get involved in the preparations in a bigger way than she was ready for. Wisely, Heath had decided to go out and buy decorations. He didn't have as much patience with the local shop owners as Ottilie did. He liked them but often found interactions with them overwhelming. It would be easier later at the party when there were plenty of other guests to dilute their effect, but for now, Ottilie was content to let him have some breathing space. Stacey – Geoff's sister and Ottilie's best friend – had stepped in for Heath and was now helping Ottilie, Magnus and Geoff to prepare the party food.

'I love parties!' Magnus said, looking so flushed and stressed as he dashed across the kitchen with a tray of vol-au-vent cases from the oven that Ottilie, despite knowing he did love parties, couldn't imagine a statement further from the truth. Right now, he looked like someone who viewed parties in the same way an aristocrat would have viewed a trip to the guillotine in revolutionary France. 'I was only saying to Geoff earlier in the year that we ought to find an excuse to have one. There hasn't been a decent get-together in Thimblebury since Simon's housewarming.'

'And then you saved us the trouble of doing our own,' Geoff called from the salad bar.

'I expect we'll still do something,' Magnus said. 'Perhaps later in the year.'

Ottilie glanced at Geoff and could read his look of resignation. He was as sociable as Magnus, but if Magnus was like this preparing for every shindig, then she could see why he might view the prospect with some trepidation.

'Oh!' Magnus tutted as he picked off three pastry cases and took them to the bin.

'What was wrong with those?' Stacey dashed across to peer into the rubbish. 'That tray looked fine to me.'

'Wrong size,' Magnus muttered.

'Huh?'

'They were bigger than the others.'

'What a waste! Nobody would have noticed!' Stacey scolded.

'*I* noticed...'

Stacey shot Ottilie a similar look to the one she'd just seen on Geoff's face. At that moment, she was presented with a startling family resemblance that wasn't always obvious, and for some reason it made her start to laugh.

'What's so funny?' Geoff asked.

Ottilie shook her head, trying to stop. 'Everything today.'

'I expect you're giddy with the excitement,' Geoff replied mildly, seemingly content with her explanation. 'I expect it's a very exciting thing you have to announce later, eh?' he added with a wink.

Ottilie grinned. She suspected everyone had guessed what their announcement was going to be – it was fairly obvious, after all, but that hadn't detracted from the pleasure she got thinking about everyone's reactions when she and Heath finally made it. The residents of Thimblebury were some of the most important people in her life.

'It might be,' she said. 'More than that I'm looking forward to a nice evening with everyone too.'

'It will be lovely,' Magnus said with a grimace as he filled a piping bag with salmon and cream cheese mousse.

Ottilie exchanged an amused look with Geoff and Stacey, and then went over to him and wrapped her arms around his shoulders in a hug.

'Thank you,' she said.

He pulled back in some surprise. 'What for? I haven't done anything.'

'You've been your usual, generous, wonderful self. I know this is a lot of work for you and Geoff, but I want you to know how much Heath and I appreciate it.'

'Oh, Ottilie.' Magnus blushed now, and for the first time that afternoon, the stress cleared from his expression. 'You know you could ask anything of us. You're like family to us now.'

'I feel the same way,' Ottilie said.

'Well...' Magnus was smiling, but Ottilie could tell he was anxious to get back to his cooking. 'That's all right then.'

'I only thought I ought to let you know,' Ottilie said, 'And that everything will be perfect and there's no need to worry.'

'I'm not worried,' Magnus said, eyeing his salmon mixture even as he said so.

'Sure you're not,' Stacey said drily, and then Geoff started to laugh and Magnus's smile faded into a frown.

'Very funny,' he said, wagging a spoon at him. 'You can

laugh, but someone's got to keep the kitchen organised. Parties don't just cater themselves, you know.'

They were interrupted by a tap at the open window. All four looked across to see Flo standing outside.

'Are you going to let me in or what?' she grumbled. 'I've been knocking for half an hour and nobody answered!'

Ottilie suspected she'd knocked once at the door and they hadn't heard her, but it was better to indulge Flo in her little exaggerations than to try to correct her.

'Come on then, Florence,' Geoff said, going to the door. 'In you come...'

She stepped in and dumped a basket onto the counter. 'I brought these for the party.'

'That's good of you,' Magnus said, going over to the basket. 'We did say we had the catering in hand, though.'

'Still,' Flo huffed. 'Better to have too much than not enough.'

Magnus looked as if he might faint as he produced a pie that looked as if it could mill corn. 'What is this?'

'Pork pie,' Flo said with some pride. 'I've been all the way to Kendal on the bus for that.'

'Pork pie...' Magnus repeated.

'It looks lovely,' Ottilie said, dashing over to take it from him before he dropped it. They'd have to go to X-ray if it landed on his foot.

'Heath likes his pork pie,' Flo said.

'I know,' Ottilie replied. 'It'll go in the fridge for now until we're ready to cut it up.'

'Not the fridge,' Flo said. 'Needs to be room temperature to be at its best.'

'But it has meat in,' Magnus protested. 'It will poison everyone if you leave it out.'

'Not you,' Stacey said with a laugh, and Ottilie held back

one of her own. If there was to be a pork pie apocalypse, Magnus wouldn't be affected. The way he was looking at it now, he wasn't even going to make contact with the pie, let alone eat it. He looked as if he wanted to deny its very existence.

Flo ignored him and dug into the basket to produce a second. She handed it to Ottilie. 'Pork and egg. These ones have some lovely jelly in them.'

'Oh dear lord,' Magnus said, and Ottilie snorted, no longer able to hold in her laughter. Flo and Magnus both looked confused.

'Sorry,' Ottilie said, doing her best to stay in control. 'Like Geoff said, I'm a bit giddy today. Everything is making me silly.' She looked at Flo. 'Does Heath like the jelly?'

'Can't get enough of it,' Flo said, and then Stacey started to laugh too, starting Ottilie off again.

'What's so funny?' Flo demanded. 'I can go home, you know, and leave you all to struggle without me!'

'I'm sorry, Flo.' Ottilie gulped in a couple of steadying breaths and tried to straighten her face. 'Please don't do that – we're ever so grateful for your help. And thank you for the pies. I'm sure they'll go down a treat.'

Magnus shot a look of deepest suspicion at the offending articles and then went back to his vol-au-vent filling.

'If we need to leave them out,' Ottilie said, 'perhaps there's somewhere a bit cooler we can store them for now.' She turned to Geoff. 'You maybe have an outhouse or something that's out of direct sunlight?'

'Leave it to me,' Stacey said, taking off her apron and gathering up the pies. 'There's an old pantry at my place – they'll be fine in there.'

'In that case, there's an old pantry at mine too—' Flo began, but Ottilie stopped her.

'Stacey can take care of it,' she said. 'Don't want to have you walking back to yours when you've just come from there. We've got plenty to do here – if that's all right with you.'

'What do you need?' Flo asked while Stacey slipped out. Ottilie was glad to see her mood improve instantly. 'Sandwiches? What sort? Cheese and onion? Has anyone been to fetch a bit of ham?'

Magnus rolled his eyes, and it was lucky Flo didn't see it. Ottilie had to admit that they had very different ideas about party catering and that there would be an interesting mix of themes when they eventually put the food out for their guests. But she liked that. It was representative of their lives in Thimblebury, of all the different and interesting people they knew and loved from all backgrounds and age groups. Their party was for everyone, and there ought to be something for everyone. So if there were delicate, caviar-topped blinis alongside hefty sausage rolls, that was OK – that, to Ottilie, was how it ought to be.

'There's cheese and ham in the shop,' Geoff said. 'Chloe's covering for us – just go and ask her.'

Flo gave a short nod before bustling out.

'Thank you,' Ottilie said. 'If you keep track of what we're having from the shop, I'll settle up later, if that's all right.'

'You don't owe us anything, my love,' Geoff said. 'Consider it our... well, whatever occasion your party is, consider the food our gift.'

'I couldn't—'

'Yes, you could. That's the end of that conversation.'

Heath arrived with the decorations an hour later, and Geoff went with him to help put them up while Ottilie continued in the kitchen with Magnus, Stacey and Flo. An hour after that, Chloe shut the shop and came through with Mackenzie. Everyone stopped to make a fuss of the little boy, who had just started to walk and was roaming around the kitchen like a drunken leprechaun while Chloe sat with a glass of water. Ottilie noticed she looked pale.

'Are you OK, Chloe?'

'She's not sleeping well,' Stacey said, scooping Mackenzie into her arms. 'Are you, Chlo?'

'Any particular reason?' Ottilie asked.

'I dunno,' Chloe replied in her usual dull way. She wasn't known for her enthusiasm in any circumstances, and today was no different. It often came across as rude or surly, but Ottilie had learned over the time she'd got to know her better that it wasn't her intention. She simply had a cynical, world-weary manner that was far older than her almost twenty years. Ottilie had once put it to Stacey – who was as cheery and excitable as her daughter was reserved – that it might be a result of motherhood and abandonment by the father at such a young age, but Stacey told her that Chloe had always been like that, even as a young girl. Ottilie knew that she'd had a tough childhood too, however, and much as Stacey preferred to overlook the fact that abandonment by her own father too, at the age of ten, might have something to do with that, it was difficult for Ottilie to look at Chloe and not think it true.

'We could keep Mackenzie here with us if you want to go and get some sleep,' Ottilie said, glancing at everyone else. Geoff and Stacey seemed happy enough. Magnus looked less certain, and Flo grimaced.

'We're busy enough,' she said.

'We're almost done, aren't we?' Ottilie asked. 'It's going to be a case of taking the tableware through to set up and then a quick drink before we go to get changed for later, isn't it? One of us can stay with Mackenzie while the others do that.'

'I'm fine.' Chloe sipped her water. 'I don't know what everyone's making a fuss about.'

'We're only concerned,' Stacey said.

'Nobody was concerned when they asked me to mind the shop.'

'Hey,' Stacey said, her tone sterner now. 'You promised to do that last week – nobody knew you were going to be knackered. And you're getting paid, so less of that.'

'I'm only saying,' Chloe grumbled.

'And we're offering to help now,' Stacey continued. 'So do you want to go home for a lie-down or not?'

'I'll take Mackenzie with me,' she said. 'He'll probably go down for a nap too if I put him in bed with me.'

After taking the little boy from Stacey's arms, Chloe dumped her glass in the sink and left. Ottilie watched her go and then turned to Stacey.

'Is she all right? She does look a bit peaky.'

'Overdoing it, probably. Back and forth to her boyfriend's house all the time, looking after Mackenzie and then all the studies for that part-time degree she's started. I told her when she signed up for that she was taking too much on, but...' Stacey shrugged. 'You know Chloe. She won't be told.'

'But it will be a brilliant career once she gets her qualification. I think she'll make a great social worker – I mean, who knows more about life throwing curveballs than Chloe?'

Stacey nodded. 'Nobody's saying it won't be, and I know she'll be amazing at her job, I just think she should have waited a couple of years until Mackenzie is at school before starting the course.'

'I suppose she feels as if she's already on the back foot,' Ottilie said. 'I bet none of the other students have a small child.'

'I think a few do, actually,' Stacey said. 'I think some of them are older than her too. I pointed that out, but she's adamant she's not waiting any longer. I suppose I can't blame her; I just worry she's not coping.'

Ottilie smiled. 'As long as you're looking out for her.'

'As long as I do it without her noticing.' Stacey offered a

wan smile in return. 'God forbid she'd realise I'm watching her like a hawk all the time.'

'Do you think it would be easier for her to talk to me if she needed someone to confide in?' Ottilie asked.

'It might, but she'd probably expect you to tell me what had been said, and that would put her off.'

'I'll try to let her know anyway, without making it too obvious, that I'm around if she wants to offload. And I didn't do the same course, but I know how punishing that kind of study schedule can be, so there's that too. If she only wants to talk to me about uni, that's something, isn't it?'

'Thanks, Ott. You're one in a million, you know that?'

'I'm only doing what you'd do for me.'

The kitchen door opened. Heath and Geoff came in.

'All done in there,' Geoff said. 'Any time you want to move the tableware in feel free.'

Magnus went to a cupboard and took out a pile of neatly folded white tablecloths with silver stars on them. 'These are lovely, Ottilie,' he said. 'If you want to get rid when you've finished today, we'd happily buy them from you.'

'You could just have them,' Heath said, looking at Ottilie, who nodded agreement. 'I doubt we'll be using them again, and you've done so much for us today.'

'In that case, thank you,' Magnus said. 'We'll definitely use them.'

'Well, this *is* the Thimblebury party household,' Stacey said.

'Given we're in Thimblebury,' Geoff replied, 'that's hardly an accolade. It's not exactly Beverly Hills.'

Flo looked at her wrist and then tapped at her watch as she held it up. 'Never mind all this yakking – have you seen the time?'

'You're right,' Ottilie said. 'Getting carried away here. Let's get everything in the other room and then we can go and get changed for later.'

'Honestly,' Heath said as he arrived at her side and smiled down at her, 'I think you're having more fun doing this bit than you will at the party.'

'You know me so well,' Ottilie said with a light laugh. 'I'll enjoy the party, and it feels like an occasion special enough to make an effort, but generally I hate being the centre of attention and I hate formal events.'

'We didn't have to do it,' he said, his expression suddenly troubled. 'You said—'

'I wanted to, and I still do. I only meant it's not a habit I could get into. I'm excited to announce our news. It deserves something special.' She grabbed his hand. '*You* deserve something special. I'm so lucky to have you.'

'We're both lucky,' he said. 'But I'm sorry to break it to you – I think I'm luckier than you. I think I definitely got the best out of this deal.'

'Shake a leg, you two!' Flo called from across the room.

'Yes, boss!' Heath grinned, slipping his hand from Ottilie's grasp. He offered her a faint look of apology, and her smile grew. She was excited to be marrying Heath, but as she glanced at Flo, she was fully aware that marriage to Heath wasn't going to be without its challenges…

Ottilie studied her reflection in the bedroom mirror and decided she was overdressed. She'd been back and forth on this dress ever since she'd bought it. In the shop, the midnight-blue satin, ruched and pinched at the waist and flaring out into a calf-length skirt, had stolen her breath. Heath had told her she looked spectacular in it when she'd modelled it and asked whether he thought it was the right one for the party. She hadn't been convinced, thinking he would only say nice things, even if she was wearing a rubbish sack. So she'd sent a photo to Stacey, who'd said it was gorgeous and perfect for her party, and that had made Ottilie feel better. But now that she had it on, she had doubts again. She was gradually convincing herself, as she looked at the mirror, that everyone would think she thought she was at the Oscars or something.

'Nobody would think that,' she told herself sternly. 'Don't be an idiot.'

'What's that?' Heath wandered into the bedroom doing up his shirt. He stopped and whistled. 'Hey, why don't we skip the party and go straight to the after-party?'

Ottilie slapped him away as he tried to grab her around the waist to pull her into a kiss. 'No time for that.' She frowned. 'You don't think it's too much, do you?'

He stood back and smiled. 'God, no! You look amazing!'

Ottilie turned back to her reflection, adjusting her neckline and feeling that it was far too low now that she was ready to appear in public in it.

'Stop it!' Heath said gently. 'I can read your mind.'

'Can you?'

'Well, not always, but I am getting good at recognising some of your expressions. You look beautiful. This is your party, your moment in the spotlight – stop feeling as if you don't deserve it because you do.'

'It's your party too.'

'Yes, it is, and I would like very much to see you at our party in that dress. Nothing would make me prouder than to walk into that room with you as you look right now. So there. Stop second-guessing everything. And even if anyone thought you were overdressed – who cares? It's your party, not theirs!'

'See,' Ottilie complained. 'Now you've put that idea back into my head again. I might try something else on—'

'Don't even think about it. Do I have to barricade the wardrobe until tomorrow?'

'You really think it's all right?'

'Yes! You've bought it with hard-earned money because you loved it in the shop. What were you planning to do with it? Pull it out to stare at it once a year and never wear it?'

'It wouldn't be the first time,' Ottilie said sheepishly.

Heath kissed her lightly. 'Wear it and enjoy it.'

She nodded. 'You're right – ignore me. I think I'm just nervous.'

'Me too, if I'm being completely honest,' Heath said. 'But we're going to be in a room full of friends, and it's going to be fine. I'll tell you one thing, though,' he added, fastening the last of his shirt buttons. 'If we're like this at the engagement party, what are we going to be like at the wedding?'

'Don't,' Ottilie said, turning back to the mirror. 'I don't even want to think about that right now.'

Heath kissed her again. 'Everything will be perfect, and you are perfect, so stop worrying and let's get over there, or they'll be starting without us!'

When they got back to Magnus and Geoff's, Stacey, Chloe and her boyfriend, Ollie, baby Mackenzie and Flo were already there.

'Simon sends his apologies – he's going to be late,' Stacey said, rolling her eyes.

'Let me guess…' Ottilie replied, 'something he needs to do at the surgery. He never stops thinking about that place.'

'Tell me about it. I mean, I love him for being so caring, but from time to time, I'd quite like him to pay as much attention to me as he does his patients.'

Ottilie offered a look of sympathy, but there was little else she could say. She knew only too well how dedicated Simon was to his patients, and that was hardly likely to change. If

Stacey wanted to be with him, she was going to have to learn how to live with that reality.

Flo came over with an envelope and shoved it at Heath. 'I didn't buy a present,' she said. 'Don't know what you want.'

'We don't need anything, Gran,' Heath said, taking the envelope and undoing it to pull out a card with two fluffy rabbits on the front and the words 'On Your Engagement' emblazoned in silver lettering across it.

'Thank you,' he said, stuffing it back into the envelope so that nobody could see the wording. He shot a look of resignation at Ottilie. Had there really been any point in trying to keep their announcement secret? It seemed that most of Thimblebury already knew, even if they hadn't divulged it to one another.

'When you decide what you want, I'll buy it for you,' Flo said.

'Honestly, there's nothing we need,' Ottilie said. 'We'd rather you kept your money – we're just glad to have you here.'

'But I have to buy something!' Flo protested. 'I don't want people to think I couldn't be bothered!'

Heath put his arm around her and grinned. 'As if anyone would think that,' he said.

Flo grunted. 'No sign of your parents yet either,' she added. 'What time are they supposed to be arriving?'

'Any time now, I suppose,' Heath said. 'I told them what time it was due to start, so I'm sure they'll be here soon.'

'Not if your mother has anything to do with it,' Flo shot back. 'She couldn't arrive anywhere on time to save her life.'

'As long as they make it before we all leave, it will be fine by me,' he said. He glanced out of the window to see a taxi pulling up. 'I think this might be your mum, Ottilie,' he said.

'It is.' Ottilie went to the door. When she opened up, Ottilie's mother, Francine, was paying the driver. As he drove away, she looked round with a broad smile.

'You look lovely!' she said, nodding approval at Ottilie's dress. 'Now I feel as if I haven't made enough effort.'

'You look great,' Ottilie said. 'I'm sorry we didn't have time to come and pick you up—'

'Don't be daft! I wouldn't have expected it! It was fine. I got a train to Windermere, and the taxi wasn't too far from there. It was quite a nice journey, actually. Scenic – very peaceful.'

'It makes a change for a train to be peaceful,' Ottilie said as they walked into the house together. 'Heath's inside with his grandma. You know the drill there, right?'

'Yes.' Francine laughed. 'I have been warned!'

'And there are a ton of other people I want you to meet.'

Everyone huddled round to greet Francine as Ottilie introduced her. Ottilie had never been prouder of her community and the welcome they had for her mum.

Heath's parents arrived shortly after, and Heath did the same, taking them around the room to introduce them to the other guests, Ottilie feeling strangely shy around them. Despite the fact that she'd been with Heath for well over a year now, she had only met them a handful of times and didn't really know them well enough to feel at ease in their company. She liked them, of course, managing to resist the influence of Flo, who had very little time for Heath's mother. She thought Flo too harsh a judge. Heath's mum, Lori, and his dad, Colin, were always friendly to Ottilie, and she had no reason to think badly of them.

'Excited?' Lori asked as she adjusted a patterned silk scarf in bright, acid colours. One thing Ottilie couldn't deny, Heath didn't get his dress sense from her. Nothing she wore matched, and not even the colours in her dress, scarf, shoes and handbag made any attempt to complement each other. It was like she'd gone to her wardrobe and pulled out the first of every item she could lay her hands on and thrown them all on, and had then left the house without a single glance at a mirror. But her expression was so sweet and wholesome that, despite also being quite dippy, Ottilie couldn't help but like her.

'Nervous, to be honest.'

'Oh, I don't think there's any need for that,' Lori said. 'Though you do strike me as a nervy type, so I suppose that's only natural.'

Ottilie wondered if she struck everyone as a nervy type and, if so, whether she ought to be doing something about that, but she didn't have long to ponder it. The door opened again, this time to mark the arrival of Fliss, her husband, Charles, Simon, Lavender and her husband.

'Will you excuse me?' Ottilie asked Lori. 'I just need to say hello.'

Over the course of the following hour, the rest of the guests arrived. The room was crowded, the temperature climbing with each extra body, until Magnus opened the patio doors and people began to spill out into the garden. The music, as anyone who knew Magnus and Geoff would have expected, was an interesting mix – everything from forties show tunes to sixties film scores, to Fleetwood Mac, to the latest Eurovision winner and just about everything in between. More than once, Ottilie had caught Chloe and Ollie sniggering in a corner, while Stacey paraded around with Mackenzie in her arms like she'd just won a gold medal at the Olympics and wanted to show everyone. Ottilie didn't mind Chloe and Ollie having their fun. She was grateful that they'd come at all – at their age, she would probably have thought being at a party where most of the guests were at least twenty years older was lame too.

The other thing she noticed about Chloe and Ollie was how they looked at each other. She was convinced, without Stacey having to say so, that they were very much in love, and that made her happy too. Chloe had been a deeply troubled and unhappy young woman when Ottilie had first arrived in Thimblebury – abandoned by her dad, and then a boyfriend who'd got her pregnant with a baby she hadn't been ready for. It was good to see her so much happier and settled now.

She made a point of giving every guest as much of her attention as she could spare. Corrine and Victor had been in good spirits, as had their daughters, though the two husbands seemed less happy to be there. Ottilie was sorry to see Ann from Hilltop Farm hadn't made it but not surprised. Darryl would have found it a difficult environment, and Ann perhaps hadn't managed to find someone to stay home with him.

A couple of hours in, Magnus came over to her, rosy-cheeked and breathless after doing an impressive tribute to Sally Bowles performing 'Mein Herr' from *Cabaret* for a select group of guests who were drunk enough to appreciate it.

'Geoff says we ought to eat soon.'

What Ottilie suspected Geoff meant was that Magnus ought to eat soon to soak up some of the alcohol he'd clearly had too much of. But she nodded and smiled. 'I think that might be a good idea. I suppose people might be getting hungry.'

'Do you want to say a few words first?' Magnus asked. 'Or afterwards?'

'Maybe we'll do it first, while we still have their attention. Once the food is available, people might drift off to eat in the garden or whatever and it might be harder to get everyone in one place. People are already drifting off...' Ottilie frowned. 'I should have thought about this happening...'

'I think it's fine if you do it soon.' Magnus twirled once and then hiccupped. 'I'll go and tell Geoff. He can do the glass-tinkle thing.'

Ottilie watched him weave through the gathering in search of his partner. From behind her came the sound of Heath's voice.

'Someone's enjoying the party,' he said. She turned to see him smiling. 'How about you? Are you enjoying yourself? I've hardly had a chance to ask you.'

'It's hectic, isn't it? But, yes. It's lovely to see so many people here.'

'They're here for you.'

'For both of us.'

Heath shook his head. 'For you, Ottilie. I don't mind that. You mean a lot to everyone here – I'm just a part of your entourage as far as they're all concerned.'

Ottilie prodded him playfully. 'Don't be silly. They all love you.'

'Not as much as they love you. It's hardly surprising when you stop to think about it for a minute.'

Ottilie was about to protest when a shout went up for quiet. Geoff was, indeed, doing a glass-tinkle thing, tapping with alarming force on a crystal goblet for everyone's attention.

'We're going to have a few words from Ottilie or Heath... not sure which, or maybe you'll be lucky enough to get both of them!' Everyone laughed and when it died off, Geoff continued. 'And then we're going to unwrap the food and you can all help yourselves.'

'Finally,' Flo grumbled from the crowd.

'Don't worry,' Geoff replied with a look of mischief. 'Your absolutely titanic pork pies are cut up and waiting for you.'

Everyone laughed again, but Flo only scowled at him. Ottilie turned to Heath. He offered her a hand.

'Together?' he asked.

She nodded, her heart hammering as she took his hand. She couldn't even say why she was so nervous. She was in a room full of people she knew and loved, and there would be nothing but goodwill and delight over their announcement, and yet, she almost felt guilty for demanding their time to make it, as if she wasn't deserving. She knew what Heath would say about that, and he'd be right, but that didn't make her feel any less stressed. At least he was by her side, and she knew he'd do the talking for her if she dried up.

Every face waited with an expectant smile. Heath cleared his throat.

'Thank you all for coming. Some of you know, and probably most of you have guessed, that Ottilie and I didn't only want to have a knees-up – though we did want that and it's turning out to be a decent one...'

There was more polite laughter which Heath allowed to fade before he continued. 'We've actually brought you here to make an announcement.' He turned to Ottilie. 'Do you want to take this?'

She shook her head. 'You're doing a far better job than I could.'

'Right... anyway, I asked Ottilie to marry me, and for some unfathomable reason that Fliss or Simon might want to make a psychiatric referral for, she said yes. So I suppose that means we're getting married, and we just wanted to let you all know.'

A cheer went up from the revellers, and then Magnus started a string of hip-hip-hoorays that were far more hip-hip-hoorays than the norm, and when it died down and Heath bade everyone to go and get food, he and Ottilie were inundated with well-wishers wanting to offer their congratulations in person.

'It was all right in the end, wasn't it?' Heath asked once the last of them had gone.

Ottilie nodded, unable to stop smiling even though her cheeks ached. 'More than all right. Thank you for doing the talking.'

'I wasn't sure if I was taking over, but—'

'Not a bit. Shall we go and get something to eat? I don't know about you, but now that's over, I'm starving.'

'Yeah, and we've got a pile of pork pie bigger than Scafell Pike to get through before we go home. If there's any left at the end of this, Gran will never stop going on about it.'

They were making their way to the tables when Geoff

called them over to the outside door. Ottilie was alarmed by the sudden look of worry on his face.

'What's wrong?' she asked, but he only nodded at a young woman waiting outside in the porch.

'She's asking to speak to you. Do you know her?'

'No... I don't think so.'

Ottilie could see that something in their brief exchange had rattled Geoff, though she couldn't imagine what. But then she looked again at the young woman, perhaps in her mid-twenties, slim and pale, and noted the anxiety in her face as she waited and knew that Geoff had drawn the same conclusion as she was currently doing. This woman was on a mission. Whatever she'd come to do or say, it was something she felt uneasy about.

Ottilie's first thought was that she might have something to do with her husband Josh's killer. It had happened before – Heath's ex had come to Thimblebury pleading the man's case and trying to get Ottilie to intervene in the court proceedings because he was her cousin, and had almost split her and Heath up in the process. This time, Heath seemed as confused as she was as he looked at the woman. It was obvious he didn't know her. Perhaps it was something entirely unconnected, though, again, Ottilie couldn't imagine what.

'You're not going out there?' Heath asked as Ottilie began to head out of the door.

'She's asked to speak to me.'

'I'm coming with you.'

Ottilie didn't argue. But the girl looked warily at Heath before addressing Ottilie.

'I'm sorry to disturb you. Are you having a party here or something?'

'It's all right. What can I do for you?'

'It's... awkward.' The young woman glanced at Heath again. 'Could we talk somewhere quiet?'

'You can say what you need to say here,' Heath cut in, but

Ottilie silenced him with a pleading look. This woman was nervous and he wasn't helping.

'Heath... can you get me some food before it goes? I'll be back inside in a tick.'

'You're not...' He paused, seemed to realise that she wasn't going to back down and that she was going to find out what this woman had come to say, and then gave a vague shrug. 'Shout if you need me.'

'I will. Thanks.'

As Heath went back inside, glancing around every couple of steps as if he couldn't decide if he was doing the right thing or not, Ottilie turned back to the young woman. 'There are some benches over by the trees if you'd rather talk there, away from the house.'

'Thanks,' the woman said, making her way as Ottilie followed. She took a seat, but Ottilie didn't.

'I'm sorry,' the woman said again.

'You haven't done anything wrong.'

'I didn't realise you were having a party. Is it for something nice?'

'Yes,' Ottilie said.

'For you? It's your birthday or something?'

'It's for... well, it's a celebration, but it's not just my party. I don't mean to be rude, but—'

'Sorry, of course...'

'You don't have to keep apologising.' Deciding that she seemed harmless after all, and that hovering over her was probably making her more nervous, Ottilie took a seat next to her on the bench and offered a reassuring smile. 'I'm sorry, but are we supposed to know each other? I hate to ask, and if I've met you somewhere and forgotten, I—'

'No, you don't know me. I only found out about you a couple of days ago. I sort of stalked you online a bit. Sorry, I didn't mean to be creepy or anything, but it seemed like the easiest way to get hold of you.'

'You went to a lot of trouble then. So whatever it is you've come to say... well, I suppose you'd better say it.'

The girl gave a short nod, paused and then spoke again. 'I think you're my sister.'

Ottilie stared at her.

'I'm sorry,' the woman said again.

'*I'm* sorry,' Ottilie replied. 'I don't know what to say. Are you sure?'

'Yes.'

'Oh...' Ottilie was dumbfounded. She stared into space, not a coherent reply in her head.

'But if you want me to go,' the girl added, 'I will. I can see it's a bad time.'

'Not yet. How... sorry, but how do you know this?'

'You took a DNA test, and you must have ticked the box to make it available to others who shared the same DNA.'

'I had no idea I'd done that,' Ottilie replied slowly. 'Didn't even know there was a box to tick. And you're really sure?'

'Yes.'

'Oh...'

'So your dad must be my dad too.'

'No, I don't think...' Ottilie paused. 'It can't be... What's his name?'

'My dad? Conrad. Conrad Greening.'

Ottilie shook her head slowly, but an idea was forming, one she didn't much care for. There were little things she'd noticed as a child. She'd never attached much importance to them, but somehow they'd bugged her. Like how little she resembled her dad. It meant nothing, of course, and people said she looked like her mum, but it had always bothered her that there seemed to be *nothing* of him in her when she looked at photos or stared into the mirror. She was hardly a carbon copy of her mother either. So where had that pointy little nose come from? Where had she picked up those freckles? Nursing had later taught her that traits could be seen from generations back, even when they hadn't appeared in the intervening ones, and knowing that had put her adult mind at rest. But now she looked at this girl and she couldn't deny that she saw some of her own features reflected there. As much as she didn't want to believe it, she was beginning to see the truth – this other man, this Conrad... he was her biological father.

'But my dad... It can't be right.'

'Here...' The girl unlocked her phone and opened a page on the company website that showed their results and the link. Ottilie stared at it, hardly able to believe what she could see – but there was no mistake.

'Is it just you?' she asked in a daze. 'I don't have any other siblings I ought to know about?'

'It's just me.'

'What's your name?'

'Fion.'

As if in a dream, Ottilie held out her hand. Later, she would realise what a strange reaction it was, but for now, she was so blindsided by the speed with which her world had changed that she couldn't think of anything else to do. All that she was, the comfort that came from knowing where she'd come from, who her family were, had been destroyed in an instant, in half a dozen sentences uttered by a girl she'd never met. 'Pleased to meet you, Fion.'

'Are you?'

'Well, it's not every day you discover a sister you never knew about.'

'Half, I suppose.'

'Still half a sister more than I thought I had.' Ottilie tried to smile for Fion's sake because she looked as if she was already wishing she hadn't come. She didn't much feel like it, though, and she had to wonder if her shock was showing, despite trying so hard to keep it to herself. 'Does your... Have you told your dad about me? Did he already know? Does he know you're here?'

'No. I was scared. Mum would have been devastated if she'd thought Dad had cheated on her.' The girl studied Ottilie for a moment. 'You're too old, I think, for that to be the case because they only met thirty years ago. So at least I can tell Mum that's true.'

Ottilie ignored what might have been an insult to some. 'You're planning to tell them?'

'I don't know. Do you want them to know about you?'

'I...' Ottilie glanced at the house.

'You want to get back to the party?'

Ottilie glanced towards the house again. How could she saunter back in and carry on as if nothing had happened? And what was she meant to do with the girl who had come all this way to change her life? Ottilie didn't have an answer for either of those questions. All she could do was what came instinctively to her – she could reach out and try to make friends. 'Actually, I was going to ask if you wanted something to drink? Or food? We've got food if you're hungry.'

'In there?' Fion looked at the house now. Heath was at the window watching them, but the minute he realised he'd been seen, he moved away.

'I can bring something out to you.'

'No, thanks. I'm all right.'

'Where did you say you lived?'

'Penrith. I came on the bus.'

'Are you going back there tonight?'

'There's a late one, I think.'

'Right.'

'I'll go. Sorry again.'

'For what? For being my sister?'

'For coming here and interrupting your party. I hope I haven't ruined it.'

'Well, you've certainly taken it in a completely unexpected direction. Listen, I do have to go back in. If you want to meet up again, I don't mind if you contact me. I mean, I'd like to if you would.'

'I would,' Fion said, looking brighter now. 'When?'

'That's up to you. Message me and we'll work out a date.'

'OK.' Fion stood up.

'You'll be all right getting back to the bus?'

'Yeah. Sorry again for—' She stopped as Ottilie shook her head. 'Sorry. I mean, I know: *don't keep apologising*.'

'Not when you have nothing to apologise for.'

'Thank you.'

'For what?'

'For…' Fion shrugged. 'Talking to me, I guess.' She stood for a moment, arms swinging awkwardly at her sides, and then she turned and walked towards the gates. Ottilie blew out a long breath as she watched her go. As she and Heath had made their engagement announcement, she'd been tipsy, but she was sober now. The minute Fion had disappeared from view behind the shrubs that bordered Magnus and Geoff's garden, Heath was at her side, two glasses of wine in his hands. He offered one to her before taking a seat on the bench.

'OK, what the hell was that about?'

She turned to him, the words seeming unreal as they came from her mouth. 'Apparently, I have a sister.'

CHAPTER SEVEN

'What I can't figure out is how she found you here,' Heath said. 'At the surgery, maybe, or even at your house, but here? How could she have known?'

'I doubt it's as big a mystery as you imagine,' Ottilie said. 'Think about it. She can see my Facebook feed. And so she can probably see my friends as well. It only takes one of them to tag where we are and *voila*. It's that easy.'

'Bloody Facebook,' Heath huffed.

Ottilie sipped at her wine, resolving to look at her privacy settings. She didn't mind that Fion had found her, but perhaps it wouldn't hurt to make her information a bit safer.

'I'd rather people were able to find me at a party here than them knowing where I live.'

'She doesn't know where you live then?'

'She didn't say so I wouldn't worry. She seems harmless. In fact, she seems sweet.'

'You still don't know anything about her.'

'True. I'll arrange to meet on neutral ground – a café or something.'

'You're determined you're going to meet her?'

'Why wouldn't I?'

'Again because you don't know the first thing about her.'

'And I'm not going to if I don't make the effort, am I?'

'I don't know how you're taking it all so calmly.'

'I don't think I am. To be honest, I don't think it's sunk in yet.'

'Are you going to tell your mum?'

'I suppose I ought to. Better to be honest from the start than have her find out another way in a few months. I don't know how the hell I have that conversation, though.'

'It's a shame your mum didn't think that when she kept your dad a secret from you.'

Ottilie shook her head. 'We don't know what happened yet. I'm not going to be angry with her anyway.'

'You're never angry with anyone, and sometimes I think that's your biggest flaw.'

'Oh God, I'm sorry. You didn't sign up for this kind of drama, and I must seem like such a lost cause right now, but...'

'I don't want you to be sorry. I don't want you to change. It's your biggest flaw but also one of your loveliest qualities. That's not to say it doesn't make me worry. You're going to grab her today?'

Ottilie paused, her gaze going back to the house. 'It doesn't seem like the ideal time, does it? Difficult not to, but I think I'm going to have to keep it to myself until this is all over.'

'Difficult is the understatement of the year!'

Their discussion was cut short by Geoff coming out to them. It seemed he'd also been waiting for Fion to leave.

'Is everything all right?' he asked. Ottilie could see he wanted to know more but wasn't sure he ought to ask.

'Fine,' Ottilie said. 'I hope you don't mind...'

'Mind what?'

'That she turned up like that looking for me. To your house, I mean. But there's nothing to worry about—'

'I'm not worried, darling. If you say it's all right, then I'm happy with that.'

'Do you mind if I don't tell you about it for the moment?' Ottilie asked him. 'I'm still trying to get my head around it; I will tell you as soon as I do.'

'Of course. It's none of my business anyway.'

'But I will – just not today.'

Geoff hesitated, and then went inside.

'Are you...' Heath paused. 'Are you happy about the idea of having a sister?'

'I don't know,' Ottilie said. 'Maybe a bit. I always felt like I missed out on siblings as a kid. I suppose I'll know more how I feel when I get to know her better.'

'So that's a decision you've already taken then. You want to get to know her.'

'She did come all this way to find me, and she does seem nice. So yes, I suppose I don't see any harm in it. I'd better talk it over with Mum first.'

'Is it anything to do with her?'

'What do you mean?'

'Is it her business if you choose to meet up with your sister?'

'I think she'd tell me to make up my own mind about that, but she needs to know. It's only fair – imagine if she found out and I hadn't said anything. She'd be so hurt.'

'You're right – I don't know why I said that.'

'We'd better go back inside – people will start to notice we've gone missing.'

'They might,' Heath said with a smile. 'But they'd probably assume we were off doing some private celebrating of our own.'

'Yes, and that's the kind of gossip I'd like to avoid,' Ottilie said.

'You're all right to go back in? You don't need more time?'

'I can't pretend I'm not in a bit of a daze, but I'm fine. I can't abandon a party that's meant to be for us, especially as everyone in there has made such an effort to be here.'

He held out his hand and she took it, and doing her best to hide the turmoil turning her inside out, she followed him back into the thick of it.

Ottilie tried to forget Fion, at least for the rest of the party, but it was hard. Their brief but meaningful conversation kept running through her head. She found herself examining every little word, every intonation, every facial expression, trying to figure out what they meant, if there was something to be read between the lines. But most of all, her world seemed entirely different than the one she'd inhabited just an hour before.

She had a sister. She was no longer an only child, as she'd always been. She had a whole new family and she knew barely anything about them. And every time she caught sight of her mum across the room chatting to someone, and every time their paths crossed briefly and they shared some observation on how the party was going, Ottilie was desperate to tell her what had happened. It wasn't the right time, and she didn't even know where she was going to start when it was. Her mum would need reassurance. She'd feel guilty and she'd fret over what this meant for Ottilie, even though Ottilie herself was feeling remarkably calm, despite all the questions racing around her head.

As proceedings started to wind up and people began to leave, Ottilie found Francine sitting in the conservatory with a cup of tea Flo had made for her.

'On your own?' Ottilie asked.

'Having a breather. Flo was in here with me, but she's gone to ask Heath something.'

'Have you had a nice time?'

'Lovely. Have you?'

Ottilie nodded. 'It's been quite an evening.'

Francine gave her a sideways look, and Ottilie wondered whether her tone had revealed more of her feelings than she'd meant to. But Francine didn't ask; she only reached for her mug and blew softly on the tea before taking a sip. Ottilie could hear people saying their goodbyes in the main room. She knew she ought to go out and see them off, but this moment, here with her mum, suddenly seemed like the moment to share her news. Or rather, to get it off her chest. Either way, she'd have to do it soon. But then Flo came back in and the moment was snatched away.

'Are you ready to go?' she asked Francine.

Ottilie raised her eyebrows. 'Where are you two going off to? Is there an after-party I don't know about? A new club opening somewhere?'

'Francine is going to stay with me tonight,' Flo said briskly.

Ottilie turned to her mum.

'I was going to mention it a minute ago. We decided it might be nice for you and Heath to have your place to yourselves... in the circumstances.'

'But—' Ottilie began.

'I'll be glad of the company, and we can get to know each other better,' Flo cut in.

'What about Heath's mum and dad?'

'They're going to be staying with me too,' Flo said. 'I've got room.'

Ottilie was silent for a moment. Her mum seemed more than content with the arrangements, and she supposed it would mean she could get to know Heath's family better – which had to be a good thing, assuming they'd all get along, and she couldn't see why they wouldn't. But it did mean the opportunity for Ottilie to talk to her mum about Fion was gone for tonight. Unless she could take her to one side before she left, but it didn't seem fair to pack her off to Flo's house with that kind of bombshell. Once again, it was taken out of her hands as Victor and Corrine came to say goodbye.

'We wanted to say goodnight before we went home,' Corrine said, coming to give Ottilie a hug. 'It's been lovely – thank you for inviting us.'

'Thank *you* for coming!' Ottilie said. 'And for the gift.'

'It was only a little bottle of something,' Victor said.

'We couldn't turn up with nothing. Congratulations, by the way. We're so happy for you.'

After another tipsy hug and a promise from Ottilie that she would visit the following week, they left. During that time, Francine had finished her tea, and Ottilie could see Flo was itching to leave too. It wasn't surprising – it had been a long day for Flo, running errands and helping out with the preparations before the party.

'I'm going to round up that silly pair,' she said, marching from the conservatory.

Francine frowned as she watched her go. 'Who's she going to find?'

'If I know anything about Flo, I'm going to assume she's talking about Heath's mum and dad.'

'Oh,' Francine replied warily. 'Don't they get along?'

'I think they get along fine, but Flo has a short fuse, and I think they both test it sometimes. Don't worry,' she added, seeing the concern on her mum's face. 'It shouldn't be a problem for you tonight. I'm sure they'll all be on their best behaviour with you there.'

'I see.' Francine looked a little doubtful.

'You can still come to stay with us if you'd rather.'

'I don't know. I think Flo will be offended now if I say I've changed my mind about staying with her.'

'I can't argue with that – it's quite likely, knowing Flo, but I thought I'd make the offer anyway.'

. . .

Once Flo had found Lori and Colin and had returned to collect Francine, almost all of the other guests had left. Ottilie and Heath were preparing to help with the clean-up, but Magnus had ideas of his own. Rather drunken ideas, but they were finding it difficult to argue with him nonetheless.

'You two' – he wagged a finger at both of them in turn, swaying on the spot – 'must go home and do whatever engaged people do. I will clean up.'

Ottilie suspected he was more likely to end up face down, snoring on a plate of stale vol-au-vents, but she didn't say so. 'We can't leave you to do all this. It'll take you all night.'

'No...' he slurred. 'Stacey and Geoff will help.'

'Even so, it's our party. You've let us use your house – the least we can do is help to clean it.'

'If you even try, I will smack your bottom!'

'Magnus!' Ottilie burst out laughing. 'It's not 1969, you know! I'm pretty sure you can't do or say that now.'

'I can, and I will if you so much as lift a rubbish bag.' He flung a hand at the door. 'Now off! Begone! Go and do romantic things!'

'Magnus,' Heath said, coming in from the kitchen with a pile of plates. 'You ought to know by now she's never going to go and leave the cleaning up for someone else, no matter what you threaten her with. That's not to say we don't appreciate the sentiment.'

'I'll help too,' Francine said, and then Magnus rounded on her and wagged another drunken finger. 'You're a guest – you can't do it.'

At the sight of her mum's disappointment, Ottilie almost laughed. 'Go with Flo...' She leaned in and lowered her voice. 'You'd be doing me a favour – she looks tired, but she'd never admit it and leave without you. If you decide to stay and clean, she will, and she's dead on her feet.'

Thankfully, Francine could see the logic, and she nodded. 'I'm ready when you are, Flo,' she announced.

Flo, who had been getting her coat on, looked relieved. She gestured for Lori and Colin to follow as she marched out.

'Goodnight, Gran,' Heath said in a wry tone. If Flo heard him, she didn't turn around. They only got a goodnight and a promise they'd see Heath and Ottilie the following day from his parents, and a kiss from Francine.

'Don't leave without coming over,' Ottilie told her mum.

'I wasn't about to.'

Ottilie wondered whether to say there was something they needed to discuss, but she didn't want to leave her mum with something that might keep her from sleeping with the worry. So she left it again, the news she wanted and needed to share growing heavier by the minute.

Once it was just Magnus, Geoff, Stacey, Simon, her and Heath, Ottilie pushed thoughts of Fion firmly out of her mind. There was nothing she could do about any of that now, and it served no purpose to fret about conversations she couldn't have right away. Instead, they got stuck into the clean-up operation, Magnus turning up the music and swilling the last of a Chilean red as they went, Geoff chastising him and complaining that he was so drunk he was making more mess than he was tidying away. Heath threw a grin at Ottilie, and her heart swelled at the sight. Her life was filled with ups and downs – as all lives were – but at least she had Heath by her side. Whatever was coming, she knew he'd stick by her.

CHAPTER EIGHT

Heath unwrapped another gift and held it up. 'What's the tally on the bottles of booze now?'

Ottilie took it from him and put it with the others on the table. 'Three brandies, a couple of gins and six bottles of wine. I don't think we'll have to buy any booze for a while.'

'We could take some over to Magnus and Geoff to repay what we drank of theirs last night.'

Ottilie nodded as she inspected the label of the one Heath had just passed to her. 'That's a good idea.'

She was calm on the outside, but her stomach was churning. Glancing up at the clock, yet again, she noted that she had only fifteen minutes until her mum was due. She had no idea how she was going to open the discussion, but she had to talk to her about what Fion had said before she let her go back to Manchester.

Then there was a knock, and Ottilie started.

'If this is your mum, she's early,' Heath said, which made Ottilie suspect that he'd been watching the clock as keenly as she had. 'I'll go.'

A moment later, he came back. Francine followed with Flo and Heath's parents. Ottilie tried to hide her vexation. She'd ordinarily be pleased to see them all, but she needed her mum alone.

'Why don't you show your mum that thing in the garden?' Heath said very deliberately, and Ottilie could have thrown herself at him and kissed him. 'I'll make everyone a snack.'

'What thing in the garden?' Flo asked. 'Shall I—'

'Could you help me with the sandwiches?' Heath guided his gran gently to the counter. 'Mum,' he added, 'You can get some plates out for me. And, Dad, if you could open some wine...'

Ottilie didn't need to be told twice. Before anyone could argue, she beckoned her mum to follow her outside. She led her to a shaded bench. The sun hadn't yet reached this corner and she pulled her cardigan tighter. Francine was still in her coat and seemed content enough.

'Let's sit down here for a minute,' Ottilie said.

Francine frowned slightly as she took a seat, and Ottilie settled beside her. 'What's this about?'

Ottilie gave a wan smile. It wouldn't have taken a genius to work out there was something going on here that was about more than showing off some plant or other.

'Something weird happened yesterday. A girl turned up at the party and told me she was my sister.'

Ottilie studied her mum's reaction, and the shock – but also guilt – told her all she needed to know.

'How?'

'That's what I want to know.'

'How did she...?' Francine looked as if she might faint. Ottilie gave her a moment. 'I don't know where to start. How did she find you?'

'I decided to do an ancestry test. I was curious. She'd used the same people and we were matched.'

'You're sure?'

'She showed me.'

'Ah...' Francine paused, her hands shaking.

'I have no Irish in my DNA. I didn't think anything of it at first, but it all adds up. Did you know? That Dad wasn't my real dad?'

'To be honest, I didn't know, not for sure. There was a possibility.'

Ottilie stared, her heart hammering now. 'Did Dad know?'

Francine nodded. 'You have to understand, for the most part, our marriage was a happy one.'

'But...'

'But there was a time, shortly before I fell pregnant with you, when things were difficult. We thought about splitting up. And then I started to work for Conrad. I was looking for some comfort... oh, Ottilie, please don't judge me.'

'I'm trying not to. It will help if I understand. Conrad... that's the man... that's Fion's dad. So he's my dad?' It felt like a betrayal to say the words out loud, but Ottilie had no choice. That was her new reality.

'Yes.'

'You had an affair with him?'

Francine wrapped her arms tight around herself. 'Oh, Ottilie, don't say it like that.'

'But you had a... relationship with him? When was this?'

'I had a little job at his kitchen showroom. I was only there a few months. What we had was so brief, hardly anything at all, and then I realised what a horrible mistake I'd made. I left the job, and your dad and I patched things up. I found out I was pregnant shortly afterwards.'

Ottilie was silent for a moment, staring into space, processing what she'd heard. In the tree above them was a rowdy nest of sparrows. She and Heath had been joking about them the day before, but she hardly noticed now.

'I should have told you this years ago,' Francine said into the gap. 'You're an adult, a sensible and intelligent woman, and I know it would have been better for me to be honest than for you to find out this way. But I was scared of what you'd think, of how it might change things between us. You understand that, don't you? I'm so sorry, Ottilie.'

'But you didn't know if Conrad was my biological dad?'

'Not for sure. I suppose the dates added up better than they did in any other scenario. I suppose I wanted to believe you were your dad's. So did he. When he caught me – that's when we decided it was make or break. In a way, I think I almost made it easy for him to catch me. Looking back, it's clear to me I wanted his attention; I wanted him to look at our marriage and to see what I saw. I wanted him to fight for it. And he did. We worked it out, and he was thrilled when I told him I was expecting. But then he started to think about things, and, naturally, he wondered if he was the father.'

'But you didn't try to find out?'

'It wasn't so easy back then. We decided that he would be your dad regardless. He didn't want to question it. He loved you so much, he didn't want anything to come between you and him. If there was ever any doubt, you might have felt differently about him, and he'd have hated that. So we never spoke of Conrad again, and we never ever talked about the possibility of Conrad being your father. After your dad died, I didn't see the point in dredging the past up any more than I had while he was alive. As far as we were concerned, you were our daughter.'

Ottilie shook her head. 'This is mad.'

'I'm sure it must be a shock. I understand if you're angry.'

Ottilie grabbed her mum's hand. 'I'm not angry; I'm only trying to take it in. I might need time.'

'Of course. I'm sorry – I shouldn't be thinking of myself.'

'I don't think that's what you're doing. You're my mum and I love you no matter what, but things have changed.'

'Do you want me to leave?'

'No. I want you to stay. Things are different, but what you are to me isn't. I'm not so naïve to think marriages are straightforward and simple. I know you loved Dad, and I understand why you both made the decisions you did. I just need time.'

'What did I do to deserve such an amazing daughter?'

'If I'm amazing, it's only because you raised me that way. You brought me up to be tolerant and patient, to understand that people have all sorts of reasons for what they do and never to judge. If I'm this person now, it's down to you and Dad. *My dad, not some bloke I've never met.*'

Ottilie was pleased to see the relief on her mum's face. She still had questions, many of them. Had her mum kept in touch with Conrad? Had she been in love with him? Would they share these new discoveries with anyone else? But those questions would wait. The most important thing now was for her and Francine to get through this, together, with their relationship undamaged.

'What will you do now?' Francine asked. 'Are you going to see him?'

'I don't know. I'm going to meet with Fion again. Would it upset you if I went to see him?'

'It would be difficult, but I can't stop you. He's not...' Francine paused. 'He's not much like your dad.'

'I didn't expect him to be. Is he...?' Ottilie shook her head. Perhaps it wasn't fair to quiz her mum on what he was like, and perhaps she didn't want to know. Or perhaps she wanted to discover for herself, build a relationship without preconceptions. 'Never mind.'

Through the kitchen window she could see Heath talking to someone out of view. And then Flo appeared and looked out.

'We've been rumbled,' Ottilie said, realising that they were going to have to go inside and pretend nothing seismic had happened.

. . .

Francine had reminded Ottilie that she didn't need her blessing – she was an adult, after all – but Ottilie had wanted it all the same. She wasn't about to do anything that would upset Francine and said so. Francine said that nothing she could do could ever upset her and that she was perfectly entitled to form a relationship with her own flesh and blood if she wanted to. And so, confident in her mum's approval, Ottilie arranged to meet Fion.

That bright morning she waited for her half-sister at the same café in Kendal she'd often taken Flo to on their drives out. She'd managed to snag a table by the vast windows, and the sun was warming her through the glass, while the higgledy stone-built high street beyond bustled with shoppers and day-trippers. It was as quaint and charming as she'd come to expect from the many Lake District towns and villages she'd been to since she'd moved to the area; busier than some, and big enough to keep Flo amused for a decent chunk of a day whenever Ottilie brought her. Before arriving at the café, Ottilie had made a point of buying some Kendal mint cake from Flo's favourite shop. She might be disappointed when she discovered Ottilie had been without her, but once Ottilie explained what she was doing there and presented her with the gift, she was sure Flo would be a little more forgiving.

Fion had seemed keen during their messages. She'd told Ottilie to choose the location and she'd get there, no matter where it was.

As Ottilie was checking the time, noting that Fion was now fifteen minutes late and wondering if she ought to phone to see what the hold-up was, she happened to glance outside and see her half-sister dashing down the opposite side of the road, looking up at all the business signs. She stood at the window and waved to catch her attention. Fion saw her immediately and broke into an anxious but also relieved smile.

'I'm so sorry!' Fion said. 'The bus was held up – some daft sheep on the road...'

'Of course it was. How very Lake District.' Ottilie smiled. 'Not to worry, you're here now. I was just about to order. What do you fancy? I'm buying.'

'Oh... um... I'll have a flat white, please. Thank you.'

'That's all right.' Ottilie took her purse from her bag. 'Nothing else? Cake or a panini or something?'

'I'm not hungry, thanks.'

'If you don't mind, I'm starving so I'm going to get a toasted sandwich.'

'Why would I mind?'

'Because I'll be munching it right in front of you and it might not be pretty.'

'Oh...' Fion smiled awkwardly, and Ottilie realised that it was perhaps too early for her jokes – such as they were – to land. Things would be strange and new for a while yet, she supposed.

'I won't be a minute.'

Ottilie went to the counter and placed her order. The barista took the payment and told her to wait at the table and she'd bring everything over when it was ready. As Ottilie rejoined Fion, she found her typing a message on her phone. She looked up.

'Sorry... some stuff I had to reply to.'

'Don't mind me. Is it work or something?'

'No, I... I just lost my job, actually.'

'Oh, I'm sorry. What did you do?'

'It was only serving in a shop. I could probably find another job easily enough. I just haven't had time to look yet.'

Ottilie smiled. The nerves she'd had driving over had gone,

but she was still finding this harder work than she'd imagined. But when she thought about it, she didn't know why she'd expected anything else. 'What are you going to do? Do you want another shop job, or do you fancy a change?'

'I can't say I've thought about it. I know I have to get something soon to get Dad off my back.'

'You still live with them?'

'Yes. Twenty-six and still with my parents. I suppose you think that's pathetic.'

'God, no! I'd have stayed with mine as long as they'd have had me.'

'That's just it – I'm not sure they do want me. Even they think I'm too old to be there – Mum doesn't say it, but Dad does. But it's hard to get a place round here on shop wages, you know? Not on your own, at any rate. If I had a partner, I could maybe afford it, but I don't, and none of my friends are in a position to houseshare, so...'

'I can imagine it must be hard.'

'I hate living with my parents, actually,' Fion said, with sudden passion in her statement. 'I wish I could find a way out. They're not bad people, but I feel...'

'Stifled?' Ottilie prompted. 'Like you're running on the spot?'

'Yeah,' Fion said. 'That's it. That's a good way of putting it. How do you know?'

'Well...' Ottilie unfolded a paper napkin and spread it over her lap, 'I might not be in the same position as you right now, but I remember what it was like living at home with my parents...' She paused and smiled. 'Vaguely anyway. I have to admit it was a while ago. But I get it – there comes a point when you're not the girl you were and you want to live in a different way than how they do.'

'But you can't because you have to follow their rules

because you're living *under their roof*, and if you don't like it, you can find your own roof.'

Ottilie got the impression that Fion was paraphrasing, and guessed it was something Conrad often said.

'That sounds tough,' Ottilie said.

'It's not so bad, I suppose,' Fion said.

The barista came over with their order. Ottilie thanked her, and she left them again.

'So you got engaged,' Fion said. 'When are you going to get married?'

'Not sure yet. We've been trying to agree on an exact date. You wouldn't think it would be so hard, but every time we think we've nailed it, one of us comes up with a reason it won't do after all.'

'I suppose everyone else wants a say too.'

'Not so much, actually. Most of our friends and family are being respectful about keeping out of it. I mean, it's second time around for both of us too, so we're a bit long in the tooth for all that kind of stuff. It's not other people being a nuisance, it's us.'

'So you've been married before?'

'Yes. He...' Ottilie stirred her coffee. It never got any easier to say, even though it was now a couple of years since Josh's death and she had Heath. 'He was a policeman. He got killed on duty.'

'Oh...' Fion's eyes widened. 'That's awful.'

'It was.' She put her spoon down and decided to change the subject. 'What about you? Is there someone special?'

'Not really. I've had a few boyfriends, but they've mostly been idiots.'

'So nobody at the moment?'

'No.'

'Ah. Have you always lived in Penrith? Your family, I mean.'

'I have. Mum and Dad are both from Manchester way. But I suppose you know that. How come your mum...?'

'You want to know how I've ended up with the same dad as you and how come I didn't know about him?'

Fion nodded.

'To cut a long story short, my mum and Conrad had a... *thing*. They split up, and my dad – the man I call Dad – raised me as his own and they never told me otherwise. That's it, really.'

'Were you pissed off when you found out about it?'

'I suppose I was shocked, but...' Ottilie shrugged. 'That's life, isn't it? It's often the way, you think you've got it all worked out and then someone comes to pull the rug from under you.'

'I'm probably not supposed to say it, but I'm sort of glad. I mean, I'm glad I have a sister now.'

'I grew up an only child too. I always wanted a brother or sister. I have to admit, I didn't expect to get one quite so late!'

'But you don't mind? That I came to find you, I mean.'

'Not a bit.'

Fion seemed to brighten at this. She took a sip of her coffee, gazing at Ottilie over the rim of the cup. 'I think we look a bit alike,' she said, placing the cup back on the saucer.

Ottilie studied her for a moment. A slightly pointy nose; freckles; fine, straight hair. 'I think you might be right. Poor you.'

'I should say poor you,' Fion said, a smile now forming at the corners of her mouth.

'Actually, let's agree that we're both hot,' Ottilie said. 'Positive vibes only here today.'

Fion's smile grew. 'You're a nurse?'

'I am.'

'That's cool. You got a good job at least.'

'It has its moments. It's not always as glamorous as people like to think.'

'Do they think that?'

'Well, if you watch half of the medical dramas on telly, you'd think so. It's better now I work in the community than it used to be when I was on the wards in Manchester. Nicer, I mean. I get to know my patients really well. Most of them are lovely.'

'What made you want to do that?'

'To be honest, I don't recall it being a decision. It was just something I grew up knowing I was going to do – I never considered any other career.'

'That must be nice. I don't have a clue what I want to do, even at twenty-six.'

'I bet there are a lot of people in the same boat. What are you interested in? Could you find a career in the things you're into?'

Fion shrugged. 'Maybe.'

Ottilie watched her pick up the cup again. She got the impression that Fion was a young woman who didn't yet know who she was and how she fitted into the world around her. It pained her to see because talking to her now, she also saw that Fion was sweet, bright and articulate, and that she desperately wanted to find her place.

'I like cooking,' Fion added.

'There has to be a career in that, I bet.'

'Dad says I'm not very good at it.'

Ottilie ignored what sounded like mean and unhelpful input on Conrad's behalf. Her father ought to have been encouraging his daughter, not belittling her. 'But you could train to be good. If you love doing it, then you can get better. Enrol on a course or something? Get a trainee chef job?'

'I might be too old for that sort of thing.'

'I don't know much about it, but you're not exactly ancient. There must be opportunities for someone a bit older, surely?'

'I wouldn't know where to start.'

Ottilie regarded her steadily. It was clear to her that Fion was a woman who needed a serious boost to her confidence and self-belief. Ottilie didn't know what her childhood had been like, and whether her lack of those things was anything to do with that, or simply something she'd been born with, but she didn't believe that Fion deserved to held back by it. What was also clear was that Fion was bright and likeable and given half a chance could be successful. Perhaps she could help her. She wasn't sure how, but there had to be a way, and it would have to be in a way that didn't make Fion feel patronised and that she'd still had a hand in it.

'We could do some investigating together,' she said. 'And Heath might be able to help. Would you fancy working in Manchester?'

'But I'd have to move there,' Fion said doubtfully. 'I don't think I could afford to do that.'

'There might be remote work. Or you could commute.'

'I can't drive,' Fion said.

Ottilie nodded. 'I suppose that might be a problem. Haven't you wanted to learn?'

'Yes. I had a few lessons, but I wasn't very good – couldn't get the hang of doing everything at once.'

'I can help with that too,' Ottilie said. 'I could give you driving lessons. We could take it as slowly as you like because you're not paying me by the hour, so it wouldn't matter how long it took to get the hang of it. We'd just keep going until it clicked.'

Fion brightened at this. 'You'd do that?'

'Of course I would. We're family. I'd love to – it would give us a chance to get to know each other too. I could come over to Penrith and pick you up whenever you like.'

'From the house?' Fion asked, doubtful again.

'I wouldn't if it's a problem.'

'I don't mind coming to Thimblebury on the bus.'

Ottilie cut her toasted sandwich in half. 'Whatever suits you is fine by me. And now the days are getting longer you can come when I've finished work and we'll have plenty of daylight

– just while you're getting used to the car I think it might be better not to drive in the dark. The roads around Thimblebury aren't very well lit at night.'

'That would be amazing!' Fion said, her face now in a genuine smile. 'Thank you!'

'It's nothing.'

'But if I can drive, it will help so much. I'll be able to come over to see you whenever I want.'

'You can do that anyway – I'm sure if there's no bus, Heath or I can come to pick you up. Or we can meet somewhere like we've done today. I want to get to know you, and I'm glad you want the same.'

'Does Heath live with you? You said he works in Manchester.'

'He's in the process of moving in with me. He just needs to get some things in place so he can remotely work and then he'll be able to. I can't wait, to be honest. We've been going back and forth to Manchester for so long it's started to feel exhausting.'

'I bet. You like Thimblebury then?'

'I love it.'

'But you used to live in Manchester, like my dad did?'

'Born and bred.'

'You don't miss it?'

'I did a bit at first. You get used to a place, and Thimblebury seemed so quiet in comparison. I enjoy visiting now, but I don't miss it. What about Penrith? It's bigger than Thimblebury. I bet there's a lot more going on, especially in the summer.'

'Oh, we have festivals and whatever. I can't say I know how I feel about living there. It's home, but I've never lived anywhere else to compare it to.'

'You've never fancied moving to a city for a while? You're younger than me – didn't you ever get bored being in a small town?'

Fion shrugged. 'I don't think I'm a city type of girl. I don't like nightclubs and that sort of thing, so I don't know if I'd like life in a big city.'

'There are more than nightclubs,' Ottilie said with a smile as she bit into her sandwich. 'There's art and culture and history and brilliant shopping – in Manchester, at least. Thimblebury is home now, but I'll always have a bit of my heart there – it was home for most of my life before this and, of course, I have family and friends there and memories of Josh.'

'Josh?' Fion gave a slight frown. 'Your husband who died?'

Ottilie nodded. 'Losing him was why I left Manchester in the first place. I couldn't bear to be there with all those memories, but time has made it easier, and when I go now it reminds me of the good things, not the bad.'

'I can't imagine what it must have been like.'

'I hope you never have to find out – I wouldn't wish it on my worst enemy. I still miss him, but my life is good again. In a different way, but good.'

'I'm glad I came,' Fion said.

'Me too. Fion...' Ottilie paused, wondering whether to ask. But in the end the urge was too strong. 'I think I would like to meet your dad. Do you think I could?'

'I don't know if...' It might have been Ottilie's imagination, but Fion seemed to pale. 'I don't think he'd be keen.'

'But you could ask him? Now we know there's no problem as far as your mum is concerned, then surely he'd want to meet me? He'd be a bit curious, wouldn't he? You could be there if it helps – we could tell him about how we're becoming good friends and it would make him feel easier?'

Fion seemed torn. She turned her gaze to the window without a reply.

'Please,' Ottilie said. 'Could you at least ask him?'

After what seemed like an age, Fion turned back with a nervous smile. 'When?'

'Whenever he has time. You'll ask him and let me know?'

'Yes.'

Ottilie tried not to be troubled by the reluctance in Fion's tone. She'd never asked for much out of life, and she rarely put herself before others, but this time, just this once, she was going to. Because she wouldn't be able to rest until she'd met the father she'd just discovered for herself.

CHAPTER NINE

It took Ottilie just over an hour to make the drive from Thimblebury to Penrith. Like many other towns across the Lake District, it was characterised by rambling, mismatched stone houses, crowding down streets like lines of unruly schoolchildren waiting for class. The one Ottilie was heading for was larger than its neighbours, a double-fronted house of grey stone, front door and sash windows painted olive green, and a vast rockery built around a wishing well in the front garden. It ought to have been cute and welcoming, but something about it as Ottilie parked outside make her feel anything but welcomed.

It was hardly surprising, in the circumstances. While her biological father, Conrad, had agreed to meet with her, from what Fion had said, he didn't sound happy about it, but Ottilie had pushed the bad vibes to the back of her mind. She wanted to know him, and despite his obvious reluctance, the very fact he'd acquiesced to this meant he wanted to meet her too. Perhaps he was curious about the daughter he'd had no clue about until a few days ago. Perhaps he would warm to her. Perhaps he had other, less reassuring reasons – but Ottilie didn't want to think about those either.

She sat behind the steering wheel, staring at the house for a moment. It was just an ordinary house, with ordinary people living in it, and yet this felt huge, far bigger than that. Her life, and the lives of everyone who lived there, were about to change forever. She wasn't sure if she was ready, or if she even wanted this now she was here. There was still time to drive away, wasn't there? Nobody had come out to greet her – perhaps they hadn't noticed her arrival. Perhaps her mum had been right – perhaps they were better off leaving the past where it had always been up until now: hidden, out of sight and out of mind. Until this point, Ottilie had been blissfully unaware of this man and this family and she'd been happy. Did she need to complicate things?

The decision was taken from her hands as the front door opened and a woman came down the garden path, smiling anxiously. She looked a little younger than her mum – perhaps around ten years or so. She wore a good layer of make-up, and her dark bob was immaculately styled, yet beneath the veneer was someone who seemed weary. Her steps were those of someone who was in some pain, the sort of pain she probably carried with her all the time. Ottilie took a deep breath before opening the door and getting out of the car.

'Hello,' the woman said. 'Ottilie, I presume?'

'Yes... you must be Caron?'

'Pleased to meet you, Ottilie,' she replied, her tone suggesting that she wasn't entirely sure she *was* pleased to meet her. In fact, it told Ottilie that she wished she could make all this go away. Ottilie could hardly blame her for that – it wasn't every day you discovered your husband had a daughter that neither of you had known about. 'Conrad is making coffee. You drink coffee, don't you?' she added, suddenly doubtful.

'Coffee sounds good. Is Fion home? She said she would be...' Ottilie asked. Suddenly she was struck by the feeling that she needed her half-sister's moral support after all.

'She's upstairs. I'll let her know you're here.'

Ottilie followed Caron inside the house. There was a large entrance, glossy wooden stairs leading to the first floor, a feature window of stained glass overlooking the garden and a period tiled floor that had clearly been cared for.

'This is lovely,' Ottilie said, though it was more for conversation than because she thought so. It was lovely, but she was finding it hard to appreciate how pretty the house was while her mind was racing with every possibility of how the afternoon would pan out. She wished she'd let Heath come with her now. He'd wanted to, but when she'd made the decision to come, it had seemed better and less complicated to do it without him.

'Thank you.' Caron pushed open a door. 'We've worked hard to renovate it for the last twenty years. It was a shell when we bought it...' She beckoned Ottilie forward. 'The kitchen is this way.'

At a counter, a man had his back to them. At his wife's announcement, he turned. Ottilie held in a gasp. He was handsome – extremely so, despite his age – and she could see immediately why her mum's head had been turned in a moment of weakness. But it wasn't a kind, warm sort of handsome, like Heath or Josh. It was hard and arrogant. If Ottilie's resolve had wavered outside in the car, now that she was face to face with her biological father, it was a heartbeat away from crumbling entirely. He looked far from pleased to see her, and she had to wonder why he'd agreed to the meeting at all.

'Conrad...' Caron said. 'Ottilie's here.'

He gave a short nod, regarding Ottilie carefully as he gestured for her to take a seat. 'So you're Francine's little secret?'

The greeting set Ottilie's nerves on edge. Immediately, her mood went from nervous anticipation to annoyance and dislike. *Francine's little secret?* As if he had nothing to do with it? All it needed was the word 'dirty' to be inserted and her humiliation would be complete.

'I'm her daughter,' Ottilie said coldly. 'I'm also your daughter. Believe me, I was as shocked to learn of our connection as you are.'

'You'd better sit down then,' he said. 'We've got a lot to talk about.'

Ottilie's eyes stayed on him as she took a seat, trying to get the measure of him, some sense of who this man was. She'd expected to come and feel some instant connection, some innate pull, but there was nothing. She might as well have been meeting a new patient. Not even that because with patients she felt some of her professional responsibilities towards them, and that included her own kindness. There wasn't even that. In his physical features she saw something of herself, but she also sensed that their personalities couldn't have been more different. His greeting had put her guard up, and no matter how she might want to let it down, as she watched him pour coffee from a pot, she realised it wasn't going to be so simple.

'How do you take it?' he asked.

'White please, one sugar.'

'Hmm. How Francine used to take it.'

Ottilie tried not to frown. She glanced at his wife, Caron, who seemed to be doing her best to pretend she hadn't heard the comment. Ottilie's heart went out to her. This was probably harder for her than it was for Ottilie or Conrad – stuck in the middle of a situation that had nothing to do with her, the thought of which probably hurt.

'How she still takes it,' Ottilie said.

'Right. And how is she?'

'Fine. As you'd expect.'

'And what exactly is that? How do you know what I'd expect?'

The frown Ottilie had been holding back finally creased her

forehead. 'If this is a problem for you, I can leave. I was under the impression that you were as amenable to meeting me as I was you, but—'

'That won't be necessary,' he said, bringing two cups of coffee to the table and putting one down in front of Ottilie. Caron went to the door and met Fion on the way in. Ottilie's attention was drawn to them as they exchanged a few words she couldn't hear. Then Fion smiled nervously at Ottilie as she came to sit with them.

'I'll leave you to it,' Caron said as she left the room.

Ottilie forced a smile for her. She wanted to call her back and tell her there were to be no secrets, but she recognised it wasn't her place. She and Fion had discussed something and perhaps that was the reason Caron had left.

'It's nice to see you,' Fion said to Ottilie.

'You too. Your house is lovely.'

'Mum and Dad did it. Nothing to do with me, I'm afraid. Did you find the house OK?'

Conrad coughed loudly and deliberately, which Ottilie took to mean he didn't want to listen to their small talk all day.

She turned to him. 'Have you been married long?'

'Why do you want to know?'

'Dad!' Fion yelped, but Ottilie gave her a reassuring smile.

'I'm only making conversation. It doesn't matter if your dad doesn't want to talk about that.'

'I wasn't cheating on Francine with her mother, if that's what you're getting at,' he said, nodding towards Fion. 'We met afterwards.'

Ottilie sent a swift glance towards the door, wondering how easy it would be to make a dash for it. Already she was wishing she hadn't come. She'd watched plenty of family reunion shows on television over the years, and they'd mostly been joyous affairs. Those people had certainly seemed happier to see each other than Conrad was to see Ottilie. He looked as if he wished he could kick her out as much as she wanted to escape. But she'd come this far now, and she was going to see it through, even if today made up her mind that this would be the one and only meeting.

'Caron's nice,' Ottilie said. 'That's all I meant. I know you weren't cheating. Do you have children? I mean, children other than Fion and me, from another marriage or—'

'What do you want?' he cut in.

'To meet you. I thought you wanted to meet me.'

'You said—' Fion began, but he regarded Ottilie coldly as he spoke across his younger daughter.

'Why would I want that? I don't know you.'

'I don't know you either. Isn't that what meeting is meant to fix? I thought... because you said yes, I thought—'

'Fion asked. I said no. For some reason, she asked again, and Caron said I ought to. She said I'd regret saying no. What do you want? Why have you come here now? After all these years?'

'I told you. I've only just found out about you. Mum never said anything, and then Fion—'

'She was right not to say anything. I don't see what good any of this does now. What do you do?'

'Do? What do you mean?'

'What's your job?'

'I'm a nurse.' He nodded slowly. Ottilie couldn't tell whether he approved or not, and he didn't say so. 'How about you?' she asked, hopeful that this was a thread that might open up a more positive conversation.

'Import export, isn't it, Dad?' Fion answered for him.

'That must be interesting,' Ottilie said. 'What sort of things do you deal—'

'There's no money for you,' he said.

Ottilie's forehead creased into the deepest frown of the day so far. 'I beg your pardon.'

'I said there's no—'

'I heard what you said. I want to know why you said it.'

'Why do you think?'

'I couldn't say. I have all the money I need, thank you very much. And if I didn't, the last person I'd come to for help is you.' She got up and pushed the cup of coffee back towards him, composed, though her heart was beating in her ears.

'Ottilie,' Fion said, getting up too. 'He didn't mean—'

Ottilie gave her a calm look. 'It's all right. I wanted to meet the man who gave me his DNA.' She turned to Conrad. 'And now I have, I realise that's all you'll ever be – a man who gave me some DNA. My father was a kind, loving, brilliant man. He wasn't a bit like you. He'll always be my father, no matter what. Thank you,' she continued coldly, 'for making me see it clearly. I won't bother you again. I wish you and your money a long and contented life.'

'But, Ottilie!' Fion began to hurry after her.

'I'm not angry at you,' Ottilie told her. 'We can still meet up. I hope you don't take it personally, but I have no desire to meet your dad again.'

'Your dad too!'

Ottilie shook her head sadly. 'Not really.'

As she marched down the hallway towards the front door, Caron emerged from one of the doors leading off it. 'You're going already?' she asked.

'Yes,' Ottilie said, mustering every ounce of courtesy she could find for her. It was hardly Caron's fault her husband was such a miserable misanthrope. 'It was lovely to meet you.'

'Oh…' Caron said faintly, rushing in her pained way to open the front door for Ottilie. 'You too,' she called as Ottilie marched down the path to her car.

Fion came outside. 'You will message me, won't you?'

'Of course I will,' Ottilie said, doing her best to smile for her sister. 'As soon as I get home. And if things are bad when I've gone today, I'm sorry. I didn't mean to make things awkward, and I didn't think... It doesn't matter. But if there's any trouble, if you need my help, all you have to do is ask.'

Fion nodded. Ottilie wondered whether she was meant to hug her, but in the end Fion walked back to the house and saved her the uncertainty.

She didn't look back again as she returned to her car. And then Ottilie started the engine and drove away. As soon as she was out of sight of the house, she pulled over and burst into tears.

CHAPTER TEN

Ottilie peered at Stacey's ankle, moving it this way and that. 'I think you might have to give up trying to get fit. You're going to end up doing yourself a serious mischief.'

'And they say exercise is good for you.'

'Good for most people; not you, apparently. How did you say you did this?'

'Turned it on the lane while I was jogging earlier. It's lucky you called round when you did. Should I go to the accident unit? I'd rather avoid it if I can, but...'

'I think it will heal. Stay off it for few days, keep it elevated and put plenty of ice on.'

'Stay off it – easier said than done when you've got Chloe and Mackenzie around.'

'Chloe's an adult; I'm sure she can manage without you until you're back on your feet. And if she says she can't, send her my way for some lessons. Have you got a bag of frozen peas or something you can use as a compress?'

'I expect so...' Stacey started to push herself off the sofa, but Ottilie let out a loud tut.

'I'll go – what did I just say about staying off it? Honestly...'

'Thanks,' Stacey replied with a sheepish grin. 'I don't expect you to wait on me, though.'

'I'm not waiting on you; I'm nursing you.'

'Well, you're more than I deserve, either way.'

'Don't be daft...'

Ottilie went to the kitchen and rifled through the freezer, through last bits of loaves and half boxes of fish fingers and chicken nuggets until she found a bag of frozen sweetcorn welded to the side of the drawer and decided that would do the job just as well. With a tug, it came away and she wrapped it in a teacloth before going back to the living room. When she got there, Stacey was typing on her phone.

'Speak of the devil,' she said, nodding at it. 'Chloe. She's staying over at Ollie's tonight with Mackenzie.'

'That's lucky,' Ottilie said. 'So there'll be no excuse for you to be on your feet for today at least. Are you expecting Simon later?'

'Yes.'

'Even better – he can do your fetching and carrying.'

'If I'm lucky, he'll be carrying me somewhere,' Stacey said, and then gave Ottilie such a saucy wink that she burst into laughter.

'Just as long as he can work around your bad ankle, you go ahead and let him carry you wherever you like. I don't think I want to know. In the meantime, do you want me to make you a drink or anything to eat. You might as well make use of me while I'm here.'

'A cuppa would be lovely. You're staying for one, aren't you?'

Ottilie glanced at the clock on the wall and nodded. 'I don't see why not. Heath's working over and he won't be in Thimblebury for ages.'

'Isn't he sick to death of all the commuting yet?' Stacey

shifted to get comfortable as Ottilie pressed the cold compress to her ankle.

'We're both getting a bit fed up with it now, but we're working on that.'

'He's definitely going to move here? What about his job?'

'They're working on a way for him to be based at home. He'd have to travel in for meetings, and he'd have to show up for the odd office day, but it will be a lot easier when they sort that for him. His boss has been great, actually. We'll have to invite him to the wedding—'

'I'm so excited for the wedding. Who are you going to have as bridesmaid?'

'Don't know yet. I don't suppose you're up for the job?'

Stacey beamed. 'Of course I am!'

'I don't know yet, it depends on how things go, but maybe I'll ask Fion too.'

Stacey paused and then realisation seemed to hit her. 'God, I'm sorry, Ott! You went to see your dad, didn't you? I forgot! How did it go?'

'It was horrible,' Ottilie said, trying to shake the memory of Conrad's looks of disdain. 'I wish I hadn't gone.'

'He didn't want to know you?'

'He wasn't what you'd call welcoming.'

'So you didn't spend much time with him?'

'About five minutes.'

'Ottilie...' Stacey shook her head sadly.

Ottilie waved the sympathy away. 'I don't care. I'm better off without someone like that in my life. I'll just go back to how I was before I knew and forget he exists. He was so rude I just... to tell the truth, I sort of stormed out.' Stacey laughed lightly, and Ottilie was forced to smile in agreement. 'I know. I'm sure it was the most pathetic storming out anyone has ever done. It's not exactly in my nature.'

'I'd still have paid good money to see it,' Stacey said. 'I'm sorry it turned out to be so shit. But on the bright side, you said it yourself – you were happy before you knew about him. So you can just go back to the way it was before. It's his loss, not yours. He's the one missing out by not getting to know you.'

'I'm sure he doesn't agree with you, but you're right about the rest.'

'Exactly. We all love you, so you don't need that tosser.'

Ottilie smiled. 'Thank you. That's honestly what I needed to hear. I keep going over the meeting in my head and wondering if it was my fault it went so badly. Like, should I have been more patient, more understanding, cut him some slack. I suppose I could have handled it better. But then I remember how rude and cold he was, and I think nothing I did would have made any difference.' Ottilie turned Stacey's compress to the colder side. 'I'm better off as I am. I've been to Penrith, I've met him and now I know I don't want to meet him again. My dad who brought me up was my dad, and as far as I'm concerned, he always will be.'

'Hmm...' Stacey regarded Ottilie in silence for a moment. 'You're really OK with it?' she asked finally.

'I'm already over it.'

'Promise? Because you know I'm here for you if you want to talk.'

'Promise. Now...' Ottilie got up. 'What about this cup of tea?'

Ottilie had discussed her meeting with Conrad with her mum on the phone. As it turned out, Francine hadn't been all that surprised.

'I did say he wasn't like your dad.'

'You weren't kidding.'

Francine had told her one or two particulars of what he'd been like to work with, although she'd been careful to avoid very personal details about the affair, and then they'd both agreed not to discuss him again. Fion was a different matter. Francine was interested. She wanted to know as much as Ottilie could tell her. Ottilie wondered if she was trying to work out if the relationship was going to be good for her or not and whether she ought to say something. If that had been Francine's intention, then she must have decided against it because in the end, she didn't.

Heath, on the other hand, had been suitably furious on Ottilie's behalf at Conrad's treatment of her. He'd told her to forget him, and she assured him that she already had, and though he also seemed to have his doubts about Fion, he didn't air them either.

Messages between Ottilie and Fion had been regular over that weekend. Ottilie had reassured her that she was completely unaffected by Conrad's hostility, but reading between the lines, she didn't feel that Fion was faring so well. She wondered if he'd taken his frustration out on her, angry that she'd engineered the meeting. She knew for a fact he was annoyed that Fion had searched out Ottilie in the first place. She was worried, but all she could do at this point was offer her support and remind Fion that she was on hand to help whenever it was needed.

The following Monday was a busy one. Ottilie had spent the morning carrying out routine weight and blood checks on some of her diabetic patients. By the time their communal lunchtime arrived, she was famished.

Fliss had brought beef-and-ale stew in, and it smelled amazing as Ottilie followed the scent into the kitchen.

'It's only leftovers,' she said as everyone sat around the table and marvelled at how delicious it was.

'Leftovers?' Lavender shot a glance at her heaped bowl and then the pan on the stove where they'd reheated it, still half full. 'How many people were you cooking for? There's only you and Charles – even I couldn't get my measurements that wrong!'

New Products Coming:

T-Shirts and Mugs Paint Your Own Protection! Great Gift Ideas

Emf-Paint your own Protection Varnish

Insoles Fully Shungited!

'Your Topia'- The Game!

'Expect Miracles' The Extended Immersive Transformational Book

Connect with us for the latest updates:

FB: Oraphim
Instagram: Oraphimuk

Oraphimshungite.com

Your Shungite adventure begins...

Thank You

oraphimshungite.com

Use discount code **SHUNGITE5**

For 5% off your next website order

'I did intend to batch cook and freeze it, but then I thought it would be nice to have something a bit heartier today.'

'It's certainly the weather for it.' Ottilie looked towards the windows, where rain beat against the glass in silver needles. 'Is this set to last? There haven't been any warnings from the Environment Agency, have there? I checked, but—'

'I'm sure it will be fine,' Fliss said. 'I haven't seen anything about flooding.'

Ottilie let out a sigh, but she couldn't dismiss the risk entirely from her thoughts. Shortly after she'd arrived in Thimblebury she'd almost been driven away again by a flood that had destroyed a good deal of her cottage, not to mention the damage it had done in the rest of the village. Everyone said it was a one-off event and unlikely to happen again, but once bitten was twice shy for Ottilie. She could never settle during heavy rain, not until it had passed. In a bid to take her mind off it, she decided to work on the plans she'd been making to help Fion.

'My sister's looking for work,' she said.

Simon reached for a slice of crusty bread from a plate at the centre of the table. 'I keep forgetting you suddenly have a sister. That must be even weirder for you.'

'It's weird to be saying those words, but I'm getting used to it. I really like her. We've talked loads recently. Quite honestly, she worries me a bit too.'

'You worry about everyone,' Fliss said. 'What's it this time?'

Ottilie paused. 'I hate to say it, but I don't think Conrad is much of a dad. At least, I don't think he's a very nice one. He doesn't seem to have encouraged her over the years – in fact, I'd say he's done the opposite, so she's not very confident. I'd go so far as to say she thinks she's totally useless, which I don't think is true at all. I think if someone did give her some encouragement, she'd find she's actually quite capable.'

'And you're the person to do that?' Fliss asked with barely disguised amusement.

'I thought I ought to try and help,' Ottilie said.

'Of course you did. You know,' Fliss said, the smile breaking free now, 'I have the perfect epitaph for your stone, in the unlikely event you should pop off before me. *Here lies Ottilie Oakcroft, who never met a problem she didn't like.*'

Lavender shook her head, and while Simon smiled, he looked as if he didn't quite agree with Fliss's summing up.

'You *do* think it's your job to fix everyone, Ottilie,' Lavender said.

'It's not necessarily a bad quality,' Simon put in.

'Nobody said it was,' Fliss replied serenely. 'It's saintly, but it must be exhausting. It's my job to fix people and even I don't want to do it all the time.'

'I'm not saintly,' Ottilie said, uncertain now whether she ought to be offended or not. 'And I don't do it all the time. I'm just trying to be nice to someone who needs it.'

'I know.' Fliss dunked a corner of her bread into her bowl. 'So what's your plan?'

'Plan?'

'To get your sister on her feet, so to speak. I'm assuming we're having this conversation because you have a plan and you want to get our take on it.'

'Not as such. I'm going to teach her how to drive.'

'Right. I suppose that's a good start. A woman of her age ought to be able to drive.'

Ottilie wasn't entirely sure she agreed with that, but it was the sort of practical thing that would figure high on Fliss's list of priorities for a successful life. Fliss was just like that. 'She's only twenty-six.'

'Exactly. If I had my way, driving would be part of the high school curriculum.'

'Yes,' Lavender said with obvious sarcasm in her tone. 'Imagine all those sixteen-year-old boys driving slowly and carefully down our roads. That would definitely end well.'

'They'd be taught how to drive carefully from the very beginning,' Fliss said.

'With respect,' Lavender said, 'that's the sort of thing someone who has never been in close contact with a teenage boy would say.'

'I know plenty of teenage boys,' Fliss said. 'I have two nephews for a start.'

Simon exchanged a brief look with Ottilie that seemed to agree that this conversation wasn't going where she'd intended it to. 'I was going to teach Chloe to drive,' he said. 'Perhaps we can pool our resources and teach Chloe and your sister at the same time.'

'That might be an idea,' Ottilie said, though she doubted that having Chloe and Fion in the same car would be pleasant for either of them. Chloe was blunt and cynical and had no time for small talk, while Fion, despite being older, would undoubtedly find her intimidating and probably off-putting as well. Ottilie and Simon might be able to pool their resources, but she wasn't sure teaching the two younger women at the same time in the same car was the way forward. It was something to think about, however. Simon's help in some capacity might be very welcome. 'I don't suppose,' she added, thinking in those terms, 'you know of any jobs she might be suited to.'

'I don't know of any jobs at all,' Simon said.

'What's she suited to?' Lavender asked.

'She's worked in a shop, but she just got made redundant.'

'I suppose you've already asked Magnus and Geoff and at the newsagent?' Lavender said.

Ottilie nodded. 'Not that they were likely to have anything, but I did ask, yes. To be honest, even if they'd been able to help, I'm not sure it would have been ideal because, of course, Fion lives in Penrith, and it would mean her travelling over every day.'

'And she doesn't drive,' Fliss said.

'Exactly. In the end, what she earned might have been swallowed up by what she spent coming back and forth.'

'There must be jobs in Penrith,' Lavender said.

'I... well, I suppose there are, but I thought—'

'You thought you'd get involved anyway,' Fliss said.

Ottilie couldn't help but feel that Fliss didn't approve of her efforts to help Fion, though she couldn't see why. More to the point, it was none of Fliss's business.

'It's not like that,' she began, but Simon cut in.

'I can see why you'd want to, given what you've told us. I can't promise it'll be any use, but I can keep my ear to the ground, and if I hear of anything that sounds suitable, I can let you know.'

'That would be great, thanks,' Ottilie said.

'Me too,' Lavender said. 'Although, I'm not sure who I'd be able to ask that you haven't thought of already.'

'We couldn't...' Ottilie hesitated. 'Never mind.'

'What?' Fliss asked. 'You might as well say it now.'

'I don't suppose we could use her help here?'

'At the surgery? Doing what?'

'I don't know, filing or something.'

Fliss shook her head. 'I can't afford to take her on. And if I was going to take on another member of staff, it would be a midwife.'

Ottilie frowned. 'But we already have a district midwife.'

'Yes, but we also seem to have something of a baby boom in Thimblebury at the moment. Must be something in the water. In any case, I've referred five new mums just this week and the midwifery service is stretched as it is. I'm sure they'll be taken care of, but sometimes I wonder if we ought to have our own midwife here.'

'They wouldn't have enough work.'

'If we put some kind of arrangement in place so they could service a few of the neighbouring villages and farms, it might make it worthwhile. I'd have to talk to someone at the health authority.'

Ottilie realised that her discussion of Fion was over. Fliss had moved on and had made it clear there was nothing she could offer Fion in the way of employment. To confirm this, the conversation turned to who was pregnant and why there might be a sudden uptick in the local birth rate, which soon descended into surreal comedy scenarios involving Magnus and Geoff sneaking around putting hormones in the water supply to increase the future membership of their film club. And while Ottilie found it amusing enough, her mind was still with Fion. Her sister had been let down enough in her life – it seemed that way to Ottilie at least – and Ottilie wasn't going to do it to her again.

CHAPTER ELEVEN

After a chat with Heath, Ottilie had decided she needed to put Fion on her car insurance and also needed to find somewhere suitable, away from any busy roads, to start off the driving lessons. It seemed simple enough, but she soon found that Thimblebury wasn't a place filled with flat, smooth, unused squares of tarmac.

Back in the days when Ottilie's dad had helped her to learn to drive, he'd taken her to the car park of a supermarket after closing time, and she'd had all the space she'd needed to manoeuvre the car back and forth and round and round until she'd got the hang of the controls and hadn't had other cars to worry about. By the time she'd had a paid lesson, she was confident that she could move the car around and only had the rules of the road and keeping up with other traffic to worry about, which was exactly what she hoped to achieve this time with Fion.

She'd asked around for ideas on where to go, and it was Victor who'd had the solution. The patch of ground she wanted lay not on Daffodil Farm but on the land he'd gifted to one of his daughters, Melanie, and her husband, Damien. They had space outside one of their barns which was flat and plenty big enough for her needs, and Victor was certain they'd be happy enough with her using it.

And so, with a low sun in the sky, with the barns on one side and Damien and Melanie's home on the other, Ottilie was in the passenger seat of her car as Fion buckled her seat belt.

'How back to basics do we need to go?' Ottilie asked. 'You said you weren't very good at driving, so you must have tried to learn before. How far did you get? Do you know what all the controls do, or shall I go over them again?'

'I know the very basics,' Fion said. She looked down at the pedals and pressed each one lightly in turn. 'Clutch, brake, accelerator. I know about the handbrake and gears. I'm not used to this car, though, so I don't know where the lights are and that sort of thing.'

'We won't worry about that yet. Let's concentrate on moving the car first. Unless you're happy with that too?'

'I haven't done it for ages, so I think that might be a good idea. Shall I start the engine and just drive around a bit?'

'I think that's a good idea. Take it steadily.'

'I wasn't going to do anything else,' Fion said with a sideways glance. 'It's so good of you to do this for me, you know.'

'I think you might have said that once or thirteen times,' Ottilie replied with a smile. 'But you know quite a lot already, so that's half our work done. I can't imagine it's going to be such a hardship. I think it might even be fun. Are you ready?'

Fion nodded.

'Don't forget to have it in neutral before you start the engine.' Ottilie angled her head at the gears to remind Fion.

'Of course...' Fion waggled the gear stick before seeming satisfied it was where she needed it. 'It's already in, I think.'

'It was, but it doesn't hurt to check anyway. I'm not a qualified instructor, of course, but I'll do my best to remember what driving by the book is like before I show you what to do. It wouldn't do to have you driving like I normally do – you'd fail your test for sure.'

Fion gave an anxious smile. 'You seem like a good driver to me.'

'I'm sure I'm safe enough, but I've definitely picked up some bad habits. We all do eventually. I'll try not to pass them on to you.'

'I'll still be a better driver than I am now.'

'I suppose that won't be hard, as you don't drive at all now. Come on – let's see if we can get started before it goes dark. If I'm telling you something you know, feel free to tell me that you know it – I won't be offended. Otherwise I'm going to assume it's useful and carry on. So when you take off the handbrake and put the car into first, don't forget to lift the clutch gradually and you'll feel the biting point where the car is telling you it wants to move. Then you can let off the brake and let it go.'

Fion nodded. Concentration was etched into her features. Ottilie could barely remember what it was like not knowing how to do any of this, but she was reminded now of just how much there was to learn. It was like second nature to her, but once upon a time she'd had that same look as Fion as she tried to get going. The car screeched and groaned a little as Fion clumsily brought it to biting point and then, a moment later, jolted forward. Immediately, it cut out and came to a halt.

'Stalled,' Ottilie said. 'Don't worry; you'll get there. Try again.'

Fion repeated the operation and then stalled again.

'See,' she said, slapping her hands on the wheel. 'I told you I was useless at it.'

'You've barely begun,' Ottilie said patiently. 'Give yourself some time. You might stall it twenty times before you get going, but you will get going in the end.'

'What about your car? I might break it.'

'I think it will take more than that to break my car. Anyway, it's an old thing; I wouldn't worry. Concentrate on what you're doing and put all that out of your head.'

Fion looked unconvinced, but she did as Ottilie asked, and this time, the car inched forward.

'There you go!' Ottilie said. 'Now bring the speed up a little – we're juddering.'

Fion put her foot down, but it was too clumsy, and the car shot forward so alarmingly that she immediately lifted her feet from the pedals and stalled the car once more, throwing them both forward in their seats.

'I'll never curse a seat belt again!' Ottilie said, laughing, but Fion only looked miserable.

'Sorry.'

'Never mind. Let's go again. You'll get it.'

After ten minutes, Fion was beaming as she brought the car to a halt after a successful, if slow, circuit of the yard.

'See!' Ottilie said. 'You can do it, and you picked it up far quicker than you thought!'

'Only because I have a good teacher.'

Ottilie was beginning to realise that all Fion had really needed was someone with patience. Whoever had tried to teach her before had perhaps been lacking. And then, to her utter surprise, Fion leaned forward and threw her arms around Ottilie's neck in an awkward hug. It wasn't unwelcome, however, and Ottilie returned it.

'Thank you,' Fion said, letting go.

'You're more than welcome. While you're on a roll, do you want to have another go at driving round the yard?'

Fion nodded and set up the controls before going again.

'Try to get used to using your mirrors to check behind before you pull off, now that you're getting the hang of that bit.'

'OK.'

'And you might need to signal when you're on a road, but we'll get to that soon enough.'

After another successful circuit, Fion put the car into neutral and left the engine idling while Ottilie started to tell her what she might do to improve things, but they were interrupted by a figure coming from the house and towards the car. It was Damien – Victor's son-in-law. Ottilie didn't know him well – he'd come to help when her house had been flooded and she'd run into him at one or two village get-togethers, but, for the most part, he and his wife Melanie kept themselves to themselves up in the hills away from the village. Ottilie had always found Damien likeable. He had an easy manner and a pleasant tone to his voice that made it sound like he was about to crack a joke. He was taller than Heath but slimmer, with thick chestnut hair and eyes almost the same colour.

She pressed the button to lower the window, assuming he wanted to talk to them, and he leaned in with a smile, pushing a fringe that looked in need of a trim back from his face.

'How's it going?'

'Good, I think,' Ottilie said. She looked at Fion, who nodded.

'I've got further today than I have before,' she agreed.

'You look as if you're doing well,' he said.

'You were watching?' Fion asked, looking mortified.

'Not exactly,' he said, seeming to read her discomfort. 'But I couldn't help noticing whenever I looked out of the window. And I couldn't help looking out of the window because I was cooking and the chopping board is right near it. I swear I wasn't watching on purpose.'

'What are you cooking?' Ottilie asked.

'Pie. Actually, lots of pies. I'm testing recipes. They're in the oven now – I could do with some guinea pigs, if you fancy being taste-testers when they're out.'

'Why are you making so many?' Fion asked.

'I'm thinking of setting up a business with them – supplying some of the shops and pubs around here. Hopefully, I'll be creating something a bit unique that they'll want to buy. That's the idea anyway. I'm sure you'll tell me if my unique is everyone else's yuk.'

Ottilie laughed, but Fion only met the remark with a nervous smile. But as Ottilie watched her, she saw something else. Awe, she thought. Fion's expression, though it was seeking approval, was also full of admiration.

She glanced back at Damien. She'd always thought him reasonably attractive, but she'd never considered it any more deeply than that because he was Melanie's husband. And she supposed now he seemed confident and dynamic because of the way he was willing to go out on a limb to make his fortune, and that was probably attractive too.

'They'll be out in about half an hour if you want to come in,' he continued. 'I'll shout you. Of course, feel free to say no if you don't have time.'

'We'd love to,' Ottilie said. 'It'll be nice to see Melanie again as well.'

'Sorry, she's not home. She's over at Daffodil with Corrine doing something or other. I expect she'll be back soon, but I don't know if it'll be by the time you leave.'

'Hopefully,' Ottilie said. 'But we're happy to help anyway.' She glanced at Fion, who nodded her agreement.

'Great,' Damien said. 'I'll let you get on for now, but I'll come out to you when the pies are ready.'

Ottilie knocked on the door of the house and Damien answered, wearing a striped apron.

'We're finished for today,' she said. 'I thought I'd let you know.'

'You're just in time,' he said. 'The first batch of pies is out and cooling. Come in. That's if you're still happy to be my testers.'

Ottilie looked at Fion. She was flushed but she seemed happy with the progress she'd made, and over the previous twenty minutes she'd been livelier and more upbeat than Ottilie had ever seen her.

'I'm happy if you are,' she said to Ottilie.

'If I'd known there was going to be all this extra food, I wouldn't have eaten after work,' Ottilie said as they went inside.

'A mouthful or two will do it,' Damien said. 'I'm not expecting you to eat it all – unless you want to, of course.'

'You'd know we liked it if we wanted to eat them all,' Fion said.

'There is that,' Damien agreed. 'Sit down. Can I get either of you a drink? There's a jug of water on the table, but I can make tea or coffee. Or I have fruit juice if you'd prefer.'

'Juice would be lovely.' Ottilie sat down and, a moment later, their old sheepdog padded over, tail wagging limply, and laid a head on her lap, looking up at her. 'Hello, Pacy,' she said, stroking his nose. 'I bet you've had a sneaky bit of pie too.'

'He wishes,' Damien called from the fridge. 'He's certainly tried to get some, but most of them have ingredients that are not exactly dog friendly. At least, I wouldn't want to clear up after him if he had too much. Should be human friendly, though,' he added. 'In case you were worried.'

'Not worried at all,' Ottilie said. 'I'm looking forward to seeing what all these unusual flavours are.'

Damien brought a bottle of juice and three glasses to the table. Then he went to a cooling rack and took three pies from it, putting them on a platter before cutting them all into slices. A symphony of aromas filled the kitchen. Ottilie couldn't distinguish all of them, but there was beef and heavy red wine, and there was chicken – she thought – and something more eastern too, perhaps lemongrass.

'So,' he said, pointing to each in turn. 'We have turkey, chestnut, sage and apple sausage. Then there's beef with red wine and shallots, and the last one is a vegetarian one, Thai style curry with chickpea and coconut milk. I've got some other flavours in the oven – pork and pear, Moroccan-style chicken with apricot and yogurt, and one with a Tuscan-inspired bean casserole filling. And honestly, if you have any more ideas while you're here, I'd love to hear them. I'm still very much in the experimental phase and would gladly hear suggestions for new recipes.'

'I don't know about that, but these look amazing,' Fion said.

He put out three plates and then a slice of each pie onto each plate before giving them both a fork. 'Dig in. I'm sorry.' He paused. 'I never asked if either of you have any allergies. Or if you're vegan. Bloody hell, some pie manufacturer I'm going to be if I forget about those things.'

Both women shook their heads.

'Nothing to worry about here,' Ottilie said. 'Which one do you want us to try first?'

'Whichever you like. How about the turkey and chestnut? Seems like it would have less of an aftertaste than the others so it might be a good start.'

Ottilie dug her fork in and popped it into her mouth. The filling was rich, and the crust was just the right mix of crisp and moist. 'Wow!' she said. 'I thought it looked good, but I never expected it to be so amazing!'

'So you like it?' he asked, clearly hoping and perhaps expecting a positive response, even as he asked.

'Yes!' Ottilie took another forkful. 'I wasn't hungry, but I could still happily clear one of these if you gave me a whole one.'

Damien turned to Fion, who had just swallowed her mouthful.

'Delicious,' she said. 'The best pie I've ever eaten.'

'That's good,' he said. 'There's nothing you'd change? More salt? Less sage?'

'It's perfect,' Fion said. 'You made this from scratch?'

He nodded.

'I could never cook like this,' Fion said.

'I bet you could,' Ottilie told her. She looked at Damien, spotting an opportunity that was too good to miss. 'Fion cooks. She's thought about training to be a chef. I bet you'll have your hands full if you start getting a lot of orders for these. What are you going to do about making them in bulk? You'll be taking on help, right?'

'I haven't planned that far ahead,' Damien said, 'but if things went that well, yes, I'd probably need help, and Melanie isn't really interested. She's got her hands full, to be honest, with running the house and helping with the alpaca at Daffodil, so even if she was keen, it would be difficult.'

'I'm not very good, though,' Fion said to Ottilie. 'I don't think—'

'Damien could teach you,' Ottilie said.

'It wouldn't be like proper cheffing, I'm afraid,' Damien said. 'It'd be more like throwing ingredients into the mixer, more industrial when I scale it up. I mean, they'll be more artisan than most, but it will still be mass production to a degree.'

'You'll make them from here?' Ottilie asked.

'I expect so, unless it gets too big, but I'd cross that bridge when I came to it. *If* I came to it. But, Fion, if you're still looking for work when I get going and you're interested, then I'd be happy for you to do some trial shifts here to see how it suits you. I wouldn't need you to be trained to any kind of official standard. I only think if you really want to be a chef, it might not suit you.'

'I'd love that!' Fion said. 'When do you think that might be?'

'I couldn't say,' he replied. 'Not right now. I hope it won't be too much longer until I'm in a position to be able to let you know. I've got customers interested already, so it's just a case of establishing those relationships to make them regulars and getting going on working out production.'

'But you'll let me know?' she asked.

'I can let Ottilie know for you.'

'I could give you my phone number,' Fion began, and at this he seemed less certain.

'Don't worry,' he said. 'I won't forget. As soon as I know something, I'll tell Ottilie and she can let you know.'

Ottilie thought it strange that he wouldn't want Fion's number to contact her himself when the time was right. He seemed keen enough otherwise. Was it something to do with his marriage? Did he think Melanie would be suspicious of another woman's phone number in his contacts? But surely that would be ridiculous? Even if their marriage was at a rocky point, business was only business.

She dismissed the question as he went back to the platter. 'Beef next, if you're ready for another slice?'

'I'm ready,' Fion said.

Ottilie nodded and shoved the leftovers of the first one to the side of her plate to make space for the new sample.

This one was as good as the first, and Damien was delighted to hear them both say so. Then they tried the last; and as they were drinking juice, ready for the next batch to come out of the oven, Melanie came in.

'Hello, Ottilie!' she said, and although her greeting was friendly enough, there was a definite shift in the atmosphere.

'This is Ottilie's sister, Fion,' Damien said, rather too hurriedly for it to escape Ottilie's attention. 'They're both taste-testing for me.'

'Poor things,' Melanie said, again, the apparent humour masking something that neither of them were saying, a coldness beneath the courtesy.

They had the air of a couple who had recently argued and hadn't forgiven or forgotten it yet. Putting that together with what she already knew, Ottilie was alarmed to conclude that they did seem strained. She wondered how Corrine and Victor would take it if they split. It would be a mess, especially as they were living in a house built on land that Victor had gifted to them. Ottilie didn't know a lot about divorce law, but she imagined that might be tricky.

However, for now, she turned her thoughts back to the conversation in the room. It wasn't any of her business, and she might well be seeing more in it than there was. Lots of couples rowed all the time and they were fine. And gossip wasn't exactly a novelty in Thimblebury, so it wouldn't be surprising to hear speculation about anyone's marriage, even speculation that missed the mark.

'They're amazing,' Fion said.

'See.' Damien threw a look of triumph at Melanie as she bent to fuss the dog.

'Well,' she replied, looking at Ottilie and Fion in turn, 'I hope you don't think me rude, but I can't stay to chat – I've got some urgent emails to look over. If you're still here when I'm done, I'll pop down.'

'Don't mind us,' Ottilie said. 'We probably won't be here much longer anyway.'

'I have to get home before the last bus,' Fion said, and Ottilie turned to her.

'Don't worry about that – I'm going to take you home.'

'You ought to drive,' Damien said. 'Good practice.'

'Oh, I couldn't,' Fion began, and from the corner of her eye, Ottilie noticed Melanie slip from the room.

'If you wanted to try, though,' Ottilie replied, trying not to let her attention wander to Melanie's exit, 'I'd be right beside you. You could do ten minutes or so along a quiet stretch, just to get a feel for it, and then drive a bit further each time you come over until you're eventually driving home.'

'Am I allowed to do that?'

'I think so,' Ottilie said. 'I can't think of any laws against it.'

'As far as I know, as long as you have someone with a licence beside you it's fine,' Damien said.

'I don't know...' Fion knotted her hands together in her lap.

'You looked as if you were doing OK when I was watching,' Damien said.

Fion didn't reply, and after a beat of silence Damien seemed to decide that the car conversation was at an end. He went to the fresh batch of pies and put one of each on the platter to bring to the table. 'Who's got room for round two?' he asked.

'For pies that good, I'm sure I could make some room,' Ottilie said.

'Take some of the leftovers for Heath and Flo,' Damien added, cutting them up into slices, as he'd done the first ones. 'I'd love to hear what they think too.'

'I'm sure they'd love to give their opinion... Flo, at least.'

'Yes,' Damien said drily, 'we all know Flo isn't backwards at coming forwards. I'm sure she'll have thoughts, and she'll go out of her way to make sure I hear about them.'

In the end, Fion told Ottilie she was tired from concentrating for so long and didn't feel confident in the fading light, and Ottilie had to agree that when she'd only started to learn how to drive, she'd probably have felt the same. And so Ottilie drove her back to Penrith. There had been a brief call to Heath, who was meant to be coming over, to let him know she'd be late, and he'd said he'd wait at Flo's for her.

As they left the boundaries of Thimblebury, Ottilie could smell snatches of the many flavours of pie Damien had sent her away with to give to Heath and Flo and anyone else who might like to try them. Ottilie had already decided to take some for Stacey, Fliss and Lavender. Fion had some for her mum and dad, though she wasn't sure if they'd eat them or not, and the notion that they'd both overlook Fion's gift made Ottilie sad for her. The more they talked – though Fion never said it explicitly – the more Ottilie saw the picture of a home that was far from happy, and poor Fion stuck there.

As the sun dipped behind a hill, Ottilie switched the headlights on. The beam swept the road ahead, lighting up scurrying shadows in the verges and hedgerows as they went by. There was so much wildlife here, and these days Ottilie often took it for granted, but on occasions such as this one, she was reminded that her home in Thimblebury was a far cry from the one she'd shared with Josh in Manchester.

'I could have made the last bus,' Fion said. 'I feel terrible making you come all this way in the dark for me.'

'I don't mind,' Ottilie said. 'It means we get to spend more time together.'

'Oh...' Fion said, and when Ottilie shot a swift sideways glance her way before focusing back on the road, she caught a smile.

'I'm glad you came to find me,' Ottilie said. 'I can't imagine now not knowing you existed.'

'Me too,' Fion said. 'It's lucky you live so close to me too. Imagine if you'd never moved to the Lake District. Like, if you lived in Australia or something.'

'I know. Seems like the universe wanted us to meet, right?'

'My dad certainly didn't.'

Ottilie processed her reply for a moment as she followed the curve of the road, the reflective dots of the markings stretching ahead. 'Why do you think it would be such a problem for him?' she asked finally.

'No idea.' Fion unzipped her bag and checked her phone. Ottilie could see it light up briefly from the corner of her eye, until Fion dropped it back into the bag.

'Do you think it's because he'd prefer it if I didn't exist?'

'I don't know. I heard him say to Mum again that you

weren't getting any money from him.' Fion shrugged. 'Maybe he thinks you'll come for backpay for child maintenance or something.'

'That's ridiculous! Like I told him when we met, I'm a grown woman – I have no need of his money, and I never have. I was provided for perfectly well by my dad.'

'You don't think of my dad as your dad, even though you're glad we're sisters.'

'My dad is the man who brought me up. Conrad is just... well, you know. How can I put it politely? He's a biological fact in my existence, that's all.'

'Sometimes I think that's all he is to me.'

Ottilie glanced at her. 'What's he like to live with?'

'Do you need to ask? You don't like him and you've only met him once.'

'I never said I didn't like him. I don't care that he doesn't seem to like or want me in his life, but that's different. I don't have an opinion either way – I can't have because he hasn't given me a chance to form one. He might be a very nice dad to you – I wouldn't know because I don't see it.'

'He's...' Fion paused. 'He's my dad.'

'He is, but as much as it doesn't mean anything to me, it doesn't have to mean everything to you. As you pointed out, he's my dad too, biologically speaking, but I don't have a relationship with him. You might have one, but I get the impression it's not a good one. Maybe not even worth your effort. From what I've seen – which isn't much – it seems to me you're the one making all the effort.'

'Like *you* said, you don't see what we're like at home.'

Fion could deny the difficulties. She might do it from some misplaced sense of loyalty for a man she felt she ought to love and respect, but Ottilie could see through it.

'But,' Fion added into the gap, 'it's been worse since...'

'Not that I think the world revolves around me, but am I

going out on a limb if I say I think you're going to end that statement saying that it's been worse since I turned up?'

'It's just that… well, you can imagine. Mum's bound to ask questions about your mum, and Dad doesn't want to talk about it. There are things I wanted to know too.'

'But he wouldn't talk to you either.'

'He says it means nothing and he barely knew your mum. Is that true?'

'They worked together. My mum was feeling a bit lost and… well, you can work out the rest. I don't think they were in love or anything. I think my mum felt the same way once it was over – she wanted to put it behind her. But then she found out she was expecting me. We haven't talked too much about that time – I'm loath to drag it all up for her when it's obvious she doesn't want to go over it. I think she feels incredibly guilty. Your dad probably does too, and he's struggling to come to terms with the fact that there are now consequences to an affair from long ago he'd forgotten about. Maybe he even feels guilty that he hasn't been a part of my life – who knows?'

'He doesn't act like someone who feels guilty. He doesn't even want to acknowledge you.'

'True, but people do weird things, don't they? We don't always act like you'd expect.'

'I don't know how you take it all so calmly.'

'What else can I do? Raging won't change anything. Besides, I have a good life, and I don't feel I'm missing out not having him in it. If he comes to me and says he's changed his mind, I'd be happy to get to know him, but I'm not going to beg. Sorry…' Ottilie steered a sharp bend. 'It sounds as if I'm talking behind his back and saying things you probably don't want to hear. I don't mean to be hurtful—'

'You're not. I'm not hurt; you're only saying things I think might be true. He'll be furious if he finds out I'm coming here to see you.'

'He doesn't know at all? You're not going to tell him?'

'It's none of his business where I go – I'm an adult, even if he tries to make me feel like I'm not.'

'What do you mean?'

'The way he goes on all the time about living under his roof and abiding by his rules, like I'm still fourteen. I wish I could get out. I shouldn't be living with my parents at my age – even if I liked living with them, which I don't. But the rents are so high and I don't have any savings, and now I don't even have a job. Dad thinks I'm a loser with no future, and he's probably right.'

'Don't you know anyone you could houseshare with?'

Fion shook her head. 'They're all either already in houseshares or living with partners. I missed the boat.'

'And it's really as awful as you say? With your parents, I mean?'

'I'm sure there are people in worse situations. They're not cruel or abusive or anything – it's just it makes me so miserable. The three of us don't even have anything in common, let alone get along. But we don't even fight to clear the air; we mostly try to avoid one another, and if we have to be in the same room, we have hardly anything to say.'

'It does sound a bit depressing.'

'There's no point in talking about it because there's nothing I can do. I'm stuck.'

'Stuck now doesn't mean stuck always,' Ottilie said, mustering her most encouraging tone.

'Stuck now is bad enough. It's hard to think about the future when your now is so miserable.'

'I'd say thinking about the future is what might save you. It's not the same, but it's what I did when I lost Josh. I was stuck, mourning, unable to move on from what happened, angry at the man who did it. I woke up one day and realised that I had to see a brighter future and that seeing it was the first step to making it happen. So I tried to imagine what might be better than where I was now, and I opened my mind to whatever opportunities came my way, even if they weren't what I'd visualised. Then I saw the job in Thimblebury and it was like a light switch going on. I knew if I got it, that might be the change I needed to get me to the better future I'd been looking for.'

'I'm sorry,' Fion said. 'Here's me complaining about living at home with my parents and you went through all that. You must think I'm pathetic.'

'I don't at all. I didn't tell you that to measure your problems against mine or say they were bigger or tougher. I told you because I hoped it would make you feel more optimistic. When you're stuck in a rut, no matter how hard it seems to see past it, there is always a way. And if you can see past it, then you have a hope of moving past it. Nobody promises it won't be hard, but at least it's something to look forward to, something to keep you motivated.'

Fion didn't reply. Ottilie hoped she was mulling over her advice. Not that it was advice as such, more that she was sharing her own experiences in a way she hoped might help her half-sister.

When a few minutes had passed and there was still no response, Ottilie glanced across and saw that Fion was staring straight ahead. If she hadn't already told Ottilie how depressing her life was with her parents, Ottilie would have guessed it easily from the look on her face.

'Here's a thought,' she said, the idea coming from her as it formed. 'Why don't you stay with me for a while?'

Fion turned to her, but she still had nothing to say.

'I know it's not all that different to your current situation,' Ottilie added. 'But it will be a change of scenery for you and maybe kick-start some thoughts about where you want to be. You might decide it's far too quiet and boring, but then you'll know that village life is not for you. It might even make you feel you *do* want to spend some time living in a city, and I know you say you can't afford to, but you never know what will change in your circumstances that might make that a possibility after all. You might decide you want to be back in Penrith. You might even want to go abroad. I just wonder whether some time away from the place that feels as if it has you captive will be the kick up the backside you need to start working out how to change things.'

'You'd really have me?'

'I wouldn't have offered otherwise.'

'But you hardly know me.'

'True, but I know you enough to get a good feeling about it. And you're my sister.'

'Half-sister. You might get sick of me.'

'You're more likely to get sick of me. Or Thimblebury. If you did, I wouldn't be offended by you saying so and moving on. Are you worried about telling your parents you want to move out?'

'I don't think they care about the moving-out part – it's the part when I say where I'm moving to that might be a problem. What about Heath?'

'He doesn't live with me yet,' Ottilie said, trying not to think about the fact that she would have to break the news of what she'd just done to Heath and she couldn't be entirely sure how he'd take it.

'And it would really be all right?'

'It would make your driving lessons easier,' Ottilie said with a smile.

'And if your friend Damien does have work for me...'

'Now you're seeing where I'm going with this. Sleep on it. Let me know.'

'But... what will I tell my mum and dad?'

'That's up to you. Do you need to tell them anything?'

'I think I ought to. They're not the easiest people to live with, but they're still my parents.'

'I'd be the same,' Ottilie said. 'So what will you tell them?'

'I don't know yet. I don't even know... I mean, it's so nice of you to offer, but I don't know if it's the best thing for me to do.'

'Of course. I don't mind what you decide, as long as it's what you feel you need. I only wanted you to know that the offer's there if you feel it will help.'

'Thank you.'

They drove on, both of them lapsing into silence again. It didn't worry Ottilie – quite the opposite. If they could already share a comfortable silence this early on in their relationship, that had to be a good thing. She'd enjoyed the time she'd spent with Fion far more than she'd ever imagined she could, and she was hopeful that the bond they were forming would only get stronger.

Heath looked into the box. 'A few pies! You weren't kidding – there's more than a few! I wish I hadn't eaten now, but I was starving and I couldn't wait.'

'Some of them are for your gran, and then I'll take the rest to work with me tomorrow. I can put yours in the freezer here if you like for when you fancy them. Damien says they'll freeze well.'

'They look good.'

'They are – Fion and I tasted all of them. There wasn't a bad flavour.'

'What's he planning to do?'

'Other than sell them at some point? Not a clue. You'd have to talk to him about business strategies and all that stuff.'

Heath laughed. 'I was curious, but not that curious. Imagine me knocking on his door: come to the pub, mate, I want to talk to you about manufacturing processes and profit margins. There's a riveting night out for you.'

'I don't know how big it's going to be, but we did ask him if he'd be taking anyone on and he said he might.'

'Why did you ask that?'

'I was thinking about Fion. She says she'd quite like to work in catering.'

'Is it really catering? Won't it be more like factory work?'

'Not the way Damien is going to be making them, no. At least, I don't see it. He might be producing in bulk, but if he's working from one of his outbuildings, it's still going to be small scale, more like cooking than an assembly line.'

Heath refastened the lid of the box. 'I suppose a job is a job when you don't have one.'

'There's that too. Even if it only tides her over, it's got to be better than nothing. I actually think she'd enjoy working up there with Damien. He seems like he'd be a good boss.'

'It'd be a long way to commute for a minimum-wage job. I'm assuming it will be minimum wage – it won't require much in the way of qualifications. Would it be worth her while?'

'That's...' Ottilie watched as Heath opened a bottle of wine and poured some into two glasses. 'I asked her if she'd like to come and stay with me.'

'Oh? For how long?'

'For as long as she wants.'

His head snapped up. 'What do you mean?'

'I mean she can live here for a while. If she wants to.'

'Ottilie... why?'

'Why what?'

'Why would you do that? You don't know the first thing about her. Helping her out with driving and jobs is one thing, but having her live with you? Is she paying rent?'

'We haven't talked about money yet. I don't think I'll ask her though.'

'Are you *insane*?'

'I don't think so. Not last time I checked.'

'Are you sure? You're going to let a girl you hardly know move in with you for free? With no time limit.'

'She's my sister.'

'You didn't even know she existed a week ago! And what about me?'

'What about you?'

'It's going to be awkward for me to come over if she's here.'

'You mean you won't be able to walk around the house naked.'

'Don't be like that – you know full well what I mean. It's going to change the way we spend time together.'

'So you're going to deny a girl who needs help because it means we might not always have the house to ourselves when we want to be intimate?'

'*Intimate*? You're not with one of your patients now! If you mean sex, then yes, it's going to be weird! This is a small house with thin walls and...' He threw his hands in the air. 'Whatever. It's your house and you've clearly made up your mind.'

'It is and I have. She might not be here for long; she only needs someone to give her a leg-up and she'll be on her way.'

'She might well settle right in and decide she's got it too easy to be on her way. What incentive would she have to leave? You said yourself she's got no job and no money and she can't afford rent anywhere decent. If I was in her shoes, I'd find this place a pretty attractive prospect.'

'She's not like that.'

'You don't know what she's like – you don't know her! Ott—' Heath took a steadying breath and smoothed his features. 'Your kindness is one of the most beautiful things about you, but sometimes I worry that you don't know when to stop giving. I'm not saying any of this to be mean; I'm trying to look out for you because you seem hell-bent on not looking out for yourself.'

'So it has nothing to do with how it will affect you?'

'I won't lie, that's on my mind too. Not only me, though –

us. We've just got engaged, and I'm meant to be moving in. We're a couple starting out, not an old married couple with a kid.'

'It won't be like that.'

'Won't it? So she won't be sitting in the living room with us when we're watching TV at night? Or at the kitchen table eating with us? Or sharing the bathroom? And this is a small house – it'll feel incredibly small with an extra person in it.'

'We'll manage, and I expect she'll be out a lot.'

'There's nowhere to go in Thimblebury – where's she going to?' He shook his head. 'Sorry, I don't see this working.'

'It has to work now,' Ottilie said stubbornly. 'We have to try because I've already offered.'

'Tell her you've changed your mind.'

'I can't, not now I've got her hopes up! Would you? Be honest.'

Heath regarded her in silence for a moment. 'No,' he said finally. 'I don't suppose I would.'

'If it gets too difficult I'll talk to her, I promise.'

'I don't believe that for a minute, but OK, if you say so. When is this going to happen?'

'I don't know. She hasn't even decided yet. It might not happen.'

'We can live in hope,' he said, taking a gulp of his wine.

Ottilie sat at the table with her own glass. She'd expected him to be wary of the plan, but she hadn't expected him to be so against it. On reflection, however, she should have expected his reaction. He was right, even if she didn't want to acknowledge it – they were starting out as a new couple living together properly for the first time, and if Fion moved in, it would change everything. But Ottilie wasn't going to withdraw the offer. Fion was already feeling overlooked and worthless at home with her parents; Ottilie wasn't about to reinforce that by making her feel unwanted here too. They'd have to at least try to make it work for as long as the arrangement might last.

He sat next to her and forced a smile. 'Look, I realise you're only trying to look out for her like you do for everyone. I also realise this is what I signed up for when I asked you to marry me, so' – he reached for her hand – 'do what you need to. It's your house – I know – and I have no right to tell you who to have here. I'm sorry.'

'I'm sorry I didn't talk to you first about it. The offer just came out when we were driving to Penrith. She seemed so miserable with her parents I couldn't bear it.'

'I can imagine.' He stroked her hair away from her face. 'What am I going to do with you?'

'If it happens, it'll be fine,' Ottilie said. 'We'll make it fine.'

CHAPTER TWELVE

Fion was still deciding what to do when they met up again for another driving lesson. This time Melanie was home and chatted to them both for a few minutes when they arrived.

'Is Damien home?' Ottilie asked as Melanie leaned against the open back door to talk to them in the yard.

'He's gone to see some potential clients.'

'Oh. I was going to tell him how much everyone liked the pies.'

'I'll tell him when he comes back.'

'So he's steaming ahead?'

'With the new venture? Yes.' Melanie folded her arms tight across her chest. The body language was unmistakable. Melanie didn't much care for the new venture.

'So there might be a job for me?' Fion asked.

'A job?' Melanie's arms visibly tightened. 'What kind of job?'

'Well,' Ottilie said, glancing at Fion before cutting in, 'we talked to him last time we were here, and he said he wouldn't be able to do everything himself and he might want help. We thought Fion might be able to, and he said he'd see.'

'If it's a problem, then it doesn't matter,' Fion added. 'It's just that I might be moving to Thimblebury, and it would be good to get something here rather than having to travel every day. At least until I can drive. But even then I suppose I might not have enough money for a car...'

Melanie waved away the comment. 'It's nothing to do with me if he takes someone on. It's his business, not mine; he can do what he likes.'

Ottilie thought it an odd thing to say. Surely any business Damien started up was something to do with her in some capacity, however small, given that they were married. 'How are your mum and dad?' she asked, feeling as if a change of topic to something far safer was needed.

'You probably see more of them than me,' Melanie said. 'They were all right last I saw them. Dad's had another girl. They'll have to get a bigger farm if they keep going like that.'

Fion looked confused as she glanced from Melanie to Ottilie and back again.

'An alpaca,' Ottilie said. 'He calls them his girls.' She turned to Melanie. 'How many is that now?'

'Damned if I know. Too many. He's too soft – can't hear about a rescue without going to pick it up.'

'What's he called her?'

'Tulip, I think. Something like that. Again, there are so many I forget what all the names are.'

'Maybe we could go and see her when we're done here,' Ottilie said to Fion. 'And then I can introduce you to the other Ottilie – alpaca Ottilie.'

'Named after you?' Fion asked.

Ottilie smiled. 'Yes.'

'Doesn't name any after me,' Melanie said. 'Or Pen.'

'Pen?' Fion frowned.

'My sister,' Melanie said. 'Penny.'

'Maybe they thought you wouldn't like it,' Ottilie said carefully, sensing a raw nerve. It was strange – she'd spoken to Melanie before and she'd never been like this. She'd always been brisk and courteous, in the way of someone who didn't know Ottilie particularly well, but she'd always been friendly with it. Today she seemed out for an argument, though she also seemed as if she didn't know who she wanted to have it with. It looked as if anyone who put a foot wrong and happened to be in her path would do. With those thoughts in her head, Ottilie didn't give Melanie a chance to reply. Instead, she looked at Fion. 'We ought to get started before we lose the light.'

'I'll be in here if you need me,' Melanie said, going inside and closing the door before either of them could acknowledge it.

Ottilie swiftly decided that it would have to be one hell of an emergency before she'd disturb her in her current mood. She walked to the car, Fion at her side.

'They're a funny couple,' Fion said in a low voice. 'Don't you think?'

'How do you mean?'

'He's so friendly and outgoing, and she's...'

'She's not always like that. Perhaps she's had a bad day. You don't know what's going on with people, do you?'

'I suppose not. So she's usually nice?'

'I'm not sure nice is the word. Usually sociable enough. It's funny, when you meet her mum and dad, you'll wonder how they're related at all. Victor and Corrine are lovely.'

'Seems to be a theme, doesn't it?' Fion said, and Ottilie had to smile.

'We certainly don't all get the family we deserve, do we? Let's say we do an hour here, and then I'll take you over to Daffodil Farm and introduce you?'

'I'd like that,' Fion said. 'I ought to get to know people in Thimblebury, especially if I'm going to be living here.'

Ottilie's hand rested on the car door handle. 'Does that mean you've decided to come and stay with me?'

'I'm not sure, but every time I come I feel a bit more like it's a good idea.'

'Maybe Victor's girls will convince you then,' Ottilie said with a grin. 'Get in and get driving, and then we'll pop over and see if they can't win your heart.'

Victor opened the gate to let Ottilie and Fion through before following and closing it behind him. One by one, his girls looked up from their various spots on the field, and as each noticed his arrival, they began to make a lazy beeline over.

'They're so cute!' Fion cried.

'Aren't they?' Ottilie exchanged a smile with Victor. He was so proud of his little herd, and he never got tired of showing them off.

'Want to give them some treats?' Victor asked, going to the shed where he kept their feed and equipment. He turned and waved them over.

The ground was hard – there hadn't been any rain for a good week. Ottilie was glad because she wasn't wearing the right shoes for mud. As they went over to the shed, Ottilie became aware of them being followed. She looked round and grinned.

'We've got company,' she said to Fion.

They were now being trailed by four alpaca, and there were more on the way.

'I love them!' Fion said. 'Can I stroke them, or will they bite?'

'I'll let you feed them first,' Victor called over. 'They don't know you yet. Gentle souls, but best to make friends first. That's just how I do it with the walkers.'

'Walkers?' Fion frowned slightly.

'Victor runs a sort of hike with an alpaca thing in the summer. Tourists come and walk round with them.'

'Oh,' Fion said.

They went into the shed, and Victor handed them both some nibbles. Before they'd been able to get outside again, the faces of the four closest girls were crowded at the door.

'As keen as ever,' Victor said, laughing as he tried to move them back. 'Come on now – don't crowd. You'll frighten young Fion to death.'

Fion went over to a black-and-white one and held out her hand. The alpaca sniffed and then began to eat. Fion let out a girlish giggle. 'I could take them all home! Where's your one, Ottilie?'

'I don't know,' Ottilie said. 'To my shame, I don't know if I could recognise her just like that. There are so many of them.'

'Over the other side,' Victor said. 'Bring the bag – we'll go over and see her.'

Fion was beaming as they went across the field, now being shadowed by at least eight alpaca. Ottilie watched her. She looked happier than ever – certainly happier than she'd looked whenever she'd spoken about her own home in Penrith. Heath had been doubtful about asking her to live with them, but as she watched now, Ottilie was more convinced than ever that it was a good idea.

CHAPTER THIRTEEN

Ottilie had just seen Mrs Icke out when Lavender appeared at her office door. 'I've booked William Tavistock in and he's waiting in the reception for you, but I've also got Chloe in reception asking to see you. What do you want to do? You want me to tell her to wait until your clinic is over, or can you spare two minutes? I can make William a cup of tea and ask him to wait if you need me to.'

Ottilie frowned. 'That's sweet of you, and he's not normally in a rush, but did Chloe say what she wanted that was so urgent?'

'She wouldn't tell me. She seems calm enough, but you can never tell with that girl. The sky could be falling down and she'd be walking round like she was bored of life.'

'Well, did she say how long she wanted me for?'

Lavender shrugged. 'Again, this is Chloe. She's not going to tell me. I did say to her you couldn't spare much time because it was in the middle of clinic, and she said that was OK.'

Ottilie rubbed some alcohol gel into her hands. 'I suppose I might as well see her now if William is happy to wait.'

She wiped down the treatment bed and tidied her supply

cupboard while she waited. A couple of minutes later, Lavender returned with Chloe in tow.

'Hi, Chloe,' Ottilie said. 'Come in and shut the door.'

Lavender left them to it, and Chloe took a seat at the other side of Ottilie's desk. Without a word, she took a piece of white plastic from her pocket and laid it down in front of Ottilie. 'Can you get a midwife for me?' she asked.

Ottilie peered at the pregnancy test and then looked up at Chloe. 'One of our doctors needs to do that.'

'I don't want them to know.'

'Why not?'

'Because Simon will tell my mum.'

'Chloe,' Ottilie said, leaning across the desk, 'I think your mum will find out sooner or later. Are you worried about telling her?'

'She'll freak out. She'll say it's too soon after Mackenzie.'

'What do you feel about that? Or Ollie... I'm assuming it's Ollie's baby?'

'Yes!' Chloe said with the merest hint of offence at the suggestion the father might be anyone but her boyfriend.

'Sorry, but I had to ask. It's a professional thing, you know – we can't make those kinds of assumptions.'

'Oh. Right.'

'So you're OK with it?'

'I'm glad,' Chloe said. 'I want the baby. I like babies now.'

'Even though it will disrupt your studying?'

'Ollie says he'll help. We'll manage between us. We're going to get a flat together.'

'Sounds like you've got it all sorted. I'm not sure what you need me for. Like I said, I can't refer you to midwifery. If you prefer not to see Simon, Dr Cheadle will do it, and she won't say a word to your mum.'

'She might say to Simon, and he might tell Mum.'

'She won't, and even if she did, Simon isn't legally allowed to say anything no matter what the relationship. That's how it is. None of us can. I'm not even allowed to tell Heath anything about his gran's medical record, no matter what it might be. In this case, I don't think any of us will have to tell your mum for her to know eventually. How far along do you think you are?'

'About eight weeks.'

'Early then. So you've got time to think about how you're going to break it to her.'

'Could you tell her for me?'

'Again, I think it would be better coming from you. She adores Mackenzie – I bet she won't be half as upset as you imagine.'

'She will – she'll say I'm throwing my career away and all that.'

'She might worry about that, but I don't think she'd say so.'

Chloe reached for the pregnancy test and stared at it for a moment. 'Can I have another midwife, do you think? I don't like the one I had for Mackenzie.'

'She's all we've got,' Ottilie said, though recalling a conversation she'd had with Fliss not that long ago where Fliss was concerned they didn't have enough cover for the sudden baby boom Thimblebury seemed to be experiencing. And here was Chloe, adding to the burden.

'She was always telling me off.'

'For your own good, I'm sure.'

'I don't think she liked me.'

'Whether she likes you or not doesn't come into it. Chloe' – Ottilie gave an encouraging smile – 'if I based my decision to treat on whether I liked the patient or not, I wouldn't be very busy, trust me. I'm sure she's the same with everyone; she's probably just a bit businesslike. Some midwives are – they have a lot of women and babies in their care, and they don't always have time for the niceties.'

'They don't have to be rude.'

'If you think she's treating you unfairly when you start to see her, you can make an official complaint.'

'Nobody will care. Can't you look after me? You did with Mackenzie.'

'I delivered him in an emergency – I'm hardly qualified to look after you through your pregnancy.' Ottilie glanced up at the clock. She realised that what Chloe needed, more than anything, was reassurance. She needed to know that she was making the right decision to continue with the pregnancy, that she would be able to cope, that she wasn't ruining her life chances by having another baby so soon after Mackenzie, that Ollie wouldn't abandon her like Mackenzie's father had done, and so many other things. But Ottilie couldn't give her those reassurances. Nobody could. And even if all she could offer Chloe was time to air her worries, she couldn't spare that right now either. She had a clinic to run, and soon there would be a backed-up list of patients, some of whom would struggle to wait around for long. She wanted to repay the trust Chloe so obviously had in her, and in a way she was flattered that she was the person Chloe had turned to before anyone else, but it couldn't be done right now.

'Fine,' Chloe said, getting up.

'Chloe, wait! I'm not trying to fob you off; it's just that I have patients waiting. If I'd known you were coming, I'd have made time to see you.'

Chloe made for the door. 'It doesn't matter.'

'It does. Come to see me later at home. We can talk about the midwife situation and what we're going to tell your mum.'

Chloe seemed torn. If Ottilie knew anything about her, she couldn't decide whether to make Ottilie stew for a bit, letting her think her confidence wasn't wanted but, at the same time, desperately needing it. 'Yeah,' she said finally. 'I'll come. What time?'

'I'll be finished here at six at the latest. I need ten, fifteen minutes to get back. How does that sound?'

'Ten past six?'

Ottilie nodded and decided she'd have to run home because Chloe wouldn't wait around if she was late. She also had to make certain now that her clinic didn't overrun. At least her worst, most time-consuming regular, Mrs Icke, was already done. Barring nasty surprises, the rest ought to go like clockwork.

'Right.'

Chloe left, Ottilie watching the door slam shut behind her. She let out a long breath and reached for her mobile phone. For a split second, she considered texting Stacey, but as she'd told Chloe, she wasn't allowed to break her confidence, and so she wondered what she could say to Stacey that would be within the rules and yet also warn her that a big shock was coming her way. In the end, she had to conclude that there was nothing, and that Stacey would just have to find out the hard way when Chloe decided to tell her.

Ottilie saw her last patient off and rushed home to be there for Chloe's arrival, but ten past six came and there was no Chloe. So she had a bite to eat and replied to a message from Heath saying he had a ton of work and wasn't likely to make it over that night, and then sent a text to Chloe to see if she was still planning to come which went unanswered. She wondered if Chloe had decided to come clean with Stacey after all and so was busy talking it through with her. If that was the case, Ottilie didn't mind at all that Chloe hadn't turned up; she only wanted to know what the situation was because she'd arranged for Fion to visit at half past seven. She thought about putting Fion off, but by now her sister was probably already on the bus that wound its way through dozens of local villages on her way over, and it seemed inconsiderate to tell her to turn around and go all the way home for the sake of another visit that might not happen.

When Fion arrived, Ottilie was glad she hadn't cancelled their plans. She seemed genuinely excited for her next driving lesson, about as animated as Ottilie had ever seen her.

'Do you want a drink or a bite to eat before we go up the hill?'

'I had a sandwich a couple of hours ago. I'm fine. We can get a drink afterwards – if you don't mind me staying a while.'

'Actually,' Ottilie said as she collected her keys, 'Heath won't be here tonight. You're welcome to stay over if you like. That is, if you don't fancy the bus back and you want to stay for a couple of drinks and a chat.'

'I don't have any overnight things.'

'That doesn't matter – you can borrow some of my pyjamas, and I have a spare toothbrush in an unopened pack. It might as well be yours. There's no pressure, but the offer is there if you want it.'

'I'm sure nobody at home will miss me,' Fion said. She beamed at Ottilie. 'I'd love to!'

'OK, so we'll have an hour in the car and then head back. Do you drink?'

'Sometimes, not all that often – I don't go out all that often these days.'

'Maybe we should pick something up from the shop before they close? Wine or beers or something. Do you mind if we call on the way up to your lesson? It's been one hell of a day and I could do with a tipple.'

'Has it?' Fion seemed concerned, and Ottilie couldn't help but smile at it.

'Don't worry – it goes with the territory when you're a nurse. Some days are more stressful than others, and some patients are definitely more stressful than others, but it's nothing I can't handle if I get a chance to let off some steam.'

'Oh, because I can leave the lesson if you—'

'Don't be daft,' Ottilie said, nodding for her to follow as she headed for the front door. 'If anything, spending an hour up the hill with you will be relaxing after the day I've had.'

'You say that, but I haven't got behind the wheel yet.'

'Come on,' Ottilie said, her smile growing, 'we'd better get a move on if we're going to catch Magnus and Geoff before they close.'

'Ottilie!' Magnus was tidying a shelf of magazines as they walked in while Geoff was counting change at the counter.

'Oh, you're not closing right now?' Ottilie asked, her gaze going to Geoff at the open till.

'In a few minutes,' Geoff said. 'It was quiet and we thought we might as well.'

'I'll be quick,' she said, dashing to a shelf with a modest but quality selection of wine on it. That was one thing Ottilie liked about Magnus and Geoff being such foodies – they didn't stock a great deal of a thing because the shop was too small, but what they did have was always very good.

'Don't worry,' Magnus said, regarding Fion with obvious curiosity now as she followed Ottilie. 'No rush.'

Ottilie grabbed a white and showed it to Fion. 'Look all right?'

'I haven't a clue about wine,' Fion said. 'I'm sure it will be.'

'Me neither,' Ottilie said. 'All I know is that if it's on the shelves here, it's likely to be nice.'

'Thank you,' Geoff said. 'We'll take compliments like that until the cows come home.'

Ottilie could see he was curious about Fion now too. People in the village had heard about the half-sister who'd suddenly appeared in Ottilie's life – she hadn't seen any point in keeping it a secret – but she hadn't gone out of her way to parade her around and introduce her to everyone as if she were some minor royal who'd come to stay.

'Fion,' Ottilie said, waving a hand from one to the other, 'Magnus and Geoff. The two most cultured people I know. And some of the kindest and most fun.'

'Wow, that's some introduction!' Geoff said. 'I don't think we could possibly live up to that now! Pleased to finally meet you, Fion.'

Magnus wandered over and took hold of Fion to give her a light kiss on both cheeks. 'We don't stand on ceremony here. It's lovely to meet you, Fion. Hopefully we'll be seeing you around a lot more?'

'I hope so,' Fion said, glancing at Ottilie. 'I think maybe you will.'

Ottilie wondered whether that meant Fion had made a decision about coming to stay with her long-term at Wordsworth Cottage. She'd have to ask later when they'd finished their driving lesson.

'So you have to come far to visit?' Magnus asked.

'Not too far,' Fion said. 'I live in Penrith. The buses are slow, but they're not too bad.'

'Penrith, eh?' Geoff smiled. 'We thought about buying a shop there, way back. The rents were higher than here and there was lots more competition, so we decided to stay put. It's a nice town, though.'

'Yes,' Fion agreed.

Both Magnus and Geoff looked expectant, like they were waiting for more from Fion. Ottilie knew them both well enough to see that beneath the polite enquiries, they were actually mad with curiosity and wanted to know absolutely everything about the new girl in the village.

'Is Stacey keeping all right?' Ottilie asked Geoff.

He frowned slightly. 'I would imagine you'd know better than me; I'm sure she must see more of you.'

'I haven't seen her for a few days – busy, you know. I'll have to pop round.'

'Hmm.' Geoff nodded vaguely. Ottilie concluded that if Chloe had broken the news of her pregnancy to Stacey since she'd been to the surgery, Stacey would have been straight on the phone to tell her brother. So it seemed Chloe hadn't done so yet. Again, Ottilie wondered what was happening and why Chloe hadn't turned up at Wordsworth Cottage when she'd arranged to, but decided she'd send a discreet message later to check all was well.

'It's the same here,' Geoff said. 'Always so busy.'

'We can't even get time to go and visit my relatives in Iceland,' Magnus said. 'It's so hard to get cover for the shop. Sometimes Chloe will do the odd few hours but nothing more.'

'I offer to cover so you can go,' Geoff said to him.

'But I want you to come with me,' Magnus replied.

'You have family in Iceland?' Fion asked. 'I've never been. Is it nice?'

'Beautiful. Not as green as it is here but beautiful in a very rocky kind of way. You must go one day.' He grinned. 'You'll probably get there before I do.'

'I could look after your shop,' Fion said. 'I know you don't have a full-time position but I'm not working right now, so I can cover if it helps.'

Magnus and Geoff exchanged a look that told Ottilie they were interested. She also understood that they didn't know the first thing about Fion. Ottilie herself hardly knew her, and it was perfectly understandable that while they'd grab any opportunity for the break they clearly needed, they'd have to get to know Fion better before they could trust her with their livelihood. She hoped that if Fion did decide to stay at Wordsworth Cottage, that would happen. They needed cover and Fion needed work, so it seemed like a very neat – if temporary – solution to both problems.

'We might talk to you about that one of these days,' Magnus said. 'It would be nice to go home.'

'I'm sure you want to talk about it,' Ottilie said. 'I can easily let Fion know if you decide to take her up on the offer.'

'And I could do some trial shifts to see if you like me,' Fion said.

Magnus smiled. 'We already know we like you.'

Fion blushed, and Ottilie gave her a fond glance. Fion had become such a big part of her life already she couldn't imagine what it might be like without her now.

'She might be working for Damien soon too,' Ottilie said.

'Damien?' Magnus frowned slightly.

'You know he's starting that business?' Ottilie asked. 'Making posh pies.'

'Oh, yes,' Magnus said doubtfully.

Ottilie laughed at the look of disbelief on his face. 'They're actually good,' she said. 'We did some taste-testing for him. You might want to stock some here when he's up and running.'

'I'm not sure how many we could sell.'

'There's only one way to find out,' Ottilie said.

'That's told us,' Geoff said with a laugh.

Ottilie paid for the wine and bid them both goodbye. As she and Fion got into the car, she could see Geoff at the door, locking up for the night.

'They're lovely,' Fion said.

'They are,' Ottilie replied.

'I thought they might be a bit weird with me.'

Ottilie started the engine. 'Why would they do that?'

'Because of the way I knocked on their house when I first met you. I suppose it was a bit... well, just turning up like that... But they seem OK.'

'The thing about Magnus and Geoff is they will gossip

about anything given half a chance, but at the same time they're not quick to judge. They'll give you the benefit of the doubt, and they'll be lovely to you as long as you don't give them reason to be otherwise.'

'It would be good if I could work for them.'

'I'm not sure they can afford you all the time, but if you don't get a job soon and they do decide to take time off to go to Iceland, it might work out well for you for a bit of extra cash. We'll have to see what happens when they talk it over. I expect Magnus will snap your hand off; it's Geoff who might be less keen.'

'Because he doesn't know me?'

'Well, because he'll worry about what's going on here, and, of course, he doesn't have the same pull to Iceland that Magnus has.'

'I see.'

Ottilie took off the handbrake and then paused. 'Do you fancy driving a bit of the way? Maybe just out of the village until we get to the bottom of the hill?'

'On the road, you mean?'

'You'll have to do it sooner or later, and it's nice and quiet here right now.'

Fion looked uncertain but then nodded. 'You're right – I'll have to do it sooner or later.'

They were swapping seats when Ottilie looked up to see Chloe walking on the other side of the road.

'Chloe?' she called.

Chloe stopped and looked across, before changing course to come over. 'Hi,' she said.

'I was expecting you earlier,' Ottilie said. 'Everything all right?'

'Yeah,' Chloe said. 'Mackenzie wouldn't go down for a sleep so...' She gave a vague shrug.

It was a questionable excuse, but Ottilie wasn't about to

split hairs now – she had her hands full with something else. She could only imagine that Chloe had been plagued by second thoughts about trusting Ottilie with her secret after her visit to the surgery or she'd decided she was perfectly capable of sorting things for herself and didn't need to talk it over after all. Either way, it was frustrating for Ottilie.

Not because she was annoyed for the no-show – she was used to that in her line of work; patients often missed appointments – but because whenever she felt she'd moved forward with Chloe, something would happen to pull the rug from under her. Having Chloe turn up and confide in her had felt like an honour in many ways because Chloe was not the sort of girl to form friendships easily, and Ottilie had worked hard on theirs. And then to have her pull back by not coming over to continue that conversation made Ottilie question their friendship all over again. It hardly mattered in the scheme of things whether Chloe considered Ottilie one of her friends at all, except for the fact that Ottilie was now so close to her mum Stacey, she almost considered them both family.

Chloe's gaze went to Fion.

'Oh,' Ottilie said. 'This is my sister, Fion. Fion, this is Chloe.'

Chloe looked from one to the other. 'Mum said something about that.' She looked back at Fion. 'You moving here then?'

'I don't know,' Fion said, seeming wrong-footed by the forthright younger woman.

'Where do you live now?'

'Penrith.'

'Any good?'

'It's nice.'

'Cheap flats?'

Fion shrugged. 'Depends what you want, I suppose. I don't think it's all that cheap.'

Chloe studied her for a moment and then seemed to decide

she had the information she wanted, and that Fion wasn't all that interesting after all, because she turned back to Ottilie. 'Shall I come later?'

'Fion and I were planning on having a drink later.'

'So I can't come?'

'I suppose...'

'I don't mind,' Fion cut in.

'Yes, but it's something private,' Chloe said. 'I need to talk to Ottilie.'

'I can be out of the way for as long as you need,' Fion offered. 'I'm sure I can find something to do.'

At that moment, Ottilie recognised in Fion the chronic people-pleaser that she had in herself. She'd lived her life that way, happy to put herself last all the time, and for the most part she hadn't seen it as a problem. It was only when others had pointed it out and told her she deserved better – that they wanted better for her – that she'd come to realise it wasn't always healthy to be that way. And here was Fion, doing exactly the same. And now Ottilie could see it from the other side, she wanted better for her half-sister.

'No,' she said. 'You won't need to do that. We'll be out for the next hour or so, Chloe, but then in for the rest of the night. Feel free to come round if you want to talk, but if you want it to be just us, then I'm afraid we'll have to make it another time.'

'Right.' Chloe shot a look at Fion that bordered on dislike.

Ottilie gave her a moment to add something to her statement, but when she didn't, Ottilie motioned for Fion to get in the car. She didn't know whether she was meant to expect Chloe later or not, but she wasn't going to worry about it.

Fion seemed flustered as she fastened her seat belt and started the engine.

'Yes,' Ottilie said, watching Chloe cross back over the street. 'She can be a bit intense.'

'I don't think she likes me.'

'I wouldn't take it personally – she doesn't like anyone.'

'She likes you.'

'Now, yes, but believe me, it's taken some effort on my part. Are you ready?'

Fion nodded and pulled away from the kerb with a little jolt.

'That's good!' Ottilie said.

'I nearly stalled it.'

'But you didn't, so it's a definite improvement. A few more weeks and it will all click into place – I promise. Then you'll be zipping around all over.'

Ottilie stood by the car, peering into the ditch where the front wheel had lodged.

'I'm so sorry!' Fion said as she stood next to her.

Ottilie tried not to show her stress. 'It's not your fault.'

'I was driving!'

'You're learning. If anything, it's my fault for persuading you to drive up to the farm. The light's fading, and I should have thought about that.'

Despite Ottilie's reassurances, Fion looked close to tears. 'I'm useless. How are we going to get it out?'

Ordinarily, Heath would have been her knight in shining armour, but she wasn't expecting him that evening, and she wasn't about to disturb his work and make him drive from Manchester to pull her out of this. 'I'll phone Victor,' she said, deciding on the next best thing. 'He'll know what to do.'

'Damien has a tractor!' Fion added. 'I saw it in the barn!'

Ottilie nodded, phone already pressed to her ear as she waited for someone at Daffodil Farm to answer. They only had a landline – Victor had got so fed up of losing mobile phones around the farm he'd given up buying them, and Corrine hardly went out enough to warrant one either.

To her relief, Corrine answered quickly, and Ottilie explained the problem. Half an hour later, Victor and Damien were with them. They hadn't brought the tractor, Victor insisting his old Land Rover would be strong enough to pull them free. Ottilie wasn't convinced. She'd been a passenger in Victor's beloved car, and whenever she'd gone up the hill with him, it had rattled so alarmingly, she was always afraid it would fall to bits. But she let them hook the tow rope to her car and stepped back with Fion to allow them to try.

Fion's hands were twisted together as she watched. Ottilie offered her a reassuring smile. Smoke poured from the exhaust as the Land Rover pulled, Victor at the wheel while Damien stood at the ditch and shouted instructions over the roar of the engine. After a few minutes, Victor turned off the engine and hopped out.

'It's proper stuck,' he said, scratching his head through his woolly hat as he stood at Damien's side, peering into the ditch where the wheel of Ottilie's car was still lodged. He looked up at Ottilie. 'You've done a good job there, lass.'

Fion glanced at Ottilie, who didn't bother to put Victor right. She didn't want to make Fion feel even worse than she so clearly already did.

'I can get the tractor,' Damien said.

'Let's have another go with Old Banger,' Victor said.

'Don't want to knacker your car as well,' Damien replied doubtfully.

'She's tougher than that,' Victor said cheerfully as he climbed back in and started the engine.

There followed more alarming engine noises and smoke, and just when Ottilie thought they were going to fail again, there was a jolt, and her car came free. Victor pulled it a little way along the road, out of the way of the ditch entirely, before coming to a halt and hopping out of his Land Rover. Damien jogged over and helped to unhook the tow rope.

Ottilie went over to inspect her car, Fion following closely behind. 'Will it be all right to drive?'

'I'll have a look,' Damien said, 'but it doesn't seem too bad from here. You might be lucky.'

'I'm so sorry,' Fion said again.

Victor turned with a grin. 'Oh, so you're the culprit? I should have known our Ottilie is a safer driver than that.'

Ottilie tried not to groan. The comment was well intentioned, but Fion would take it personally for sure. It would dent her confidence behind the wheel too – the last thing they wanted.

'We all had to learn once, right?' she said with forced cheeriness. 'I can't even think how many mistakes I made when I was learning. And it was getting dark.'

'It's not that dark,' Victor said, not seeming to get the memo.

'Were you still thinking of using the yard at our place?' Damien asked.

Ottilie glanced at Fion. 'I'm not sure. Maybe we ought to call it a night.'

'I think I've done enough damage for one day,' Fion said.

'Like Ottilie says' – Damien wandered over to her and smiled – 'everyone was a learner once upon a time.'

Fion looked up at him, and Ottilie could have sworn there was a strange, charged moment before he tore his gaze away and up towards the hill.

'If you've come all this way, you might as well call to see Corrine,' Victor said. 'I was ready to take the girls up to their pen for the night too, if you want to see them before they go.'

'The alpaca?' Fion asked. 'Oh yes, they're so cute!'

'They're trouble,' Victor said. 'But we can't help but love them. A bit like Ottilie.'

'Is that me?' Ottilie asked. 'Or are you talking about my namesake up the hill?'

Victor laughed. 'Both! But we wouldn't change either of you. Corrine's been baking – she'd be happy to see you.'

'She's always baking,' Damien said. 'The poor woman doesn't do anything else.'

'She likes it,' Victor sniffed.

'I'm sure she'd like a holiday where she doesn't have to do anything but lounge by a pool too,' Damien replied, and Victor waved an impatient hand.

'Farmer's wife – she knew how it would be when she said yes to me. It's not so easy to go on holiday every five minutes when you have land to tend and animals to look after. You can't just give it to someone else to do – it's not like taking your dog to the kennels or whatever.'

'I've told you a million times we'd see to the animals for you,' Damien said as they began to walk back to the Land Rover. Then Damien stopped and turned back. 'Sorry... do you want a lift up? You're going up to Daffodil? Or do you want to go up in your car and see how it drives?'

'You'll be on hand if I drive up there now and it's not quite right,' Ottilie said. 'It seems a good idea.'

'Right,' Damien said. 'Who's going to be driving this time?' he asked in a playfully mocking tone.

'Ottilie,' Fion said firmly. 'I'm not going near that steering wheel until I know I haven't wrecked it.'

'You wouldn't want to tackle that gradient just yet anyway,' Ottilie said, making her way to the driver's side.

'We'll go up behind you,' Victor said, 'just in case.'

Damien joined them in Victor's kitchen as Corrine made tea and dished out cake to everyone. Ottilie thought it odd he didn't message Melanie to tell her he was there – after all, Corrine and Victor were her parents and he was visiting. Perhaps it was simply what they did, but she knew if she was visiting Heath's parents and he was only down the road kicking his heels, she'd message him to see if he wanted to come. What was stranger still was that neither Victor nor Corrine remarked on it. Neither of them suggested that Melanie might want to pop in too. Instead, they made a fuss of Ottilie – as they always did – and were as interested in Fion as Magnus and Geoff had been.

'I think it's wonderful' – Corrine poured yet more tea into Ottilie's cup – 'you two finding each other like this. Imagine, your whole life thinking you were an only child and there was your sister not thirty miles away.' She put down the teapot and regarded them both. 'I can see the resemblance too. You both have the same nose and skin tone. Something about the eyes too. Does your dad have those greyish eyes?'

'I'm not sure,' Fion said.

Corrine looked surprised. 'Haven't you ever looked?'

'Probably, but I can't recall. I suppose they must be – my mum has brown eyes.'

'Oh, Corrine,' Victor said gruffly, 'they didn't come here for the Spanish Inquisition.'

'Nobody expects the Spanish Inquisition,' Damien said with a grin – one that only Victor returned, nobody else seeming to get the joke.

Ottilie had noticed that Victor and Damien got on well. If there was a problem in Damien and Melanie's marriage, it seemed his in-laws were doing their best to stay out of it. They certainly didn't appear to be taking sides with their daughter.

Ottilie silently chastised herself. She was seeing intrigue and gossip wherever she went these days – she had no evidence there was anything wrong in Damien's marriage apart from hearsay and some probably faulty intuition. She was starting to think she'd spent too much time around Magnus and Geoff.

'So you're going to see a lot more of one another?' Corrine asked, ignoring Victor.

'That's the idea,' Ottilie said.

'What about you?' Corrine asked Fion. 'You live in Penrith. I expect you have lots of friends there, a lovely girl like you. I expect Thimblebury seems boring in comparison.'

'A lot of my friends are living with partners or have babies or have gone to live elsewhere. I still see them, but it's not the same as it used to be. And I like Thimblebury. It doesn't feel boring to me. Everyone's really nice.'

'I suppose you have a boyfriend,' Corrine said.

'Or girlfriend,' Damien cut in. 'You can't assume anything, Cor.'

'Yes, yes...' Corrine stirred her tea and then let the spoon clatter into her saucer. 'I'm sure Fion would have put me right – don't make me look like an old fool.'

'Oh, no, I don't have a boyfriend or girlfriend,' Fion said. 'I had a boyfriend, but we split up. I haven't been with anyone since.'

'That's a shame,' Corrine said. 'I'm sure you won't be single for long.'

'I'm not all that bothered,' Fion said.

'Sworn off men for a bit?' Corrine said, shooting a glance at both Damien and Victor. 'Can't say I blame you.'

Ottilie smiled, her own gaze going to the ruby ring Victor had bought for Corrine on the occasion of her all-clear from cancer the year before. The glow from the wall lights glinted from it, hinting at the fact that although Corrine was active all day, baking, doing housework and helping on the farm, she paid great attention to keeping Victor's gift polished. Corrine might say such things, but she didn't mean them. She was as devoted to Victor as he was to her.

'Hey!' Victor half laughed and half grumbled. 'Less of that!'

'Not really,' Fion said, flushing. 'It's just that I have other things to think about.'

'How's the job hunt going?' Damien took a gulp of his tea.

Fion shook her head. 'I'm applying for things, but there's

not much around at the moment. A lot of it is part-time or casual work too. It's all right to keep my head above water for a bit; not really what I want long-term, though. I can't get a place of my own on part-time or casual work – I need to know there's definite money coming in every month.'

'I hear it's tough out there,' Damien said.

'It is,' Fion agreed. She brightened. 'I'm sure I'll find something soon. Ottilie's been helping, haven't you?'

'I wouldn't go that far,' Ottilie said. 'I've only put the feelers out here and there, and it hasn't amounted to anything so far.'

'Magnus said he might have a bit of work for me.' Fion reminded her.

'I wish I could help you there,' Victor said. 'There's a million things here I'd love to give to someone else, but there isn't the money to pay them.'

'That's a shame,' Fion said. 'I'd have loved a job feeding the alpaca.'

'I know you just said you wanted full-time,' Damien said. 'But I might have some work going forward. It will be a couple of weeks before I know for sure. Would you still be interested if that happens?'

'Making the pies?'

He nodded. 'I've come to realise it's going to be far too labour-intensive for me to manage alone, and Mel has her own work to do. So...' He drained his teacup. 'If you're interested, then I'm sure we could chat about it, work out pay and hours and that sort of thing.'

'That would be amazing! I mean, I have to keep looking in the meantime, but I would love that.'

'Won't it be a bit far to come?' Corrine asked. 'All the way from Penrith every day.'

'We've got the caravan out back,' Damien said. 'It's cosy enough, and we don't use it. I'd be happy for Fion to stay there in the week while she's working, maybe go home for weekends or days off.' He looked at Fion. 'If that's a thing you'd want to do. It's not luxury, but it would save you travel costs.'

'She can also stay with me,' Ottilie said.

'Ah.' Damien nodded. 'The caravan's all right, but I know which I'd prefer.'

'Thank you, though,' Fion said to him. 'It is a good idea, and if not for Ottilie, then I would have said yes.'

'Rather you than me,' Corrine said. 'All right in the summer, but I'd want bricks and mortar around me come the cold weather.'

Damien stood up and reached for his jacket from the peg by the door. 'I'd better get back. Thanks for the cake, Cor.'

'Thanks so much for helping with the car,' Ottilie said.

'Yes,' Fion added. 'I won't be doing that again.'

'I hope not,' Damien said. 'Why don't you come and see me next week about that work?'

'Shall I message you about what day?' Fion asked.

He zipped up his coat. 'Can do. Ottilie can give you my number – my phone's at the house right now so I don't have it here.'

'I don't think I have it,' Ottilie said.

'Don't worry – we do,' Corrine said. 'I'll let you have a note of it before you go.'

As the car came to a stop outside Wordsworth Cottage, Ottilie turned to Fion with a smile. The short drive home had been filled with lively discussion, most of it centred around Fion's decision that if Damien offered her some work, she'd move in with Ottilie. It seemed likely that he would. After he'd gone, Corrine and Victor had told them he'd had positive responses to his pie samples and many local businesses were interested in being supplied.

Fion unclipped her seat belt. 'Do you really think Heath won't mind?'

Ottilie couldn't be certain of that. He'd had doubts, but in the end, he'd pledged his support for whatever decision Ottilie made. But that was then, and this was now. His opinion might well have changed – opinions often did. He might not have viewed it as a realistic possibility, or events since that conversation might simply have changed his mind. But she'd made the promise to Fion, and she was going to keep it. If she had to, she could talk Heath round. It wouldn't be forever, and if she could reassure him of that too, perhaps he'd be patient with the situation.

'He said he didn't when I last spoke to him about it. The bigger problem is your parents.'

'They'll understand I can't live with them for the rest of my life.'

'It's not the moving out they won't like – it's who you're moving in with.'

'They can't tell me what to do and who to see.'

'Seeing me is one thing; living with me is another. They'll be offended – you've chosen me over them.'

'It's not like that. You're not my mum; you'll be more like a roommate in a shared house. One who just happens to be my half-sister.'

Ottilie pushed open the car door. 'I suppose that's true.'

'I'll put it to them like that. Dad won't care what I do.'

'I'm sure he will. What about your mum?'

'She won't like it at first, but I think she'll come round.'

'She'll miss you.'

'I suppose so. I'll miss her too, but...'

Ottilie understood. Much as Fion worried that her mum would be left alone with Conrad in a house that was far from happy, she needed to get out. Ottilie could only imagine, from what she'd been told, how stifling the atmosphere there was, how miserable it was making her sister's life. She unlocked the front door and switched on the hall light as Fion followed her inside.

'I'll put the wine in the fridge and grab a quick shower. It should be chilled by the time I'm done.' She opened the fridge door and then turned to Fion, who was hovering uncertainly by the table. 'If you go into my bedroom, you'll find some pyjamas in the drawers. Help yourself if you want to get comfy. Unless you want a shower first? In which case you're welcome to jump in before I do, and I'll get on with some snacks here.'

'Could I?' Fion asked. 'I don't want to be a nuisance.'

'Don't be daft,' Ottilie said. 'You're going to have to get out of that mindset too if you're going to be living here. This will be home for a while – I want you to feel comfortable treating it as such. You take the shower first, and I'll cut some bits for dips with our wine. You'll find towels in the airing cupboard in the bathroom and a hairdryer in my bedroom on the dresser if you want it. Shout if you need anything else.'

Fion gave her a grateful smile. Ottilie watched her thoughtfully as she left the room. She wasn't often lonely, and it would change things with Heath, but she couldn't help feeling she was going to like having Fion around a bit more.

CHAPTER FOURTEEN

'I need to stop letting you talk me into these things...' Ottilie panted. She glanced at Stacey, who was jogging at her side wearing a full and proper workout kit, while she was in the first pair of old joggers she could find and a T-shirt that was so ancient it deserved a merciful rebirth as a pile of cleaning cloths.

'I know, but you said you'd get fit with me. And now that my ankle's better...'

'I'm more likely to pass out right now. I don't feel any fitter.'

Stacey slowed to a walk and dragged a sleeve across her forehead. 'To be honest, I'm not feeling it either. I was just waiting for you to say so.'

'I wish you'd told me that a mile back,' Ottilie said, slowing down too. 'Should we go back to hiking?'

'I don't know... I don't think I'm cut out to be fit. Simon keeps saying how I need to build muscle mass and get my cardio up, and it will help me look after my bones so I don't get osteoporosis and all that, and I love him for it, but I wish he'd shut up.'

'He's just looking out for you.'

'Don't get me wrong – it's lovely to have someone do that, but it's starting to feel like hard work. The only upside is I can eat more chocolate in the evenings now.'

'I'm not sure if that's the objective of a fitness regime,' Ottilie said with a laugh. She sniffed. 'Maybe we should do something a bit more sedate. We could rejoin those wild swimming ladies in Windermere.'

'They were bonkers. And it was freezing.'

'Isn't that kind of the point?'

'To be bonkers?'

'No, that it's cold.'

'Ugh. I don't think I fancy that. We could go to the baths, I suppose.'

'We could, but we'd have to get up early to drive there.'

'We could join a gym.'

'Ditto.'

'Yoga?'

'Where?'

'Anyway,' Stacey said, and Ottilie immediately noticed the subtle shift in tone, 'I might not have time for any of this soon.'

'Why?'

She paused. 'Chloe's pregnant again.'

'Is she?' Ottilie hoped her own tone would convey enough surprise to convince Stacey that she hadn't known about Chloe's pregnancy for days now. 'How does she feel about it?'

'She seems pleased, to be honest.'

'That's good, isn't it? How about Ollie? Is he happy?'

'He seems pleased too, yeah.'

'Then it's fine, isn't it?'

Stacey let out a breath. 'They're so young and they don't have anywhere to live, and Chloe has her studies – I suppose they'll go out of the window now. To me it's terrible timing.'

'It was an accident? Or do you think they meant to get pregnant?'

'I don't know – I haven't asked. You know what Chloe is like. She keeps saying how it will be good for Mackenzie and how they'll be a proper family now because Ollie will have his own child with her.'

'Then if they're happy – as they sound – is there any reason to worry? There are obstacles, but if it's what they both want, then they'll find a way around those.'

'You just know I'll end up getting involved in the childcare. Don't get me wrong, I love Mackenzie more than my own life, but he's hard work, and to add another baby to the mix…' She fished in her pocket for a pack of gum and offered a piece to Ottilie before folding one into her own mouth.

'You know you have a support network right here you can call on. Everyone will rally around.'

'I know. I'm sure I'll get used to the idea and when the time comes we'll manage.'

'Presumably Ollie's parents will want to be involved this time too. Hopefully that will lighten the load.'

'True. It's crazy, I haven't even met them yet and soon we're going to be connected by a baby.'

'I suppose you'd better get your finger out and get to know them.'

'It's not my fault I haven't – it's Chloe. She kept putting me off. Must be ashamed of me or something.'

'I doubt that,' Ottilie said. 'Maybe she's nervous about it and that's why she's been putting it off. I suppose it's a big deal what if you and Ollie's parents don't like each other? And once you've met them, that means their relationship is serious.'

'I think a baby might make it serious,' Stacey said with a sideways look.

'Fair point.'

'She was hoping to see about getting a different midwife from the one she had last time. I don't suppose you'd be able to help there?'

'Funnily enough, it's a conversation I've had with Fliss. Believe it or not, Thimblebury is in the grip of something of a baby boom.'

'So three women are pregnant at the same time? However will we find the room?'

Ottilie laughed. 'Anyway, we did talk about how stretched the district resources are. I don't know if she's decided what to do yet, but she might try to put something in place for us to have our own midwife, or at least someone to work alongside the existing district midwife. It won't be for months yet, though. Not sure if it will be soon enough for Chloe.'

'She says she's only eight weeks, so she's got time.'

'Has she been to see Fliss? Or Simon? Officially, I mean, so they can refer her to the midwifery service.'

'Not yet. She says she doesn't want to talk to Simon about it.'

'I suppose that's understandable – he's a man and he's also your partner. It might feel awkward. But she needs to make an appointment to see Fliss, and the sooner the better. She needs care in place in case anything goes wrong.'

'I've told her that. As usual, Chloe will do what Chloe wants in her own time. If I nag, she'll leave it even longer, even if she thinks I'm right.'

'Want me to talk to her?'

Stacey sent Ottilie a grateful look. 'Could you? I know she thinks a lot of you – she'd have more time for your suggestions.'

'I don't know about that, but I could try.'

'Thanks.' Stacey prodded the screen of her fitness watch. 'Hundred and fifty calories.'

'That's all we've burned?'

'Yeah. What do you reckon is in a bacon sandwich?'

'Five,' Ottilie said, 'give or take a few hundred.'

'That's good enough for me,' Stacey said with a grimace. 'I

don't know about fit – this exercise is making me so hungry all the time I'll be getting fat, not fit.'

'I suppose if you're going to be running around after two grandchildren soon, you'll be getting exercise enough.'

'Which reminds me, I said I'd pop into the mother and baby group later to give them a hand with the weekend play party.'

'Is this a new thing?'

'They started it last week but I couldn't go. You should come with me; I think you'd enjoy it, and the girls were only saying the other day they haven't seen you in ages.'

'Don't – I feel guilty about that as it is. I started that group and now I don't have time to go.'

'Everyone knows how busy you are.'

'Even so. I should pop in and at least pretend I'm bothered, shouldn't I?'

'I know one thing – I'm going to be there a lot more in a few months.'

'But at least there'll be a lot of you to help each other out.'

'Safety in numbers, eh? Right...' Stacey reset her watch. 'Let's try to do half a mile more and then back to mine for elevenses. Sound good?'

'Sounds good to me!'

CHAPTER FIFTEEN

Ottilie rested her hands on her hips and surveyed the bedroom. In one corner, there was a neat pile of unopened boxes, a large suitcase sitting alongside. 'It seems a bit too small now that you've got everything in, doesn't it?'

'It'll be fine once everything is unpacked and in cupboards,' Fion said. 'It only looks like there isn't enough room because all those boxes are there.'

Ottilie turned to her. 'You can say if it's not. I'd rather you did. I might be able to find some room in my wardrobe for you, or—'

'I'm not doing that. It's perfect. Stop worrying – everything will fit. It's kind of you to have me here in the first place.'

'I'm glad to. Is this it? Nothing else to come from your parents' place?'

'There's a bit, but Mum said I could leave it there for as long as I needed to. It's not stuff I particularly need day to day – more like old scrapbooks and shoes I don't wear and that sort of thing. If I do need anything, I'm not all that far away; I can go and get it.'

Ottilie wondered what Conrad had thought about her car

sitting outside as Fion loaded it up. According to Fion, Caron was out shopping. Fion had thought it best to move her stuff while she was missing because she knew how upset her mum would be to see it. Conrad, if he'd cared at all that his youngest daughter was leaving home, didn't show it. But, Ottilie supposed, that would have meant having to acknowledge her too, and she was beginning to realise he'd never do that. She pretended not to care, but it was difficult not to feel rejected by his actions. They were blood, after all, whether he wanted to admit it or not. She'd wanted to go in to speak to him, explain their plans, reassure him that she'd look out for her half sister, but Fion had begged her not to. Perhaps he hadn't even been aware of Ottilie waiting on the road outside in her car as Fion brought her belongings out.

'If you want to decorate, feel free,' Ottilie said. 'It's never been done since I moved in – not this room at any rate – so you'd be doing me a favour if you did fancy giving it a lick of paint and some fresh wallpaper.'

'I wouldn't want to do something you wouldn't like with it.'

'I'm sure you'd choose something nice. If it makes you feel better, we could choose it together. That way, when you leave, I'll still have something I like in here.'

Fion nodded. 'That would be nice. When do you think I should go and see Damien? He said any time.'

'It's up to you. Maybe in work hours, before teatime? Otherwise you're more likely to disrupt his evening with Melanie.'

'You're right. I'll finish putting everything away here and then I'll go.'

'Do you want to make it a driving lesson? I could come with you and see Corrine for an hour. Then we could drive down together.'

'It's still light at least,' Fion said, her gaze going to the window where a heavy sky was dotted with darker patches of grey. 'I'll be able to see where I'm going today and hopefully miss the ditch this time.'

'I think I'd prefer you to avoid the ditch too,' Ottilie said. She moved out of the doorway and onto the landing. 'I just need to do some quick bits in the house, so I'll see to those while you finish here, and then we can get going.'

She was on the stairs when there was a knock at the door. Then the letterbox was flipped open and a voice travelled through.

'Hello! Ottilie?'

With a wry smile, Ottilie opened the front door to find Flo on the step outside.

'Oh,' she sniffed. 'I didn't know if you were in.' She glanced past Ottilie and into the house. 'On your own? Not moved your sister in yet?'

'Yes, actually,' Ottilie said, knowing perfectly well that Flo knew Fion had moved in because there was no doubt she'd seen them bringing their things in and was only pretending she hadn't. At least, if there was a world in which that hadn't happened, then it was also a world in which candy-floss trees and flowers made of jam existed. 'She's just settling in now.'

'Where is she?' Flo said, tottering down the hallway. 'I thought I might say hello.'

'Upstairs. She's unpacking. Do you want a cup of tea while you wait for her?'

'You could tell her I'm here.'

'So you don't want a cup of tea?'

'Well, yes... if you're making one.'

'I *could* be making one,' Ottilie said, thinking also of all the other things she could and should be doing which would now have to wait. 'If you want one.'

'If it's not too much trouble.'

'No trouble at all for you. Come and sit in the kitchen. I've got some leftover chicken if you want a sandwich with it.'

'I wouldn't want your chicken to go to waste, so if you're offering...'

Ottilie smiled to herself as she went to the kettle and filled it. She looked round to see Flo had already taken her coat off and was getting comfortable at the table, but her head was cocked to one side like a dog, clearly trying to listen for noises on the floor above.

'Oh dear,' Ottilie said, giving her a look of overplayed sympathy, 'do you have a stiff neck? It looks like it. I'm sure I have some rub or something in my first aid box if you—'

'Oh, no...' Flo straightened up, and Ottilie tried not to laugh. 'Is Heath coming over today?'

'Later,' Ottilie said. 'Have dinner with us if you like.'

'You mean tea?'

'Well, yes, whatever.'

'What are you having?'

'Curry, I think.'

'No thank you then. I'm out of charcoal tablets.'

Ottilie frowned. 'What?'

'Charcoal. You know.'

'I don't think I do.'

'But you're a nurse!'

'I know, but you've still lost me. Charcoal tablets? What's that got to do with curry?'

'They stop you having wind!' Flo tutted. 'I thought you'd have known that.'

Ottilie shook her head. 'Never heard of that. Does it work?'

'Why do you think I buy them?'

Ottilie decided she'd had quite enough of that conversation. For one, she had no desire to go into any more detail about the effects curry might or might not have on Flo's digestive system. She wondered vaguely where on earth Flo bought charcoal tablets, but that was another line of questioning that was probably best left alone.

'Can you have something else tonight?' Flo asked.

'I don't know. Heath is bringing some food, so it depends on what he buys.'

'I'll phone him,' Flo said, primly folding her hands in her lap. 'I'll tell him to get some sausages. Do you have any of those pies left in your freezer?'

'Afraid not.'

'Sausages will do then.'

'Right.' Ottilie had no clue if Fion would like sausages for dinner, but it looked as if she was getting them anyway.

'How long is she going to be?'

'Who?'

'Your sister.'

'I don't know. You haven't had your sandwich yet, so there's no rush, is there?'

'I've got to get my papers.'

Ottilie glanced at the clock. They had ages until the newsagent closed, but she decided not to bring that up either. Talking with Flo was like that – lots of half-finished conversations where reaching any kind of conclusion would take so much mental energy that it was easier not to bother. Instead, she went to the fridge to get the leftover chicken and some salad.

'Not too much butter,' Flo said.

'OK. Do you want mayonnaise?'

'Salad cream if you have it.'

Ottilie went back to the fridge. They had a bottle of that they kept especially for Flo, and she got it out and put it on the table. 'You can pour it – I always put too much on.'

As she waited for the kettle to boil, Ottilie cut the chicken for the sandwich, and when she turned back to say something else to Flo, the old lady had her head angled at the ceiling once again, as if listening. 'You really ought to let me look at your neck,' she said wryly.

'What?'

The kettle boiled, and Ottilie made Flo a drink.

'Aren't you having one?' Flo asked as Ottilie put it in front of her.

'I've not long had one.'

'Oh. So I'll be sitting here slurping and eating, and you're going to sit there watching me?'

'More or less,' Ottilie said.

'I'll feel guilty.'

Ottilie suspected she wouldn't feel a bit guilty, but it was another of those observations best kept to herself. She finished making Flo's sandwich and gave it to her before going to the door.

'I'll see how Fion is getting on. I won't be a second.'

She left Flo tucking into her sandwich and went to the stairs. Fion was already on her way down.

'Flo is in the kitchen,' Ottilie said in a low voice. 'You're about to have the *interesting* honour of meeting her.'

'Heath's grandma?'

Ottilie nodded, and Fion took a deep breath.

As they went into the kitchen, Flo put her sandwich down and wiped her hands on her skirt. 'Ah.'

'Hello,' Fion said.

'Hello.'

'I won't bother with introductions,' Ottilie said. 'I don't think there's a need.'

'Fion?' Flo sniffed with an obvious look up and down. 'Short for Fiona, is it?'

'No, it's just Fion.'

'Flo is short for Florence. I don't like Florence, so don't call me that. Are you having a sandwich?'

Fion shot a questioning glance at Ottilie. 'I don't think...'

'We were meant to be going up to Daffodil Farm,' Ottilie said to Flo. And then she turned to Fion. 'But it looks as if we're not going anywhere just yet, so if you're hungry, we've got time for you to eat.'

'I, um…' Fion sat at the table. 'I suppose so.'

Ottilie went to the counter, but then Fion got up again. 'I can do it,' she said.

Ottilie almost argued but then understood that Fion wanted to make her own sandwich, and if she was going to settle in as part of the household rather than a temporary guest, it was better that she felt she wasn't being waited on as a guest would be. So she stepped away and took a seat at the table.

'Do you want one?' Fion asked.

'I'm fine; I had something before I picked you up.'

'But that was ages ago.'

'She's like this,' Flo said, looking with some disapproval at Ottilie. 'She'll waste away.'

'I don't think that's likely,' Ottilie said with a chuckle. 'Anyway, when we get up to Daffodil Farm, I'm sure Corrine will make up for my lack of a sandwich with her cake.'

'Could you get some of those pies for me?' Flo asked.

'I can ask,' Ottilie said. 'I'm not sure if Damien is making them all the time just yet – the ones you had before were samples for testing.'

'Did you enjoy them?' Fion twisted from buttering her bread to smile at Flo, who simply shrugged and picked up her own sandwich again.

'They were all right. Handy to have in and heat up when I don't feel like cooking.'

'I'll tell Damien you thought they were very tasty,' Ottilie said. 'Does that mean if Magnus and Geoff stock them, you might buy some?'

'Depends how much they cost. Prices of things now are ridiculous. What time will Heath get here?'

'Not sure yet,' Ottilie said. 'Do you need me to phone and ask?'

'No,' Flo said. 'I'm sure I'll see the car when he's here.'

'I'm sure you will,' Ottilie replied, shooting a glance at the clock and resigning herself to the fact that the day's schedule was now well and truly out of the window no matter what time anyone had planned anything for.

Fion had been living at Wordsworth Cottage a matter of hours and already Ottilie could see what a juggling act her life was going to be for the foreseeable future. She'd expected it to take time for everyone to get used to the new household, but she hadn't reckoned on how quickly the teething problems would reveal themselves.

The trip to Daffodil Farm had been pleasant enough – Corrine had made a fuss of them as she always did, and shortly after they'd arrived, Damien came with good news about some work for Fion the following week. He'd warned it would be bitty and he was in the dark about the early process of setting up the business almost as much as Fion would be, but if she was willing to be patient, then so was he. Fion was thrilled, and as they sat and worked out hours and pay, Ottilie had gone with Victor to see the alpaca while Corrine went to watch a television programme she'd wanted to see. Once again, Ottilie thought it was odd that Damien wasn't conducting his business at his own house, but she supposed that as they were already settled in the kitchen of Daffodil Farm, there hadn't been much point in moving.

While she was at the pen making a fuss of Victor's girls, Heath had messaged to say he was on his way to Thimblebury, and so she'd headed back home, leaving Fion to be brought down by Victor or Damien later when they'd finished their discussions.

Ottilie and Heath were currently in the pub they often went to, just outside the village. It hadn't been the plan for that evening, but shortly after he'd arrived, Flo had come back to eat with them, Fion returning in the middle of their meal, and all the while Ottilie could see that Heath had wanted to talk to her about more private things, things that had happened to him that day, things that were bothering him, or simply things that were for their ears only. Instead, with a house full, he was forced to make small talk and listen to everyone else's news.

He'd been patient, and he'd done his best to be courteous, but Ottilie could tell he was finding it frustrating. And so, as they'd seen Flo home and then cleared the kitchen, she'd suggested they take a drive out somewhere, leaving Fion to finish organising her bedroom. Heath had jumped at it, and so here they were forty minutes later, with two shandies on the table in front of them. Already Heath was more relaxed, but Ottilie could foresee a time when he might feel resentment that they had to vacate the house just to get some alone time.

The pub was a favourite haunt. Ottilie had always liked the stone walls of the snug and the solid wooden tables. It felt cosy, the ambient orange glow of the lamps dotted around making it feel warm and inviting too.

'I'm sorry tonight's been a bit hectic,' she said.

'I've told you it's all right.'

'I don't feel you mean that.'

He reached for his glass. 'I do. I can't say the situation is ideal for us as a couple, but I promised to support your decision and I will. Let's not talk about that now. I wanted to talk to you about something else.'

Ottilie nodded, her instincts from earlier confirmed. He'd had something on his mind that he hadn't felt able to discuss with Fion and his gran there. 'OK.'

'It's work. It's funny, I thought they'd be a bit put out about the fact I want to start working remotely so I can move to Thimblebury, but a weird thing happened today. I was offered a promotion.'

Ottilie smiled. 'But that's brilliant! How would it work? Are you going to take it?'

'That's just it – I will have to be on site more than we were planning after the move. I might have to travel too. But it's a heck of a pay rise.'

'Travel?' Ottilie tried not to frown. She wanted to be pleased for him – she wanted him to know she was pleased and proud and that she'd support his decisions the way he was supporting hers. 'How often?'

'Once every couple of months for about a week or so at a time. They want me to help set up a new office in Germany and then have a hand in its management. Liaise regularly with their onsite management team, that sort of thing, and they think the best way to keep good working relations is to have regular in-person contact. I happen to agree, but I'm not sure about all that time away from you.'

'It's not so bad, I suppose. We'd get used to it.'

He placed a gentle finger to tilt her chin up and studied her. 'I'm not going to do anything that makes you unhappy. I can't deny I think I want the job, but not if it affects us.'

'It wouldn't,' Ottilie said.

'It would also mean more commuting – which is what we'd said we wanted to reduce when we first mooted the idea of me working from Wordsworth Cottage.'

'I suppose,' Ottilie said slowly, 'while Fion is with us it might not be a bad thing. She's got the room that was going to be your office, after all.'

'Yes,' he said, and in his tone she thought she detected just the tiniest hint of the resentment she'd feared. If it was there, she appreciated that he was doing his best to keep a lid on it for her sake. The life they'd been planning had been put on hold, after all. 'And I'm wondering whether I ought to keep hold of my place in Manchester for days when I finish late and it's easier to stay over.'

'But we were going to use the money from the sale for the wedding.'

'I know that, but things have changed since we made that plan. If I'm earning a lot more,' he continued thoughtfully, 'perhaps it would pay for a little flat there or something. A bolthole, you know?'

'Seems a bit of an unnecessary expense to me. Isn't there someone in Manchester who doesn't mind you staying over with them if you need to?'

'Depends how often it will be. I don't want to take advantage.'

Ottilie nodded. She understood that only too well – she'd have felt the same. This development complicated things, but how could she forbid him to take the opportunity that was being offered?

'The MD has told me to come and talk to you and take some time to consider,' he continued.

'How long?'

'A couple of weeks. I suppose it could be more if I needed it, but I'd hate to keep him waiting too long, especially if it's going to be a no – that would piss him right off.'

'Do you think it will have any bearing on our wedding plans? I mean, we could go for a longer engagement if we needed to – I wouldn't mind. There's no rush, is there?'

'Anyone would think you don't want to marry me,' he said with a faint smile.

'More than anything, but I'm also trying to avoid creating more stress for you than is necessary. For either of us, for that matter. Life isn't as calm as it was when we first started to plan it – I don't think it would be all that bad an idea to give ourselves some breathing space for things to settle before we get on with a big event like that.'

'I don't want to put it off. Unless you absolutely do. I want us to be married. I don't even know if me taking this job is the best thing for us yet – that's why I wanted to get your take on the offer. And I want you to be honest with me. Don't just say what you think I want to hear. If you're not happy with me doing it, then I won't.'

'How could I say such a thing?'

'That alone tells me you have doubts.'

'Of course I have doubts – there's no point in lying about that. But what kind of girlfriend would I be if I stood in the way of your career?'

'Talk to me about your doubts.'

'I don't want to because they're probably silly. You know how cautious I am in just about everything. Any doubts I have come from my annoying nature, not you.'

'You could never be annoying, and I'd rather you talk to me.'

'It's only that I worry it will be a mistake for you to move to Thimblebury after all because it will make life a lot harder work if you're doing this new demanding role that needs you to be on site more often. And I worry we'll end up seeing less of one another than we do now.'

'I would never let that happen.'

'You might not have a choice. If the job demands it, you'll feel obliged to be there. I know what that's like – it's how things were at the hospital. It's only since I came to Thimblebury and started at the surgery I have any kind of work-life balance at all. But I wasn't going to say that to you because I don't want it to influence your decision.'

He nodded, deep in thought as he reached for his pint. 'I know,' he said finally. 'I'll have to give it some thought.'

'What's your gut telling you?'

'That's just it.' He looked over the rim of his glass with a droll expression. 'Even my gut can't decide. I'm flattered by the offer, and I think the pay rise would be amazing, but the thought of all that time away from you... I wonder if it will be exhausting to be travelling so much, and I might soon get sick of it. I suppose the only real way of knowing if it's going to be the right thing or not is to do it. But once I do it, it will be difficult to get out of without basically ruining all my future career prospects. If the MD thinks I'm unreliable and prone to changing my mind...' He shrugged, and Ottilie nodded.

'Whatever you decide, you know I'll back you up.'

'At least you'd have Fion with you,' he said. 'That would make me feel better about being away from home when I have to travel.'

Despite her fondness for Fion, Ottilie would rather have had Heath. But she didn't say so because she didn't want to influence his decision-making process either way. The conclusion he came to had to be his because what she wanted had to take a back seat. This was his career, and only he could decide what to do with it.

CHAPTER SIXTEEN

It was raining again. Ottilie had left Fion in bed and headed up to Hilltop Farm for her daily call to check on Darryl, and then down to Thimblebury surgery to start her official working day. Fion had a later start with Damien, where they were going to work out some production systems together, but he was going to collect her from Wordsworth Cottage. She'd been so jittery the night before that Ottilie guessed she hadn't slept well, so when her own alarm had gone off and Fion hadn't emerged from her room, she hadn't worried. She supposed that their working days would overlap and clash at times, and it was just another thing they'd have to get used to.

The morning's load for Ottilie had been straightforward enough, patients coming in and out of her treatment room with brisk regularity. Lunch was chicken soup made by Fliss, the bread and butter provided by Ottilie, with a pudding brought in by Simon and freshly squeezed orange juice provided by Lavender, shared, as always, between the four of them at the surgery's kitchen table.

The afternoon promised to be as routine as the morning, until Ottilie opened her list and realised it had been overbooked by a considerable amount. Before seeing the first patient of the afternoon session, she dashed through to the reception to talk to Lavender about it.

'I told you not to take the safeguards off,' Lavender said. 'The system is supposed to flag up when the session is full, but you will insist on disabling it to fit your sneaky extras on. And then I forget to enable it, and then we're both booking people in at the same time and this is where it gets us.'

'Sorry.' Ottilie offered a sheepish and apologetic smile. 'I'm usually more careful.'

Lavender pulled up the clinic list and displayed it on her computer screen so they could both study it. 'A lot on your mind, I suppose. This once I'll let you off, but I don't know what we're going to do with all these people.'

'I could ring round to see if any of them can come another time.'

Lavender glanced at the clock. 'It's probably a bit late for most of them; they'll be on the way in.'

'My fault again – I should have checked the numbers this morning, but...' She shrugged. 'I suppose I could try to see them. Clinic would overrun, of course, but it can't be helped.'

'You'd be here until midnight trying to see this lot.' Lavender shook her head. 'Leave it with me. I'll see how many I can catch and get them to come later in the week. It will mean rejigging some of your other clinics too, though.'

'Lavender, you're a star. I don't know what I'd do without you.'

As they began to discuss who they might be able to put off, the door to the surgery opened and Melanie walked in. She seemed anxious as she approached the desk.

Lavender nudged Ottilie. 'You can leave the list with me and see your next patient if you like. I'll do it in between reception stuff.'

Ottilie thanked her and then nodded briefly to acknowledge

Melanie. She didn't ask how she was because, in her line of work in her current environment, it could prove to be a loaded question. Ordinarily, when out and about it was a courtesy. Here it could lead to an unasked-for life story and an impromptu and badly timed request for a diagnosis.

As Ottilie left the reception, she could hear Melanie ask for a prescription that was waiting for her to pick up. She sounded as anxious as she looked. It was funny, Ottilie hadn't been aware of Fliss or Simon seeing her in their clinics for anything, let alone prescribing. But she supposed they didn't tell her everything that went on, and she was often too busy to notice without someone pointing it out. But she was so distracted by her uncharacteristic curiosity that she almost forgot to call her first patient through and had to go back out to the reception to get them. When she got there, Melanie was leaving.

'What is it this time?' Lavender asked as she raised her eyes to the heavens.

'Forgot Mr Bond, didn't I?' Ottilie grinned, waving the old man over.

'I think you might need a holiday,' Lavender said.

'I think you might be right!'

Clinic did overrun, despite Lavender's efforts to move the excess patients, and when Ottilie arrived home, Fion had already done her day's work and was cooking. The kitchen was a mess, with potato peelings and discarded cartons littering the draining board, but Ottilie bit her tongue.

'What are you making?'

'Cottage pie.'

'I'd have thought you'd be sick of pies after today,' Ottilie said, putting her bag on the chair and taking off her coat.

Fion smiled. 'I didn't eat any today. We mostly just talked

about how we were going to set up the kitchen and protocols and stuff.'

'Protocols?'

'Like rules for how we're going to do things.'

'Yes, I know protocols; we have them in the health service. I just didn't think you had them to make pies.'

'Well, you know, we have to order things. Like how long the meat's going to be in for one thing in one pan and then what that means for making other stuff. So we're putting charts together and sizing up ingredient lists and that sort of thing.'

'Sounds complicated.'

'It's really interesting.'

Ottilie raised her eyebrows as she stole a slice of raw carrot from the chopping board where Fion was working.

Fion laughed at her expression. 'It sounds boring, but honestly it wasn't. How was your day?'

'Busy.'

'Anyway, Damien gave me some minced beef and you already had potatoes in, so I thought I'd make a start on tea. You did say you hadn't got anything planned, didn't you? Is Heath coming?'

'That was nice of Damien. Heath's not coming over tonight – he's got some works do on. Someone retiring or something.'

'You didn't want to go?'

'Not especially. I don't know any of them. And I'm shattered, so I'm glad I don't have to go over to Manchester tonight. I'm happy with a quiet bite here with you.'

'Damien's wife was around a bit today too.' Fion went back to her chopping. 'I don't know why, but I don't think she likes me much.'

'I don't think she's in the best of places right now,' Ottilie replied, instantly regretting her words as Fion's head snapped up.

'What's wrong with her?'

'Nothing,' Ottilie said. 'Forget it.'

'OK,' Fion said, but Ottilie could tell that she was far from forgetting it. 'I suppose you saw her at the surgery and you're not allowed to tell anyone anything about it. She had a prescription in her hand when she came in, so...'

Ottilie went to the kettle without replying.

'I'll make tea for you,' Fion said. 'Or do you want coffee? Go and have a shower or a sit-down if you like. I'll shout you when it's ready.'

'I can—'

'I want to. It's my way of thanking you. Please, let me do things around the place. So far you've looked after me and I haven't lifted a finger.'

'You've worked today too.'

'Yes, but it hasn't been as hard as yours, and to be honest we spent quite a lot of it having drinks and talking.'

'Sounds lovely. Maybe I should get a job with Damien.'

'He's so nice,' Fion said with such earnestness that Ottilie almost had to do a double take. 'I'm so lucky to have the job. He's made me feel as if I'm helping to invent the company. Sounds silly, doesn't it? But it's sort of exciting to be there at the start.' She was thoughtful for a moment as she scooped the chunks of carrot into a pan on the stove. 'It's weird how Melanie doesn't seem to care about it. You'd think she'd want to be involved, but whenever she comes in and Damien says something to her about it, you can tell she doesn't want to hear it. She pulls her face or changes the subject.'

Ottilie recalled how distracted Melanie had been earlier that day in the surgery. It was difficult to deny something was going on with her – perhaps a problem with her marriage – but it was none of her business. Unless either of them specifically brought it up to her, and even then it was probably wise to stay out of it. Knowing that and dismissing her curiosity, however, were two very different things.

She couldn't deny she was also concerned about Fion getting too involved. It already seemed to Ottilie that her sister was becoming embroiled in a situation that was nothing to do with her, simply by spending her days in the middle of it. She was beginning to wish she hadn't helped engineer this job opportunity for her.

'I wonder if Magnus has made up his mind about going to see his family in Iceland yet,' she said.

Fion took the kettle to the sink. 'I don't know if I could cover for him now. I think I might have too much to do with Damien. I'm not going to remind Magnus, I'll wait to see what happens. Maybe he doesn't want me after all.'

Ottilie didn't like Fion's plan, but she didn't see how she could say so without seeming unreasonable. Fion was right – Magnus hadn't mentioned taking time off and having Fion look after the shop since they'd first thrown the idea around, and for all they knew he and Geoff had decided against it. In a way, the onus was on them to come and ask if they wanted her to work, and they knew she had a job with Damien now, so the matter wasn't as straightforward as it had been.

'So you don't want me to have a word with them?' she asked.

Fion turned to her. 'I don't think you should have to keep fixing things for me. I could speak to them; I just don't see any point. If they wanted me, they'd ask. They haven't asked and so they must not, and as I now have work, I don't see why I should chase them.'

That summary seemed a bit on the harsh side to Ottilie, but she couldn't argue with the logic. And so she simply nodded, and Fion hummed softly as she got on with cooking their meal.

While Fion had settled into life in Thimblebury during the four weeks since her arrival, Ottilie couldn't say it had been plain sailing. She'd enjoyed having her half-sister at Wordsworth Cottage and she'd loved getting to know her, but keeping her, Heath, Flo and just about everyone else who had an opinion on Fion's presence happy was proving to be something of a juggling act. Heath was doing his best to be patient, and when he wasn't feeling it, he tried to hide it for Ottilie's sake. But if Flo was in the room and spotted the tiniest darkening of his mood, she wasn't afraid to call it out and pontificate on the reason – usually something to do with Fion – whether Fion herself was there or not.

As for Thimblebury itself, the yearly ritual of hikers appearing on the hills had begun, which meant summer had properly arrived and brought with it the tourists. The closest they had to a tourist trade was the odd one of those hikers finding themselves in the village because they were lost, occasionally taking advantage of the meagre facilities to refresh and regroup before moving on to more famous landmarks.

Magnus and Geoff had taken advantage by installing a coffee machine in their shop – which had caused some hilarity among the older residents of the village – along with a pair of wooden benches outside so anyone who wanted to take a load off while they drank their machine coffee could do so. And Victor was now walking the hills for hours every day himself with his alpaca, and snaking lines of children and parents leading each one could be seen from the village below. When Corrine had time, she'd help him maintain order, sometimes Melanie or Penny would do it, and now, when everyone else was busy, Fion had been only too happy to step in and lend a hand. The first time Victor had come to Damien's barn to see if anyone was available, she'd leaped at the chance, and Damien had sounded only too happy to let her go. From what Fion had told Ottilie, he was turning out to be a flexible and considerate employer, and Fion appeared to be very happy working with him – some mornings even excited to go up there.

'I wish I could feel like that about work,' Ottilie said one bright morning as she prepared for her trek up to Hilltop to check on Darryl and Ann.

'Don't you love your job?' Fion buttered toast at the table. 'It always seems like you do.'

'I do, but I also love days off. When you have a day off, you're miserable as sin.'

'I'm not!' Fion gave a self-conscious laugh. 'It's all new and the business is getting going, and it's exciting to be a part of that. It almost feels like my business. That sounds daft, doesn't it?'

'No. But remember it's not, so don't wear yourself out because you'll get paid just the same in the end.'

'I don't.'

'You fell asleep on the sofa as soon as you got in last night.'

'It's all that fresh air up on the farm. And I went out with Victor and the girls for a couple of hours too.'

'Hmm...' Ottilie looked unconvinced as she pulled on a light jacket, more to keep her uniform clean than because she needed one. A glance out of the window promised a day that might be the hottest of that year so far. 'Heath's coming over tonight, by the way.'

'That's all right. I might be out anyway.'

'Out?'

Fion nodded as she put the lid back on the butter dish. 'I'm going for a drink in Kendal.'

'Kendal? Oh. Who with?'

'Just...' It wasn't the name that caused alarm in Ottilie when Fion said it, more the pause, heavy with forced casualness that came before it. 'Damien's taking me. He's going to let me drive there for some practice, and then he's buying me a drink to say thank you for all my hard work. We did ask Melanie,' she added, rather too hastily for Ottilie's liking. She'd heard evasion before, and the information Fion was providing reeked of it. It wasn't what Fion was telling her but what she wasn't that might be a problem.

'Melanie's going then?'

'I don't know.'

Ottilie studied Fion carefully as she cut her toast into triangles. Over the weeks, though she'd tried to deny it, she'd noticed every conversation about Damien had Fion speaking of him in tones that were warmer, fonder, perhaps, than they ought to be for a man who was her boss. A *married* man who was her boss. She'd thought about issuing a warning, but she wanted to believe that Fion didn't need one, that she had enough sense of her own to keep away from a situation that might end messily for everyone. Was this the time for that warning?

'Is she around a lot?' Ottilie asked.

Fion looked up, toast halfway to her mouth. 'Who?'

'Melanie. Is she around much when you're up there?'

'She's in the house mostly, so I don't see her unless she wants something and comes to the barn, or I need to go to the house to get some bits. She doesn't bother all that much with the business. Damien says she has work of her own – she books trips or tours for walkers or something. He says she says she had enough of getting her hands dirty on a farm growing up so she doesn't want to be elbow-deep in pie filling all day. What time will Heath be here? Do you think I'll see him before I go?'

'I don't know. What time are you going?'

'Damien says he'll pick me up at seven thirty.'

'He's going to pick you up? From here?'

'Yes.'

'Do you think that's a good idea? Especially if Melanie isn't in the car with him?'

'Why not?'

'This is Thimblebury!' Ottilie said, aware that her voice was rising but struggling to contain it. 'What if someone sees you?'

'We're not doing anything wrong.'

Ottilie folded her arms tight across her chest. 'That's not how it's going to look. You know what people are like around here – they don't need any excuse to turn the most innocent thing into gossip.'

'They can gossip all they want. Damien and me will know it's not true and we're not doing anything wrong, and that's all that matters.'

'If you say so.' Ottilie shook her head as she studied Fion. The timid girl who'd arrived at Wordsworth Cottage a month before wasn't sitting at her table now. This girl had unmistakable traits of Conrad, the dad they shared, a man with the sort of arrogance and disregard Ottilie had seen during their brief meeting and hadn't cared for at all. 'I'm only saying don't underestimate how miserable some of these people can make your lives if they get the bit between their teeth.'

'They can try; I won't take any notice.'

She wanted to say more, but Ottilie could tell that it wouldn't make any difference. Fion had made up her mind. In a way, she was right too – it was hard to argue the logic. If they were only going for a friendly drink, two colleagues getting to know one another outside work, there was no harm in it. The village gossips might whisper about it, but there'd be no truth and nothing for Fion or Damien to feel guilty about.

'I'm going to call at Stacey's on the way home,' she said instead. 'See how Chloe's doing.'

'Has she stopped being sick?'

'I don't think so. I'm sure it's miserable, but she's an old hand at this now – it's her second, after all. I'll pop my head in and see if they need me anyway. So I was going to say I might be in late to cook, but if you're going to a pub, I'm assuming you'll eat there?'

'The pub we're going to has started to serve our pies,' Fion said.

'I'd have thought you'd be sick of the sight of those,' Ottilie replied, checking her phone before dropping it into her satchel.

'I suppose we might have something else,' Fion said. 'But it feels like cheating on our business to do that. It'll be nice to see them on the menu.'

Our business? Ottilie resisted the urge to remind Fion that it wasn't hers at all. 'That's fine then,' she said. 'If you're not going to be with us, Heath and I might have something quick and go out for a walk or something.'

'You could come and meet us at the pub.'

Ottilie suspected that Heath, even if he didn't say it, had seen quite enough of Fion the past few weeks. His initial fears had been confirmed – whenever they'd felt like being intimate, they were reminded, by a sound or an actual appearance, that Fion was in the house. When they'd needed to discuss something private, she'd come into the room. When they'd wanted to watch something on television, she'd sat with them and dropped passive-aggressive hints that she was watching this programme with them but really wanted to see something on another channel. It was all minor stuff in the grand scheme of things, but these small incidents were snowballing into what Ottilie feared might turn into constant irritation, the sort of state that would eventually lead to him actively disliking her half-sister.

'That's all right,' she said, hoisting her satchel onto her shoulder. 'We don't want to muscle in on your work thing. We'll probably have a quiet one here doing something or other. We've still got things to sort out for the wedding now we've set a date. It'll probably be a boring night looking at caterers or something – you'll be glad you're out.'

Fion gave a vague nod before going back to her toast. Ottilie left the house feeling uneasy and not really able to pinpoint why – it was more a general bad feeling about things that might be waiting somewhere down the line. But she had work to do, and there was no point worrying about what might never happen. So she put Fion out of her mind and headed to the hills.

Ottilie lay on Heath's chest, his steady heartbeat in her ears. He was propped up on his pillows, a thumb idly stroking tiny circles over her shoulder. The day had been warm, and through the open bedroom window came the first hoot of an owl they heard often, beginning a night of hunting. The odd moth bumped against the glass and there was one chasing the light of the floor lamp. It wasn't bothering Ottilie, but Heath had promised to put it out before they went to sleep. Other than that, the village was quiet. The tourists were in hotels or guesthouses or chalets in the more famous towns, and Thimblebury was once again, for the night-time at least, a small inconsequential village in the middle of nowhere. Though she never minded the summer visitors, that was always the way Ottilie liked it best. Her home: calm, tranquil, where life was at a pace so slow it was hard to get stressed.

Then again, at that moment, though she wasn't exactly stressed, she was preoccupied with things beyond their life in the village.

'The MD is happy at least,' Heath said. 'Obviously it was my choice whether to take the job or not, but I think he'd have been a bit annoyed if I'd turned it down. I'm guessing I'd figured in some grand management plan somewhere and I would have messed it up if I'd said no. They'd probably have never given me another opportunity either.'

'I'm sure they would have done – you work hard.'

'But you don't look a gift horse in the mouth, do you? I suppose it might have looked ungrateful to some.'

'Now that you have more details, are you still glad you took it?'

'It's never been about me. I'd always take it because it

furthers my career. It's how you're affected – that's always been my only concern.'

'I'll be fine.'

'You're just saying that?'

'No. I'd love for you not to have to go away so often, but we'll get used to it. And...' She trailed a finger up his chest and twisted to look up at him with a cheeky smile. 'You know what they say about absence making the heart grow fonder.'

'Remind me,' he said, sliding down the pillow and pulling her into his arms.

They relaxed into a lazy kiss, and then the sound of the front door slamming took Ottilie out of it.

Heath let out a groan. 'Perfect timing. It's like having a teenager.'

'I wouldn't know.' Ottilie threw back the covers and sat up.

Heath propped himself up on an elbow and frowned. 'Where are you going?'

'To see how she got on at the pub...' She glanced at the bedside clock. 'They must have stayed until well after last orders.'

'What does that matter?'

Ottilie gave a vague shrug. 'It's later than I expected. I want to see if... well, something might have happened.'

'Something was about to happen here,' Heath grumbled, flipping over to face the wall. 'I suppose I might as well go to sleep.'

'We both ought to have been asleep before now.' Ottilie poked her feet into a pair of slippers. 'We've both got early starts tomorrow.'

'Yeah,' Heath said, sarcasm dripping from his tone, 'living the rock-and-roll lifestyle.'

. . .

She found Fion in the kitchen, at the table with a glass of water in front of her, typing on her phone.

'Good night?' she asked from the doorway.

Fion looked up and smiled. It seemed bright, but there was also something in it that was forced and anxious. 'Yes. You?'

'The usual. So you stayed for last orders?'

Fion went back to her messaging. 'Uh-huh.'

'You went somewhere after?'

'No.'

'But it's a lot later than I thought—'

'Well, we stopped to look at the moon.'

'What?'

Fion glanced up from her phone again. 'It looked massive over the hills. Did you see it?'

'Not really.'

It was an odd thing to do. At least Ottilie thought so. Romantic. Not the sort of thing she'd do with *her* boss, no matter how well they got along. She waited for more, but Fion simply locked her phone and stood up.

'I think I'll go to bed. I thought you'd be asleep by now.'

'We were just about to turn the lights out when we heard you come in.'

'Oh, good. As long as I didn't wake you.' She went over and gave Ottilie a peck on the cheek. 'We're starting work late tomorrow, so I probably won't be up when you are for breakfast. Don't worry – I can fend for myself. I'll make sure to stack the dishwasher before I go out.'

Ottilie watched her as she sidled past and took the stairs. Something was up. Ottilie wondered if she ought to try and get to the bottom of it. She wondered if she even wanted to. Whatever it was, it looked as if she wasn't going to get anything more from Fion tonight. With a last cursory check of the kitchen, she sighed deeply, turned out the light and headed back upstairs.

CHAPTER SEVENTEEN

Someone was hammering on the front door. Ottilie squinted as Heath bolted up and turned on the lamp.

'What the hell? What time... It's two in the morning!'

He threw the covers back, then yanked a shirt and trousers from where they were draped over a chair and stamped onto the landing. Ottilie grabbed a dressing gown and followed him.

Heath opened the front door a crack, and as he did, it was pushed open from the other side. Melanie stepped into the hallway. Ottilie could smell alcohol on her breath, even from where she was behind Heath.

'Where is she?'

'Melanie,' Heath began. 'What the hell—'

'Where is she? That stupid little cow, Fion; I want to talk to her.'

Ottilie stepped forward and tried to stop Melanie from going down the hall to the kitchen. Though it was only a gentle hand to her chest, Melanie slapped it away and glared at her.

'Where is she?'

'You can't come in now,' Ottilie said. 'It's the middle of the night.'

'Come back tomorrow when you've sobered up,' Heath added.

'Don't tell me what to do!'

'I'll tell you what I like in my own house,' Heath said with a calmness that Ottilie was proud of. He didn't always know when to hold his temper, especially in a situation like this, but this time he could clearly see what Ottilie could also see. Melanie wasn't acting like someone in her rational mind. She'd been drinking, and something upsetting was at the root of that. Something that involved Fion, and it didn't take a genius to finally confirm what Ottilie had been fearing since the day Fion had met Damien. Dealing with Melanie now required patience. It wouldn't do any good to meet her aggression with more of the same.

'How did you get here?' Ottilie asked, peering around the front door to see Melanie's car outside on the road. 'Ah. You drove?'

'How else was I going to get down here?'

Ottilie and Heath exchanged a glance. Melanie was lucky to be down here in one piece. Her journey could easily have ended in a tipped-up car on the hillside rather than in their hallway now. Someone would have to drive her back up there.

'I'll take you home,' he said.

'Don't want to go,' Melanie slurred, trying to get past Ottilie again.

'You have to.'

'I want to see *her*!'

Ottilie let out a groan as Fion's voice came from the top of the stairs.

'Ottilie...? What's—'

'You!' Melanie hissed.

'Go back to bed, Fion,' Heath told her.

'No,' Melanie shouted. 'I want to talk to you! He says he's

leaving me! He says he wants to be with you! Why? What does he see in a ratty little runt like—?'

'Hey!' Heath snapped. 'Enough of the personal stuff! Coming here to talk is one thing; coming here in the middle of the night is out of order, and insulting Fion is something else again. Keep it civil or we will throw you out and call the police.'

Melanie turned to him, her eyes swimming. 'Why?'

She might have been questioning any number of things.

Ottilie turned to Heath and spoke in a low voice. 'Maybe we ought to make her a coffee and see what we can do?'

'What can we do?'

'I don't know, but we can at least sober her up before we take her home. We might even get some sense out of her.'

Heath glanced up the stairs, to where Fion stood anxiously gripping the balustrade and watching the drama below. 'I think we both know what's been going on. I don't think we need Melanie to explain it to us.'

'Still, it would be better to calm her down a bit. For a start, if she's all over the place like this, she might endanger whoever is driving her home.

'Melanie...' She beckoned as she made her way down the hall to the kitchen. 'Come through. I'll make a coffee, and you can get everything off your chest.'

'Get her down!' Melanie said, glaring up at Fion, who was still hovering and seemed to be deciding whether her presence downstairs would make things better or worse.

'She'll come when you calm down,' Ottilie said. 'So it's up to you if you see her or not.'

Melanie made to climb the stairs. Heath looked as if he might make a grab to stop her, but Ottilie took Melanie firmly by the arm and led her to the kitchen. 'It's this way. Heath will go and get Fion once you're sitting down and drinking your coffee.'

If Melanie didn't calm down, Ottilie had no intention of

letting Fion anywhere near the kitchen. She gestured to Heath. 'Go and tell her not to come down until we say so,' she said in a low voice as she herded Melanie down the hallway.

Heath went to speak to Fion while she filled the kettle. When she turned around again, Melanie was staring at her.

'*You* started this.'

'How did I start it?' Ottilie said, doing her best to clear away some cutlery which had been left on the draining board without being too obvious about it. She didn't want any sharp implements within reach, given Melanie's current mood.

'You brought her here. We were all right before that. We were working on things.'

Ottilie dropped the knives into the drawer and moved in front of it to close it with her backside. 'You and Damien?'

'We'd have worked things out.'

'What has he told you? You said you'd spoken to him. Tonight? He was at the pub, wasn't he? You didn't go?' Ottilie glanced towards the door at the sight of Heath coming into the kitchen. He nodded once, and she took that to mean he'd convinced Fion to stay out of the way for now.

'I don't know where he was. He said it was a work thing. They were going to sort out some process or other. I knew it was weird to be going out in the evening to do that.'

'Why didn't you go with them?'

'He said I didn't need to.'

At Heath's wordless behest, Ottilie went to sit at the table with Melanie while he took over making the coffee.

'You weren't tempted to insist?' she asked as she took a seat.

'Yes.' Melanie laid her arms out on the table and flopped onto them. 'I didn't know what to do.'

'Melanie...' Ottilie asked gently. 'Are you on medication?'

'What?'

'Are you taking something? I'm worried if you're drinking while you're on tablets where you're not meant to drink.'

'I'm not drunk.'

'That's not what I was saying. I don't want anything bad to happen.'

'I might die?' Melanie lifted her head and blew out a laugh. 'That'd be funny, wouldn't it?'

'Not for us it wouldn't,' Heath cut in as he poured boiling water into a mug. Ottilie frowned at him, and he shrugged. 'Just saying.'

'There might be a reaction,' Ottilie continued. 'What's your prescription for?'

'I don't know. Some nutty pills or other. Something maxy-maxymaxy... tron, thon, ethylate... nobody can ever say those names.'

Ottilie mentally ran through a list of what she thought Melanie's medication was likely to be. It didn't make her feel any easier, but as the drinking had clearly already occurred, all she could do now was keep a close eye on her condition. 'OK,' she said, nodding thanks as Heath put a coffee down and then sat next to her. 'It doesn't matter for now. Do you want to talk about what happened with Damien?'

'No.'

'Are you sure?'

Heath butted in again. 'What are you here for if you don't want to talk?' Ottilie shot him another warning glance. When he spoke again, it was aimed at Ottilie. 'When she got here, she wanted to talk to— I mean, she said she wanted to talk, and now she doesn't.'

Ottilie rolled her eyes at him before turning back to Melanie, who had her head on the table again and didn't seem to be taking any notice of their exchange. She was very drunk and now seemed groggy with it. She wondered whether to phone Simon or Fliss to get some advice, but she didn't want to do that unless she really had to. Either would come over in a flash, but she'd feel terrible waking them for nothing. She gently nudged Melanie. 'Drink some of your coffee. You'll feel better.'

Melanie didn't respond and so Ottilie nudged harder. 'Are you all right?'

An incomprehensible mumble came in return. Ottilie looked up at Heath.

'I think the only thing we can do is take her home,' he said.

'I don't like that idea.'

'Why not?'

'I'm worried. She's had too much to drink and she's on some pills, and I don't know what they are or how they're mixing with the booze.'

'She won't be on her own. Damien is there to keep an eye on her.'

'Oh, yes,' Ottilie said in a withering tone. 'Because he's exactly who she needs right now.'

'Look at her!' Heath flung a hand at the seemingly unconscious Melanie, head and arms sprawled across the table. 'She won't notice who's there. Let's take her home to sleep it off. Damien can phone for an ambulance if anything happens. Ott, you can't be on duty all the time, and it's not your responsibility to keep everyone from harm.'

'It is, actually,' Ottilie snapped. She didn't like the way Heath was trying to palm this off. Melanie was there, in front of them, clearly in need of help. 'I made a promise when I qualified as a nurse.' Then she let out a sigh. 'Sorry, I'm tired and I'm stressed about this. I know you're only trying to find the best solution – I'm just not sure that's it.'

'I'm not sure there's any other,' Heath said. 'If it makes you feel happier, take her back now, wake Damien, explain what the problem is, make sure he knows to keep an eye on her and then go up there tomorrow when you have a minute to see how things are.'

'We're meant to simply drop her off and not discuss any of the other stuff with Damien? Knowing what we know?'

'It's none of our business. Melanie being here now is, but not that.'

'That's the thing – I think it will become our business.'

'Their marriage isn't. Even if the stuff about him and Fion is true, they're both adults, so I don't see how that is either.'

Ottilie nodded slowly. She was too tired to argue, but she still thought he was wrong. If Damien and Fion were having an affair, then it would become their business. They'd be dragged into the slipstream whether they liked it or not, no matter how much distance they tried to create. Melanie was right about one thing – Ottilie had brought Fion to Thimblebury. She'd introduced her to Damien. She'd worked hard to get Fion a job with him. And while all those things had been done with the best of intentions, what had followed was as a direct result of her meddling. If Melanie and Damien's marriage was in trouble and Fion was a part of that, Ottilie couldn't help but feel that she was a part of it too, however indirectly. And so it was her job to do what she could for everyone involved, to try and smooth it over.

'Look at her,' Heath repeated, breaking into her thoughts. 'She's nowhere. It's pointless trying to get any sense out of her. While she's calm let's take her home.'

'Maybe we should take her to Daffodil Farm?'

'Wake Victor and Corrine for this?' Heath shook his head. 'I wouldn't thank you if I was Victor. Who wants to see their daughter in this state?'

'I'm sure they'd rather see her safe, whatever state.'

'Damien will do that. The guy might have slipped up – and we don't know exactly what's happened yet – but he's not a monster. She'll be fine with him.'

Ottilie paused, but then she looked again at Melanie and

she was forced to agree. It wasn't ideal, and she was far from happy with the plan, but for all the reasons they'd just covered, there wasn't much else they could do.

'Come on then,' he said, getting up. 'Let's get her to the car before she comes round and starts swinging for you again.'

Ottilie's smile for him was bleak. Perhaps, one day in the future, they might look back at this and see some humour in it, but she couldn't see that day right now.

Ottilie couldn't decide if it was good or not that Melanie had been out cold for the duration of their journey to take her home. She'd checked her over more than once, and though she'd been satisfied that she was only sleeping off the effects of her booze, niggling doubts had plagued her all the way back to Wordsworth Cottage. Neither of them had quizzed Damien on what had made her come down, all guns blazing, for Fion, though he'd looked guilty enough as he'd thanked them.

In the car once they'd left, Heath made his disapproval clear. 'He didn't even have the decency to get off his backside and find out where Melanie was. He knew she was missing and why. She could have been anywhere. Whatever had happened between them, he might have made an effort to make sure she was safe.'

'We don't know that he didn't try to find her,' Ottilie said, rubbing her eyes. 'And we don't know how often she does this sort of thing. It might be a regular event.'

'What, for him to tell her he's having an affair?'

'No, but when they argue, she might make a habit of running off. I suppose if she does it a lot, he's used to it and he doesn't wonder where she is. She might usually sulk somewhere before she comes back.'

'I don't think that's likely.'

'You don't know.'

'How do you always want to see the good in people?'

'It's not often there isn't any good to be found. And when you think someone is neglecting someone else, it's not often as straightforward as it looks from the outside.'

'Well, that's good because this whole thing isn't painting him in a good light from where I'm looking. It's not exactly doing a lot for your sister either, for that matter.'

'I know,' Ottilie said. She didn't want to admit it, but she was forced to agree that Fion had some explaining to do. She was also forced to recognise that this was only the beginning. This situation wasn't about to go away, just because they'd dropped Melanie off at home to sober up. The situation would get far more difficult before it was resolved – if it was ever resolved. 'I wonder if Fion is still up.'

'She'll be up,' Heath said as he took a bend in the road with more speed than Ottilie would have liked. She wasn't about to say so. He was as tired as she was, probably tetchier than he was letting on, and the last thing she wanted was for them to have an argument on top of everything else. 'We'll have to talk to her – we can't leave it.'

'I'll talk to her. If she's up, I'll do it tonight. If not, I'll try to catch her tomorrow, somehow.'

'You'll be at work by the time she wakes.'

Ottilie turned to him. 'Do you think she'll go to work tomorrow?'

'How should I know? I think she's an idiot if she does. I think the best thing now is for her to quit.'

'That's what I thought. It'll be difficult for her to carry on working for him now.'

'Do you think she'll want to?'

'The only way to know is to ask her.'

'Ott…' Heath began slowly.

There was a pause, too long for her liking.

'What?'

'Do you think she can even carry on living with you? If this is going to be—'

'It wasn't her fault.'

'It wasn't ours, but we're still clearing up the mess. It must have crossed your mind that if things escalate, we're going to have a lot of trouble landing on the doorstep.'

'We can handle Melanie. I'll talk to her.'

'It might not only be her.'

'Who else would it be?'

'I can't say Victor and Corrine will be pleased if this gets back to them. They're your friends. Do you want to fall out with them?'

'We won't fall out – they're both too sensible for that.'

'But you might end up being forced to take sides. They're going to side with their daughter every time, and you're going to side with your sister, and if Damien and Fion insist on continuing with—'

'It won't come to that,' Ottilie insisted, though she was far from convinced. 'I'm not going to ask Fion to leave just in case some of my neighbours are annoyed with her.'

'It's up to you, but I'd at least put it to her that it might be sensible for her to go back to Penrith if she does want to continue her relationship with Damien. I wish them all the luck in the world if this is for real between them and it will survive her moving back to her parents, but if it's not…'

'We don't know what it is right now.' Ottilie closed her eyes and rubbed her fingers over her temples. 'There's no point in talking about any of this until we know how serious things are.'

'How old is he?' Heath asked.

'I don't know. I think he's about thirty-five, thirty-six or something.'

'Old enough to know better.'

'She's not a child,' Ottilie said. 'She's old enough to decide what she wants.'

'But still younger than him.'

'She's an adult,' Ottilie repeated. 'We can't tell her what to do.'

'Can't we? When it interferes with our lives? We can tell her to leave if she's going to bring trouble to our doorstep.'

'Heath,' she said, holding on to every ounce of patience she still had left. 'Wordsworth is my house. I decide who lives there.'

He was silent. She gazed out onto hedgerows where she could make out only the barest of details, bathed white in the glow of their headlights. When he spoke again, she could hear resentment in his tone. She hadn't wanted this problem to spill out into an argument with him, but she sensed one coming anyway.

'Right. I see how it is. I'm glad we've cleared that up.'

'Cleared what up?'

'It's your house. It will always be your house, and here was me thinking we'd been planning to make it our home. What an idiot, eh?'

'That's not what I meant.'

'Isn't it? Sounds that way to me.'

'I only meant I can't just throw Fion out, not after I asked her to live with me.'

'I had thoughts back then, but you wouldn't listen.'

'Heath, don't. She's been great to have around, no trouble—'

'No trouble? What do you call tonight? What would you have done if I hadn't been here?'

'I'd have managed. I'm not totally helpless.'

'You wouldn't have been safe – either of you.'

'Ah, so that little misogynist who hides in your brain has decided to come out to play. I thought I hadn't seen him for a while.'

'Tell me I'm wrong!'

'I don't have to tell you anything!'

'No because thankfully we'll never find out. I don't want a rerun. If I have to be the sensible adult in the room, then I'm going to say that if Fion stays, you might get a rerun and it might not end so tidily.'

'What does that mean? What could Melanie possibly do that's so bad?'

'I don't know, but she's obviously not right in the head!'

'Congratulations, Freud, on another textbook diagnosis. How *do* you do it?'

'Snipe all you want, but you know it as well as I do.'

'I don't know anything.'

'Then why were you asking her about medication?'

'You think the only sort of medication that exists is for mental illness?'

'Of course not, but I think that's what she's on. You must know.'

'How would I know?'

'You work at the surgery.'

'Yes, but I don't know the details of every consultation that goes on there!'

He didn't reply. In the gloom of the car interior, she could make out the shadow of his chin, his mouth set in a hard line. He was angry. So was she, and she didn't see why she ought to back down this time.

'Do you want me to go home?' he asked after a few excruciating minutes.

'Tonight? Don't be ridiculous.'

'I'm just checking. It's your house, after all; I wouldn't want to outstay my welcome.'

'Now you're being childish. I didn't mean it like that and you know it.'

'I don't know how you meant it. I only know what you said. How else am I supposed to interpret it?'

'I don't want you to go home, and I want you to treat Wordsworth as your home too – of course I do. But I can't throw Fion out. I won't throw her out.'

'Yes, you've made that clear. But we're going to have to talk to her. If she wants to stay, then she's going to have to end this business with Damien.'

'We're going around in circles, aren't we? I'm not going to ask her to leave, and I'm not going to tell her who she can and can't see. That's my final word on it.'

'You're taking her side?'

'Over what?'

'Mine.'

'There is no side! Heath, stop it now. I'm tired and my head is swimming, and I don't want to have this conversation any longer.'

'I only—'

'Please. I've got enough to think about as it is.'

'Fine,' he said, in a tone that suggested he was anything but.

Ottilie closed her eyes and leaned back in the seat. She'd talk to Fion. She might even suggest her moving back to Penrith or ending things with Damien, but not because Heath said so. She'd suggest those things only if they seemed like the best course of action once she'd established the facts. And while she wanted Heath to treat Wordsworth Cottage like home, it was her house. She'd bought it from the money Josh had left to her. Viewed that way, it was more than bricks and mortar; it was a part of Josh, a part of her, a reminder of a life she'd once had, and no matter how much she loved Heath, no matter what their future held, she would always treasure those years. Wordsworth Cottage was far more than a house to her. It was her safety net, her security, her sanctuary. It was her insurance in case the future she was planning with Heath didn't work out. It was hers no matter who else lived there with her. She'd said this to him once before and she couldn't understand now why he found the notion so upsetting.

'Ottilie.'

She opened her eyes to see that Heath was slowing down. There was a light on in one of the upstairs windows of Wordsworth Cottage. It looked as if Fion was up. She drew in a weary breath. She was too tired for this conversation, and yet she knew Heath wouldn't be able to rest until they'd had it, not now they knew Fion was awake. She looked across at Heath to see that he seemed calmer.

'I'm sorry we argued.'

'Me too,' he said stiffly. He was calmer, but he hadn't quite forgotten what they'd said. What *she* had said. She wasn't going to backtrack, but she'd have to make it up to him when things were more settled.

Fion was at the top of the stairs as Ottilie stepped into the hallway.

'Did she get home OK?' she asked.

'Yes,' Ottilie said. 'We left her with Damien.'

Heath followed Ottilie inside and then shut the front door. He looked up at Fion and then at Ottilie.

'I know,' she said in reply to his unspoken question. She stood at the bottom of the stairs and called up. 'You know we're going to have to talk about this.'

'Now?'

'We're all still up, and I don't see any of us getting much sleep tonight. Do you? As far as I can see, we might as well get it out of the way.'

Getting it out of the way implied that there would be one discussion of the matter and that would be the end of it. But Ottilie wasn't stupid enough to think that was likely. Fion hesitated, her hands wrapped around the balustrade. But then she nodded and came down.

They all moved into the living room. Heath offered to make drinks, but neither Ottilie nor Fion wanted one. All Ottilie wanted was to hear Fion's side of things, hoping that what she heard would make it easy to forgive the trouble she and Damien had caused. She and Heath sat on the sofa, with Fion on the armchair across from them, fingers knotted together as she pressed her hands between her knees.

'I'm really sorry,' she said. 'I didn't know any of this was going to happen.'

'Melanie says Damien has come clean, that you're having an affair.'

'That makes it sound seedy, and it's not like that at all. We're in love.'

'In love?' Heath said, his derisive tone barely disguised. 'You've known each other ten minutes.'

'We are,' Fion insisted. 'It doesn't matter how long we've known each other.'

'He's a lot older than you.'

'That doesn't matter. We get on, we've got lots in common. I'm not a baby.'

Ottilie shot a look of warning at Heath. She'd told him not to patronise her.

'How serious is it?' Ottilie asked. 'You have my full support if this is something meaningful. But there are lives that stand to be ruined – not least yours – if this is only messing around. I want to know it's worth standing by you when the backlash comes... and it will come. It's only a matter of time.'

'You should want to stand by me anyway.'

'I do want to; you're my sister. In the same way, if I'm going to stick my neck out for you, then you should want it to be for something worthwhile. You're telling me you're in love with him. He definitely feels the same?'

'Yes.'

'Only that wasn't the impression we got when we dropped Melanie at home just now.'

Fion's forehead creased into a deep frown. 'What did you expect him to say? You'd just taken Melanie home in a mess. Even I wouldn't expect him to tell you a thing like that in front of her.'

'I suppose you've got a point,' Ottilie said. 'So what's next?'

'I don't know. I didn't know he was going to tell her about us tonight – I don't know why he did that. It wasn't the plan. We were going to wait until the right moment.'

'I don't think there could ever be a right moment for news like that,' Ottilie said. 'I suppose he must have come to the same conclusion. Something happened after he dropped you here and went home, presumably, that made him come clean. You had no clue he might do this?'

'No. When I left him, we'd decided we were going to talk some more and work out what was the best way of doing it before he told her.'

Ottilie was thoughtful as she glanced at Heath. She had no doubt Fion was telling the truth. Whatever had prompted Damien to break the news as soon as he'd got home didn't matter. The fact was, the genie was out of the bottle and there was no way it was going back in now. What they had to figure out was how they handled it – though Ottilie didn't have a clue what to think about that either. Was there a way to handle a situation like this? Or would they all simply have to weather the storm that was coming?

Heath spoke into the gap. 'Are you going to carry on working for him?'

Fion's fingers knotted tighter together. She hunched forward with a helpless shrug. 'Do you think I should quit?'

'I don't know how you're meant to show your face up there after tonight.'

'Then I won't have a job and he'll have nobody to help him. He's got orders. How's he going to get them out?'

'He should have thought about that before he went—'

'Heath,' Ottilie cut in. 'I'm sure neither of them planned things to go this way. Fion's got a point. He's got a business to run whatever else is happening. His marriage is on the brink; surely you wouldn't want to see his livelihood go down too? I think that's a punishment too far.'

'Of course I don't,' Heath said. 'I've got nothing personal against the guy, but I don't see how Fion can go back up there like nothing has happened.'

Ottilie turned to Fion. 'Why don't you call him tomorrow and see how things are up there?'

'I suppose I could do that. Could you go and talk to them?'

Ottilie shook her head. 'I don't think that would necessarily help. I do want to see how Melanie is doing, but I don't think I should get involved in what's going on with you, Damien and her. Sorry.'

Fion stared into space. 'OK,' she said finally. 'I'll message him. I suppose Melanie might be all right tomorrow. She might have had time to get used to what he's told her.'

Ottilie doubted that. She didn't say so. She was tired, glad to have reached some sort of placeholder conclusion to their discussion, ready to go to bed. She had no doubt they were nowhere near finished here, but she had nothing left to give at this point. She got up and pulled Fion into a brief hug. She didn't hold her responsible for any of this. People couldn't help who they fell in love with, and never had a fact been truer than it was in this instance. Fion hadn't fallen for Damien to cause trouble. And if Damien's affections were genuine, as Fion believed they were, then Ottilie was quite sure he hadn't fallen into what some might see as an inappropriate affair with his employee to cause trouble either.

'I think we all need some sleep,' she said, patting Heath on the shoulder. 'Coming?'

He nodded.

'Goodnight,' Fion said as they left the room. 'I *am* sorry, you know.'

'We know,' Ottilie said. 'Let's talk some more tomorrow when we all have clearer heads.'

CHAPTER EIGHTEEN

'What happened to you?'

Fliss peered at Ottilie as she walked into the surgery's reception the following morning.

'Huh? Oh, bad night. A bit tired. You don't mind if I skip lunch in the kitchen with you today?'

'I made chickpea curry.'

'I know; I'm sorry. I've got some things I need to see to.'

'Everything's all right, isn't it?' Fliss asked, her tone far more serious now.

'Yes. I think so.'

Ottilie wasn't foolish enough to think that Fion and Damien's affair would stay secret for long, but it wasn't her job to break the news to anyone, not even Fliss, who would be as practical and stoic about it as anyone could be.

'Because if you need some time off for something—'

'I don't. Thank you, but it's really fine. It's full clinics all week anyway, and it would only cause problems further down the line if I had to cancel today's and try to fit everyone in another day.'

'Well,' Fliss replied, seeming satisfied, 'you know where I

am if you need me. If you change your mind or you simply need to talk, my door is always open. Don't forget that.'

'I know. Thank you.'

As Fliss went back to her room and Ottilie turned to go to her own, Simon arrived. She could hear him bidding Lavender a good morning. As he left the reception area and came into the hallway where Fliss had just left her, he noticed Ottilie and gave her a cheery wave. But then he stopped and stared.

'You look exhausted,' Simon said.

'I'm all right – didn't sleep very well.'

'Things on your mind?'

'Yes, but too much to go into right now.'

'It's fine.' Simon said. 'Tell me about it at lunch if you like.'

'Sorry, I won't be staying for lunch.'

'That's a shame. I've got one or two things to get off my chest.'

'Oh? Do you need me to listen now?'

'No,' he said with a light laugh. 'It's only grumbling about Chloe and her mood swings. I never knew a pregnant woman could be so disruptive.'

'Right,' Ottilie said. 'Sorry. Another time.'

'Another time.' He started to walk to his room but then turned back. 'You're OK? Nothing you want to tell me about?'

'I'm fine. Thanks, Simon.'

'Right. So I'll see you at some point today, just not at lunch. More curry for me then.'

Ottilie forced a tired smile and went to her room. She switched on the computer and then logged into her clinic list. First patient was the notorious Mrs Icke. Then Flo for a blood pressure check. Ottilie laid her head in her hands and closed her eyes for a moment. Wasn't it Sod's Law she'd get the people who were the hardest work when she was at her lowest ebb?

. . .

Ottilie was halfway through one of Lavender's 'two-scoop specials' by the time Flo had arrived. It was a coffee Lavender always made when anyone was in need of a pick-me-up, and it had definitely done the job. Ottilie was sure she could run on caffeine for the next week if she needed to.

'How are you?' she asked Flo as she led her back to the treatment room.

'Same as ever,' Flo replied. 'What were you up to last night?'

Ottilie gestured for Flo to take a seat and shut the door. 'Oh, you know, the usual. Why?'

'Why was there so much noise coming from your place?'

Ottilie frowned. How could Flo have heard anything from where she was? There was no way her house was close enough to Wordsworth Cottage for that to be the case. And though Melanie had knocked loudly and had raised her voice, it surely hadn't been that bad? 'Noise? What noise?'

'I don't know. Magnus told me this morning something had been going on.'

'He did? Nothing was going on.'

'Then what was Melanie Tate doing there?'

Ottilie got the blood pressure reader out of the cupboard. 'Roll up your sleeve for me.'

'Something to do with Fion?' Flo asked.

'Your sleeve,' Ottilie repeated with as much patience as she could muster. 'Please.'

'It was, wasn't it?'

'You know I can't talk about any of this now,' Ottilie said. 'I'm at work, and right now I'm your nurse. I've got a busy clinic, and I don't have time to sit chatting about what might have happened at my house last night.'

'That's all right.' Flo pulled up the sleeve of her cardigan and flopped her arm out for Ottilie. 'I'll call later for tea if that's all right.'

'Can you make it the day after? It's film club tonight.'

'I suppose I'll have to. Will Heath be there?'

'I don't know yet.'

'If he is, then I can see him too. What are you having? Not pie again, I hope.'

They might never eat another one of Damien's pies, but Ottilie thought better of saying so, even in jest. 'What would you like?' she asked. 'I could do toad in the hole. How does that sound?'

'That'll do,' Flo said.

Ottilie undid the cuff and removed the monitor from Flo's arm. 'All good. No problems with taking your tablets?'

'Melanie is moving in with Victor and Corrine at Daffodil Farm.'

Ottilie froze. 'Is she?' she asked carefully.

'So I've heard.'

Ottilie wanted to ask who'd given out this news, but she realised that if she began this line of enquiry, then it would end up eating into her clinic schedule. It would have to wait. 'Oh,' she said, not knowing what else she could say at this point. 'She must have her reasons I suppose.'

'I'm sure she has,' Flo said, and Ottilie suspected from the mischief in her expression that she knew more than she was letting on about that too.

'You're all done,' Ottilie said. 'I'll pop a follow-up appointment in the post for you, if that's OK.'

'Toad in the hole, you say?' Flo asked as she got up and put her coat on. 'Peas, not broad beans. Can't stand broad beans.'

'Peas – got it. See you later then.'

'What time?'

'Come whenever you want as long as it's after six,' Ottilie said. It was pointless giving Flo a time because she wouldn't stick to it anyway.

Flo marched out of the room and Ottilie let out a sigh. She

opened the page with her clinic list and marked Flo as seen before typing a few notes on the appointment.

Despite her annoyance at Flo's inopportune interrogation, she couldn't help but wonder what had happened with Damien and Melanie since she and Heath had dropped her off the night before. She also wondered what Victor and Corrine were making of it all. She hoped they wouldn't be too hard on Fion when the truth came out.

Ottilie dashed out of the surgery, closing and locking the front door behind her. The kitchen had smelled amazing as she passed on her way out, and she wished she'd been able to join her colleagues for their curry, but if she didn't go up to Daffodil Farm now, she'd be dwelling on her worries all afternoon.

She couldn't be certain that what Flo had told her about Melanie moving in with Corrine and Victor was correct, but it seemed a safe bet that there'd be some truth in it. As a temporary fix, perhaps to allow Damien and her some space, it seemed like the most sensible idea. If Ottilie had been in their situation, probably the thing she'd do too.

Jumping in her car and starting the engine, she wondered again if she ought to have phoned ahead to say she was coming. She'd considered it a few times during the morning but had decided against it because she didn't want Corrine or Victor to put her off. They'd tell her all was well, not to worry, and there was the added awkwardness that she'd have to admit she'd heard about developments in gossip that was clearly already on its way around the village. She didn't think Corrine or Victor would be happy about that, even if Melanie herself didn't care. So she'd invented another reason for going and would see how the atmosphere was when she got there. She also wondered if one of them would start a discussion for her. They'd know by now, presumably, about Melanie's trip down to Wordsworth

Cottage the previous night, and surely they'd have something to say about it.

The rain was heavier as she made her way further up the hill, the distant skies grey and grizzled with yet more. Ottilie passed a group of soggy walkers, hoods pulled tight around their faces, water dripping from the hems of their raincoats. There was mud on the lane, making it hard for the car, but there wasn't time to park up and phone the farmhouse to see if Victor could come and get her. All in all, the view around her seemed to reflect her situation just perfectly: battered, grey, uncertain and difficult.

None of their current situation was her doing, and yet, as Ottilie pulled up outside Daffodil Farm, she was anxious. Victor and Corrine had been such good friends to her since she'd moved to Thimblebury that the thought of causing them strife – even indirectly – upset her. As she got out of the car, she could see Corrine at the kitchen window. Not looking out but head down. Probably doing something at the sink. But as Ottilie walked across the yard, she looked up. Where ordinarily she would have broken into a broad smile, today she barely had one at all. It didn't help Ottilie to feel any better.

Before she'd knocked, Corrine had opened the door. 'I wasn't expecting to see you at this time of the day.' She dried her hands on a teacloth and stepped back. 'Come in.'

Ottilie stepped inside and closed the door behind her. Corrine was alone in the kitchen. 'I won't stay long,' she said. 'I just wanted to—'

'Melanie,' Corrine said, taking all need of pretence right out of the conversation. It was the sort of practical approach that Ottilie should have expected from Corrine. Now that she thought about it, she wondered why she'd concocted any kind of ruse for her visit at all. 'You want to know how she is and what's happening between her and Damien. Ottilie, my love, I'm sorry you've been dragged into all this trouble.'

'It's not your fault,' Ottilie said.

'It's not yours either.'

'Some will say it is, I'm sure,' Ottilie said ruefully.

'They might – because they don't know any better. You won't hear it from me or Victor. You've been nothing but a good friend to our family.'

'Maybe.' Ottilie waited for Corrine to elaborate. She clearly knew some of what had passed between Melanie and Damien, but did she know the whole story? Fion's involvement? How much did she know of that? Some, it would seem because she'd have worked out that Melanie had gone to Wordsworth Cottage for a reason. But Ottilie was afraid of making the situation worse by airing things that might have been better coming from someone else – or not being said at all.

'We don't blame your Fion,' Corrine said. 'But we do wish it had been someone else. It makes things difficult, doesn't it? Between us all.' Corrine let out a sigh as she flopped onto a chair at the table. 'I don't know what the fool was thinking. Starting... *this*. With the girl who was meant to be working for him. And so much younger too. It looks bad – nobody can deny it.'

'What's Melanie told you?' Ottilie asked. She wondered whether to sit down. It was telling of Corrine's state of mind that today there was no smell of cake coming from the oven, no offer of tea or sandwiches... Ottilie watched as she wiped her brow. She looked exhausted. Ottilie wondered if Melanie had turned up at theirs overnight, perhaps almost as soon as she'd sobered up enough to leave the house she shared with Damien. Her arrival might even have been his doing. Perhaps he'd persuaded her it was the best place for her to be while they decided what to do with their marriage.

'Ottilie?'

They both turned to see Melanie herself at the doorway to the kitchen.

'I know,' she said as she went to the sink to get water. 'I look like death. I feel like it too.' She took a sip from her glass. 'I'm sorry about last night, Ottilie. I shouldn't have come to your place – I feel like a total idiot. I should say thanks for getting me home too.'

'Are you feeling better?' Ottilie asked.

'Better in terms of my hangover or life in general? Actually, doesn't matter. Whichever you're asking about, the answer is no, I don't feel better. I feel like shit about everything.'

'I'm sorry,' Ottilie said.

'What for? You didn't do anything.'

'That's not what...' Ottilie flushed, realising that the next bit of her sentence was hardly going to help.

Melanie finished it for her. 'That's not what I said last night, huh? I can't remember everything that I did and said last night, but I remember that. Listen, you can't help what your sister does. I've got issues with her but not with you.'

'She didn't set out to make any of this happen, you know,' Ottilie said. From the corner of her eye, she noticed Corrine get up. She went to a drawer and took out a stack of teacloths, folding them and putting them back, despite the fact they hadn't needed it.

'She didn't exactly walk away from it. You want to say it was all Damien's fault, is that it? I suppose you might have a point. I don't think he was trying too hard to put her off either.'

Ottilie wanted to point out that their marriage must have already been on thin ice. If not, she was certain Damien wouldn't have encouraged Fion in the way he'd clearly done. And Ottilie had heard and seen things that she now knew were clues to the state of things, even before Fion had got involved. She doubted Melanie wanted to hear it, though, and she recognised that even if that were true, being betrayed in such a way would still hurt.

'Is she there now?' Melanie asked into the gap. 'With him?'

'I don't know. I've been at the surgery all morning. She didn't say she was going up there, but...' Ottilie shrugged.

'They do have work to do,' Corrine said, and while Ottilie was grateful for her trying to be reasonable, Melanie just offered her mother a withering look.

'Do you think any work will be going on today?'

Ottilie couldn't dispute Melanie's logic. They might have every intention of keeping work and their personal lives separate, but it wasn't likely to happen. Things would be horribly tangled. Time, she supposed, might help ease the situation, but she didn't think that was likely either. It would take a big decision. Something was going to have to give, whether that was their working relationship or their romantic one. Fion had mooted leaving Damien's employment, and as far as Ottilie could tell, that was becoming the most sensible course of action. It really didn't seem as if either of them wanted to break off their affair. Was it even an affair now? It was out in the open, and when Ottilie thought of affairs, they were always clandestine, secret, sneaking things. But if it wasn't an affair, what was it?

'You're not going over there, are you?' Corrine asked.

Melanie shook her head. 'Because that's exactly what I need right now. To see them together.'

'I don't suppose you know what you're going to do?' Ottilie asked her.

'Right now?' Melanie sipped at her water. 'I hardly know what day it is right now, let alone what I'm going to do.' She pulled a blister pack from the pocket of her dressing gown and held it up. 'I could down a few more of these to numb things. As a nurse, how many do you reckon is too many?'

Ottilie gave a start as she recognised the anti-depressants.

So that was the medication? 'I'd say don't exceed the recommended dose,' she said carefully, knowing full well that wasn't the reaction Melanie wanted. But she couldn't give the reaction Melanie wanted without alarming Corrine.

'That's what I thought,' Melanie said, putting them back in her pocket. 'I have thought about it, though. It would solve a few problems.'

Not for you, Ottilie thought, but she only glanced at Corrine, who was, thankfully, busy with her teacloths.

Should she discuss it with Fliss? She had to be careful here, and she wasn't sure if she ought to do anything or not. Despite her words, Melanie seemed exhausted and upset, but she did seem stable. Was it worth rocking the boat? Might it make things worse if Ottilie got involved in her nursing capacity?

Melanie got up. 'I'm going back to bed. Not much to stay up for, is there?'

Corrine spun round. 'You're not having breakfast? Not even a cup of tea?'

'It's lunchtime. And I don't want any of that either. You can't feed away a broken heart, Mum.'

It was the most vulnerable and the most telling thing Melanie had said since Damien and Fion's affair had come out into the open. All she'd done so far was lash out and blame. She'd been angry and she'd been vindictive, but she'd never said how she was truly feeling about it, how she'd been affected as a wife – until this moment. Ottilie wanted to hug her and tell her it would get easier, but she knew she wasn't the person Melanie needed for that. She doubted Melanie would welcome it, even if it did come from the right person. It would be some time before she'd be drawing those claws in enough to let anyone comfort her.

Corrine shook her head and watched sadly as Melanie left the kitchen with her glass of water. Then she turned to Ottilie.

'I don't know what to do with her.'

'I'm sure. I wish I could help, but I don't know what to say.'

'It was good of you to come up.'

'I don't feel as if it's made a lot of difference.'

'Probably not,' Corrine agreed. 'I appreciate you trying. Don't be too hard on yourself or Fion. It wasn't all down to her. If the truth be known, if not her, it would have been someone else. They weren't happy. They hadn't been happy for a while, not since...'

Corrine switched the kettle off. Ottilie could tell there was more, things she wanted to say but didn't think she ought to. She wasn't going to push it. She wasn't even sure she wanted to know what those things were. Her thoughts went back to more pressing matters. Like the afternoon surgery that would be running late if she didn't make a move to get back for it.

She stepped forward and hugged Corrine briefly, and when she pulled away, Corrine had tears in her eyes.

'Don't mind me,' she sniffed. 'A little cry will do me the world of good. I might have one when you've gone.'

'But you'll be all right? Because if you need me to stay a bit longer, I can phone Lavender to—'

'No, no...' Corrine forced a watery smile. 'Don't be daft. You have patients to see. On your way. Oh...' She looked around the kitchen as if suddenly dazed. 'I didn't offer you anything.'

'I think you might have had a reasonable excuse today,' Ottilie said. 'You've got my number. If you need anything, any help with...' Her gaze wandered to the doorway Melanie had just disappeared through. 'Call me.'

'Thank you,' Corrine said.

Ottilie left her and walked to the car. Corrine was thanking her, but for what? None of this was her fault, and everyone had gone out of their way to reassure her of that. So why did she still feel as if it was?

CHAPTER NINETEEN

The timing could have been better, but Ottilie had promised Magnus and Geoff she'd be at film club that night. She'd been exhausted when she'd finally seen the last of her patients and the last thing she wanted as she headed home was to go out again. It was tempting to cancel, but apart from disappointing Magnus and Geoff, she had another reason for making the effort to go. She wanted to find out how far the gossip about Fion and Damien had spread, and film club would be a reliable clue to that.

Fion was in the kitchen. The guilty expression as she looked up from peeling onions was all Ottilie needed to see to know she'd seen Damien at some point that day. Whether they'd done any actual work was doubtful. Ottilie didn't want to know, and she didn't ask.

'I thought I'd make bolognese,' she said. 'Is that all right?'

'Film club tonight,' Ottilie said. 'Remember? Magnus usually makes food for everyone.'

'Oh, of course.' Fion hesitated. 'Do you mind if I don't go?'

In the circumstances, Ottilie had hardly anticipated anything else. 'I don't mind. Will you be all right here?'

'Yes.'

Ottilie put her satchel onto a chair and took off her jacket. 'What do you have planned then? While I'm out. Will you be...?' It was her turn to hesitate. 'Will you be seeing Damien?'

Fion shook her head. 'He says he needs to talk to Melanie.'

'I think that's sensible. You've seen him today?'

'We went for a drive. We had a lot to talk about.'

'Not a working day then.'

'No. He said it would be weird trying to work under the circumstances.'

'What did he say to Melanie last night? You told me he was supposed to wait.'

'He said he couldn't wait. Something happened when he got in. I don't know what – he didn't say. But I suppose it made him want to tell her about us. You know she isn't an angel?'

'Damien told you that?'

'Yes. But it wasn't to make him feel better about being with me, if that's what you think. She's been as bad as he—'

'Fion, I don't think I want to know. I definitely think it's better if I don't – at least for my own sanity.'

'I'm trying to tell you why it's not all Damien's fault.'

'I never said it was. You're all adults, and it's nothing to do with me. I don't need the details; I just want you all to sort it out and for things to settle. I need to get showered if I'm going to make film club on time.'

'Oh, right...'

Ottilie could sense Fion watching as she left the room. Perhaps she'd seemed harsh when she'd told Fion she didn't want any of the details, and perhaps she wanted them more than she'd like to admit. But she didn't know if having that information would change the way she felt about the situation, and from a purely practical point of view, she didn't have time to stop and listen. What she wanted, more than anything else right now, was for this whole situation to go away.

. . .

'No Heath?' Magnus kissed Ottilie on both cheeks and took the bottle of wine she'd brought for him.

'No, he's got some work meeting tonight.'

'How dull.'

'Very,' Ottilie said, forcing a bright smile. 'I know where I'd rather be.' She was tired and far from in the right frame of mind to be here, but skipping it would only feed the gossip monster, and so she'd decided to appear as carefree and normal as possible.

'No Fion either?' Magnus asked, and this time the subtext was unmistakable.

'No, she's got a headache.'

'Oh dear. I hope she feels better soon.'

Magnus went across the garden to the cinema room that he and Geoff had built there, and Ottilie followed. She couldn't help but notice as she walked in that many of the people she'd normally spend film night with were missing. There was no Heath or Fion, of course, but also no Flo, no Lavender, and strangely no Geoff, Simon or Stacey. Ottilie smiled briefly at the other members of the club. She knew them well enough from around the village or when they'd been to her clinic, but they weren't people whose company she sought out under normal circumstances.

She was wondering whether to text Stacey to find out whether she was coming when her friend walked in with Simon and Geoff. Magnus was fiddling around with the projector at the back of the room. When he saw Geoff, he waved him over, gesticulating at the equipment with a frown. While they tried to fix what had evidently gone wrong there, Stacey left Simon getting drinks and made a beeline for Ottilie.

'Are you all right?'

'Fine. Are you?'

'For a nice change, I'm not the one being talked about everywhere I go.'

'You're saying I am?' Ottilie asked, trying not to feel alarmed.

'Well, not you, exactly. But you're sort of being mentioned.'

Ottilie nodded slowly. What was the use in trying to deny it? And there was no need to hide anything from Stacey of all people. 'What's the word on the street then?'

Stacey gave a pained but sympathetic smile. 'Fion and Damien have run off together.'

'They haven't exactly run off. Fion's at my place right now, and he's at his.'

'But they're having a fling?'

Ottilie sighed. 'I think it's more than a fling. If it was a fling, I could cope. I'd give her a good talking-to and tell her not to be so daft, and that would be the end of it. I think they're... well, I know Fion has genuine feelings. As for Damien...' She shook her head. 'I don't know what's going on with him. She says he feels the same, but it's far more complicated there than it is for Fion, isn't it? Whether he has genuine feelings for her or not isn't the point where he's concerned.' Ottilie narrowed her eyes slightly. 'Who told you?'

'You can take your pick.'

'Great...' Ottilie let her gaze wander the room. Was it her imagination that the rest of film club were paying her far more attention than they usually did? She hadn't noticed it when she'd walked in. She shook the thought. It was far too easy to get paranoid in a situation like this. But if people were gossiping and it was getting round the village at the rate Stacey seemed to be suggesting, she might find paranoia about it the least of her worries. She turned back to Stacey with a grimace. 'Does *everyone* know?'

'I'd say it might be easier to list who doesn't know.'

Ottilie took a breath and straightened up. 'Right then! I suppose all that's left to do is look like I don't care.'

'Ottilie, this is you we're talking about. You always care.'

'But they don't know that.'

'Honestly, it makes a nice change for it not to be me or Chloe being talked about. I wouldn't let it worry you. They'll have their fun, and in a couple of weeks it'll be forgotten.'

They looked round as Simon came over with two glasses of wine and handed one to Stacey. 'Ottilie, what's going on?'

'What do you mean?' Ottilie asked, even though she already had a fairly good idea.

'I don't remember her name but that woman who runs the newsagents has just been asking me about your sister.'

'Asking what?'

'All sorts. How old she is, where she lived before she came here, has she been married... I mean, how should I know all that? More to the point, why do they want to know and why are they asking me, of all people?'

'Because,' Stacey said, knocking back a mouthful of wine and sending a barbed look in the direction of the culprit, 'she knows she won't get any of that information out of me.'

'Surely if she's that interested, she should ask Ottilie,' Simon said.

'Again,' Stacey reiterated, 'she'd get the same response from Ottilie as she got from me.'

'In fairness, she probably wouldn't,' Ottilie said ruefully. 'We all know I have no backbone when it comes to things like that.'

'I wouldn't go that far,' Stacey said. 'You're just too polite to tell people to bog off and mind their own business.'

Simon studied Ottilie for a moment. 'you still look exhausted.'

'Thanks.'

'You know I didn't mean it like that.'

Ottilie gave a wan smile. 'I know. I'm messing with you. I've just got a lot on my mind.'

'Want to share?' Stacey asked. Ottilie considered keeping it to herself, but Stacey was her most trusted friend these days and there didn't seem to be any point. She swiftly checked for eavesdroppers and then lowered her voice. 'Melanie came to our place last night – that much you probably know. She was a bit worse for wear. She wanted to see Fion, but we wouldn't let her.'

'Bloody hell,' Stacey breathed.

'I assume,' Simon cut in, seeming to piece it together, 'that's where you went at lunchtime.'

'I wanted to check she was all right. She's Fliss's patient, right?'

Simon nodded.

'I wonder if I ought to talk to Fliss about her.'

'You think she's struggling?' Simon asked.

'I don't know. I don't think it would hurt to give Fliss a heads-up, though. What do you think?'

'I don't think you can ever be too careful,' Simon agreed. 'But if you don't feel it can come from you for whatever reason, I can speak to Fliss. Tell her a little birdie told me – that sort of thing.'

'You can take your pick from a whole flock of little birdies around here,' Stacey said with a wry sweep of the room.

People had started to notice their conversation and kept looking their way while they had conversations of their own. Ottilie couldn't imagine how she was so interesting, but she was glad now that Fion wasn't here.

'I'd appreciate that,' Ottilie told him. 'I think you're right – probably better coming from someone other than me, in the circumstances. I think I'm too close.'

Magnus's exclamation of triumph from over by the

projector caused everyone to forget about Ottilie. They all looked round to see him smile as he addressed the room.

'Crisis averted! My hero Geoff has fixed the projector and we're ready to go!'

Ottilie didn't think she'd ever been so pleased to take a seat and have the lights switch off in a room. But even as they went to sit down, she could feel the curious stares of the other film club members. She'd been subjected to them before when she'd first moved to the village, but that time they'd been sent her way with far kinder intent. This wasn't so nice. Once again, she was glad Fion had decided to stay away. Clearly, her sister had understood the trouble she was beginning to cause even better than Ottilie did.

'Two hours of my life I'll never get back. Who chose that rubbish?'

Ottilie couldn't help but overhear the comment. She'd chosen *that rubbish*, and everyone knew it. At least they ought to. And for what it was worth, the unspoken rule of their film club was that people were respectful of the films others picked, even if they didn't like them.

'There's a way of saying things like that,' Stacey said in her ear as she eyed the audience leaving their seats. 'And that's not it. I ought to have a word with Geoff.'

'He probably heard it,' Ottilie said wearily. 'It's not worth bothering.'

'I think it is.'

'I'd rather you didn't, though.'

But when Ottilie looked round, she noticed Geoff pull someone to one side. Though she couldn't hear what he was saying, he was speaking to them with an expression that told her he was giving them a dressing-down. Inwardly, she groaned. She hoped it wasn't about her or the comment she'd just heard.

She'd had enough unwanted attention for one evening, without making it worse. And despite what Stacey had said, it hadn't bothered her all that much anyway – not enough to make a fuss over it.

She tried not to make it obvious she was watching, but every time she dared a glance, she could see that they weren't exactly seeing eye to eye on whatever they were discussing.

Deciding she'd seen enough and if there was trouble she'd rather not know, she turned to Stacey. 'Are you staying for drinks and nibbles?'

'I will if you will. Chloe's got Ollie over, and I think they'd probably appreciate having the house to themselves for a bit longer. To be honest, I'm starting to feel as if I'm in the way every time I'm in with them.'

'Still love's young dream then?'

'God yes! I don't mind. He makes her happy, and that's a feat in itself. I ought to be giving him a medal.'

'They're still planning to rent a place of their own when the baby comes?'

'I think that's the idea. Chloe says they're going to wait until the very last minute so they can save as much money as possible. If not for that, I think she'd have moved in with him weeks ago. As it is, looks like I'll have her and Mackenzie at my place for a while longer yet. You won't see me complaining about that. Chloe's a pain in the backside, but Mackenzie is an absolute sweetheart.'

'You'll miss them both when they move out.'

'I will. I've told her she can't go too far. I don't want to miss out on the new baby either.'

'Is she going to find out what she's having?' Ottilie asked, her attention once again drawn to another conversation in the room that seemed to be about her, despite trying her best to ignore it and concentrate on this one. An uninformed shrink, she thought wryly, would accuse her of narcissism.

'I think she might this time, if only to work out what that means for a flat and whether she can keep any of Mackenzie's old clothes. I think she'd like a girl, but I don't think she minds if it's another boy; it'll make life easier with bedrooms and reusing Mackenzie's things.'

'I suppose so...'

Stacey followed Ottilie's now wholly distracted gaze. 'What's wrong? You're not still stressing about that comment on the film? Forget it – Geoff will remind them of the rules.'

'I think he already has. I don't think they took kindly to it.'

'It'll blow over.'

'I know. I don't care about that. I just... well, I can't help but wonder... I mean, I've chosen films nobody else has liked before and I've never had anyone be so rude about it. I suppose they might be rude in private, but I've never heard it, and nobody's ever made it so obvious.' She grimaced. 'Am I being paranoid? Seeing more in it than there really is?'

'I expect so,' Stacey said. 'You know when you got here and said you were going to act like you didn't care? How's that working out for you?'

Ottilie was forced to smile. 'Terribly, by the looks of things. I never said I'd be any good at it.'

'Take it from someone who has been the focus of more gossip than I care to remember – don't take it home with you. I know you – you'll spend all night fretting about it, wondering how you can make it up to all the people you think you've offended.'

'Not this time. I'm not really the one who's offended them, am I?'

'Then you'll worry about how you can protect Fion from it, and you can't. She's going to have to ride it out.'

'You're right, but it's easier said than done, and I do think I'm being a little bit tarred with the same brush if tonight is anything to go by.'

'Ah well, you can't do anything about that no matter how nice you are to people. Small-minded is as small-minded does. If they want to gossip about you, they'll find something no matter what you do.' Stacey grinned. 'Not everyone in Thimblebury is as nice as me, you know.'

Ottilie's smile returned. 'You can say that again. You'd only have to be a fly on the wall in my clinic for a morning to see that.'

Magnus called everyone through for nibbles. The food was as much a part of film club as the movie was, and chatting with the other members while they sampled new things that people had brought to share was often more enjoyable than what they'd watched. But tonight, despite wondering if it was in her imagination, Ottilie detected a frisson of something in the room. Little cliques of people she wasn't exactly close to but knew well enough were gathered at corners away from her. They were chatting, animated conversations, and every so often a look would come her way, only to be followed by another one that was either guilty or accusing, and sometimes both. It was hard to accept that all of this was in her imagination. She'd be in conversation with someone else and could swear she'd hear her name from across the room.

After ten minutes, as she was going to use the bathroom, she was certain she caught someone talking about outsiders bringing trouble. Surely not? She'd never seen this side of her community before, and she refused to believe it existed. Yes, people gossiped and often it crossed a line – as far as Ottilie was concerned, at least – but it was never overtly hostile. As she passed by, the group fell into silence. One or two forced smiles came her way.

In Magnus and Geoff's guest bathroom, Ottilie washed her hands and decided that she was tired and the events of the previous twenty-four hours were making her see and hear things that weren't coming across as they were meant. Thimblebury just wasn't like that.

She leaned on the sink, staring in the mirror at the dark circles beneath her eyes, and took a moment to collect herself. On reflection, perhaps she should have made an excuse to miss tonight's film after all. She could think of a reason to leave now and get the early night she so clearly needed. For the briefest moment, it crossed her mind to phone Heath and ask him to come over, but she was reluctant to disturb him after he'd put in such long hours at work that day. It would have been a comfort to have him there, but he couldn't always be there, and she wasn't about to start relying on him all the time. Besides, Fion would be at home, and she might feel like talking. Ottilie was sure that, as much as Fion wanted to be with Damien, the situation was as stressful for her as for anyone else.

After doing her best to tidy herself up and giving her reflection one last critical look, Ottilie went back to the gathering. But as soon as she stepped back into the room, she knew something was off. Geoff had his arm around Magnus and was trying to comfort him, while a few others were standing around them, offering support, including Simon and Stacey. Ottilie went over and, when they noticed, she could see strained expressions looking back at her.

'What's wrong?' Ottilie asked.

'Oh, nothing,' Magnus replied, pushing an unconvincing smile across his face.

'Something's wrong,' Ottilie insisted.

'Nothing for you to worry about.' Geoff glanced at Magnus, who gave a brief nod before heading out of the room.

'Where's Magnus gone?'

'He's gone to get more wine,' Geoff said.

Ottilie looked across at the counter where there seemed more than enough wine already.

'If he's an ounce of decency, he's gone to apologise!' someone called from across the room.

Ottilie spun round to see who it was. She couldn't tell – there was more than one person staring at her.

'If you've got something to say,' Stacey snapped, 'don't be shy. Come and say it to our faces.'

There was no reply. Ottilie looked from one group of villagers to another.

'Come on!' Stacey goaded. 'I get it – you don't want to say it where everyone can see because you know you'll get kicked out too.'

There was a pause, and then three people walked out together.

'Good riddance!' Stacey shouted after them.

'Stacey...' Geoff warned, but she spun to face him.

'Come on – you're not going to lose sleep over that lot, are you? They're not even regulars. They don't support the community – they don't even buy anything from your shop! Let them go – nobody in here will miss them.' She turned back to those still left. 'Anything else you want to say?'

Her expression was as confrontational as Ottilie had ever seen it. She'd had a few drinks and that was probably making her braver – though Ottilie had always known Stacey to be able to hold her own. She'd had to grow a hard skin over the years when her own personal life had been so turbulent.

There was some murmuring, and then a few more people decided to leave. But this was a more sheepish exit. Some of them said goodbye to Geoff and mumbled excuses about dogs to walk or early nights. Some of them shuffled out with a guilty look. And when they'd gone and Stacey had backed away from the fight, there was a strange hush over those who were left. Despite them staying on, Ottilie wondered if someone ought to call time on the evening anyway because it was going to be odd and forced from now on. As for her own departure, in the circumstances, she didn't feel she could leave now without some kind of explanation, and without making sure everyone was all right.

With that in mind, she drew Stacey and Simon to one side.

'What was all that about?'

Simon exchanged a look with Stacey that put Ottilie on the back foot. They didn't say so, but she was forced to conclude that it had something to do with her.

'Stacey.' Ottilie's tone was urgent. She was so tired and so stressed, she felt she could burst into tears at any moment, 'I'd rather know if it's something…'

'Geoff lost his temper with something he overheard,' Simon answered for her. 'Then Magnus got involved. There were words…'

'What kind of words?' Ottilie asked.

'I'm not sure,' Simon replied, but Ottilie could tell he knew more than he was letting on.

'Magnus asked them to leave,' Stacey said.

Ottilie stared at her. 'He did *what*?'

'He asked them to go,' Stacey repeated. 'Good for him, I say.'

Ottilie was silent as she processed the information. Magnus was always the perfect host. He loved entertaining, being popular, and having everyone happy around him was what he lived for. He'd never ask someone to leave a gathering. Whatever had made him take such drastic action must have been bad. And it had clearly upset him. 'Where is he now?'

'I don't know. Probably gone to cool off,' Stacey said.

'Who was it?'

'Mo Taylor.'

Ottilie knew Mo to say hello on the street, but she wasn't a regular at the surgery or at film club. 'What did she say?'

'I didn't hear it,' Stacey said.

'Me neither,' Simon added.

'But,' Stacey continued, 'whatever it was, it pissed Magnus right off.'

Ottilie studied the two of them and decided that at least one of them did know what had been said and simply didn't want to tell her. Which made her suspicious. Much as she hated to think it might all have been about her – or, more specifically, Fion, as had been the case so many times that evening – there was no other conclusion she could draw. People gossiping about her had been bad enough, but she could bear it. That same gossip dragging her friends in and upsetting them? That was something else entirely. She couldn't allow it. 'Was it about Fion?'

There was an awkward silence.

'Right,' Ottilie said. She glanced around the room. People had gone back to their drinks and nibbles, and it looked calm enough now, despite the strange atmosphere still hanging over the room. 'I think I ought to go.'

'Why should you go?' Stacey asked. 'You're not the one causing trouble.'

'I think I am. Sort of. Magnus only felt the need to defend me because he was worried it would hurt my feelings if I overheard anything. And quite honestly, while I appreciate it, it's a bit too late for that – we've all heard stuff, right? Even if we've ignored it and pretended we haven't. I'm done. I can't be bothered with it, and I'm not about to ruin everyone else's night even more than it already has been.'

'If you go, then they've won,' Stacey insisted.

Ottilie shook her head. 'I don't think it's that simple. I probably ought to talk to Fion too.'

Stacey looked set to argue, but Simon only nodded and offered a strained smile. 'I think you're right. Probably best to take yourself out of the situation until things have calmed down.'

'She can't hide away for the next few weeks,' Stacey said.

'No,' Simon agreed. 'I know you don't want to hear this, Ottilie, but it might be wise to ask Fion to lie low for a while. Perhaps even go back to her parents for a spell. Just until it all blows over.'

'I wouldn't give anyone the satisfaction of knowing it had got to me,' Stacey said.

Simon turned to her. 'That's you,' he said with such obvious pride and fondness it cheered Ottilie a little. 'I'm not sure Fion is as resilient as you are.'

'And you're not seen as an outsider,' Ottilie added. 'People might gossip about you, but they're more tolerant. I don't know if that's part of the problem with Fion, but I'm sure it's not helping.'

'You really think people are that small-minded here?' Simon asked.

'Yes,' Stacey cut in.

'No,' Ottilie said. 'At least, I hope not. I don't really want to ask Fion to leave. I get the impression life in Penrith isn't any better for her.'

'I wasn't only thinking of her,' Simon said.

Ottilie blew out a long breath. 'I'd better mention to Geoff that I'm leaving. I'd like to say goodbye to Magnus too, make sure he's OK.'

'Want us to come with you? Walk you home?'

'There's no need. No point in cutting your night short as well.'

'You're sure?'

Ottilie nodded and forced a smile. 'Absolutely. I'll see you at work tomorrow.' She turned to Stacey and gave her a hug. 'And I'll see you when I see you.'

'That better mean tomorrow,' Stacey said. 'Don't let this crap get to you.'

'I won't. And even if everyone else in the village hates me, I still have you, right?'

'The only one worth having, quite honestly,' Stacey said with a faint smile of her own.

'Exactly.'

Ottilie went to let Geoff know she was leaving. She didn't mention the incident because she didn't want him to think it had ruined her evening, and as he didn't address it either, she had to assume he didn't want to talk about it. Then she went to find Magnus.

He was in the cinema, tidying up. As the door opened he turned around.

'Hello.' His tone was bright enough, but Ottilie could tell that was for her benefit.

'I just came to say thanks and that I'll be off now.'

'So soon?'

'I'm a bit tired, and I've got an early start tomorrow, so...'

Magnus nodded. 'Of course. Ottilie...'

'Yes?'

'You know that everyone here loves you.'

'Of course.'

'That's all right then. As long as you do.'

'I'm fond of you all – you know that.' Ottilie paused. 'I'd hate to think anything I was doing was a problem for you. Or that it might cause you upset. If that happened, you'd tell me, wouldn't you?'

'You could never do that,' Magnus said.

'But you would tell me?'

'I'm sure that won't ever happen.'

Ottilie wondered whether to bring up the altercation she'd missed while she'd been in the bathroom but decided that Magnus, like Geoff, really didn't want to talk to her about it. If he had, he would have said something by this point, and she'd given him enough prompting.

'Goodnight, Magnus.'

He held up a hand. 'Thanks for coming.'

'You know I wouldn't miss film club.'

'Bless you,' he said with a vague smile before going back to his cleaning. Ottilie paused for a moment, wondering whether she ought to say anything else, but then decided to leave him to it.

CHAPTER TWENTY

An unfamiliar car was parked outside Wordsworth Cottage when she got home from film club. Ottilie stopped on the pavement for a second, trying to recall if she knew it and who it might belong to. The sight did nothing to settle her uneasy mood, but she dismissed it quickly, deciding that she really did need a good night's sleep. Perhaps then she'd stop seeing bad news wherever she went.

But as she opened the front door she could hear voices in the living room. She went in to find Fion sitting with her mum, Caron.

'Oh...' Ottilie looked from one to the other, fingers twisted around the door handle. 'Hello.'

'Ottilie...' Fion got up. 'I'm sorry... you don't mind Mum being here, do you?'

'Of course not. I wasn't expecting—'

'I know, I didn't say,' Fion added. 'It was a spur-of-the-moment thing.'

Ottilie wondered what had made Fion bring her mum out here. They'd stayed in contact while Fion had been living in Thimblebury, as Ottilie would have expected, but neither

Caron nor Conrad had seemed interested in visiting. Ottilie had told Fion she could ask them, but she'd got the impression that Fion would rather they didn't. Something had changed, and Ottilie wondered if it was to do with her affair with Damien and its fallout.

'I'll leave you to it,' Ottilie said.

Fion looked awkward, but Caron looked more relieved.

'Please don't think you can't come and go,' Fion said. 'It's your house.'

'It's no problem – I'll go and make a drink. Does anyone want anything?'

Caron shook her head.

'We've just had one,' Fion said.

Ottilie went to the kitchen. As she closed the door, she could hear their conversation resume. Caron's tone had a note of entreaty in it. She was asking Fion for something? It sounded that way. Perhaps Fion would put Ottilie in the picture once her mum had gone, but Ottilie had to wonder how long Caron was planning to stay. It was already quite late, and she had a drive of at least forty minutes home. It looked as if Ottilie's plans for an early night were out of the window.

She put the kettle on and texted Heath, just to see how his day had been. His reply was almost immediate:

Boring as always, but meeting was useful. How about you? How are you holding up? Did you go to film club or straight to bed after work? I know I didn't want to wake up this morning.

A text message wasn't the place to fill him in on everything that had happened in Thimblebury since his departure that morning, so she sent a brief note to say she'd found the day a slog too, that she'd been to film club, and that she was planning to get some sleep just as soon as she could. She didn't tell him that Caron was there and that she was trying to stay out of her and Fion's way while they discussed something that sounded important.

He sent one more in response, telling her he loved her, to which she replied in kind, and then her thoughts went back to the conversation taking place in the living room. Should she pop her head round and say she'd be going to bed? Then they could take as long as they wanted and they wouldn't have to worry about her being around.

Just as she'd decided that was what she'd do, she heard the front door being opened and murmuring in the hallway. Then the door closed and Fion came into the kitchen.

'Mum's just gone. I'm sorry I didn't... I didn't know she was coming until the very last minute, and I thought you'd be out at film club longer... I hope it's OK.'

'It's your home as much as mine,' Ottilie said. 'Of course you can have your mum visit.'

'I thought you might be angry that I'd given them your address.'

'Why would I be angry?'

Fion took a seat at the table with her and shrugged. 'Because of my dad. I mean *our* dad.'

'I hardly think he's going to rush over here for Sunday lunch,' Ottilie said. 'You could subliminally implant my address into his brain while he was sleeping and I'm quite sure it wouldn't make him want to come over. He made his feelings quite clear when I went to meet him. Sorry,' Ottilie added as she picked up her mug. 'I know he's your dad.'

'He's your dad too – you're entitled to say how you feel.'

'In that case, he might be my dad, but it doesn't feel that way to me. To me, he's just a man I once met who wasn't very nice to me.'

'He's not very nice to anyone,' Fion said.

Ottilie had to wonder, not for the first time, what her mum had seen in him. Her marriage must have been at rock bottom for her to stray to someone like Conrad because it couldn't have just been his looks. She had to reflect on the parallels of that situation with Fion, Melanie and Damien. It wasn't the same, but there was more than an element of history repeating itself. Then again, there didn't seem much chance of Damien and Melanie patching things up, as her own mum and dad had done.

Fion's voice broke into Ottilie's thoughts. 'Mum wants me to go home.'

Ottilie didn't immediately respond. She was meant to say that she didn't want Fion to leave. She didn't, but logic was telling her that it might be the best solution to their current predicament. It would take her away from the gossip and allow time for the dust to settle. Perhaps it would even help Fion and Damien reflect on their affair with more clarity, and perhaps they'd both decide there was no future in it. As harsh a conclusion as it was, Ottilie couldn't help but feel it would be the easiest way out. For her or for Fion? Selfish, yes, but Ottilie had to admit that it would probably make her happier than Fion if they called it off.

'I don't think I will,' Fion continued. 'Unless you want me to.'

Ottilie shook herself and offered a vague smile. 'I've got no intention of asking you to leave. It's up to you. There's a room here for as long as you want it.'

'I feel I'm making things difficult for you.'

'Is that why your mum came? Because she wanted to persuade you to go back to them?'

'I phoned her. I wanted to talk to her... I miss her, even though I don't want to go back. I was feeling...' Fion's sentence trailed off.

'I know,' Ottilie said. 'It's understandable. You can't let people get to you.'

'I don't care about them getting to me; I care what people say to you.'

There was a flash of rebellion in Fion's tone. Ottilie recognised that streak of granite she'd inherited from Conrad, the same steel she'd seen once before. She wasn't as weak as she sometimes seemed.

'You don't need to worry about that,' Ottilie said. 'The people who have bad things to say aren't ones worth listening to.'

'But if me being here was a problem, then I could go. I don't think Heath—'

'Heath's fine with you being here,' Ottilie cut in. 'He's got no time for gossip either. If you want to leave, neither of us would try to stop you, but we're happy to have you if you want to stay.'

'You're sure?'

'Positive,' Ottilie said, though she wished she could feel it as forcefully as she'd just said it.

Despite her tiredness, Ottilie had struggled to sleep that night. Yet more rain was forecast, but the morning was bright and cloudless, and the air was clean and sharp in her lungs. Ottilie parked her car on a plateau and walked the rest of the way up to Hilltop Farm, knowing that the wet weather they'd had overnight would have made the path that was barely a road too muddy to drive safely. She never minded climbing that last bit of the hill. The scenery up here was breathtaking, like she could see the entire world – rolling carpets of green scored by dark valleys and silver rivers stretching out as far as she could see.

At the house, she knocked on the back door to announce her arrival, as she always did, before pushing it open and walking into the kitchen. Darryl was at the table, head bent over his favourite train book, gulping down a glass of juice, as always, while Ann cooked bacon and sausage for him.

She turned with a smile. 'Morning, Ottilie. How are you?' She paused. 'Oh dear, you look a bit peaky. Didn't sleep well?'

'Not the best night I've ever had.'

'I suppose there's no surprise there,' she replied mildly before turning back to the pan. 'Do you want a sandwich this morning? There's plenty here.'

'No, thank you.' Ottilie put her bag on the table. 'What do you mean, "no surprise"?' She was aware that her tone was perhaps a little sharper than she'd intended.

Ann didn't seem to notice. 'All the trouble you're having. It would be enough to keep anyone up at night.'

'Trouble?'

Ann nodded as she turned over the bacon. 'It's a shame. Must be a worry.'

There was only one conclusion Ottilie could draw. Somehow, the village gossip had even got as far as the remote Hilltop Farm. Ann rarely went into the village. Ottilie couldn't imagine how it had travelled so far. Unless she'd heard directly from Corrine or Victor, who were friends of hers. In which case, at least it would be a fair and balanced picture rather than the titillation she was sure was spreading around the village even as she thought about it. She had to admit, Ann didn't seem too concerned by what she'd heard. She only seemed sympathetic.

'Has Victor been over to see you?' she asked, keeping her tone casual.

'I ran out of kindling yesterday so I went over to see if I could get some. Victor was at the house.'

'Oh. So you stayed to have a chat with Corrine?'

'A few minutes. She was busy, you see. With her Melanie. She's staying with them for a while.'

'I suppose they told you all about that.'

'Oh, yes,' Ann said. 'They don't blame you.'

'Oh...' Ottilie glanced at Darryl, who, as usual, took no notice of their conversation. 'Is everything all right here? Darryl had his insulin this morning?'

'I think so. He doesn't try to hide it so much these days. Since he got that book from Dr Stokes, you can do anything with him. Put that thing in front of him and you can let a bomb off next to his head and he wouldn't even notice.'

'That's good. You don't need me today then.'

'Oh, we like to see you.' Ann looked up now with vague panic on her face. 'You're not going to stop coming up, are you? Only he'd notice that. Routine would change, you see. You think he's not taking stock, but he is – when it comes to routine, he always knows.'

'Oh, I didn't mean that. Of course I'll keep coming up. As much as I can, in any case. Things aren't always in my control, you know...'

'You're not going to leave Thimblebury?'

'No – who said that?'

'Corrine said she wouldn't be surprised with all the trouble here for you. And then you just said—'

'I only meant things like holidays and sick days. Even I get sick.'

'That's a relief.' Ann went back to her cooking. 'Are you sure you won't take a sandwich? I've made far too much bacon, as usual.'

Just to make Ann happy, Ottilie agreed to the sandwich. She took a seat as Ann went to get some bread from the crock. 'Will your sister leave?'

Ottilie didn't reply straight away. She watched Ann place slices of bacon on the bread she'd just cut from her home-made loaf and wondered what she was meant to say. Did Ann want her sister to leave? Was that how people in Thimblebury felt?

'None of my business, I suppose,' Ann said as she wrapped Ottilie's sandwich. 'I didn't mean to pry. I'm sure Damien and

Melanie were already in trouble before she arrived. Corrine hasn't said so, but it's obvious, isn't it? Something happened with her last year. I don't know what, but I know it was something.'

'Happened with who? Melanie?'

Ann nodded as she put Ottilie's parcel on the table in front of her.

'What happened last year?'

'I don't know, but something did. Or maybe it was before that. Around the time Corrine was poorly. You remember – that wasn't long after you got here.'

'That must be the year before,' Ottilie said thoughtfully. She'd never heard of anything like Ann was telling her. Then again, she had been new to the village and preoccupied with settling in and getting to grips with her new job. And if Ann was talking about Corrine's skin cancer, Ottilie supposed she and Victor were going to have been preoccupied with that. If something had gone on with Melanie, depending on what it was, it might not have been uppermost in their minds either. They certainly wouldn't have been telling Ottilie about it. She wondered what Ann was talking about and how she knew so much. Maybe it was as simple as her living alone up here with time to notice the comings and goings of her nearest neighbours.

'I wouldn't worry about any of it,' Ann said. 'People have nothing better to do.'

'Did you see Melanie when you were over there?'

'She came into the kitchen for a minute. Didn't say much. Never did, to be honest, so no surprise there. I've never met your sister, but if she's like you, I daresay I'd prefer her to Melanie anyway. It's funny how people as nice as Corrine and Victor could have a daughter like that.'

Ottilie recalled hearing that from someone else, though she couldn't remember who. She hadn't been around Melanie all that much but had always found her courteous enough. Apart from their encounter the other night, of course, and nobody could accuse her of not having a good reason for being less than amiable that time. 'But she looked all right? She didn't seem ill or anything?'

'She could have done with a hairbrush and was in her dressing gown, but other than that, she seemed all right.'

'Hmm...' Ottilie collected her sandwich. 'Thank you for this,' she said, holding the parcel up as she stood to go.

'So you'll be here tomorrow, like always?' Ann asked.

'Don't worry – I'll be here.'

'Good. Darryl will be glad.'

Ottilie had always suspected that her regular visits were more appreciated by Ann than Darryl, but she never said so. She only left with an airy wave and headed back to her car, deep in thought.

At the surgery, Lavender greeted Ottilie with the news that Fliss was on a house call. This was cause for remark because while Simon was happy enough to venture out into the community when it was necessary, Fliss never went on house calls if she could help it. And then Lavender, with more glee than Ottilie was happy about, revealed who she'd gone to see.

'I'm surprised you didn't pass her car on your way down from Hilltop. You must have crossed paths. She's gone to see Melanie at Daffodil.'

'Melanie? What for?'

'I don't know. I took the call from Corrine, but she didn't want to say what it was about, only that it was for Melanie.'

Fliss wouldn't have said either. She might not even want to tell Ottilie. It all depended on what the visit was for.

'So,' Ottilie said, trying to be professional about it, despite her racing thoughts, 'is there anything I need to do while she's out? Someone I can see to ease her load when she gets back?'

'I don't think so. She didn't say so. Simon said he could cover any emergencies here while she's missing.'

'I'm surprised Simon didn't go.'

'Corrine was very specific that she wanted Fliss. I suppose it must be an ongoing problem that Fliss has already seen her for. Do you want a coffee?' Lavender asked as Ottilie made her way to her room. 'I'm making one anyway.'

'A two-scoop special sounds good about now, if you're offering.'

'Ooh, bad night then? Again?'

Ottilie didn't need to tell Lavender she had good reason for losing sleep – she'd have heard as much in the village gossip as everyone else by now. And so she simply turned back with a nod.

'Two-scoop special coming up. I can bring you a biscuit if you like?'

'Ann's given me one of her doorstops,' Ottilie said. She rifled in her bag and held it out to Lavender. 'Actually, I'm not all that hungry, if you want it.'

Lavender grinned as she took it. 'Don't need to tell me twice! Thanks, Ann!'

Fliss was busy catching up on paperwork at lunch and so didn't come down to the kitchen until it was almost over. Ottilie sensed some irritation, and she was reluctant to bring it up in case it had been caused by her visit to Melanie – and, by default, Fion or herself. Fliss gobbled the carrot soup that Lavender had kept warm for her while Ottilie finished hers and helped to tidy the kitchen. By the time she'd eaten, everything else was cleared away. Fliss took her empty bowl to the sink, but Lavender grabbed for it.

'Don't worry; I'll wash it. I know you've got a lot to do.'

Fliss gave her a grateful smile. Simon had already gone back to his room and, as Fliss left, Ottilie went after her, catching her in the hallway.

'I know you're busy, but do you have time for the quickest word?'

Fliss turned to her with a wry smile. The impatience was still there, but Ottilie appreciated that she was trying to keep it bottled. 'Would this be anything to do with my home visit today?'

'Um...'

'It's all right,' Fliss said. 'I'm happy to speak about it, though there's not all that much to tell. I think Corrine's concerns were worse than any actual medical problem. Melanie is fine. Down, of course, in need of some counselling, perhaps – which I have put a request in for – and some rest with as little excitement as possible.'

'That's the part that worries me,' Ottilie said.

'I can imagine.'

'But she's not in any immediate...' Ottilie paused, searching for the right word. Danger wasn't it, and yet she worried that there might be danger of some kind – for Melanie herself at least. Distress? That much was obvious so there was no point in hoping for anything other. 'There's nothing in her behaviour right now that makes you think we need to keep a very close eye on her? Perhaps even remove things that might cause her stress to bubble over?'

'I don't think it ever hurts to remove those,' Fliss said. 'But it's rarely that simple. I don't see her stress bubbling over, as you so eloquently put it. I think she's exhausted – emotionally – and I think what she's getting now, some quiet time under the watchful eye of Corrine and Victor, ought to do the trick eventually.' She put a hand on Ottilie's shoulder. 'Does that put your mind at rest?'

'Honestly?' Ottilie gave a vague shrug. 'Not really. Will you keep me updated? I don't need to know specifics, only if things are going in the right direction.'

'I'm sure Corrine and Victor will do that. I imagine you'll know more most of the time than I do.'

'As things are, I don't feel I can ask them.'

'I think they'd appreciate you asking. In times of crisis, don't we all find it a comfort to know our friends are thinking of us?'

Ottilie hadn't thought about it that way.

'Sorry to cut you off,' Fliss added. 'But...' She nodded at the door to her room.

'Oh, yes, of course. Sorry. Thank you.'

Fliss acknowledged her thanks and went to start her afternoon clinic, leaving Ottilie rooted to the spot, deep in thought. Should she be encouraged by Fliss's assessment of the situation at Daffodil Farm? Would it be a good idea to go over there later to see for herself?

A voice snapped her out of her musings.

'Having clinic in the hallway this afternoon?' Lavender asked.

Ottilie turned to her with a distracted smile. 'Sorry... I'm on my way to start now.'

'Looks like it. Do I need to force another two-scoop special on you?'

'Give me an hour,' Ottilie said. 'If it all goes quiet and you come in to find me face down on the desk, you might have to.'

CHAPTER TWENTY-ONE

Flo shovelled a roast potato into her mouth and chewed as if the plate were about to be snatched away. Ottilie and Heath exchanged a look of humour. It was the second time in a week they'd entertained her. Ottilie was of the opinion that once a week was more than enough, but she supposed Flo was entitled to be spoilt on her birthday like everyone else.

'Are you enjoying your dinner, Gran?' Heath asked.

'It's all right,' Flo said, scooping up some peas to follow the potato. 'Not like home-made, but it never is at these places.'

'I think it is home-made,' he replied. 'They still cook from scratch here.'

'But it's the pub kitchen, not a house, so it's not home-made, is it? It's pub made.'

'I can't argue with that logic,' Heath said with a light laugh. 'As long as you're having a nice time.'

'At least someone remembered my birthday,' Flo said.

Ottilie glanced at the card they'd brought along to give her, standing on the table in between their glasses and plates. She was glad Heath had reminded her because she'd clean forgotten, just like all the other people Flo was grumbling about.

Ottilie didn't blame her for being a bit offended. Even in her eighties, Ottilie would probably be hurt if everyone appeared to forget her birthday too. Although, Ottilie suspected the reports of Flo's forgotten birthday may have been exaggerated because she was certain most of the residents of Thimblebury would have remembered, and if they hadn't, she'd have had no qualms reminding them. And in her defence, Ottilie thought as she reflected on the week she'd had, hearing whispers and gossip everywhere she went – whether real or not – she could be forgiven for it having slipped her mind. 'If you like, we'll go shopping sometime next weekend.'

'It won't be my birthday next weekend,' Flo replied.

'Not necessarily for your birthday, just because. We haven't been over to Kendal for a while. We could go to that place where they sell the mint cake you like so much.'

'Don't put yourself out for me.'

'I want to.'

'You'll probably have something going on with your new sister,' Flo sniffed as she speared a carrot and shoved it into her mouth. 'She takes up all your time these days.'

'I'm sure that's not true,' Heath said. 'But they're bound to want to spend time together – they're still getting to know one another.'

'I think we all know her by now.'

Ottilie held back a frown. She wasn't about to ask what Flo meant because she was afraid she wouldn't like the answer, and the way every discussion around Fion seemed to go lately, she was certain that would be the case.

'Beef is nice,' Heath said. 'Really melts in the mouth, doesn't it?'

Ottilie shot him a grateful look. He'd had enough practice with his gran over the years to know when to steer a conversation to a new place, and he was doing that now. Usually, it worked too, but today, Flo seemed to have other ideas.

'I bet you wish you'd never set her up with Damien and that pie business,' she continued, eyeing Ottilie keenly. 'You meant well, I know, but you must be kicking yourself now. Sometimes it's better to keep out of these things, eh? If you had, there'd be none of this trouble.'

'Gran,' Heath warned. 'Do we really want to bring that up?'

'I don't blame your sister,' Flo added, as if she hadn't heard him. 'I blame that Damien. Any young woman would have her head turned by flattery from him. You could see she was all starry-eyed the first time she saw him.'

'I don't know how you could say that,' Heath replied drily. 'You weren't there.'

'I've seen it well enough since,' Flo said. 'I've seen it over the years with stronger women than her too. The first sniff of attention from a man and they're falling all over themselves.'

'I don't think it's quite like that,' Ottilie said, unable to hold off any longer. 'Fion's not a brainless pushover.'

'She's very young.'

'She's twenty-six! She's an adult, and I'm not going to patronise her by telling her she's not.'

'He's an older man, more experienced. She didn't stand a chance—'

'Gran, can we drop this now?' Heath reached for his beer and gulped some back.

'Hit a nerve, eh?' Flo said, and in her voice there was a note of triumph so obvious it took every ounce of strength Ottilie had not to let fly with her feelings on Flo's observations.

There was gossip all over the village – Ottilie didn't have to hear it to know it was going on – and now she was beginning to wonder how much Flo had contributed to it. She'd hoped for better from Heath's grandmother, not least because she was practically family. But perhaps, she reflected for a moment as Flo went back to her meal, there was no guarantee that family would offer a haven from judgement and intolerance.

. . .

Earlier than they'd planned to, Ottilie and Heath saw Flo to her house and went back to Wordsworth Cottage.

'I'm sorry about her,' Heath said as Ottilie unlocked the front door. She didn't reply for a moment, listening in the hallway to see if Fion was home. The house was silent and the lights all off.

'Fion?' she called, but there was no reply. She beckoned Heath in. 'It's not your fault.'

'It still feels like it at times. You'd think by now I'd be able to get her to shut up when she starts, but no, not even at my age.'

'She wouldn't listen, even if you tried. Flo says what Flo wants to say – you know that.'

'Doesn't mean I don't want to gag her at times.'

Ottilie couldn't help but smile. 'I think I'd be obliged to inform social services if you did.'

'I think they'd come round with a medal if they'd met her.' He took her into his arms and held her tight. 'From this branch of the family, I apologise for that one. How can I make it up to you?'

'There's no need.'

'There is.'

'It's not me getting it in the neck from everyone, is it?'

'But it's getting to you, I can tell.'

'Of course it is.' Ottilie let out a sigh as she laid her head on his shoulder.

'Why don't we have a weekend away?'

'When?'

'Next weekend? We'll pack the car and go to stay on the coast. You choose.'

'I can't – there's too much to do.'

'Like what?'

'I just can't. I'm needed here.'

'Fion will be fine.'

'I know that, but...' Ottilie's feelings were vague, and she didn't know how to express them. There was nothing in particular holding her back, only an inexplicable but inescapable sense that if she wasn't around to keep an eye on things, life at Wordsworth Cottage would somehow go off the rails.

'OK,' Heath said. 'Why don't we go out tomorrow?'

'I don't have time—'

'If the phrases housework, wedding planning or washing uniform come out of your mouth in the next thirty seconds, then the wedding is off. All those things can wait, and you need to let off some steam. And don't try to persuade me otherwise because I can tell it's true. You don't want to go away for the weekend and that's fine, I understand, but you need a break. We're in the Lake District. For once, let's take advantage of it. When was the last time we spent some time outdoors?'

'I don't think it was all that long ago.'

'For you, maybe, but for me I'm sure it's weeks, if not months. Let's go out – the forecast is good. Picnic, a bit of walking, maybe...' He paused and then, as Ottilie looked up at him, he broke into a broad smile. 'That swimming hole. You know the one in the hills Gran used to go to as a girl.'

'Where you came to rescue us that time with a face like thunder when I couldn't get her down?'

'That one!' He laughed. 'It's about time we made a different memory for that place.'

'I suppose it is, though I do like that one, even though you were really grumpy about having to come up for us. Isn't it a bit cold for wild swimming?'

'It's warm enough. We don't have to be in there for long; we can take towels and robes and a flask and some snacks and make a day of it. The good thing is, it will be peaceful. Hardly anyone knows it's there.'

'Locals do. So Flo says.'

'They might, but for most it's too much of a trek. Even we haven't been back up there since that day with Gran. Come on, what do you say? An outdoor spa day – it might be just what we need.'

Ottilie shook her head slowly as she smiled up at him. 'I don't know how I deserve you.'

'In a good way or a bad way?'

'Good,' she said. 'Always good.'

'So that's a yes?'

'Yes. It'll be fun. And if it's not fun, it will be a change of scenery. I think you're right – that's exactly what I need at the moment.'

CHAPTER TWENTY-TWO

Though the morning was warm and promised to get warmer still as the sun climbed the sky, there had been rain the day before, and so the path up the hill to the swimming hole was muddy.

'At least it's not crumbling away under our feet,' Heath panted, holding out a hand to help Ottilie negotiate a particularly uneven section. 'I've been up here with Gran as a kid during really dry summers and it was one step forward and two steps back. Once I thought I'd slide all the way down to the bottom.'

'I can see she was a responsible adult when you were in her care.'

'Not a bit,' Heath grunted as he pulled Ottilie up. 'But she was always fun. That's what makes me sad about how she's behaving now.'

'Let's not talk about that today.'

'No...' Heath stopped for a moment and gazed out over the view as the sun skimmed a distant hillside. 'You're right. We said we'd come out today and forget everything else for a while. Looking at that, shouldn't be too difficult.'

Ottilie stood at his side and hitched up her rucksack. 'You were right. We don't take advantage of having this on our doorstep half as much as we ought to.' She shaded her eyes and took in the path that continued to wind upwards. 'How much further? I can't exactly remember – Flo led the way last time, and I just followed.'

'I can never tell you where it is until I'm almost on top of it, but I'd say about half an hour more. The ground levels out a bit and there's a twist in the path. You can hear the waterfall before you see it.'

'Do you think we should have told your gran we were coming up here? She does love it.'

Heath began to climb again, and Ottilie followed. 'We came up here to get away from her, remember?'

'Not just her.'

'No, but she's included in the stress package that is Thimblebury right now. What she doesn't know won't hurt her, and I won't tell her if you don't.'

'I wouldn't dare now.'

'There you go then...' Heath stepped over a high tussock of grass that was obstructing the path. 'You've answered your own question.'

They climbed for another twenty minutes, stopping every so often to take in a new version of the heavenly view, across the valley and the road below and over to the opposite hills, until Ottilie heard a faint rushing, roaring sound.

'I think we must be getting close if that's the waterfall.'

Heath paused to listen and then nodded. 'The twist in the path must be around here somewhere. Keep a look out for it in case I miss it. I don't fancy climbing any higher than I have to.'

'I thought you said you were half mountain goat.'

'Yeah.' He grinned. 'That was at the bottom of the hill. I changed my mind – I think I'm half sloth after all.'

They found where the path forked, one direction continuing upwards and the other around the hill, until the ground levelled out onto a plateau and they could see water gushing from the hillside above and into a rocky cauldron of water. Ottilie smiled as the memories of her day there with Flo came flooding back. She turned to Heath.

'Still nice and secret,' he said, noting, as she'd done, that they were there alone. 'I hate to gatekeep, but some things are better kept that way.'

'I feel guilty for agreeing. Flo said the same when I came up with her before. As soon as somewhere like this gets out on social media, it's ruined by too many people coming at the same time.'

'And half the time it's only for an Instagram pic anyway...' Heath clambered over the rocks to get up to the pool, offering a hand to help Ottilie as he went.

'I can probably climb it easier by myself if I take my time and watch my feet,' she said.

'It's not too bad once you get past where they're a bit more pointy.'

'Is that the technical term?' Ottilie asked as she picked her way through a gathering of tiny mountainous peaks and onto where the rocks levelled out. 'Pointy?'

'Yes, it's mountaineer speak – I thought everyone knew that.'

At the edge of the pool, they found a boulder to sit on. Ottilie stripped down to the swimsuit she'd worn beneath her clothes and pulled on a pair of rubber shoes. The first time she'd been up here with Flo, she'd been unprepared and she'd been nervous about getting into the water. This time, she had the right equipment, and she had Heath to help if she got into trouble.

Once they were both ready, Heath tucked their rucksacks into a dry corner and helped Ottilie over the lip of the pool, where she sat and dangled her feet in. As she pondered the best way to enter the water without simply dropping in like a stone, she recalled that last time Flo had shown her a natural step that allowed easier access. She cast around for it, and Heath seemed to realise what she was looking for and pointed.

'It's easier to get in over there if you're worried about jumping.'

'I don't want to jump; I have no idea how deep this is, and I don't know how long I'd be sinking for.'

He started to laugh. 'It's not a journey to the centre of the earth, you know. I don't know how deep it is, but I'm pretty sure you'd come back up after a few seconds.'

'I'd rather not find out. I like my swimming to be on the surface, with my head above the water at all times.'

She got up and made her way cautiously to where the rocks allowed her to walk in a way. 'Oh my God, I don't remember it being this cold!' she yelped.

'Better to get straight in,' Heath said, holding his nose and leaping with a splash so large that it soaked her. A moment later, he resurfaced, grinning. 'It's cold but not so bad when you get used to it.'

Ottilie brushed water from her eyes and glared at him. 'Thanks!' she said, making him laugh again.

'Come on – better if you don't dither.'

Ottilie took a breath and steeled herself, and then pushed off the side and into the pool.

The cold stole her breath, and she gasped as she struck out. 'Remind me again why we thought this was a good idea!' she panted.

'But just look at it!' Heath said, swimming to the rocks and leaning over them to gesture at their view.

Ottilie made for him and grabbed the same rocks to steady herself, shivering but still awestruck by the vista. The sun was above the hills now, and everything was different shades of green, dramatic pockets of light and shadow where the geology changed, and the sky was a cornflower blue, clear and vast above them. She kicked to keep herself warm as she bobbed in the crystal waters that had perhaps travelled for years and years through the rocks of their Lakeland home to reach her skin at this point.

'You'd pay thousands for a view from a pool like this on holiday, and then it would never be this exclusive,' he continued. 'No wonder people would flock here if it ever got discovered. If I saw this on a post, I'd want to come here too.'

'It is incredible,' Ottilie agreed, turning to plant a kiss on his chilled lips. With her shoulders out of the water, the sun was warming them enough that she could manage the cold now she was getting used to it. 'We're the luckiest people in the world right now.'

'I think we might be.' He returned her kiss with one that was longer and more passionate. 'I love you so much, Ottilie. I think I might be the luckiest person in the world. And not just now – whenever I'm with you.'

'Silver tongue,' Ottilie said with a laugh. 'You think I'm falling for that. What do you want?'

With a grin, he let go of the rocks and pushed off, gliding through the water on his back. 'I want to swim, and then maybe I want to fool about with you. And then lunch.'

'Sounds like every teenage boy's dream.'

'Deep down, we're all still teenage boys, you know.'

He held out his hands for Ottilie to join him. She paused, still warier of the depths than he was. It unnerved her not to know what was beneath them or how far it went down, but she wanted to be brave. Heath always made her want to be brave, and so, after a moment, she shook the fear and swam over.

'Aren't you glad we came?' he asked as they trod water together and he wrapped his arms around her.

'Yes.' She smiled, safe in his embrace, the peace of their surroundings seeping into her soul. 'Very.'

CHAPTER TWENTY-THREE

It had been a wonderful few hours, and by the time they'd arrived back in Thimblebury, Ottilie felt as if she'd had the weekend away that she'd refused. They swam until they were too cold, and then wrapped up and gazed out at the glorious quilt of hills and valleys and distant lakes as they'd warmed up with hot coffee from a flask and snacks Heath had packed for them, and then they'd gone back into the water and done the whole thing all over again.

They'd talked, longer and more honestly than they'd talked in a long time. Heath had been completely open about his feelings on what was happening – not only with Fion and Damien and the village at large, but how he felt it was affecting them, what their futures might look like, and how hard he was prepared to work to make sure they would be this happy forever. They'd laughed, recalling things that had happened the last time they'd been here. It felt like the early days of their relationship all over again. Ottilie had worn a smile all the way back to the car, even when her legs had been aching and her feet were sore. They'd stopped at a pub for a quick drink and yet more food, contented and happy as dusk followed them into Thimblebury.

At the same time as they arrived at the house, Damien's car pulled up too. Ottilie looked across at Heath. As relaxed as she'd been only a moment before, it was like their day out had never happened. Instantly, she was tense again, wary of what might unfold in the next few minutes.

But the car didn't stop for long. Fion got out and waved as it pulled away again. She turned to watch as Heath killed the engine and he and Ottilie got out of the car.

'Have you had a nice day?' she asked. She looked so happy it made Ottlie's heart ache for her. Why did people have to judge her so harshly? Her intentions hadn't been to hurt anyone, and Ottilie felt she knew enough of her now to know she would have tried hard not to, even if she hadn't been able to fight the attraction to Damien in the end.

'Lovely,' Ottilie said. 'Did you?'

'We've just been on a driving lesson. Damien says I should think about putting in for my test. We've done hours and hours of practice today.'

'That's brilliant,' Ottilie said cautiously.

'I think we're out of bread,' Fion said. 'Want me to go and see if the shop is still open?'

'Magnus and Geoff won't be open now,' Ottilie replied, 'The newsagent might be.'

'I'll go,' Heath said, but Fion started to walk.

'Don't worry – I've got it! Won't be a minute!'

Ottilie opened up and let Heath in. 'I think I'll go and put something comfier on.'

'Want some help?'

'No.' She laughed, prodding him in the chest. 'You can make yourself useful and go and make drinks.'

'Can't I go and get something comfortable on?'

'When you've made me a drink.'

'Spoilsport. All right then, what do you want?'
'Something warm. I won't be a minute.'

Ottilie came back downstairs a few minutes later in some old leggings and a fleece. She liked that they were at the stage of their relationship where she didn't have to worry about what she wore in front of him. She'd joked that as soon as he'd proposed, he'd waived the rights to sexy lingerie and sitting around in full make-up and stiff clothes whenever he was around. He'd joked that if that was the case, she'd waived the right to clean boxers and socks. He'd made cocoa from a jar of very expensive chocolate Fliss had bought her for Christmas, and it smelled amazing as she took a seat at the table and wrapped her fingers around the mug.

'I feel quite spoiled today.'

'Good,' he said, playfully nudging her leg beneath the table with his foot. 'That's what I was aiming for.'

She leaned across to kiss him but a second later was jolted away by the sound of the front door slamming. Expecting Fion to skip into the kitchen with the bread, she turned and smoothed her expression into one that didn't give away the raunchy thoughts that had just been whirling around her head. But all steamy thoughts were chased out when she saw the anguish on Fion's face.

'What's happened?' she asked, leaping up to embrace her. 'What's wrong?'

'It's nothing,' Fion sobbed. 'I'm fine…' She dragged in a breath and pushed herself free of Ottilie's arms.

'You don't look fine. Has somebody upset you? Fion—'

'Please, Ottilie, I'm really fine. I'd rather not talk about it.'

It was then that Ottilie noticed Fion didn't have the bread she'd gone for. Narrowing her eyes, she held Fion by the shoulders and looked at her squarely. 'Did they say something in the newsagent's?'

'No.'

'Was it shut?'

Fion shook her head.

'Then where's the bread?' Heath asked. 'Didn't they have any?'

'I don't know...' Fion started to cry again. 'I didn't... I didn't go in.'

'Someone said something to you,' Ottilie insisted. 'What did they say? Was it about you and Damien?'

'It was...' Fion gave a tiny nod. 'But don't make a fuss about it, please!'

'Who was it?' Heath asked.

'Nobody.'

'Who?'

Fion looked up at him, and there was a horrible moment where realisation hit and Ottilie went cold. Ottilie saw that Heath had worked it out too.

'Gran?'

'You can't say anything to her,' Fion pleaded. 'She didn't mean anything. She said... she said it was you two she cared about.'

'And she told you the best thing you could do was to break it off with Damien, I suppose?' Heath said.

'She told me I ought to move back to Penrith,' Fion replied.

'There's progress,' Heath said grimly. 'I'll go and see her.'

'You can't!' Fion yelped.

'It'll only make things worse,' Ottilie said to him. 'Fion's right, you can't.'

'But look at her!'

'I know. Still, we're going to have to let it go.'

'No.' Heath grabbed his jacket from the back of a chair. 'This has gone too far.'

'Where are you going?' Ottilie ran after him as he marched into the hallway. Her feet were bare, and she cast around for the nearest pair of shoes as he yanked open the front door. 'You're not going to Flo's now? At this time?'

'There's no point in talking to my gran about it because anything I've got to say would fall on deaf ears,' he said, reaching into a pocket and pulling out his car keys. 'I'm going to the source.'

'What?' Ottilie stepped onto the path, the ground beneath her bare feet cold and hard. She winced as she stood on a sharp stone. 'What source?'

He turned to her. 'Go inside.'

'Not likely. Not until you come back in too. What source?'

He nodded at the distant hill, where Damien and Melanie's house was.

'Heath, this isn't your fight. It isn't your business.'

'It's my business when it upsets your sister because that upsets you. And you are very much my business. There's only one way to put a stop to all this. Damien' – there was a hard emphasis on the name – 'needs to be a man about it and accept some responsibility.'

'And what does that mean?'

Heath unlocked the car, and Ottilie followed him out onto the pavement. At this point, Fion was also on the path, watching anxiously. Ottilie didn't know how much of their altercation she'd been there to hear but suspected that if she'd heard all of it, she'd be trying harder to stop Heath from getting into his car too.

'Please,' Ottilie said, glancing back at Fion before grabbing him by both hands. 'Don't. It's not going to help. We've had a lovely day – why ruin it like this?'

He paused, and Ottilie could tell she was getting through. While she loved and admired his sense of right and wrong, his need to step up, whether it was his business or not, she felt that sometimes it was misjudged, and sometimes it was too much. This was one of those times, and if ever she needed him to step away and think for a moment, it was now. She was convinced that no good could come from him storming up to see Damien and demanding he break things off with Fion. If nothing else, it was surely up to Fion who she chose to love. And Ottilie had no doubt that Fion did love him. Whether Damien's feelings were as strong, she couldn't say, but it wasn't her or Heath's business to pass judgement on that.

'Tomorrow,' she added in a voice meant to soothe him, 'we'll talk about it – you, me and Fion. It might even be a good idea to get your gran over too and all sit together. We'll decide then if anything needs to be done. I know you want to do something, and I understand it's frustrating to sit around watching all this and not be able to do anything about it, but it would make me happier if we didn't rush in all guns blazing.'

After another long pause, he gave a reluctant nod.

'Thank you,' Ottilie said, and as they turned to go back into the house, Fion scurried inside and ran up the stairs to her bedroom. Perhaps, with Heath in his current mood, that was for the best.

CHAPTER TWENTY-FOUR

Ottilie had slept fitfully. It seemed to be a problem most nights now, ever since the trouble with Fion and Damien had begun. She lived in hope that the dust would settle soon as people got used to seeing Fion and Damien together, but it was taking so long she wondered if she'd be able to cope much longer. But she also realised that it wasn't about her at all. If she was feeling the stress, then she could only imagine what it was like for Melanie, or Corrine and Victor, or even Damien and Fion.

She'd seen Heath off early that morning and then got ready for work herself. Thankfully it had been uneventful, and her patients had all managed to stay away from any contentious remarks.

The day was warm, if grey and humid. There was rain in the air but nothing that promised to be heavy, and at least it stayed light now until well after nine, which meant far more time to enjoy the countryside Ottilie had been blessed with outside her home. Just before lunch, Ottilie sent a text to Stacey.

Wondering if you fancy a quick stroll later on? I could do with clearing my head. We could get some food afterwards. You're welcome to eat at mine if you like.

Won't you be with Heath?

He's got stuff to do, will probably be late. He won't mind anyway.

Walk sounds fun, dinner even better. There'd better be chips.

Ottilie grinned as she typed a reply. She could do chips, no problem. There was no better confidante in Thimblebury than Stacey. Ottilie could air some of her doubts and tire herself out in the process, and hopefully it would mean a better night's sleep. And at the same time she could get an update on Chloe, her pregnancy and the plans for her to move in with her boyfriend. Ottilie couldn't deny that although she knew Stacey would miss them, it was about time – for Chloe's sake, at least – that she left home. She suspected that Stacey and Chloe's relationship would be better for it, even if it didn't seem that way to Stacey yet.

After helping Lavender to clean and lock up the surgery, Ottilie rushed home to change and then dashed over to Stacey's house. Chloe answered the door, looking as bored and jaded as ever.

'Yeah. Come in. Mum can't find her shoes.'

Ottilie stepped over the threshold. She stood in the hallway and watched Chloe yell up the stairs.

'Ottilie's here!'

Stacey's head appeared at the top. 'Hey!' She grinned. 'Give me a minute. Is it raining out there?'

'No,' Ottilie said. 'Not yet, but it might later – best to get something waterproof on.'

'Right...' Stacey disappeared again, and Ottilie heard her add, 'if I can find anything.'

Chloe left Ottilie in the hallway and went into the living room. Ottilie wondered whether to follow and start a conversation but then heard her talking and decided she was probably busy messaging her boyfriend, so she didn't bother. Instead, she got out her own phone and checked in case anyone wanted her. There was nothing new, apart from a few replies to enquiries about wedding venues. She'd go through those later when she saw Heath, so they could look together.

She'd just put her phone away when Stacey came down the stairs.

'What's with the plastic poncho?' Ottilie asked with a grin.

'I couldn't find my cagoule,' Stacey said. 'This was the best I could do. It's Chloe's – she went to Alton Towers. Must have been for the rapids or something.'

'I can see that.' Ottilie nodded at the huge logo emblazoned on the chest of the cover-up.

'Nobody's going to care,' Stacey said, taking it off and stuffing it into a pocket, even as she did.

'It's cute,' Ottilie said.

Stacey opened the door and stepped out, Ottilie following her onto the path. 'Where do you want to go?'

'Shall we head towards Daffodil Farm?'

'That hill?' Stacey blew out a breath. 'We'll be knackered!'

'Where do you want to go?'

'Circuit of the village? It's flat at least, and if it starts to rain, we can call at the shop and get Geoff to make us a cup of tea.'

Ottilie laughed lightly. 'I thought you wanted to get fit.'

'*Simon* wanted me to get fit. I think I've already peaked, so might as well give up now.'

'Come on.' Ottilie took her by the arm and began to lead her towards the road out of the village. 'Let's at least have a go at the hill, and if we get fed up or the rain starts, we'll come back down. A circuit of the village will take us five minutes.'

'That was the idea,' Stacey said, shooting Ottilie a sideways look but following her lead all the same.

They chatted as they walked, and it only took ten minutes of Stacey's company for Ottilie to feel lighter. Chloe's morning sickness had got worse, but other than that she was fine and healthy, and despite their intentions to wait, they'd found a flat they liked, though it was in Keswick, and Stacey thought that although it wasn't too far by car, by public transport was a lot more difficult, and as neither Oliver nor Chloe could drive, Stacey worried she wouldn't see much of them. Stacey and Simon were still madly in love, and though they hadn't got as far as engagement, Ottilie and Heath's upcoming nuptials and Chloe's plans to move out had turned Simon's thoughts to perhaps him and Stacey living together too.

As they reached the outskirts of the village, they could hear voices. And then they noticed a group of people speaking in earnest tones. Ottilie noticed Victor at first and then was surprised to see Corrine there – she didn't venture into the village as often as he did. Then she saw Damien, Melanie's sister, Penny, and her husband Leon.

'What's going on here?' Stacey asked in a low voice.

'I know,' Ottilie replied. 'Is it just me or do they seem stressed?'

'They do a bit. Do we slip away and pretend we haven't noticed, or do we go and ask?'

Ottilie glanced across at her, and Stacey smiled. 'OK, I forgot who I was with for a minute. Of course we're going to ask them.'

'Hello,' Ottilie said in a bright voice as they went over.

Corrine spoke first, her features taut with anxiety. 'Oh, Ottilie. You weren't coming up to see us, were you?'

'Not especially, though we were going that way. Is everything all right?'

'Nothing for you to worry about, lass,' Victor said gruffly, though there was no unkindness in it.

'Are you sure?' Stacey asked.

Penny, Leon and Damien all exchanged a look that wasn't lost on Ottilie. Victor and Corrine might have wanted to keep her and Stacey out of whatever this was, but they didn't.

'I don't suppose you've seen Melanie on your travels?' Damien asked.

'Tonight?' Ottilie frowned. 'No. Should we have done?'

'We, um…' Victor hesitated. 'Well, we don't know where she is.'

'You're going to look for her?' Stacey asked.

'We thought we'd split up and see if we could find her,' Leon said. 'The weather's moving in, and if she's in the hills…'

'She might not have the right clothes on,' Penny finished for him. She looked like her mum – far more than Melanie did – and as she spoke, Ottilie could see the same expression of worry.

'How long has she been out?' Ottilie asked.

'It's hard to say,' Corrine replied. 'I thought she'd gone to bed for a nap. When I went to see if she was still asleep, the bed was empty – but I didn't see her go out.'

'And she hasn't answered her phone?'

Damien held one up, and Ottilie went cold at the sight. She didn't need to ask who the phone belonged to, and now that she saw it, she realised just why everyone looked so worried.

'Want us to help?' she asked.

'Lass…' Victor began, but she silenced him with a frown.

'What I meant to say was, we're here to help. Let us know what you want us to do.'

'I think we should split up,' Victor said. 'See if we can't spot her wandering somewhere. She hasn't taken a car, so she can't have got too far.'

'Sounds like a good idea.' Damien was doing his best to keep it together. He was trying to be calm and authoritative and acting as if everyone present didn't recognise that he was a part of the problem. Ottilie could see it in his eyes, in his body language, in the way he forced himself to be vocal when it was clear he wanted to stay quiet. He felt responsible for Melanie's disappearance, and the truth was, no matter how they were pulling together right now to find her, everyone agreed that he was. Even Ottilie, who couldn't possibly hold it against him, could see that he'd played his part.

'What if we go and look around the village?' Stacey suggested.

'We've already been up and down the streets,' Corrine said.

'Still,' Penny said, 'she might have doubled back, and now there are more of us, we can make sure. Me and Mum will do that.'

'We'll head up towards Hilltop,' Ottilie said. 'She might have gone to see Ann.'

She could see in Corrine's expression that the possibility of Melanie being at Ann's place was doubtful, but it had to be worth a try.

'I'll go along the river,' Leon said.

Damien nodded. 'Want me to go with you?'

'Maybe go out towards Windermere. She might be on the road.'

Victor looked at Leon. 'The river's too big to do by yourself. We'll do it between us.'

Everyone agreed to keep in touch and then fanned out to start searching.

'This isn't what I had in mind when I said I would go for a walk with you,' Stacey said as they began the climb up to Hilltop Farm.

'It wasn't exactly what I had in mind either,' Ottilie agreed. 'Do you think she's all right?'

'Who knows? She hasn't been herself, has she? Not for a good few weeks.'

'I didn't realise things were this bad, though.'

'Joke's on us if she's in Ann's kitchen having a brew and we're all up and down looking for her.'

'I presume Corrine rang the neighbours first of all. Honestly, I doubt she'll be at the farm, but we have to start somewhere, don't we?'

'Don't you have Ann's number?'

'Yes, but Corrine—'

Stacey stopped on the path. 'Call anyway. It's got to be worth a minute just to see if she's turned up there since Corrine checked.'

Ottilie got out her phone and dialled Ann's number, but there was no reply. She locked it again with a shrug. 'She's not in.'

'That's weird,' Stacey said. 'She hardly goes anywhere.'

'Well, if she's in, she's not near her phone. So there's someone else for me to worry about now.'

They continued to trudge the steep path. The further up they went, the steeper and more uneven it became. Ottilie knew it well, but even though she went to Hilltop most mornings, she still struggled. It was almost as if the urgency in the situation was adding to the burden, testing her limits. She hoped to find Melanie up there, in Ann's kitchen, with some mad excuse for why nobody had answered the phone, but not for a second did she think it likely.

After a minute or two where she and Stacey had fallen silent, it started to rain. Stacey groaned and then pulled the plastic theme-park poncho from her pocket.

'At least you've got something,' Ottilie said, zipping her own raincoat up. 'Let's hope Melanie has too, if she's out in this.'

. . .

They were close to the top when Ottilie spotted a figure hurrying towards them. It was a woman but too far away to recognise. For a moment, she held her breath, praying that it would be Melanie. And then was almost disappointed to see it was Ann, until she got closer and could see the same worry in Ann's face as she'd seen in Corrine's earlier.

'Am I glad to see you!' Ann panted. She was in a woollen cardigan, and her hair was wet from the rain. She looked as if she'd left the house in a rush. 'I can't find Darryl! You haven't seen him on the way up, have you?'

'Darryl?' Ottilie's forehead creased into a deep frown. 'No. We can help you look if you're worried.'

'He never goes anywhere without me. I can't imagine what would have made him leave the house and not tell me.'

'We're looking for Melanie,' Stacey said. 'We might as well look for the both of them while we're up here. I'm beginning to think something weird is happening around here,' she added, though Ann didn't react to the joke. She only nodded.

'Could you? I'd appreciate it.'

'I take it you've searched all the obvious places he might be?' Ottilie asked.

'Oh, yes. It would only be the outbuildings anyway.'

'There's nowhere else you can think of?'

'No.'

Ottilie paused. This new development had changed things. Harsh as it seemed, right now she was more concerned for Darryl than Melanie. His difficulties meant he didn't function like other boys his age. If he was lost, he'd be stressed and possibly out of control. He couldn't think his way out of situations like others did, and the world outside his home scared him so much he rarely left it. He needed safety and security. She couldn't imagine what had tempted him out of the house to disappear like this. As for Melanie, there was a cry for help all right, but there were lots of people out looking for her and she was, at least – Ottilie hoped – a functioning adult. For all they knew, she'd simply taken herself out for a walk and left her phone behind for some privacy.

'Is it worth checking the fields past the woods?' she asked.

'I don't know if he'd be there, but I don't have any better ideas.'

'What about the other side of the hill?' Stacey asked.

'The path that goes to the river?'

Stacey nodded. 'Why don't I take that one? You and Ottilie check over by the woods. Phone me if you find anything.'

'You'll be all right?' Ottilie asked. 'I daren't let you out of my sight in case we lose you too.'

'I'll be fine – I'll stay in touch.' She looked at the sky. 'The sooner we sort this mess, the sooner we can get out of the rain.'

Ottilie didn't like them splitting up, but it made sense. She let Stacey march off in one direction, while she and Ann headed to a loose gathering of tall trees, hardly a wood at all, really. It was surrounded by fields owned by Hilltop, but since the death of Ann's husband, they had lain fallow, Ann unable to farm them by herself. They were now overgrown with wild grass and flowers, and followed the contours of the land so that there would be hollows where it might be difficult to see someone walking. The boundaries were marked by low stone walls, some with sections crumbling or even missing entirely. Ann kept apologising for the state of her property, as if Ottilie somehow disapproved, and Ottilie couldn't help but reflect on how surreal the situation was. Two people were missing – one her vulnerable son – and she was explaining why she hadn't been able to cut the grass. Looking past the anxious chatter, however, Ottilie could see that Ann was scared and it was the only way to take her mind off her fears.

As they left a dip and walked onto a higher section, more of the walls became visible. And then Ottilie saw a flash of blue. She glanced to her side to see Ann had noticed it too.

'Darryl!' she cried, her stride quickening.

Ottilie kept pace as they dashed over the uneven ground, doing her best to watch where she was going. With her gaze on her feet as often as it was ahead, she was taken completely by surprise when a second figure appeared and climbed onto the wall to join Darryl.

'Is that Melanie?'

'Darryl!' Ann shouted. This time her son turned around. He didn't wave; he simply sat on the wall and watched her approach.

When they reached them, Ottilie noticed that Darryl was in a raincoat and wellies. It seemed he'd intended to go out and had prepared. Melanie, on the other hand, was in a soaking blouse, some tracksuit bottoms and was barefoot apart from some discoloured, mud-caked socks.

'Darryl!' Ann huffed, pulling him into an unwanted hug. 'What are you doing? I've been looking everywhere for you!'

He pointed at Melanie. 'It was raining.'

'It's still raining!' Ottilie looked at Melanie. 'Are you all right? People are looking for you too.'

'Are they?'

'Yes. Your mum and dad are worried. They couldn't find you, and you left your phone there.'

'I went for a walk.'

'I can see that.'

She couldn't quite work out the connection between Melanie's impromptu walk and Darryl wandering off, but for the moment she was happy both had been found safe and well. At least, as well as could be expected. Perhaps it wasn't quite the word for the state Melanie was in right now, but she seemed physically unharmed, thank God.

'I've been all right,' Melanie added. 'Darryl's been keeping me company.'

Ann frowned from one to the other, and Ottilie could

imagine her surprise. Darryl didn't really do social situations. He didn't go and chat with people of his own accord, but something had drawn him to Melanie. It didn't explain why he'd gone out, though. Had he noticed her wandering and gone to investigate?

'I'd better phone Stacey,' Ottilie said. 'And text the others just to let them know they can relax.' She looked at Ann. 'Are we all right to go back to yours? Melanie can dry out, and Corrine and Victor can pick her up from there, if it's OK with you.'

'Of course,' Ann said, taking Darryl gently by the arm. 'I'll get a pot of tea on.' She glanced at Melanie, her face full of sympathy. 'We can have a chat while we wait.'

Ann lit a fire and sat Melanie next to it and then bustled in the kitchen. She was clearly as perplexed as Ottilie at the events of the day, but she was so happy to have Darryl safe at home again that she didn't seem as if she was going to let it worry her. Darryl was at the kitchen table with a mug of hot blackcurrant juice, looking at a book. Ottilie was sitting with Melanie.

'Would it help to talk?' she asked.

Melanie turned to her with a vague shrug. 'What is there to say? You know it all.'

'What about today? You really just went for a walk?'

'Yes.'

'With no shoes or coat?'

'I forgot them.'

'You weren't...' Ottilie paused, wondering whether to ask her next question. 'You weren't planning to do anything... you know. Anything that wouldn't end well for you?'

'What do you mean?'

'Never mind.'

Melanie stared into the yellow flames of the newly built fire.

The wood was still damp, and tendrils of black smoke unfurled into the chimney. 'I've lost him for good, haven't I?'

'He's been out looking for you.'

'Only because he feels guilty. If something did happen to me, he'd only care because it made him look bad.'

'I don't think that's true.'

'It's my fault.'

'It's nobody's fault.'

'It's mine.'

Ottilie wondered what had changed. For the past couple of weeks she'd been only too happy to point the finger at Fion for the collapse of her marriage. Damien too, and even Ottilie at one point, but this was something new. Something had made her re-evaluate. Something she'd been denying until now?

There was a lot Ottilie didn't know, and perhaps would never know, but one thing was clear – Melanie needed help. Fliss had requested an intervention, but after today Ottilie was convinced they would have to upgrade it to urgent because she needed that help now, not a few months down the line. When she got back to work, she'd speak to her and fill her in.

There was a knock at the door, and a moment later Stacey came in. Ottilie couldn't help but smile at the daft plastic poncho she was still wearing.

'All's well that ends well then,' she said cheerily, studying Melanie as she did.

'Yes,' Ottilie said. 'Victor and Corrine are on their way over.'

'So, Ann says it was Darryl who saved the day.'

Ottilie nodded. The funny thing was, Darryl had saved the day, and he wouldn't have even known it. He'd seen Melanie go past the window, and something about it had intrigued him enough to go out and follow her. He'd been quizzing her on what she was doing when they'd found him and Melanie on the wall. Ann had been as puzzled about his behaviour as Ottilie, and when they'd asked him what had made him go out, other than seeing Melanie, he hadn't been able to give them an answer. At least, he hadn't seemed very interested in giving them an answer. It appeared his adventure had been too much, and the first thing he'd wanted to do when he got back was sit at the table with some juice and look at his beloved train books.

Stacey pulled off her poncho and sat down. 'So much for our walk. Do you think Victor will give us a lift home?'

'I think he might have other things to worry about,' Ottilie said, watching Melanie as she stared into the fire. 'I'll see how close Heath is, if you really want a lift.'

'Simon might be free,' Stacey said. 'I'll call him.'

CHAPTER TWENTY-FIVE

If Ottilie hadn't known Chloe was pregnant, she wouldn't have been able to tell. Keeping a promise to Stacey to make up for the evening that had been hijacked by the search for Melanie, she'd gone round there after finishing work and grabbing a quick shower, feeling exhausted, as she always seemed to be these days. Simon and Heath would join them at some point for a drink at the pub.

'She's going to get taken away,' Chloe said. 'In one of those jacket things that have buckles on to hold your arms. That's what I heard.'

'You ought to know you shouldn't believe everything you hear,' Stacey said briskly as she bounced Mackenzie on her knee. 'Especially not in this village.'

Chloe stretched to take up the entire length of the sofa, shrugged and went back to her phone. Stacey frowned from the opposite armchair.

'I'd better go to talk to her when I get time,' Ottilie said. 'I told Victor and Corrine to let me know if they needed my help.'

'They must be managing then,' Stacey said.

'It doesn't sound like it. Who told you she went missing for hours on the hills?' Ottilie asked Chloe, who simply looked up from her phone and shrugged again.

'Don't know.'

'You must have some idea.'

'I think I heard someone say it at the playgroup. She's lost the plot.'

'I wouldn't worry about it,' Stacey said. She reached for her phone and unlocked it to show Ottilie a website. 'I found this shop. It's in Sheffield – a bit far I know, but look at these dresses!'

Ottilie took the phone. She thumbed through images of tulle and silk fairy tales. Some were white and some were muted pastel colours.

'The prices aren't too bad either, considering,' Stacey said.

'Am I going to be a bridesmaid too?' Chloe asked.

'I haven't worked out the budget for dresses yet,' Ottilie said, hoping that would be enough of a hint to tell Chloe that she didn't have the money for more than two – and that they would be Stacey and Fion.

'Oh.' Chloe went back to her phone. She typed rapidly. Ottilie assumed she was messaging Oliver.

Ottilie handed the phone back to Stacey.

'You don't like them?' Stacey asked.

'They're lovely. I'm struggling to concentrate right now, that's all. Can we look again another day?'

'We could drive over there if you get a day off.'

'That sounds nice.'

'Does it?' Stacey asked. 'You don't seem keen.'

'I'm sorry...' Ottilie sighed. 'It's just all this stuff. Do you think I ought to go and see Melanie anyway?'

'And do what?'

'Not a clue. I feel as if I ought to at least try.'

There was a knock at the door. Stacey put Mackenzie on

the floor with a pile of toys and got up. A moment later, she returned with Heath and Simon.

'I don't think Ottilie wants to go,' Stacey said.

'I didn't say that.' Ottilie got up.

'You didn't have to.'

Simon glanced at Stacey and then back to Ottilie. 'Listen, we can do the pub any night. If you two want to... well, if you need to do other things, we don't mind, do we, Stacey?'

'But I don't—'

'Honestly, it's all right,' Stacey said. She turned to Heath. 'Take her home, will you? She looks knackered.'

'Come on,' Heath said gently. 'They're right. You should have phoned me; I would have told you to have a quiet one – we could have given it a miss tonight.'

'I don't want to give it a miss, but maybe a quiet one is a good idea.' Ottilie sent a look of apology to Stacey and Simon. 'I'm sorry—'

'Don't be daft!' Stacey smiled. 'Call me – we'll rearrange. Go home and get some rest.'

Heath and Ottilie stepped out onto the pavement. 'You don't mind not going to the pub with them?' Ottilie asked as she slipped her arm through his.

'Of course I don't. It was only a casual arrangement; we can do it any time, can't we?'

'I thought you might have something to say about me letting circumstances get the better of me.'

'They're bound to.'

'You haven't said anything to your gran, have you? About her having a go at Fion?'

'No. I've thought about it, but you're right – what's the point? She won't think she's done anything wrong.'

'And she's not the only one saying things. Chloe just told us people at the playgroup were saying things about Melanie going off the rails.'

'You did find her wandering the hills in her socks,' he said. 'Most would say that's going off the rails.'

'But if it's what people are saying, it's not fair – especially not to Victor and Corrine.'

'Or you,' he said, concern etched into his features as he looked down at her.

'I'm all right.'

'Liar.'

'I'm more worried for Fion.'

'To be honest, as time goes on, I'm worried for her too.'

Ottilie was about to reply when she felt him stiffen beside her. And then, before she could stop him, he marched towards a figure across the street. Ottilie reached out to grab his arm, but he shook her off. 'I want a word with you!'

Damien turned in surprise. He may not have known what Heath's problem was, but he couldn't have mistaken the fact that there was one, or that he was at the centre of it. 'Heath...?'

'What the hell are you playing at?'

'I don't know what you mean.'

'Don't you? Do you want me to spell it out? You' – he prodded a shocked-looking Damien in the chest – 'causing trouble. Worrying Ottilie. Taking advantage of her sister. Take your pick. It's got to stop.'

Damien backed away, hands in the air in a gesture of surrender. 'I'm not trying to cause trouble, and I'm not looking for it.'

'If you don't back off and leave Fion alone, you're going to get it.'

'Heath, I don't have an argument with you – why are you starting one with me?'

'I just told you why!'

'You don't understand—'

'I understand all right. Your marriage is on the rocks and along comes a good-looking girl who thinks you're all that and you take advantage. You think, why not? My missus isn't interested in me. Well, she's the one getting all the grief around here, and you're sitting pretty in your house up the hill out of the way. She comes home crying, and me and Ottilie have to pick up the pieces. It has to stop.'

'Or what?'

'Don't make me show you.'

'Heath,' Ottilie pleaded, her voice low as she checked out who might be on the street to see. 'That's enough. This isn't going to help.'

'It is.'

Both Ottilie and Heath turned to Damien with surprise.

'It does help,' he repeated. 'I suppose this is what everyone thinks? I'm the older man leading an innocent girl astray? I'm using her, having a bit of fun on the side because my wife isn't interested in me? That maybe Fion is the reason my marriage is in tatters? Is that what everyone thinks?'

'Are you surprised?' Heath asked. 'You must know that's how it looks.'

'I suppose I do, but I'd hoped the people of this village would be more open-minded. I should have known they wouldn't be.'

'There's open-minded and then there's open-minded,' Heath replied. 'You're trying to say people have it wrong?'

'Yes. You live with Fion. Surely you know how it is?'

'She only tells us so much,' Ottilie said, ignoring a look of warning from Heath. 'It might help us to hear it from you.'

She supposed Heath was doing the macho thing, wanting to be the fixer, wanting to protect his lady and her sister. While she appreciated that it came from a place of love, she didn't appreciate how patronising she found it. She hadn't asked for Heath to defend her honour like this, nor Fion's when it came to it. They were both perfectly capable of defending their own. She also felt she knew enough of Damien to see there was more to this than Heath was assuming. She'd heard what Fion had to say, her defence of Damien, which Heath – along with the rest of the village – hadn't given any credence to. She thought Damien deserved to tell his side of the story too. 'You must have known how people around here would react to what's going on with you and Melanie, and how Fion's now involved. It looks bad.'

'It only looks bad because nobody has bothered to find out what the truth is. Mel's going around telling people this and that, making me out to be the villain, making out like Fion is a victim, like I'm some degenerate or something, but it's not like that. Mel started this. She was the one who had an affair, last year.'

Ottilie stared at him. She glanced quickly at Heath and could see the shock in his face too. 'Is that true?'

'Why would I say it otherwise? She'd have left me, if it weren't for the fact he wouldn't leave his wife. We decided to give things another go, but it's not as easy as saying you'll try to get back to what you had before. When the trust is gone, it's only a matter of time before everything else falls apart. Our marriage was already over long before Fion arrived – we were just making a show of keeping it going.'

'Why? What good does that do?'

'I don't even know why – it seemed easier, I suppose. There's the house on Victor's land, and the farm…'

'It doesn't change what you've done to Fion,' Heath said. 'You're older – you should have known better.'

'I'm older, yes, but there are bigger age gaps, and Fion's not a child. She can make up her own mind about who she wants to be with. I don't get why it's such a problem to everyone.'

'Melanie's struggling,' Ottilie said, and Damien grimaced.

'I know. Do you think I don't feel guilty about that? I still care about her. I care about Corrine and Victor too, but what can I do? I didn't want any of this.'

'But your intentions are genuine?' Ottilie asked. Fion had said as much, and now she felt like she was the patronising one for not taking her sister seriously. Despite the way they'd gone about things, Damien was right. Fion was a grown woman with her own mind – she'd said it enough times to others, so why did she have such a hard time believing it for herself?

'Of course they are!' Damien threw his hands in the air. 'What did you think? All this trouble and you're asking me if I'm genuine? Of course I am! I want to be with her more than anything!'

'You're not saying that because we're here confronting you?' Heath asked.

'Throw a punch if it will make you feel better,' Damien said in a withering tone. 'It's obvious you're itching to. Beat me to a pulp – it won't make any difference. Believe me or don't, but my feelings for Fion are genuine. I care for her, and she cares for me.'

'You care for her?' Heath said. 'That's all very well. I cared for a cat I had when I was fourteen.'

'Do you love her?' Ottilie asked.

'To put up with all this?' Damien said. 'I suppose I must do. Yes, then, since you're asking, I love her.'

Ottilie had no reply. Faced with his words, she didn't understand how she'd misjudged his intentions so badly. Perhaps the pressure from a disapproving community, or the misplaced desire to protect a younger sister who was capable of protecting herself had coloured her judgement. Why had she found it so hard to believe that what Damien and Fion had was genuine? Was it because she thought herself older and wiser than Fion? Again, she had to conclude that her actions had been horribly patronising. If someone had treated her in the same way, she'd have been angry and offended. And yet Fion had been patient and understanding, even when she was trying to offer an explanation that was only falling on deaf ears.

'Neither of us thought it was going to be easy,' Damien continued. 'We both knew there would be people who'd take a dim view of what we were doing. What I didn't count on was how hypocritical Melanie would be. If you want someone to blame for the village being turned inside out over this, she's where you want to look.'

'I'm not sure that's fair,' Ottilie said. 'She might have made a mistake before, and she might be the reason the trouble in your marriage began, but she's going through her own pain.'

'I'm sorry; you're right,' Damien said. 'And what makes me sad is what it's doing to her family as well. We were all close once. They're still speaking to me, and I don't think they blame me, but it's never going to be the same.'

'Do you want me to talk to Melanie?' Ottilie asked.

Damien shook his head. 'No point. She doesn't want to listen. In some ways, I think it's best to let her have her version. Let her believe that's how it is, if it makes her feel better. My reputation's already in the gutter – there's not much further down I can go, so why worry? I'll be the villain if that's what she needs, as long as she leaves Fion alone.'

'What are you going to do?' Heath asked, and Ottilie could tell from his tone that he felt as guilty about his treatment of Damien as she did. 'You can't carry on as you are.'

'I'm going to talk to Fion. If she wants to, we could look at moving away.'

Ottilie's eyes widened. 'Leave Thimblebury? But you've just got your business up and running! What about that? And Fion? She's only just moved in with me, and I...'

Ottilie wanted to say that she didn't feel she even knew her sister properly yet, that she'd miss her, but then she was forced to remember that it wasn't about her.

'It's not what I want,' Damien said. 'But if it's what we have to do, then...' His sentence trailed off. There was no need for him to finish it because they all knew the reality.

'Perhaps it's for the best,' Heath said. 'Even if it's only temporary until the dust settles. People have got short memories and they'll soon move on. Then you can come back.'

'I don't know about that,' Damien replied ruefully. 'People might have short memories, but I don't know if mine is short enough to forget what happened here. There's Victor and Corrine too. Do they want to be reminded of all this trouble every time they see me and Fion around the village? It's a small place, too small to avoid one another for long.'

'They're not the sort of people to hold a grudge,' Ottilie said.

'It's not what I'm saying.' He shook his head slowly. 'There must be a bit of you that thinks your life would be easier without all this too.'

Ottilie exchanged a loaded glance with Heath. It was obvious he was thinking the same as her – there was no denying that life would be easier for them.

'It's not about us,' Ottilie said. 'You know we'll support you, whatever you decide.'

Damien looked at Heath. 'So you've changed your mind about knocking my block off now?'

'I'm sorry,' Heath said. 'You have to understand—'

Damien halted him. 'I'd have probably done the same.' He held out a hand, and Heath paused before shaking it. 'I'm sorry for all the trouble this has brought to your door.' He looked at Ottilie, and she forced a smile. 'You have to believe this wasn't what I wanted. I want to do right by Fion, though, and if you have concerns about that, you don't need to have.'

Ottilie nodded and pulled at Heath. Damien had talked of leaving Thimblebury with Fion, but the way she was feeling right now, perhaps she and Heath ought to think about it too.

CHAPTER TWENTY-SIX

Ottilie frowned at the message. Joanna Maidstone – she hadn't heard that name in a long time. Joanna had been the matron in charge of the ward Ottilie had been working on when she'd lost Josh. They'd never had much to do with one another socially, although they'd got along well at work. They'd exchanged a few brief messages after Ottilie had moved away from Manchester but not for a long time now. Wondering what on earth she could want, Ottilie opened it up and started to read.

'Everything all right?' Heath asked. He was lying beside her, pillows propping him up as he watched a movie on his laptop. 'You've gone quiet. I don't like it when you're quiet – you're supposed to be talking over the top of my film.'

'Cheeky,' Ottilie said, vaguely recognising she was meant to react to a joke he'd made but absorbed by Joanna's message.

'What is it then?'

'I don't know yet. Give me a minute...'

She was silent again, and Heath paused the action to wait for her. When she was finished, she locked the screen of her phone.

'I've just been offered a job.'

'You've got a job.'

'In Manchester.'

'Manchester?'

'It's a good one too. Clinical nurse specialist. I mean, when I say offered, I've been told I *really* should apply, which means she really wants me but can't say so. Reading between the lines, if I went for it, then I'd get it. Good money too. Very good money. She'd put me on the top of the pay band.'

'This is all great, but surely you don't want to start commuting to Manchester. Especially not now I'm getting ready to move here.'

'You wouldn't have to move at all if I took it, would you? And you could take your promotion. We could live in Manchester.'

Heath closed his laptop and sat up. 'You're serious? But you love it here, and you love working at the surgery.'

'Yes, but I can't deny things have got sticky since Fion started this business with Damien. Some people have shown their true colours, and I feel as if… well, somehow I feel like the villain, even though I've done nothing wrong except bring her here.'

'There's nothing wrong with that.'

'You'd think, wouldn't you?' She opened the message and read it again. 'It's tempting.'

'I never thought I'd hear you say that. You can't really be thinking of putting in an application?'

'I don't know. Part of me thinks there's no harm in it. If I don't get it, then I was wrong about how badly she wants me for her department. It's weird timing, isn't it? Feels as if there's a reason it's come through now.'

'And if you do? If you get the job, what then?'

'Then I can think about it.'

'Leave yourself with an impossible choice, more like. I know you – you'll drive yourself mad agonising over it. And whatever decision you make, you'll torture yourself afterwards worrying it was the wrong one. As for leaving Thimblebury...' He shook his head. 'I don't see it.'

'I've loved being here, but when I arrived, I was broken and lonely. This village was what I needed back then. But now... Now I have you. If you're with me, I can live anywhere and be happy. Thimblebury, right now, doesn't even feel like the same place that was so good to me when I first arrived. Everyone's at odds, and somehow I seem to be caught up in it all.'

'That will pass.'

'It will, I'm sure. But it's so stressful I don't know if I have the energy to ride it out until it does pass. Living here at the moment feels like hard work. And I'm sure it looks like running away, but I don't care. I hate seeing this place the way it's become – it's ruining the memories of the good times I've had here. And think about it – this might be the perfect timing, regardless of anything else. It will be easier for you to do your new role if we're both living in Manchester. If I'm working there, we can see a lot more of one another than we'll be doing if I stay here.'

Heath put his laptop to one side and slid down the pillow to lie next to her. 'You'd really be up for this?'

'Yes... I think. I don't know. There's a lot to think about, but I don't feel I want to say no straight off.'

'It would be amazing.' He smiled. 'Not that I don't like it here – I do, it's great, but you're right: life would be easier without all the back and forth. I'm not sure Gran would agree, but...'

'She will *not* be impressed,' Ottilie said. 'I'm sure she'll never forgive either of us. Other than that, it does feel like a bit of a magic bullet, doesn't it? All our problems here sorted in one fell swoop.'

'Not sorted, but out of reach, that's for sure.' He paused,

studying her for a moment. 'I know you, though. Doesn't it feel a bit like running away?'

'I don't know when that ever stopped me. I ran away from Manchester in the first place – that's what brought me here. And it didn't end too badly, did it?'

'No,' he said, kissing her lightly. 'I don't think it did. Not for me, in any case.'

He pulled her into his arms, and she lay wrapped in his embrace. Thimblebury had been very good to her for so many reasons. Perhaps returning to Manchester would feel like running away, but it wasn't as if she could never come back to visit. Her patients would be sad, some of them upset even, but when she'd first arrived, they'd felt that way about their previous nurse, Gwen, and that had passed as they'd got used to Ottilie. It would pass again once her replacement had settled in. Fliss would be upset, but surely she'd understand, and, besides, she didn't have so many years to go until she retired, and then she'd be the one leaving the surgery. She thought about all her friends. She'd miss them, but they'd all understand too, wouldn't they?

If anyone had told her she'd feel this way, even a month ago, she'd have laughed in their face. But, perhaps, regardless of the job, it was time to move on anyway.

It had been a couple of months since Ottilie had visited her mum in Manchester. They'd kept in regular contact over the phone and via messages, but life had been hectic. Francine had been only too pleased to hear that Ottilie planned to drive over that weekend, and Ottilie felt guilty for not warning her of the reasons for such a sudden house call.

'You've had new curtains,' Ottilie said as she walked into the living room.

Her hair was greyer than the last time Ottilie had seen her

too, but there was good reason for that. It was naturally an ashy brown – a colour her mum had called mousey – and over the years she'd dyed it various colours, but during the previous twelve months, she'd read an article about toxins in hair dye and had stopped. Now the last application was almost out and it was a pretty palette of greys and whites. She was slimmer than Ottilie, which she had always been too, petite and almost fragile looking now she was older. The trousers she was wearing looked a little too big around the hips, but they were stylish.

'Been to the church jumble sale recently?' Ottilie asked.

'Oh yes, actually,' Francine said. She smoothed a hand down the front of her trousers. 'Picked these up yesterday. They're a good brand, hardly worn. And the curtains too.'

'They look nice,' Ottilie said. 'The trousers and the curtains.'

'I thought it was time for a refresh. Do you want a drink? Something to eat?' She ran a critical gaze over her daughter. 'You look like you've lost weight. I hope you're not skipping meals like you used to at the hospital.'

'We always sit down together for lunch at the surgery. Trust me, I'm eating more than enough.'

'I can't think why you look thinner then.'

'I don't think I am.'

'Shall I make us a sandwich before we go to the cemetery? You might get hungry while we're out. I've got some tuna in. The bread's fresh.'

'I can wait. I'd rather go now and eat later.'

Francine looked as if she might argue but then nodded. 'I'll get my coat.'

Ottilie was glad her mum was taking fresh flowers regularly. Josh's grave was well tended and looked well loved, although there was guilt too, that her life these days made it hard for her to come. It almost felt as if she was betraying Josh, though she was sure he'd never have seen it that way.

'They look nice,' she said, adding her own to a spare vase. 'Thanks for picking them up for me.'

'I thought it would save time.' Francine peered closely at her. 'You don't look well to me. A bit pale.'

'Thanks,' Ottilie said with a half laugh. 'It's nice to know I can rely on my mum to make me feel good about myself.'

'I didn't mean anything by it, but you do look tired. If I can't tell you, who can?'

'It's been hectic.'

'With your half-sister?'

'With a lot of things,' Ottilie said, still wondering if telling her mum the whole saga about Fion and Damien had been the right thing to do. 'Heath and I have been talking...' she continued, wondering if this was a good idea too. 'We might be coming back to Manchester.'

Francine stared at her. 'I thought you loved it where you are? You said it was your forever home.'

'It was, but things have changed. Heath's working his notice so he can take his promotion, and I've had a job offer at the hospital here, and things have been... well, they're not the same as they used to be.'

'I'd love to have you back,' Francine said. 'As long as you're sure it would make you happier.'

'You don't think it will?'

'I don't know. I hear how you talk about it. When you first went, I was devastated, but as time went on, I could see how good it was for you. I would hate to think you'd stop and take a breath in a year or so and realise you'd made the wrong choice.'

'Of course I'm going to miss it, but I think it's the right choice. It's the most practical one, in any case.'

'Yes,' Francine said wryly, 'because practical always makes us happy, doesn't it?'

CHAPTER TWENTY-SEVEN

It was hard to fathom how such a small house could take so long to clean, and when Ottilie had finished, it still didn't seem enough. She kept on top of it as much as she could from week to week, of course, as most people did. But having it clean and tidy enough to live in was one thing, and showing it to an estate agent – who would probably want photos to list it – was another thing entirely. Even so, when she'd finished, she was so tired she could happily have crawled into bed for a sleep. One thing she wasn't going to get was sleep, however. After this – which she'd taken time off from work for, swearing Lavender to secrecy to organise it – she had a full clinic and it would probably overrun.

Fion was out, and Ottilie had planned it that way. She couldn't say why, but she hadn't yet told Fion of her plans to sell up and move back to Manchester. She didn't want Fion to feel it was somehow as a consequence of things she'd done, and she didn't want to have to break the news that Fion would either have to go to Manchester with her or make some other arrangements, but there was more to it than that. Perhaps because, despite discussions with Heath and an agreement that she'd apply for the nurse specialist post and that they'd take his job offer and hers as a sign that they were meant to return to Manchester together, Ottilie had still to tell anyone else. Saying it out loud like that felt too hard and made it a real fact she wasn't altogether ready to face. Whenever she'd thought about it, her mind had gone back to the many wonderful things that Thimblebury and its residents had given her, and she knew it was going to be hard to let go of such an amazing place.

The knock at the door came bang on time. Ottilie opened up to find a woman of around fifty on the doorstep.

'Ottilie?' she asked, sticking out a hand anyway.

'Yes. Ali?'

'Pleased to meet you. I hope you don't mind, but I've just had a snoop around from the outside. This is a gorgeous property. I took a few photos too – while the sun's out and it's looking extra lovely. I can delete them, of course, if you decide not to list.'

'I'm quite sure I will list,' Ottilie said, opening up and beckoning her inside. 'My fiancé has been offered a job in Manchester and the commute is probably going to be too much.'

'You'll have no trouble selling. Properties here are hot. I doubt it'll even make the website before someone snaps your hand off for it. You'll get more than your asking price too, I'm sure.'

'That's good to hear,' Ottilie said, trying to sound pleased but not feeling it. Hearing the estate agent talk about Wordsworth Cottage like that made her feel sad, almost as if she were betraying the little house that had changed her life.

As they went from room to room, Ali cooed and ahhed and made enthusiastic comments about this little detail or that little selling point, on how pretty and well maintained it was, what a perfect location and how confident she was that Ottilie wouldn't have to wait long for an eager buyer.

'The floor in here is stunning.' Ali gave it a once-over before getting out a device to measure the room. 'Did you put it in?'

Ottilie nodded. 'Shortly after I moved in.'

She didn't mention the flood that had almost sent her packing once before, but Ali's comment about the floor brought back vivid memories of laying it, of friends from all over the village coming to help, of the fun they'd had despite the hardship of the event, of Heath helping with the woodwork, sending looks of longing that she'd still to recognise her way. He'd sat on the bare boards with her for hours while she'd wept over Josh, and he'd comforted her without asking for anything in return.

A knot of sadness pushed up into her throat. This house was so special. What she'd said to Heath was true – she could make anywhere home if he was there, but it didn't change the fact that Wordsworth Cottage had been the most perfect home before he'd come into her life. She tried to tell herself that it was silly to get sentimental over bricks and mortar, but as she looked around the room, at the floor her neighbours had laid and the walls she and Heath had painted together, it was hard not to.

Ali snapped a few more photos from different angles and then handed Ottilie a business card. 'I'll email you when I've put together a mock listing and worked out a definite valuation. All you have to do then is let me know if you want to go ahead. I hope you do – we've already got clients waiting who are looking for something exactly like this.'

'Thank you.'

Ottilie saw her out and waved her off. Once the car was gone, she closed the door, but it hadn't quite shut when she heard a voice calling from outside. She opened up again to see Flo storming down the path, shoulders hunched and head forward as if she was planning to batter her way in.

'Who was that?'

'Who?' Ottilie asked, knowing full well who Flo was talking about.

'That car – it said estate agent on it. You're selling up!'

'We haven't decided yet,' Ottilie began, ushering Flo inside.

But Flo folded her arms and stubbornly stuck to the outside step, glaring at her. 'Nobody told me!'

'That's because there's nothing to tell yet.'

'They don't come round for nothing. How much are you going to make?'

'I have no idea,' Ottilie said patiently. 'It's not about money.'

'Isn't it? A fast buck – that's all everyone wants nowadays. Strangers come, they buy our houses and then sell them for a profit, and before you know it, the village is full of strangers!'

'I'm not a stranger.'

'You were once.'

'Lives change. What you wanted or needed once isn't always what you want or need forever.' Ottilie glanced up and down the street. 'Come in, Flo. I've got to be at work in half an hour, but have a cup of tea and we'll talk about it properly.'

'So you can persuade me not to make a fuss.'

'So I can explain to you what's happening. It's not just about me or the village or even this house.'

Flo continued to glower at Ottilie. But after a moment she relented and stepped over the threshold.

'Heath's got a promotion at work,' Ottilie began as Flo followed her to the kitchen.

'I know that. He told me that ages ago. He never said anything about moving away. He said you were both going to live here when you got married.'

'We were, and we thought we could make that work, but now I have the opportunity of a new job in Manchester too, with a boss I worked for a while back, helping to establish a new service at the hospital. It looks like an amazing role, and I'd like to try it. If I get it, then it makes sense for us to go back to Manchester. What's the use in us both rushing back and forth every day when life could be easier living where we both work?'

Flo's mouth fell open as she stood at the kitchen doorway. 'You're leaving the surgery?'

'I don't know. None of this is in stone yet, but...' Ottilie filled the kettle. 'I'm going to apply for the other job and see what happens.'

'What if you get it?' Flo squeaked.

'Then I'll have to decide what to do.'

Flo was silent for a moment, and Ottilie could see the cogs turning as she worked scenarios through for herself. 'But if you don't get it, you'll both stay in Thimblebury?'

'I don't know if it's that simple. Things are a bit messy here, if we're being honest, aren't they?'

At this, Flo at least had the decency to look slightly ashamed. 'It was all right before your sister arrived.'

'That doesn't change that they're not really all right now.'

'Nobody's got any truck with you.'

'We're still stuck in the middle of it, and sometimes it feels as if people do have a problem with me. Fion's my sister – do you really expect me not to be hurt on her behalf?'

'You barely know her.'

'Doesn't make any difference. I know her enough to know I love her. It hurts to see people whispering about her. She's done nothing wrong. Damien and Melanie were already on rocky ground, and they would have split up without Fion eventually. Everyone seems happy to overlook that little detail.'

'We didn't know that!' Flo said tartly, and Ottilie raised her eyebrows.

'Really? The way gossip flies around this place? Everyone seems to know everything else, so I find it hard to believe nobody knew this.'

'We didn't!' Flo insisted. She folded her arms tight and huffed. 'I suppose that puts a different complexion on things.'

'Good,' Ottilie said. 'Perhaps if you could spread *that* around the village, it might help.'

'It would make you stay?'

'I didn't say that. I think it's only fair, though.' She gestured to a seat. 'Do you want that cup of tea?'

Flo seemed torn and then shook her head. 'No thank you. I'll let you get on.'

Ottilie had been distracted throughout the afternoon clinic. She'd paid attention to her work – she would always be conscientious of that above all else – but when it came to chit-chat with her patients, she didn't have the energy for it. Her mind went over the appointment with the estate agent and Flo's subsequent visit. She could understand why Flo would be upset at the thought of her and Heath leaving Thimblebury. She'd felt abandoned once before by her family and in particular by the grandson she doted on, and she'd been thrilled at the prospect of Heath moving in with Ottilie at Wordsworth Cottage. The situation had taken an about-turn. It wasn't anyone's fault, Ottilie reasoned, simply a result of the circumstances they'd found themselves in, but part of her wondered if she was being too hasty to take the easy way out.

But then, Heath had his promotion and they'd talked it over. Living close to work would be easier for him – easier for both of them – and allow them to spend more time together. He'd been willing to make sacrifices for Ottilie, willing to relocate when it made life easier for her. It was only fair she ought to be willing to do the same for him, wasn't it?

It wasn't often, but today she was glad when she was able to see the last patient out and turn off her computer. With a brief, distracted goodnight to her colleagues, she hurried home.

Fion was in, curled on the sofa with a cushion to her belly watching a soap. She looked up and gave a smile that seemed as vague as the one Ottilie offered in return.

'I'll cook in a minute,' she said before going back to her programme.

She hadn't been to work for Damien for the past week. They'd skulked around, trying to see one another for the odd evening in secret, away from the eyes of the village, but other than that, Fion had kept away. Ottilie could tell that having no work again, being forced to hide, was getting her down. She didn't know what to do to help, other than persuade an entire village that she wasn't a villain after all, and that hadn't gone well so far.

'Don't worry,' Ottilie said. 'I'm not hungry yet. No rush.'

After making a drink, Ottilie sat at the kitchen table and opened her laptop. She looked over the job description for the position she'd been invited to apply for at the hospital, and then she began to work on a personal statement to attach to her application. It had been a long time since she'd had to write one, and every time she constructed a sentence she ended up deleting it to try again. It didn't help that her heart wasn't in it, even though there was a deadline. A few sentences and half an hour later, Fion's voice interrupted her.

'Do you need the table for a while? Because I can use the kitchen later if...'

'No.' Ottilie closed the laptop. 'I'll do this when my brain is working. Let's eat first and I might have a bit more energy.'

'What is it?' Fion asked. 'Something for work?'

'Sort of.'

'Oh. I've been thinking – I suppose I ought to get another job. I don't know where, to be honest. I asked Magnus today about looking after the shop for him, and he said they'd decided not to go to Iceland this year.'

Ottilie wasn't surprised. Even if Magnus had wanted to take Fion up on the offer of cover, things were so fraught in the village, it would have ended up causing more problems than it solved. 'You're not working for Damien now?'

'It's...' Fion let out a sigh. 'He has to move the business somewhere else, so it's not running at the moment. He says he's going to hand the house over to Melanie because it's on her dad's land and he doesn't feel right living there now.'

'Where's he going to go?'

'He doesn't know.'

Ottilie patted the chair next to her, and Fion came to sit. 'You love him, don't you?'

'Yes.'

'And he loves you.'

'You're the first person who says they believe that. Everyone else thinks he's...' Fion's fingers twisted together on the table.

'He's not serious and he's only having fun with you because his marriage has only just ended. I know. People believe what they want to believe. It's hard because most of them have known Melanie her whole life and they've only just met you. Their sympathies are bound to be with her, even if that's not right. It's not what you deserve – you or Damien – but...'

'We'll prove them wrong. They'll see when we're still together years from now. But I don't...'

Ottilie turned to her. 'Don't what?'

'I don't want to leave you, but Damien is going away from here, and...'

'Fion, I would never force you out, but while we're on the subject, I've got something to tell you. I'm putting Wordsworth Cottage up for sale. Heath has his new job in Manchester, and I've been offered... well, there's an opportunity I'm thinking of taking there too.'

'But you love it here!'

'I do, but it just feels like the right time to go.'

'Because of me? Ottilie, I didn't mean to—'

'It's not because of you. It's because sometimes life is telling you it's time to move on, even if you don't want to listen.'

'Then I'll have to leave anyway.'

'I'm so sorry, but yes. If it helps, I'm sure there will be a room for you with us in Manchester.'

'No,' Fion said, staring down as she knotted and unknotted her fingers. 'I'm not your kid – you don't have to find room for me.'

'You'll go back to your parents?'

'Mum wants me to, but no, I don't belong there either. Wherever Damien is going, that's where I'm going to go. I wasn't sure, but now I know your plans, it's a no-brainer. We'll be all right. We'll find a place to live, and we'll get the business running together. You don't have to worry.'

Ottilie smiled. 'I'm not worried. I think you're smarter and more resourceful than anyone realises. But… you know where I am if you need me. At least, you will as soon as I know where I'll be.'

'I won't come back to live with you no matter what happens. I've loved it, but I need to find my own way now. You helped me to get started, and you helped me to see that I'm braver than I thought I was.'

'I don't know how I did that. There's nothing brave about me – I'm the most cautious, sensible person you'll ever meet.'

'I always thought that about myself, but I don't now, and I don't think that about you either. I suppose we're more alike than we realised.'

'That must be it,' Ottilie said. Her smile was tired, but it was full of affection. 'I'll miss not having you around all the time.'

'I'll miss you too, but this is how it's meant to be, isn't it? We couldn't live together for ever anyway, could we?'

'No, I don't suppose we could. Be honest with me – you're not going to follow Damien just to get out of my hair, are you?'

'I'm following him because I want to. People can think what they want, and I know we haven't been together long, but he's everything to me, Ottilie. I don't know how, but I just know he's the one.'

Ottilie nodded. 'I understand. I felt that way about Josh.'

'And Heath?'

'Well...' Ottilie gave a light laugh as she went to the cupboard to get a bottle of wine, which she then put in the fridge. 'That took a bit longer, I have to confess. We didn't exactly see eye to eye in the beginning. But now... yes, now, I know he's the one.'

Fion went to shower, and Ottilie tried again with her job application. Heath was due to arrive in the next hour. She had the wine chilling, and she'd messaged to tell him they'd wait for him so they could all eat together. Ottilie wanted Fion to tell Heath her plans over their meal, so they could all discuss ways to help her.

She wasn't much further on with her statement when she glanced up at the clock to see Heath was running late. Only half an hour, but he'd normally let her know if there was a problem on the roads. She tried not to worry and turned her attention back to the open page on her laptop. And then she began to type.

Why do I want this job?

Why did she want it? She'd been flattered by the offer. It was the best move for her and Heath. She'd wanted a way out. As she sat there, trying to dream up a convincing argument, she was forced to recognise that she was lying to herself. She didn't want the job. She didn't want to leave Thimblebury at all. Even if Fion hadn't been leaving, even if things continued to be as difficult as they'd been, when it came to the day where she'd have to hand the keys of Wordsworth Cottage to someone else, would she be able to do it? Her gaze ran over the kitchen, warm peachy walls and solid wooden furniture, rescued stone floors and windows dressed in pretty curtains. And then her thoughts went to the majestic hills and vast, sparkling lakes just outside her front door, and she didn't know if she could.

Ottilie closed the laptop again, elbows on the table, chin resting on her fist as she stared into space. Maybe she had too much on her mind to write this statement tonight. Better to wait until the morning, perhaps, when she'd be fresh and her head would be clearer. She was tired, that was all.

Tired again. She'd had a lot on, but it didn't seem right. Something else had been bothering her too. Something was late, something unexpected. She'd had her suspicions, but she'd shrugged them off. She was beginning to wonder if she was in denial.

She reached for her phone, unlocked it and sent a quick text to Stacey.

I need help.

Stacey's reply was immediate.

Are you OK?

Not sure. I don't suppose you have a pregnancy test lying around???

Instead of a text, the phone began to ring. Ottilie answered to a squealing Stacey.

'No way!' she cried. 'For you? Please say it's for you and not for Fion because I'm sure it's lovely, but I don't think I can take any more drama!'

'It's probably nothing. I'm a bit late, that's all. I thought maybe Chloe might have a spare test from before. You can buy them in twin packs, right? Not that I've ever had to buy one.'

'As it happens, we do have one. Want me to bring it over?'

Ottilie glanced up at the clock. Would she have time to do it before Heath's arrival?

'I'll come to you,' she decided. 'I'll have to be quick – Heath's due any time.'

'You'll want to be able to tell him?'

'I suppose I'd have to!' Ottilie said. 'I think he might need to know!'

To save time, she drove to Stacey's, grabbed the test, promised to call once she'd done it and then raced home.

Fion called from the living room as she got back. 'Heath's not here yet!'

'That's OK!' Ottilie shouted back as she dashed to the bathroom. 'Traffic, I expect.'

With trembling hands, doubting that it would be anything but a negative result but her stomach churning all the same, Ottilie ripped open the packaging of the test.

Ten minutes later, Heath walked in, a bouquet in his arms.

'Sorry I'm late,' he said, handing the flowers to her and kissing her lightly. 'I had something to do.'

'That's all right. I've been trying to get my head around this job application since I got home. I was about to message you, but only because I was a bit worried.'

She was doing her best to be normal, but she was dazed. She doubted she even knew what normal was right now.

'I should have phoned. I had a meeting with the MD and things ran over so I thought I'd just get here.'

'But you stopped to get me flowers too,' Ottilie said, glancing at the bouquet. 'Softie.'

'You deserve them. I don't treat you often enough.'

'Yes, you do, but thank you.'

'So...' Heath sat down as she went to put the flowers in water. 'You haven't done the application yet?'

'No. It's so hard – I can get all my qualifications and experience down easily enough, but I have to write a personal statement too – like a mission statement type thing, you know. What I want to achieve and what I envisage bringing to the role and all that. And I don't know what to say.'

'But you do still want it?'

'Yes.' Ottilie gave an emphatic nod as she took the wine from the fridge. She poured a glass for him and took it over.

'So you might be angry when I tell you what I've done.'

She frowned as she ran the tap for some water for herself. 'What have you done?'

'I told the MD I've changed my mind about the promotion. I've told him I don't want it.'

Ottilie joined him at the table. 'Why would you do that?'

'Because' – he took her hands in his – 'I don't think you really want to leave Thimblebury, do you?'

'But we said—'

'I know what we said, but I can tell your heart's not in it. Honestly, when I thought about life in Manchester with you, it would have been all right and we'd have been happy, but I don't think my heart was in the move either. When we were out at the swimming place, I looked out and I thought how I'd never want to leave all this behind.' He kissed her fingers. 'Are you mad at me? I should have asked you first, but I didn't because I thought you'd pretend to be OK with it for my sake.'

'You know me too well.'

'I do that.'

She wove her fingers into his to lock hands and smiled. 'I'm not mad at you, not one bit. You're right – I was only thinking about it before you came home.'

'*Home*,' he said. 'That's why we could never leave – because of the way you call it home, like you really mean it. Not like a house, but like... like...' He shook his head. 'You know what I mean even though I don't know how to say it?'

She did. Wordsworth Cottage – and Thimblebury – had long felt like more than a house she called home. It was a place that felt like home for her soul, where she truly belonged.

'Did I do the right thing?' he asked. 'I know there are still things we need to sort out—'

'You did. Fion's decided to move out anyway.'

'She has?'

'She told me earlier. She and Damien are going to leave the village. He's giving the house back to Melanie.'

Heath's eyes widened. 'He's just going to give her the house?'

'It's on land that belongs to Daffodil Farm anyway, so it was never really his. I don't know if it ever belonged to either of them, but if anyone has a claim, then I suppose it's her.'

'It's big of him. I've got to hand it to him – there aren't many who'd be so... *noble* about it. So what? He just walks away with nothing and starts again? That's going to be hard.'

'The other side of that is it means he must really love Fion. He's giving up everything to be with her, after all. It would make his life far easier to give her up and patch things up with Melanie. He'd have the house back, and they'd carry on as before.'

'He must. That's good then. One less thing to worry about.'

'While we're on the subject of worrying, I'm going to add one to the list. Your gran. She saw the estate agent's car outside here this morning. She wasn't very happy when she worked out why.'

'I know,' Heath said with a grin. 'She phoned me at work. I told her we hadn't decided yet.'

'I told her that too, but I don't think she believed me. I almost feel sorry for the agent now we've decided not to sell – she was quite excited about this place. She liked your floor.'

'Good.' He grinned. 'A lot of sweat and tears went into that floor.'

'There's something else,' she said. 'Another reason I don't think I can take the job in Manchester now. I mean, I could, but it complicates things. I hope it doesn't complicate things for us too much, but...' She drew in a breath, though her heart was hammering and her chest was so tight she didn't think she could ever take one big enough to fill her lungs. 'I'm pregnant.'

Heath stared at her. And then his face transformed into the biggest, brightest smile. 'You are? When...? How long...? How pregnant are you?'

'Considering I only found out about two minutes before you arrived, I don't know any of that other stuff.'

He kissed her full on the mouth and then downed his wine in one. 'I'm going to be a dad!'

Ottilie laughed. 'Yes. It's crazy. I never thought I'd be a mum, and here we are! You're happy?'

'God yes! I'm so happy!'

Ottilie smiled, her worries dissipating. She didn't even know why she'd been worried because Heath was always going to be pleased. The news was a shock to both of them, but it was more than welcome. Fion would leave, and Ottilie would be sad about that, but she would have a whole new person to think about and care for, and she couldn't be anything but excited for that.

'I'll have to make some calls,' she said. 'Let my mum know and Stacey and everyone at the surgery...'

'Have you told Fion?'

'Not had a chance yet. We'll do that shortly. I want to enjoy the moment with you first,' Ottilie said, kissing him. 'You'll want to call your parents too. And I suppose we'd better go and see Flo before we do any of that.'

'Are you going to try again with Conrad? Maybe give him a chance to meet his grandchild?'

Ottilie was thoughtful for a moment. 'Maybe,' she said finally. 'It seems like a good place to start building a relationship with him, doesn't it? He might be more willing to try for the baby's sake, if not for mine.'

'He's a fool if he doesn't,' Heath said. He put a hand to her belly. 'I still can't believe it.'

'Neither can I.'

'I can't believe how lucky I am. I love you so much. And I'm going to love being a family with you and our baby.'

'Me too,' Ottilie said. She was smiling like she might never stop, so happy that tears were filling her eyes.

Many things were still uncertain and were yet to work themselves out, but some things she knew for sure. She loved Heath with all her heart. She was going to love having his baby, and most of all, she knew for certain she was exactly where she was meant to be. In Thimblebury, the little village that had saved her when she'd been at her lowest, the place that had been her new start. It was the perfect place to bring up their baby, and she knew now that, no matter what, she never wanted to be anywhere else.

A LETTER FROM TILLY

I want to say a huge thank you for choosing to read *A Family Surprise for the Village Nurse*. If you did enjoy it, and want to keep up to date with all my latest releases, just sign up at the following link. Your email address will never be shared and you can unsubscribe at any time.

www.bookouture.com/tilly-tennant

I hope you enjoyed *A Family Surprise for the Village Nurse* and if you did I would be very grateful if you could write a review. I'd love to hear what you think, and it makes such a difference helping new readers to discover one of my books for the first time.

I love hearing from my readers – you can get in touch on my Facebook page, Goodreads or my website.

Thank you!

Tilly

https://tillytennant.com

facebook.com/TillyTennant

ACKNOWLEDGEMENTS

I say this every time I come to write acknowledgements for a new book, but it's true: the list of people who have offered help and encouragement on my writing journey so far really is endless and it would take a novel in itself to mention them all. I'd try to list everyone here, regardless, but I know that I'd fail miserably and miss out someone who is really very important. I just want to say that my heartfelt gratitude goes out to each and every one of you, whose involvement, whether small or large, has been invaluable and appreciated more than I can express.

Most importantly, I have to thank my good friend Paula Chell for her invaluable advice and help with this book. She's not only a brilliant and dedicated nurse but also a gorgeous human being. I'd also like to mention all the other incredible nurses I worked alongside during my ten years at University Hospital North Midlands. Those people, and all the others that work so hard to keep us all well, were the inspiration for this series.

I also have to thank the remarkable team at Bookouture for their continued support, patience and amazing publishing flair, particularly Lydia Vassar-Smith – my incredible and long-suffering editor – Kim Nash, Noelle Holten, Sarah Hardy, Peta Nightingale, Mandy Kullar, Lizzie Brien, Alex Crow, Louisa Pagel and Alba Proko. I know I'll have forgotten many others at Bookouture who I ought to be thanking, but I hope they'll forgive me. Their belief, able assistance and encouragement mean the world to me. I truly believe I have the best team an author could ask for. Signing with them changed my life and I don't think I'll ever be able to thank them enough for taking a chance on a daft little woman from Staffordshire.

My friend, Kath Hickton, always gets an honourable mention for putting up with me since primary school and Louise Coquio deserves a medal for getting me through university and suffering me ever since, likewise her lovely family.

I also have to thank Mel Sherratt, who is as generous with her time and advice as she is talented, someone who is always there to cheer on her fellow authors. She did so much to help me in the early days of my career that I don't think I'll ever be able to thank her as much as she deserves.

My fellow Bookouture authors are all incredible, of course, unfailing and generous in their support of colleagues – life would be a lot duller without the gang!

I'd also like to give a special shout-out to Jaimie Admans, who is not only a brilliant author but is a brilliant friend. There's also an honourable mention for my retreat gang: Debbie, Jo, Tracy, Helen and Julie. I live for our weeks locked away in some remote house, writing, chatting, drinking and generally being daft. You are the most brilliant women and my life is better for knowing you all.

I have to thank all the incredible and dedicated book bloggers (there are so many of you, but you know who you are!) and readers, and anyone else who has championed my work, reviewed it, shared it or simply told me that they liked it. Every one of those actions is priceless, and you are all very special people. Some of you I am even proud to call friends now – and I'm looking at you in particular, Kerry Ann Parsons and Steph Lawrence!

Last but not least, I'd like to give a special mention to my lovely agent Hannah Todd and the incredible team at the Madeleine Milburn Literary, TV & Film Agency, especially

Madeleine herself. I'm so lucky to be a part of such a dynamic agenting powerhouse!

I have to admit I have a love-hate relationship with my writing. It can be frustrating at times, isolating and thankless, but at the same time I feel like the luckiest woman alive to be doing what I do, and I can't imagine earning my living any other way. It also goes without saying that my family and friends understand better than anyone how much I need space to write, and they love me enough to enable it, even when it puts them out. I have no words to express fully how grateful and blessed that makes me feel.

And before I go, thank you, dear reader. Without you, I wouldn't be writing this, and you have no idea how happy it makes me that I am.

PUBLISHING TEAM

Turning a manuscript into a book requires the efforts of many people. The publishing team at Bookouture would like to acknowledge everyone who contributed to this publication.

Audio
Alba Proko
Melissa Tran
Sinead O'Connor

Commercial
Lauren Morrissette
Hannah Richmond
Imogen Allport

Contracts
Peta Nightingale

Cover design
Debbie Clement

Data and analysis
Mark Alder
Mohamed Bussuri

Editorial
Lydia Vassar-Smith
Imogen Allport

Copyeditor
Anne O'Brien

Proofreader
Laura Kincaid

Marketing
Alex Crow
Melanie Price
Occy Carr
Ciara Rosney
Martyna Młynarska

Operations and distribution
Marina Valles
Stephanie Straub
Joe Morris

Production
Hannah Snetsinger
Mandy Kullar
Ria Clare
Nadia Michael

Publicity
Kim Nash
Noelle Holten
Jess Readett
Sarah Hardy